THE STORYTELLERS' COLLECTION

TALES *from* HOME

the STORY TELLERS' Collection

Collection Two

COMPILED BY KAREN BALL

Multnomah®Publishers *Sisters, Oregon*

THE STORYTELLERS' COLLECTION 2
Published by Multnomah Publishers, Inc.
© 2001 by Multnomah Publishers, Inc.
International Standard Book Number: 1-57673-820-5

Cover design by The Office of Bill Chiaravalle
Cover image by FPG International LLC

Scripture quotations are from
The Holy Bible, New International Version © 1973, 1984 by International Bible
Society, used by permission of Zondervan Publishing House
Holy Bible, New Living Translation (NLT)© 1996. Used by permission of
Tyndale House Publishers, Inc. All rights reserved.
The Holy Bible, King James Version (KJV)

Multnomah is a trademark of Multnomah Publishers, Inc., and is registered in the
U.S. Patent and Trademark Office.
The colophon is a trademark of Multnomah Publishers, Inc.

Printed in the United States of America

For information:
Multnomah Publishers, Inc.•Post Office Box 1720•Sisters, Oregon 97759

01 02 03 04 05 06 07 08 — 10 9 8 7 6 5 4 3 2 1 0

TABLE OF CONTENTS

Forewords 7
A Place Like No Other, A Story by *Chuck Colson* 11

The Northwest

1. The Huckleberry Patch, *Robin Lee Hatcher* 18
2. Homecoming, *Shari MacDonald* 23
3. The Orchard, *Karen Ball* 30
4. A Matter of Perspective, *Jefferson Scott* 41
5. The Darkest Night, *Lauraine Snelling* 50
6. On Account of a Skunk, *Melody Carlson* 62
7. Home Is the Sailor, *Robert Elmer* 68
8. Cicely's Hats, *Janet Chester Bly* 79

The West

1. Connor Sapp's Baseball Summer, *Deborah Bedford* 92
2. I See Things Deeply, *James Scott Bell* 103
3. Fall in the Valley, *Kristin Billerbeck* 110
4. The Day the Wind Stopped, *Stephen Bly* 118
5. When You Wish upon a Star, *Dave Jackson* 128

The Southwest

1. Grapes without Seeds, *Jane Orcutt* 142
2. Fragments of Truth, *Carol Cox* 147
3. Jessica's Gift, *Karen Kingsbury* 161

The Midwest

1. Lime around the Outhouse, *Jane Kirkpatrick* 172
2. Home to Southfield, Mourning, *Carole Gift Page* 182
3. The Pride of Freedom, *Tracie Peterson* 191
4. The Wedding, *Denise Hunter* 198
5. Communication, *Lori Copeland* 207
6. Heart's Treasure, *Colleen Coble* 215
7. Fences, *Neta Jackson* 223

8. Prairie Lessons, *Deborah Raney* 232
9. Lonely Christmas in Chicago, *Lyn Cote* 239
10. The Coward, *Athol Dickson* 248
11. Aunt Pert's Folly, *Lois Richer* 256
12. The Smell of Green Apples, *Nancy Moser* 268

The South

1. The Blue Convertible, *Terri Blackstock* 276
2. The State of Incorporation, *Angela Elwell Hunt* 285
3. Diary of a Farmer's Wife, *Patricia Hickman* 292
4. Brothers, *Randy Alcorn* 298

The Northeast

1. A Seed for Tomorrow, *Doris Elaine Fell* 314
2. In the Matter of Grace, *Judith McCoy-Miller* 324
3. Just Fourteen Days, *Gayle Roper* 333
4. The Crab Garden, *Lisa E. Samson* 343

FOREWORD ONE

KAREN BALL INTRODUCES SOME WRITING FRIENDS

*Y*ou're about to embark on an adventure…

Contained in these pages are fascinating tales of the here and now and of ages past, of humor and tragedy and everything in between, of people and places you'll want to visit over and over again. These are tales from the hearts and souls of a very special breed of folks: novelists.

Novelists are great. It was such a relief, the first time I talked with another novelist, to discover two things: 1) I'm not alone, and 2) I'm not crazy. Or maybe I am, but it's okay. Novelists are *supposed* to be…unique. They're supposed to see things in ways no one else ever has, to have their own special brand of humor no matter how odd (translated *warped*) it may seem to others. Novelists observe and experience and absorb—and whatever comes to them, good or bad, they're driven by one powerful thought: *Someday…I can use this in a story.*

We've written these stories in part because novelists enjoy a challenge. And there are few forms of writing as challenging as short stories. Using a scant number of words to create worlds peopled by believable characters…well, it ain't easy. But it's fun.

Another reason for this collection, though, is that we wanted to make a difference. To take part in ministry and outreach in the name of the One who called each of us to write…the One we seek to serve wholeheartedly. The first collection, *The Storytellers' Collection 1, Tales from Faraway Places,* has already had a wonderful impact for The *JESUS* Film Project. In fact, we've been delighted with how well it's done. It is our hope and prayer that this second collection will be equally beneficial for Prison Fellowship Ministry.

So get ready to enter an entire universe of new worlds…of hometown places where we hope you'll have fun, be challenged, and take part in something wonderful. And maybe, just maybe, where you'll discover your all-time favorite novelist.

KAREN BALL

FOREWORD TWO

RANDY ALCORN EXPLAINS
THE PRISON FELLOWSHIP CONNECTION

*W*hen ChiLibris authors collaborated on our first book of short stories, *The Storytellers' Collection,* we decided to designate all the royalties to reaching the lost and needy for Christ. Those royalties continue to go to The *JESUS* Film Project, bringing the good news to the far corners of the earth.

With this second book we wanted to support an equally Christ-centered and strategic ministry. After nominating a number of worthy organizations, we chose Prison Fellowship Ministries.

Chuck Colson founded Prison Fellowship in 1976 for the purpose of bringing together Christians to share their faith and God's love with prisoners, ex-prisoners, and their families. Colson came to grips with his own need for Christ in the long months prior to his conviction for Watergate-related offenses, and he experienced the difference that redemption can make. He became convinced that the ultimate solution to crime is not in therapeutic interventions, institutions, or legislative reform, but through spiritual renewal.

Prison Fellowship Ministries now encompasses organizations in more than eighty-three countries. It has regional offices in Switzerland, Zimbabwe, New Zealand, Singapore, and Peru. Another division of the ministry led by Chuck Colson, the Wilberforce Forum, is a respected Christian worldview think tank, extending the ministry of Prison Fellowship even further through dialogue with lawmakers, public figures, and opinion leaders in the nation's capital. PF is the largest and most extensive association of national Christian ministries working within the criminal justice field. By the grace of God and the labor of more than fifty thousand volunteers, prisoners worldwide are being evangelized, discipled, taught God's Word, counseled, and linked with local churches. Men and women are being delivered from emptiness and despair and are learning new ways to think and live.

Like many, I daily receive the e-mail version of Prison Fellowship's brief but incisive radio program, BreakPoint (http://www.breakpoint.org). The subjects addressed include not just prisons, but family, ethics, pro-life issues, cultural concerns, and matters of discipleship. Prison Fellowship has embraced not only the cause of reaching prisoners but also of teaching a Christian worldview and accurately representing Jesus Christ in every corner of culture.

Many readers have heard of Project Angel Tree, one among many exciting PF ministries. It provides Christmas gifts to children of prisoners who otherwise wouldn't receive them. With the gifts comes personal contact with Christians who are there to serve and offer spiritual and material help to needy wives and children.

Many of us writers receive letters from prisoners who read our books. After responding to prisoners' letters, our own ministry often gives their names to the Oregon chapter of Prison Fellowship. Through letters and visits they faithfully follow up on these men and women. For years my family and our ministry have supported Prison Fellowship. It's high on the list of Christian organizations that we trust.

Each of the contributors to this second *Storytellers' Collection* is honored to partner with Prison Fellowship and delighted that 100 percent of the royalties from this book will go to this outstanding ministry. We consider this an investment in eternity and look forward to seeing in heaven the exciting results of the Holy Spirit's ministry not just through this book, but through the proceeds given to Prison Fellowship.

We encourage readers to pray for and consider supporting Prison Fellowship. For information, see www.pfi.org, or contact Prison Fellowship, P.O. Box 17500, Washington, DC 20041-7500 (703-478-0100).

As ChiLibris authors, we hope you enjoy *Storytellers' Collection 2, Tales from Home,* and that your heart is drawn to our Lord and King. We also hope it encourages you to know about the powerful ministry your purchase is helping support. Thank you, from all of us, for sharing in this important outreach.

A PLACE LIKE NO OTHER

A Story by Chuck Colson

t was more than a pastime or a diversion. Larry had been a visitor in prisons for a long time now, and it was an important part of his life. It was part of how he defined himself. He could hardly remember what it was like before he started these regular visits.

It wasn't a job, either. It was his ministry, and that made it different.

It was like the first time he picked up a guitar. From the very first moment, he knew that coming here and meeting with these men was something he would do forever, and he simply took each step, one by one, until he mastered the process.

Even though he was an ordained preacher, many people thought of him as a musician. The guitar player. The gospel singer. He sang and played and talked about Jesus. He was a poet and writer, and whenever he went to visit folks, he would sometimes sing or tell stories and then pray for them. And in the prisons, he would preach and sing for the men. Mostly, though, he talked to them, and he went out of his way to reach those that other people would prefer to just ignore.

A lot of these prisoners were damaged men. They were angry men. But he went anyway, and he loved going. Truth be known, going behind those concrete walls and wire fences was more than a ministry. It was also Larry's passion. And there were moments he would never forget.

Early one Saturday morning, Larry and a group of volunteers asked to be taken to "Level Five," the maximum-security section at the

Missouri penitentiary. It was a place for men serving long-term sentences under the tightest security possible. They wanted to share their Christian faith. Larry and a couple of the others had visited deep solitary before, so they had a pretty good idea of what to expect—it wouldn't be easy. They knew the risks and they accepted them.

They were told that some of the inmates would be hostile and angry. It was inevitable. Tough guys deep inside the prison would never admit to the pain they felt, and preachers were particularly subject to verbal abuse. There were some who might be interested, maybe even anxious to talk to visitors like Larry and his friends. But the men had to be careful about seeming too eager. Inside the prison, the system feeds on the weak ones. Those who took kindly to preachers and gospel singers could easily become victims.

There were three hundred inmates in the segregation units because of discipline problems. Often more like animals than men, they were locked up twenty-four hours a day in small, single cells. These were the ones with nothing to lose. Most showed no signs of remorse or restraint; they expressed no moral sentiment of any kind.

As they approached the cell block, Larry and the other volunteers were taken to the security office and told to sign in. They handed over their personal identification, removed their shoes, and passed in single file through the metal detector. A guard handed them back their shoes and then rapped on the steel door with his fist. After a long pause, the metallic buzzer sounded and the door swung open. Then, once again, the visitors lined up to pass through to the next checkpoint.

"Harder getting in than out," Larry said, smiling at the others.

"Don't you believe it," the security officer said, returning his smile.

The guard nodded. "These men have earned the right to be here."

Larry glanced down the long, bare corridor ahead of them. Dimly lit, it was a place like no other, shadowed by a sense of profound bitterness and gloom.

He looked over at the young, muscular guard who carried the keys. "Well, maybe they have earned the right to be here," Larry said, "but so have I. So have we all." The guard looked at Larry. "Except for the love of God," Larry said, "this is about the best any of us could hope for." The guard snorted and looked away.

"This is the spitters' wing," the guard said. "You'll find out what these guys are made of soon enough. They'd as soon spit on you as look at you. On a bad day, they'll throw things at you, too, including body waste."

Larry had seen this before, fully believing the stories he'd been told. The officer confirmed his fears. "Sometimes the only way to clean this place is to just hose it down."

Each man was locked in a separate cell, and from the looks of them, some had been in the same place for years.

"You don't have to visit these guys," Larry had been told by prison officials. "But if you insist, you've gotta wear protective gear—like the white suits and face shields." Those discouraging words were like fire in Larry's bones, so he asked if he could leave the face shield off so the men could see his face.

The guard beside him smiled and laughed out loud. "Hey, it's your life! If that's what you want, I won't be stopping you! But, if you're smart, you'll put on the suit." Larry nodded as he pulled on the white protective clothing.

When he stepped into the wing, Larry found himself ankle-deep in trash and filth. The halls echoed with shouts and curses. Above the roar he could hear the sound of one man violently kicking his steel cell door. The sound was so loud, Larry half expected the door to come off its hinges.

But he kept walking, filled with the sense that God was with him.

He slowed and looked into the first cell. The inmate inside stared back silently, apparently surprised by the presence of a visitor. He couldn't believe that anybody would come down here to the spitters' wing.

Larry moved closer and began to share his faith in Christ with the prisoner. The hardened criminal told Larry that a man had hanged himself in that same cell just a week before—and now he had been moved into the cell.

As they talked, as their conversation went a little deeper, Larry learned that this man, John, had become a Christian at a young age, but had turned away from God in his early twenties. He led a rough life after that—a life that led him to Level Five. After hearing his story, Larry asked if they could pray together. He asked John if he would pray with him and renew the relationship with Jesus that he'd abandoned.

The prisoner nodded and bowed his head. They each prayed, and when Larry looked up, he could see an immediate change in the young man's face and eyes.

Larry smiled and told John he wanted to go a little farther now, to talk with some of the other guys, but the prisoner reached toward the glass and stopped him. "Larry, I haven't prayed in years, but you're going into a pretty tough place down that way." He paused and cleared his throat. "Would you let me pray for you and these men, that they will listen to what you have to say?"

Humbled, Larry reached out and touched the glass between them as they prayed. Both men had tears in their eyes. Larry looked at John and smiled, praying silently, *Lord, this is one of the lost sheep you talked about, that turned away, and he's come back.* Larry could see that God was already at work.

As Larry walked from cell to cell, talking with each man and praying for them, the unit became perceptibly quieter and calmer. Soon, each man was waiting with anticipation for Larry to come to his cell. Nothing was thrown. No spit. There was not one curse or threat or shout. The hall was hushed…except for the one prisoner who still violently kicked the door of his cell.

Several of the prisoners called to him, trying to calm the angry inmate, but to no avail. One man whispered to Larry, "That's Suicide Man."

Finally, Larry reached the man's cell door. The large inmate inside immediately stood up and demanded, "Who are you?"

"I'm Larry Howard. I'm from Prison Fellowship."

"No! I mean, who are you *really?*"

"I'm a Christian," Larry said simply. "I came here to let you know that God loves you, and we care about you very much."

To Larry's amazement, the big man started to cry.

"I've been here so long I've gone crazy," he said through his tears. "I know it. They all know it." He took a long breath. "Last month my wife died, and I couldn't go to the funeral or even say good-bye. I've sat here on that bed and cried every day and night for the last month." He paused, then stifling a groan, he muttered, "The pain's been more than I can bear."

Larry was moved but he didn't speak. He waited. There was more.

"Last night," the prisoner continued, looking into Larry's eyes, "I had a dream."

"Is that right? Would you tell me about it?"

"God talked to me," the man said. "Not in a voice like us, but I could still hear Him, just the same. He said He was gonna take away my pain…and He said He was gonna send somebody to pray for me."

Suddenly tears welled up in Larry's eyes, but he didn't brush them away. He let them flow.

"When I woke up this morning," the prisoner said, "I felt a little better, but then I got to thinking and I thought I'd just dreamed all that or I just made it up 'cause I was so angry and lonely. And I started to get mad at God."

Larry nodded and whispered, "I know."

"And I shouted at God. I said, 'Who are You kiddin'? Nobody ever comes down here! Nobody even knows I'm here. How is somebody going to come down here and pray for me in this hole?' And that's when I started kickin' and yellin' and trying to get out…"

Larry's chest was on fire by now, and big, wet tears were rolling down his cheeks. The entire wing had grown silent. Every hardened inmate along that cell block was glued to every word coming from Suicide Man's cell.

Larry brushed away his tears and told the big man that God knows all about the pain and suffering in each of our lives. "Christ died for us and He's gone on ahead to prepare a place for us…a place where there'll be no more tears or pain." Larry told him that all anyone has to do is accept Christ as his Savior, and God will accept him just as he is…even down in Level Five.

The big man was visibly moved.

Larry reached out and put his hand on the glass.

The prisoner wasn't crying or angry now. He seemed to understand that God had heard his cry, and that sooner or later he would have to do something about it. As Larry turned to go he watched the big man sit down on that bed, pick up the Prison Fellowship book Larry had given him, thumb through it, and then start to read. It was a booklet called *Running the Race*, a one-week introduction to Christianity, and Larry knew it was to be a first step back from hell.

As the security officer took Larry back outside, away from the spitters' wing that day, the gospel singer could hardly restrain the joy or the tears. The electronic doors snapped shut behind him…and it was the only sound in a place that, just an hour earlier, had been a chaotic hellhole.

In the sunshine outside, Larry stopped and looked up at the brilliant white clouds. *I've always said that the peace of God can penetrate even the deepest of dungeons, and today I've seen it happen.*

That morning, Larry saw God's hand at work, and he was part of it. God cared enough about one prisoner and his pain to cut through the most extreme isolation.

And He used a simple gospel singer to do it.

ABOUT THE AUTHOR

Charles W. Colson, founder of Prison Fellowship Ministries, had this to share with the Storytellers' Collection readers: "Throughout history, the actions and beliefs of men have been shaped by stories. It is from tales and legends that we discover our heroes and embrace beliefs worth defending, and that's why I have always used them in my books and other writings. Stories touch us deeply and change lives in ways mere words cannot. Nowhere is this more evident than in this remarkable volume, and I am grateful to Randy Alcorn, to the publishers at Multnomah, and to each of the distinguished contributors to this volume to be included. And that the proceeds from the work should be dedicated to a ministry that has for a quarter century motivated my life and work, I am humbled and deeply grateful. Thank you."

The Northwest

THE HUCKLEBERRY PATCH

Robin Lee Hatcher

Aunt Dodie—Dorothy Mae Collins to those outside our extended family—was an original. God broke the mold after making her, and that's for certain.

For her entire adult life, Aunt Dodie lived in the central Idaho mountains in a cabin overlooking Payette Lake. She never married, never had kids of her own. But there wasn't a one of us—in any Collins generation—who didn't know where to turn when we needed help or advice or a bit of loving concern.

I suppose if she'd been born a southerner, they'd have called Aunt Dodie a "steel magnolia," for she was as strong as she was beautiful. However, we don't have a comparable description in our Idaho vernacular—unless you count "tough old bird." And that doesn't fit Aunt Dodie.

I was thirty-two the year I experienced my greatest need for a dose of Aunt Dodie's wisdom. I'd broken up with Barry, my fiancé of three years, after catching him in a, shall we say, *questionable* situation with my best friend. So much for being a keen judge of character. Then the firm I'd worked for longer than I cared to admit—in a rather boring position to boot—decided to close their Boise office and relocate to Spokane, Washington. I had no desire to go with them, not for the salary I earned. Of course, they didn't offer me a job there either, so that was a moot point. The final blow came when I learned that the apartment complex where I lived was to be torn down to make room for a grocery superstore.

Life was the pits—and it had nothing to do with cherries.

Aunt Dodie to the rescue.

"You come stay with me for the rest of the summer, hon. We'll have us a good time while you wait to see what it is the Lord has in store for you."

That was another thing about Aunt Dodie. Nobody had more faith than she did. She looked for—and found—God in everything around her. Maybe that's because she was a painter and sculptor and had a special way of seeing the world with those artist's eyes of hers. But I believe it's because she looked at everything through the Artist's eyes rather than through her own.

It was a clear, hot August afternoon when I drove my fifteen-year-old Ford up the dusty, bumpy driveway to Aunt Dodie's home. She must have been watching for me. The door opened and out she came onto the deck, her face wreathed in a smile of welcome.

Aunt Dodie was in her seventies, thin as a model, with hair as black as pitch—"thanks to Lady Clairol," she would tell anyone who commented on her lack of gray. She didn't make excuses. You always knew where you stood with Aunt Dodie. That's what I desperately needed right then, to know where I stood.

But not with Aunt Dodie. With my Creator.

It sure seemed to me that I'd been sent to the woodshed without being told the reason why. Worse, I felt abandoned, rejected, alone.

That evening, while we sat at the table eating a supper of fried chicken with mashed potatoes and gravy and fresh-cut green beans, Aunt Dodie let me pour out my confusion and heartache and anger. She listened attentively while I whined and railed. I complained about Barry. I complained about my former boss. I complained about the superstore mentality that had swept across America, wiping out all the little guys in the name of big bucks and big business. And finally, long after the food on the table had grown cold, I complained about God.

"What did I do wrong to deserve all this, Aunt Dodie? Why is everything going wrong? I've prayed and asked, but He doesn't answer me."

"Doesn't He?" She lifted one of her finely arched eyebrows. "Perhaps you simply aren't listening."

Ah, something new to complain about. Now I could complain about Aunt Dodie!

"God never promised us a rose garden, hon."

I sank into a mire of my own misery.

Aunt Dodie rose from her chair and began to clear the table. "We'll go huckleberry picking tomorrow. About six."

"In the *morning*?"

She laughed, and that was answer enough. I groaned.

"My dear," she said, leaning toward me, "you might be surprised at the many ways God can speak to you in a huckleberry patch."

The forest was hushed, almost reverent, at six in the morning. A light breeze whispered through the tops of the lodgepole and ponderosa pines. Dew sparkled on the underbrush. Dried leaves and needles crunched underfoot, and the air smelled of rich soil and wood smoke.

I followed Aunt Dodie up the trail, climbing ever higher on the mountainside. Her stride was surprisingly long and sure for a woman her age. I, on the other hand, had a hard time keeping up while carrying two large plastic buckets, one in each hand. I was panting from the exertion by the time we stopped.

Aunt Dodie glanced over her shoulder. "We're here."

Golden sunlight filtered through trees that surrounded a small clearing, gilding the bushes, warming the dark brown earth.

"Some years, there's a bumper crop." Aunt Dodie took one of the buckets from me. "And some years you have to look hard to find even a few. Let's see what sort of crop we have this year."

I stood there, feeling tired and cranky.

She leaned over and plucked a purple huckleberry from beneath a leaf. She held it out toward me. "The berries are tiny and the bushes they grow on seem so scraggly and worthless, it's easy to overlook them." She popped the huckleberry into my mouth, then added, "But they're wonderfully sweet to the taste."

She was right about that. The burst of flavor on my tongue left me wanting more.

"When I was a girl, back in the forties, my father used to bring the family to McCall in his Studebaker. Your grandfather loved huckleberry season, loved his huckleberry pancakes with huckleberry syrup. So up we came, every August." She set to work then, bending over the nearest bush. "It took much longer than two hours for the drive back then. But oh, the view from the mountaintops. It always made the journey worthwhile."

I began to pick, too.

We worked in silence for a long spell, moving through the brush, leaning over to pluck berries, one at a time, from their hiding places. My back started to ache, and I worried about the size of my bucket. At this rate, I would never fill it.

This wasn't why I'd come to be with Aunt Dodie, I grumbled silently. I could have stayed in Boise and been miserable.

One more lousy thing happening to me in a string of lousy things.

But while I silently bemoaned the condition of my life—*poor me, poor me, poor me*—Aunt Dodie sang. It took time for me to really hear her voice through the cacophony of my complaints. It took even longer to recognize the words. They were from the Psalms. She wasn't singing them to herself or for my benefit. She was singing them to the Lord, singing words of praise for His faithfulness, words of trust in His love.

And somehow, in a way I can't describe, her song, her words, touched a place in my wounded heart and soul. Like waking from a deep sleep, I suddenly remembered that God was loving and just, that He had promised to walk with me in the valleys of my life, that I need only seek Him to find Him.

How had I allowed myself to forget all that for even a little while?

"Look," Aunt Dodie whispered.

I blinked away the tears that had momentarily blinded me, then lifted my gaze. There, at the far end of the clearing, I saw a small doe and her fawn staring back at us. I held my breath, struck by the wild, delicate beauty before me. A few heartbeats later, the deer and fawn bounded away, hopping over fallen trees and underbrush until they'd disappeared from view.

"So many wonderful things of God to see," Aunt Dodie said, "if we just remember to look up every once in a while."

I turned toward her.

"God's blessings are all around us, hon, but sometimes we get so focused on our lives that we miss the beauty of the journey. All the steps aren't easy, and sometimes the climb is hard, but the journey is still beautiful because He's with us."

Last night Aunt Dodie had said that I might be surprised at the many ways in which God could speak to me in a huckleberry patch.

So what have I learned today? What have You said to me?

I pondered all the things Aunt Dodie had shown me, all the things she'd told me as we'd shared these morning hours. I pondered the golden sunlight and the scrawny-looking huckleberry bushes that had produced a surprisingly sweet crop. I pondered the whisper of God's voice, carried on a mountain breeze into a woman's broken heart.

Then I smiled. For you see, I'd learned I couldn't find the huckleberries until I leaned over and searched for them. Many of God's blessings were like that, tiny and hidden from view. But not recognizing them—the huckleberries or the blessings—didn't make them any less there, any less bountiful, or any less sweet.

Strange. Knowing that didn't change the circumstances of my life. Barry still had a new girlfriend, and I was still jobless and without a home to call my own. Yet knowing it seemed to change everything.

Aunt Dodie was right. God hadn't promised me a rose garden…

But I think He might have promised me a huckleberry patch.

ABOUT THE AUTHOR

A native Idahoan, Robin Lee Hatcher has spent many a summer day plucking huckleberries in the forest that surrounds Payette Lake. She is the Christy Award and RITA Award winning author of over 35 historical and contemporary novels—many of them set in Idaho—including *Ribbon Of Years* (Tyndale), *The Story Jar* (Multnomah), *Patterns Of Love* (Zondervan), and *The Shepherd's Voice* (WaterBrook). Robin and her husband, Jerry, live in Boise, as do her children and grandchildren.

HOMECOMING

Shari MacDonald

$\mathcal{S}$o one day I'm basking in the sun—literally, not figuratively, you understand—living the kind of perky, toothy-smiled existence that screams "Southern California" to rusty, rain-worn native Pacific Northwesterners like me. The next, I'm kissing my barely-used husband good-bye—literally *and* figuratively—and hopping a train back to the land of timber and spotted owls, Starbucks and Ben & Jerry's, Nordstrom and Nike. A place where it rains so fiercely and relentlessly, it's entirely possible that no one will even notice my tears.

Stop! screams the internal sensor. *Enough melodrama already!*

I always have had a flair for the dramatic.

All right, then. I'll skip the dare and give you truth. With a bag of honey-roasted peanuts from the Amtrak snack car clutched in one paw, I'm spending more time licking salt from my fingers than wiping brackish tears from my cheeks. I'm more hacked than heartbroken, more grouchy than grievous, more vengeful than mournful.

Not that I haven't run the gauntlet of melancholy. One does not just pull the plug on a still-wet-behind-the-ears marriage without some degree of soul-searching, believe you me. I've been through the disappointment, the disillusionment, the weekly visits from the *How-could-this-happen-to-me's?*

What can I say? I always thought "The honeymoon is over" was a figure of speech. Chump. *How could this happen to me?* indeed. Within months of the wedding, it became obvious that "how" was really beside the point. Shortly after I exchanged vows with the love of my life—soon to be unmasked as the love of my year, the bum—I realized that the husband I'd chosen so carefully could no longer stand me.

What led me to this cheery conclusion? A number of things, really, thanks for asking, but mostly the fact that I was seeing even less of him than I had before we'd started dating—a neat trick, since I hadn't even known him at the time. Ba-*doom*-ching.

The problems started out simply enough—and, of course, since I've set a speed record for separation, you can well imagine that they never ended. The first week after we returned from Maui, Rick told me that he didn't feel "at home" in the cozy little love nest I'd prepared for us not far from his accounting office in Newport Bay, California. Say what you will, I took that little revelation pretty well, smiling demurely as I pulled the dagger from my chest cavity, placing it neatly in the dishwasher.

Happy Homemaker, eat your heart out.

And speaking of happy homemakers, there's one waiting for me right now at Portland's Union Station, a thin smile stretched over her dentured teeth—a grin not unlike that of a ventriloquist's dummy—looking frighteningly as though there were rubber bands running from her ears to the corners of her lips.

Don't get too close, folks, there's no telling when those babies could snap!

I don't even have to see her to know this is the case. I've seen this happy-at-all-costs look of hers before. I've *lived* with that look nearly my entire life. That look was, in fact, the best reason I had for walking out on Rick. Frankly, I've seen what a bad marriage can do to a woman, and let me tell you, what I witnessed is *not* for the weak of heart. PG-13 at the very least. So it's ironic—*n'est-ce pas?*—that my running away is driving me straight back to that unsettling, if not terrifying, grimace. But hey, at twenty-two years old, where else am I gonna go?

Don't answer, please. It's a rhetorical question.

I'm not crazy about people who have all the answers—perhaps because I grew up in a house where no one was allowed to wonder, but was ordered to believe what he or she was told, no matter the cost. Having an interior life comprised almost entirely *of* questions, this was a bit awkward for me. And that's putting it mildly.

Not that there's anything wrong with religion, mind you. Some of my best friends are believers. Rick and I were both Christians ourselves—

lapsed, in a sense, but that's more due to a problem with organized religion as we've experienced it than a legitimate beef with God Himself.

Anyway, my friends have heard the stories of how I was raised, and they know better than to cram structured religion down my throat. They know I'm more interested in being loved than being judged. They know I want to be supported, not shamed. They've heard my pleas for acceptance and they've listened, thank God.

But I digress.

The point is, I'd heard that marriage was hard, but I always thought folks were talking about the kind of hard that builds character. Like when you say you want to put your spouse on a plane bound for Burma and that he can come back in six months when he's got his attitude straight, but secretly you're thinking about the fact that he's so cute in the morning when his hair sticks up in that goofy Dennis-the-Menace way that maybe you'll keep him for a while after all, if for no other reason than the smooching.

No one ever told me that as soon as I got married, my spouse would start demanding enough "space" to build a space shuttle in. No one ever said that I would realize I was bound to a man *completely* unlike the one I'd gotten attached to while dating. Frankly, no one ever said I'd wonder if I was really loved, if I'd chosen a man who would adore me for life, what I would do if I *hadn't*, or if I'd ever find true happiness now that the prospect of finding true happiness "out there" was truly gone.

All right, so maybe I *am* a little teary—hand me a Kleenex, would you?—and can you blame me? As if it weren't bad enough that my marriage has ended after six months—all right now, don't roll your eyes like that!—I'm about to be paraded in front of the Morality Patrol, and I haven't even decided yet what I want for my final meal. A doomed woman's got rights, you know.

I listen to the solid *chug-chug* as the train pulls into the station and I try to imagine I'm someone else, *anyone* else, somewhere else at some other time in history: a freedom fighter in the French Revolution, perhaps. Maybe a wealthy widow traveling on the Orient Express in the early 1800s.

But, no, I'm just plain ol' Libby Gresham, known in this part of the world as Libby King since long before I found myself stuck with some man's name. And not just *any* man's name. The name of the man I loved and lost—like I need *that* reminder hanging around my neck like an albatross. Not hardly.

I get off the train and follow the other passengers into the massive station. *Ah, home again,* I think purposefully, but it doesn't feel like home yet. I still feel like I'm in an elaborate, spacious European train station. I fight the urge to turn to a stranger and murmur the few phrases I've retained of my high school French.

"Eh, bebe, boit ton lait." Hey, baby, drink your milk.

Or perhaps: *"J'aime beaucoup t'maillot."* Never mind that there wasn't a swimsuit in sight to admire.

Or even—

"Libby." My mother's voice. Her eyes are snapping, but she's still smiling, the trouper. "Still the daydreamer, I see. What's the matter with you? Didn't you hear your father calling you?"

Ah...*now* it feels like home.

"Mmm." The verbal flogging is going to get a lot worse. I decide to conserve my energy.

"Hurry, now. Your grandmother is waiting in the car."

"Gran's here?" The one relative who doesn't use me as a scratching post? Even though she lives with Mother and Dad now, I hadn't dared hope she'd come along for the ride. I wonder at my uncommonly good luck.

My father gives me an awkward side hug, then grabs my duffel bag and heads toward the main entrance. No sloppy sentimentality here, no siree bob.

Mother fills in the silence with a running commentary.

"I hope you don't interpret our taking you in as an approval of your actions, Libby—"

"Oh, I would never interpret anything you did as that, Mother," I say as sweetly as I can.

She does not even pause for breath.

"—you are, however, our daughter, and we are not about to shirk our responsibility—even if *you* are willing to shirk yours."

Ouch. Good shot, Mom.

Of course, she's been practicing in the car.

When I see the tan Accord, I break away from Mother's diatribe and grin at the back window.

"Move over, Gran," I say, but she's already on the far side of the seat.

I tug the back door open and leave it gaping behind me as I climb into the empty space behind Mother's seat, a space that even at twenty-two years old still feels like mine.

"Hello, gorgeous," I grin at my seat companion. I still can't get over how beautiful she is. I myself am not looking forward to aging, but Gran has done it like a pro, her hair white and soft, dancing round her head like a dandelion gone to seed.

"Hello, my little macaroon." Gran beams.

I look into her eyes, cloudy gray within faded sapphire.

"So, are you disappointed in me, too?" I whisper as Mother barks instructions at Daddy outside the car. My heart does a little cha-cha beat. Their opinions all matter to me, no matter how hard I try to pretend they don't. But Gran's matters most of all. That's the power of love, I suppose.

"You are never a disappointment to me," she says, jutting out her chin. "Nor are you a disappointment to God. We both may be disappointed *for* you, honey, but that's not the same thing at all."

"No?" I lay my head in her bony lap. I can feel her femur through her skirt and skin beneath my ear, and I try to hold my head up ever so slightly, to carry my own weight.

All my life I've felt like such a terrible disappointment to my parents, to God…and now to Rick. For the first time in months, I allow myself to consider the remote possibility that I'm not a complete loser after all.

"Is it such a terrible loss, Gran, to lose a husband who doesn't really love me anyway?" Now that I am being held by someone whose love I *don't* doubt, I begin to think that maybe it *is* a terrible loss—and I feel the tears begin to rise for real.

Gran looks straight ahead. Her image blurs as I watch her watch my mother and father arguing about something—me, no doubt—outside the car.

"It's hard to know when someone really loves you, Libby," she says after a while. "They don't always show it the way you'd like."

"You mean like Mother and Dad?" She's always understood my pain at the way I was raised, but she hasn't been as inclined to judge my parents as I have.

"I mean like…fill in the blank, sweetie. Do you know anyone who *does* show love the way you'd like?"

"You," I say without hesitating. I snuggle in closer. Gran's sweater, thrown across her lap, smells comfortingly familiar—a blend of Ivory soap and denture cream.

"Yes, well…" Her papery lips twitch. "We can't all be *me*, can we?"

I giggle. I am not a giggler, but so help me, Gran brings them out of me, she really does.

"We certainly cannot," I agree.

"But you can be *you*, Libby." Her look is compassionate, sharp.

"Mmm. Meaning?"

"Meaning you're not a victim. It's true that you don't have to be mistreated. Neither do you have to run."

"What makes you think I'm running?"

"Baby—" Gran scratches me over the ear, like a puppy—"you've been married six months and you come back home with little more than the clothes on your back. That's not running? It certainly doesn't look like a well-planned vacation. Far be it for me to tell you what to do, but I think you should go back to your Rick and give it another try."

"Gran, I hate to break it to you, but that *is* telling me what to do."

Still, my heart catches in my chest as I consider the prospect. I'm surprised to find that in this moment, I actually want to do as she suggests. Not because I'm horrified by the idea of living with my parents again for *any* length of time—though, having a few brain cells in my head, of course I am—but because I can finally remember what it does feel like to be secure, safe, and loved. Because when I'm honest with myself and let my guard down, I realize that I really do want Rick to provide those feelings for me and—heaven help me—I want to provide them for him as well.

"How did you get to be so wise, Gran?" I grumble.

"You know the answer to that, baby."

I think about this for a moment.

"God, huh?"

"God, huh," she agrees.

It occurs to me—for about the zillionth time in my life—that Gran's relationship with God is very different from that experienced by my parents, and I feel a faint burst of compassion as I hope they someday find what Gran has.

I hope the same thing for me. I suspect maybe I've just come the tiniest bit closer.

"I think I'll call Rick when I get to the house," I say to Gran. I say it confidently, like it was all my idea. Like I'm a young wife on a short trip away from her loving husband—which, with a little grace, I suppose I could very well be.

I think about going back and telling him all that's happened between us is both our faults. Or no one's fault.

Maybe I won't talk about fault at all.

Maybe I'll just talk about love.

Maybe even promise that I'll give him space enough to build that space shuttle.

Just at a little closer distance.

ABOUT THE AUTHOR

Shari MacDonald (www.ShariMacDonald.com) has authored numerous Christian novels, including *Love on the Run*, *A Match Made in Heaven*, and *The Perfect Wife* (WaterBrook). She is also the coauthor of *Our God Reigns: The Stories Behind Your Favorite Praise and Worship Songs* (Kregel). Shari's articles have appeared in such publications as *CCM* and *Aspire* and on Websites such as Beliefnet.com. Shari and her husband, photo-journalist Craig Strong, live in Portland, Oregon, with their emotionally challenged "pound puppy," Ellie.

THE ORCHARD

Karen Ball

"A tree is identified by its fruit. Make a tree good, and its fruit will be good."
MATTHEW 12:33 (NLT)

ad?"

Nick Wilson paused, fighting the frustration that assaulted him at the small voice. He turned slowly, frowning.

Jimmy was sitting there, already decked out in his beloved soccer gear. Typical ten-year-old. Couldn't get him dressed on time for school or church or anything important. But there he sat, an hour before the game, ready to go.

"What is it, Jim?"

The boy's set jaw trembled slightly, but he caught himself, steadied his voice. "You sure—?"

"We talked about this last night." Nick winced at the harsh tone in the words—and at the way his son's lips started to tremble. With a heavy sigh, Nick set his briefcase down and went to lay a hand on Jimmy's now-stiff shoulder.

"Son, I know how much this game means to y—"

"It's the finals, Dad!"

Nick tried not to let the desperate appeal in his boy's voice and eyes get to him—as if there were any way he could prevent it. He felt his heart constrict. But on the heels of regret came a far more familiar emotion: irritation.

He dropped his hand. "Jim, you're getting old enough now to understand this. I'm a realtor. I have to work hard, long hours to keep my business strong. But you know I'm doing it for you—"

"Never asked you to," came the mutinous mutter.

Nick gritted his teeth and continued—"and your mother. For this nice house and the clothes you wear and food you eat and the bike you ride and the fees to play in the soccer league…"

Jimmy turned away from his father's pointed look. "The game starts in an hour, Dad. At ten. Maybe you could make it…you know, just for a little bit?"

"Jim, I'm sorry. I can't. I've got this meeting, and then paperwork—"

"What good does it do to play? You never come to see me. Everyone *else's* dads are there. All the time." Those accusing eyes—eyes that were twins to Nick's in shape and color—brimmed with tears. The sight pierced Nick to the core. "You like your stupid job more than you like me."

Heat shot up Nick's face, and he drew a breath before he shook his head and stepped back. "I don't have time for this today."

He grabbed his briefcase and stalked to the door, jerking it open and walking out without another backward glance. But he didn't need to look back. He knew what he'd see…what would be filling his only child's eyes and face and stance.

Disappointment.

In him.

Nick shook his head as he jerked the car door open and tossed the briefcase on the passenger's seat. He slid in, jammed the key into the ignition, and jolted the gearshift into drive, feeling a slight satisfaction as the tires squealed their way out of the driveway.

This wasn't the first time he and Jimmy had fought about all this. Probably wouldn't be the last. At least Annie hadn't got in on it this time. Last thing he needed this morning was her green-eyed glare. He loved that woman to distraction, but she could make him feel like a worm faster than a heartbeat. Jimmy's disappointment was tough, but it was a walk in the park compared to Annie's.

It would be nice if his wife at least supported him at times like this, but no. They didn't fight about a lot, but they didn't need to. The battles they'd had over his work hours were more than enough. And last night, they'd gone at it again.

Annie had spoken in that soft but resolute tone—iron sheathed in velvet. The woman didn't yell. Nick almost wished she would. At least then he could feel justified in yelling back. "Bad enough you work on Sundays when you don't have to—"

"Who says I don't?"

"—but you haven't made it to *one* of Jimmy's games. Not one, Nick."

"You go."

Her lips—lips that smiled with such beauty—thinned. "He wants *you.*"

"Annie, I'm building a business here. Southern Oregon is growing fast, and there are lots of people moving in. If I'm going to be a part of all that, I can't just be taking time off. I have to invest in our future."

Her eyes flashed. "What about investing in your son?"

Nick wanted to explode, but he settled for shaking his head. "You don't understand how much there is to do!"

"Maybe not, but I know this: You're letting what's most important slip away because of things that don't matter a whit in light of eternity."

Eternity. That's how long it felt when he and Annie—and he and Jimmy—were fighting. An eternity of cold, dark, heavy days.

Nick slammed his hand on the steering wheel. "Why doesn't anyone *get* it? I'm doing this for *them,* for cryin' out loud."

He knew, as Jimmy couldn't—as he'd make sure Jimmy never had to—the importance of working hard. Of *making* something of yourself. Of sacrificing everything for a while so your family didn't end up on food stamps to be stared at with those sideways why-don't-you-worthless-freeloaders-get-a-job glances in the grocery store…

He cleared his throat against the lump suddenly lodged there. *Forget it. That was another time. Another lifetime…*

Forcing his attention to the road, he turned the car into the parking lot. It was hard to disappoint his family. He hated it. But if he'd learned nothing in life he'd learned this: A man didn't get ahead by going to kids' soccer games all the time.

All the time? How about once in a while? Or ever?

Nick ignored the mocking questions and leaned back against the seat. He realized he was gripping the steering wheel until his fingers ached, and dropped his hands into his lap.

Breathe…relax…you can't face Mr. Able looking like you're about to pop a gasket.

Willard Able, owner of Able Orchards, would know in a flea's sneeze that Nick was upset. And sure as the sun burned down on the valley in

August—they didn't call 'em dog days for nothing in this area—the old man would want to know what was up. As much as Nick had come to like the man, he just wasn't up to going into it again.

Slipping from his car, briefcase in hand, Nick glanced around the parking lot and frowned. What were all these cars doing here? The orchards weren't operating any longer…so it couldn't be employees. Not this many, anyway.

He looked at his watch. Had he written the time down incorrectly? No, Able had told him to stop by early that morning so he could sign the final papers. Straightening his tie, Nick walked up the steps and pushed open the front door.

The sight that met him stopped him cold in the doorway. There were people everywhere in the reception room, adults and children. Faces turned to look at him, and a laughter-filled voice rose above the hum of conversation.

"Nick! Welcome!"

He turned to find Willard Able coming toward him, hand outstretched, face wreathed in the smile that seemed to reside on the man's wrinkled features day in, day out. Had he ever seen Able frown? Nick didn't think so.

"Glad to see you, m'boy. Come on in. Meet the family."

"The—?" A quick glance revealed that the warehouse had been transformed to a balloon repository, and more people were gathered there at tables spread with food. "Mr. Able, I can come back later if you—"

The man waved his words away. "Don't be silly. I told you to come by, didn't I? 'Course—" those pale blue eyes sparkled with a glee that reminded Nick of Jimmy on Christmas mornings—"I didn't know my family had planned a surprise celebration breakfast for me."

"How about some fresh-squeezed orange juice, Nicholas?" Marie Able joined them, a glass of juice in her hands.

Nick was about to refuse, but Marie didn't give him the chance. She handed him the glass even as she linked her arm with his, then led him to the tables. There she introduced him to the family.

Willard's sons and daughters welcomed Nick warmly, and soon they were all seated. Willard held his hands out to his wife, on his right, and his eldest son, on the left. Everyone reached out to hold hands, and then bowed their heads.

"Heavenly Father," Willard's deep voice drifted over Nick, "we thank Thee for the abundance of these Thy blessings. For nourishment, for friends and family, we thank Thee. Amen."

A resounding chorus of "Amen" echoed around the room, and then it was as though conversation exploded all around Nick. He couldn't help laughing as first Don, then Vaughn, shared story after story of their father, the orchards, growing up. Stories of holiday celebrations, school events, summer jobs in the orchards, births, marriages…and in the center of it all, Willard and Marie Able. They made the Easter eggs, writing each child's name on one to ensure no one was left out; they herded their brood up the mountains, through knee-deep snow at times, to cut down the perfect Christmas tree; they gathered the fireworks through the year, ensuring an Independence Day display beyond compare.

Every event centered around the elder Ables. Just like now, Nick thought, watching Willard as he sat at the table, smiling at his children and grandchildren. The man was clearly in his element, trading story for story, joke for joke.

"Mom, how have you endured him for nearly fifty years?" Carol, one of their daughters, said with mock dismay after yet another groaner of a joke.

"God gave me an extra measure of patience, dear." Marie Able's smile was a delightful mixture of imp and serenity. "And an abundance of opportunities to refine it." As she laid her hand on her husband's, the action a benediction of love, Nick thought his heart would break.

Was that how Annie would look after fifty years of being married to him?

The delicious food suddenly tasted like sawdust, and Nick bolted from his chair, making his way back to the reception room.

"Nick?"

He steeled himself, then turned to face the man who had followed him. "Really, I should go—"

"Wouldn't hear of it."

"But these are your friends…your family…"

The man's eyes were as gentle as his words. "And so are you. You're more than welcome here, son."

Son… The lump was back in Nick's throat, and he could only nod wordlessly and accept the glass of punch someone held out to him. How often had he longed to hear that word spoken with affection, with a tender, even prideful tone? How was it this man, whom Nick had only known a matter of months, could say it with such conviction when Nick's own father…

Forget it. The bitter thought was almost as familiar to Nick as breathing. *Forget it. It doesn't matter.*

But he couldn't forget it. It was as though someone had jabbed a long, jagged shard of glass in his chest and was slicing him to shreds. He cleared his throat and lifted his hand to tug at his tie as he fought for air.

"Nick?"

He looked at Willard Able, and their gazes connected….held. Something flickered deep in the older man's gaze, and he reached out to take Nick's arm in a gentle grip.

"What say you and I take a ride?"

Nick started. "A…a ride?"

Willard just smiled and steered him back out the door.

"Hey, Pop! You runnin' out on your own party?"

Able waved at his son. "Hold the fort, Don. I'll be back in a shake." He paused. "Just don't go eating all of your mother's scrambled eggs."

"Wouldn't dream of it," Don replied with a chuckle.

"Woman never lived who could make better scrambled eggs than my Marie. Culinary work of art, that's what they are."

Nick didn't reply. He couldn't seem to find his voice. He just followed Willard outside to his old silver Scout. It was, to Nick's way of thinking, an antique, but Willard declared it the most dependable vehicle he'd ever owned. "You can have your flashy SUDs—"

"SUVs." Willard's grin told Nick the old man had known exactly what he was saying.

"You say SUV, I say SUD. Sport Utility Duds. You can keep flashy. Give me dependable anytime."

Nick slid into Old Reliable, then stared out the window in silence as Willard drove out of the parking lot. The sun was warm as they traveled south on Old Pacific Highway, crossed I-5, and then headed into the hills. Nick watched as houses and businesses gave way to acre after acre of fruit orchards.

He remembered, years ago, when he and Annie used to go for Sunday drives after church. They loved this area—Fern Valley. In the spring, when the pear trees were in full blossom, it was like an ocean of fluffy white and pink blossoms. There was even a big parade and celebration to honor the budding of the orchards: the Pear Blossom Festival. Jimmy had marched in his school band in this year's parade…or so Annie had said.

Nick hadn't been there to see it. He'd been working.

"Did you know they call this area the Banana Belt?"

Nick started, then turned to face his companion.

"Yup," Willard went on, not waiting for Nick's reply. "It's one of the only areas in this region warm enough to grow bananas. They used to have palm trees here, too. When I was a kid, you couldn't have told the old Rogue Valley from California or Florida." He chuckled. "'Course, now there's plenty of difference. Though with the vineyards coming into the valley, we'll look like California again before you know it."

Nick grimaced. "Just what we need, more Californians."

Willard's hearty laugh echoed in the cab of the Scout and drew a responding smile from Nick.

"Why, son, you sound like an Oregonian, born 'n' bred." He turned the Scout onto a rutted road, gray, bare-limbed trees dancing past as they bumped along.

Nick glanced around. "Willard? Where are we—"

"Almost there. Ahhhh…here we go." With that, the Scout rumbled to a halt, and Willard killed the engine. He gave Nick's arm a pat and jerked his thumb outside. "Come on, son."

They walked along in silence, and Nick lifted his face to the warmth of the sun. He could hear birds chirping away, their song carried on the soft breeze along with the smell of earth and a hint of wood smoke. He'd say one thing for the orchards…they were peaceful when you were out in them like this. He could see why a man like Willard had spent his life, as his father had before him, nursing and caring for the orchards.

Nick looked off to the south. On a clear, cloudless day, you could sometimes see the majestic tip of Mount Shasta. He looked to the west, where the Coastal Cascade mountain range reached to the heavens…

Nick had never really understood the line "purple mountain's majesty" until the first time he stood there, all those years ago, with Annie, looking out at scenery that he'd thought only existed on postcards. He felt like he was on top of the world out here.

Willard halted, and Nick came to stand beside him. They'd come to a small rise, and from here the view was breathtaking. Willard drew in a deep breath. "My father planted these orchards," he said, that familiar smile tugging at his lips. "And like him, I've spent most of my life tending and working, harvesting and planting, plowing under and seeding, smudging against frost, working in fog so thick you couldn't see more than a few inches in front of your nose."

Nick slid his hands into his pockets, staring at the swells of trees around them, trying to take in that much of it would be gone soon. For all that he was a realtor, for all that he was the one who'd handled the sale of the orchards to the contractors, he couldn't quite see it...couldn't make himself see this area dotted with houses and developments rather than trees.

Oh, some of the orchards would stay. But for all that fruit was still one of the Rogue Valley's main industries, more and more privately owned orchards—like Able Orchards—couldn't make do any longer. Nick couldn't imagine how Willard must be feeling, knowing his life's work...his *father's* life's work...would soon be erased from the hillsides they'd occupied for generations.

"Willard...I'm so sorry..."

At his choked words, the older man turned to him, placing a large, strong hand on his arm. "No, Nick. No regrets. Not from you, or from me." The smile that touched his face was filled with something that made Nick ache.

Peace. Willard Able was a man at peace.

Nick wondered what that was like.

"I love the orchards," Willard said. "Loved working in them with my father, and then with my children. But the work here is done. And the fruit has been good. Very good." His voice all but vibrated with a joy Nick couldn't understand.

"The fruit...?" He looked out at the trees, the barren branches, the dry, cracking ground.

Willard shook his head. "Not here, Nick." He nodded west, toward town. "Back there. My work, my father's work, it's not about trees. Or fruit."

Nick frowned. "But..."

"It's about them. My family. My family and the family that has worked for Able Orchards all these years." He reached out to rest a hand on a nearby pear tree branch. "These orchards, the fruit they bore, that was our product. But the people... Ah, Nick. The *people* are the fruit. They are what really matters. Believe me, as much time as I spent working the orchard, I spent a lot more time on the soil in which my family would grow. Now—" he gave the rough wood of the tree a pat and moved away—"the orchards will be gone. But my family?" He drew a breath, looked up at the sky, and smiled. "They'll always be there. And you know, when it's all said and done, that's all you have left, Nick. Family. That's what matters in light of eternity."

The echo of Annie's words jolted through Nick, and he turned to stare at the orchards and beyond…past the mountain range…past even the vast ocean…to a yesterday where a young boy wanted nothing more than to have his father love him, accept him, be there for him. To have him be a dad. Alcohol had rendered Nick's father incapable of meeting his son's needs. The man hadn't been able to care for or to provide anything for them, emotional or financial.

Nick had sworn long ago that he'd be a real father to his kids. A provider. A dad. He'd been so sure that was what he was doing. But now…

Now he saw what Annie had been trying to say all along. Fear had become to Nick as much a prison as liquor had been to his father. Fear of failure, fear of poverty, fear of letting his ideals down.

What he really should have been afraid of was letting his family down.

His throat constricted. What would *he* have left when it was all said and done? He was very much afraid he knew the answer.

"Never too late, you know."

Nick jumped at the quiet words. He looked to find Willard kneeling down, holding a small pile of dirt in his hand. "I…you…for what?"

Willard tipped his head, studying Nick. "For working the soil, making it fertile." He let the dirt trickle to the ground. "For building a foundation that will last." He stood, brushing his hand against his pants, then angled a look at Nick and chuckled. "Why I'm telling you all this, I can't say. I just had a feeling I should. Kinda like when the weather report said sunny and fair, but I knew it was time to fire up the smudge pots." He chuckled. "Like my kids always say, I'm just this side of crazy."

Nick put his hand out and gripped Willard's shoulder. "No. You're not crazy." An odd feeling was stirring deep in Nick's gut. A churning excitement. A certainty of what he needed to do.

Never too late…

What he needed to do. Now.

"You're not crazy at all," Nick repeated, and he suddenly felt like laughing. "You're probably the sanest person I've ever known." At

Willard's quizzical look, Nick finally gave in to the laughter. It felt good. Almost as good as it was going to feel to see the look on Annie's face.

And on Jimmy's.

"Look, Willard, I'll explain later. But right now…listen. I have to be somewhere." A quick look at his watch told him he had time. Just.

He met the older man's gaze and felt a wave of gratitude so powerful it almost knocked him to his knees. Amazing. He'd thought he was coming to see a man to close a deal.

Instead, he'd come to open his mind. And his heart.

"Willard, can you give me a lift to the park? Hawthorne Park?"

The man didn't hesitate. "Sure. We can be there in fifteen minutes, tops."

Another glance at the watch. Perfect. The game started in twenty minutes. Nick could hardly wait. As he followed Willard back to the trusty Scout, he found himself almost skipping. He hadn't been this excited since…since…

Okay. He'd never been this excited. Even the realization that changing his priorities this way could hurt their finances didn't change things. Not a whit. What good was a healthy bank balance when your family was ailing?

Willard's words echoed in his mind, his heart: *You can keep flashy. Give me dependable anytime.*

A smile worked across Nick's face. Dependable. A dad who didn't let you down. A dad who was there for the special times. And for the everyday times. A dad like Willard.

That's what he would do, from this day on. Give his son dependable. Anytime.

He leaned his head back against the seat and smiled. He might not own an orchard, but he knew, with a certainty that both shattered and lifted his soul, that he was about to start working the soil. And the fruit?

It would be sweet.

ABOUT THE AUTHOR

Author and award-winning editor Karen Ball grew up in her story's setting, the beautiful Rogue River Valley of southern Oregon. She found it a joy to write not just about a region she considers one of God's true masterpieces, but about a father's love. Karen considers herself greatly blessed, for both of her parents are, to this day, two of her closest friends, her most-trusted source of wisdom, laughter and love, and her most treasured blessings.

Another blessing in Karen's life is her vocation in the world of publishing. As an editor who specializes in fiction, Karen has had the delight of working with such authors as Francine Rivers, Gilbert Morris, Angela Elwell Hunt, Robin Jones Gunn, Liz Curtis Higgs, Catherine Palmer, Karen Kingsbury, Diane Noble, Sharon Foster, Deborah Bedford, Robin Lee Hatcher, and many others. As an author, Karen has written more than a dozen books, fiction and nonfiction. Her novels and novellas share several common threads: faith, adventure, humor, and animals—domestic and wild—of all sorts, shapes, and sizes. Karen and her husband, Don, live in Oregon with their "kids," two mischief-making Siberian huskies.

A Matter of
Perspective

Jefferson Scott

ine sap, wonderful."

Garreth Adamson flicked a pine needle off the yellow-speckled roof of his Buick Century and plopped in. He had the car moving before his briefcase had even come to rest on the seat beside him. The wheels crunched around the circular gravel drive, and he pulled onto the paved street in a cloud of Central Oregon dust.

He actually had to wait for cars to go by at the corner where the road to his subdivision met with the highway. McKenzie Pass was only open from about July to October, but for those few months every year, there was traffic on this road. Garreth had a theory that the cars all waited until he showed up at the corner to decide to head on into town.

He pulled out behind an SUV pulling a trailer with two jet skis. There wasn't really a gap between cars, but Garreth was tired of waiting. When the truck behind him honked, he just lifted his palm, as if to say he had no choice.

Sunlight and shadow strobed his vision painfully as he drove through the narrow forest highway. A big Coachmen motor home passed him going the other direction, a map spread out over the steering wheel.

Garreth shook his head. "Just don't take me with you when you run off the road, okay, buddy?"

The cars finally broke out of the trees and into the morning sun.

Sisters High School, on the left, was empty. Wouldn't be long before school started up again, though, and he would have to start slowing to twenty when he went by here. He couldn't wait.

On his right were the first tourist traps this side of Sisters: an elk farm and a llama ranch. Sweeping fields of green grass, kept verdant by constant watering from those rolling multi-sprinkler machines. Fifty or so elk grazed near the fence, and in the next field a gaggle of llamas was giving somebody's lapdog a serious look. Twenty cars were pulled off onto the grassy margin. Garreth had to hit the brakes when the car ahead of him decided he had to stop, too. *Tourists.*

As he punched the accelerator, he glanced at the plates on the parked cars. California, of course. He should've known when he'd seen the pudgy slobs heaving themselves out of the gas guzzlers they drove, posing for photos from ridiculous telescoping cameras held by equally lumpy photographers. Sure, the Three Sisters mountains looked good behind the green fields populated by exotic animals, but come on, how many times could that same photo be taken?

Something like a sneer pinched Garreth's mouth as he raced by. It was Californians who had driven so many good people from Sisters. It was one thing to visit Sisters as a vacation destination; it was something else entirely to move here. Thanks to Californians and their expectations for what property and homes ought to cost, the cost of housing here had gone through the stratosphere. Now natives of Sisters couldn't afford to live in their own hometown. It was sickening.

At the far edge of the llama ranch, Garreth noticed the fresh white pine frames of two new buildings being built. That made seven new digs in what four months ago had been an open field abutting the ranch. Just what they needed: more apartments for more Californians to move here. He thought of the book that had come out five years ago ranking Sisters among the top ten spots in America for raising a family. The author ought to be taken out and executed.

Garreth had to wait for traffic again when the highway merged with the main road coming from Santiam Pass and heading into downtown Sisters. A seemingly endless caravan of recreational vehicles and eighteen-wheelers. He drummed his fingers on the wheel, bemoaning for the ten thousandth time the lack of a traffic bypass around Sisters. He'd voted for it, but it had failed.

He spotted a small gap and plunged in. The main drag through

Sisters had lost its charm for Garreth. How could he enjoy the 1880s Western motif of the buildings when the sidewalks were crowded with trash-throwing, cigarette-tossing out-of-towners? Even Hotel Sisters, the two-story yellow restaurant that looked like something straight out of *Gunsmoke,* looked cheap with so many tourists taking snapshots of it.

He sat there for three minutes and counting, waiting for someone to stop so he could turn left. He glanced at the clock on the dash: 8:03. Wonderful.

Finally, a woman pushing a stroller braved the crosswalk, and traffic stopped for her. Grudgingly, Garreth blew air through his lips. How long before the city council saw the need for some kind of pedestrian safety in Sisters? The bypass would've solved the problem. Then, when the international quilt show and the national rodeo came, when the jazz festival and all the rest happened, they could just shut the town down to cars and let people walk everywhere. Would someone have to get hit before the council took action? He used the traffic gap the woman had created and turned left.

Garreth pulled into a less-than-desirable parking space at ten after eight. He spotted a vice president crossing the parking lot, so he snatched his briefcase and hopped out.

"Morning, Jim," Garreth said. "Glorious day in the Lord, isn't it?"

Jim Echols, VP of Sales for Cascade Christian Gifts, inhaled deeply. "That it is, Mr. Adamson. That it is. How was your weekend?"

"Wonderful. Just spent time with the family, praising God for what He's created out here."

"Mmm," Echols hummed as they entered the building. "Wise man. Have a good day, all right?"

"You too!"

Nobody noticed Garreth as he made his way through the cubicles to his office. He shut his door with a sigh. Maybe they'd think he'd been in there all morning.

The usual array of phone messages, e-mails, and mysterious packages had accumulated on his desk since Friday afternoon. Garreth fell into his chair and flipped on the radio. Another day of so-called ministry.

The Christian gift industry, too, had lost its luster for Garreth. Internal squabbling, the demands of the market, and the behavior of celebrity artists—all the trappings of the secular gift market—were in full force here, too.

He cruised through the day in a funk. Everything he did, he did well—it just didn't have any meaning for him. He was bored and bitter. Most of the time his thoughts strayed to other things: other jobs, other places he might live, other men's wives… Somewhere he'd lost his way. He knew he was out of step with God, but he had no clue how to get back.

The knock physically startled him. His afternoon coffee sloshed in his company cup. "Come in."

It was his manager, a tall, model-type recently up from (you guessed it) California. "You got a sec, Garreth?"

"Sure, Dominic. You want to sit down?"

"No. Tell you what, why don't you finish up what you're doing and step into Ted's office."

Ted was Garreth's vice president. "Okay. Be right in."

Dominic and Ted stopped speaking when Garreth walked in. "Hey, there, Gare," Ted said. "Pull up a chair."

Garreth sat. He felt himself begin to sweat.

"How was your weekend, Garreth?" Ted asked.

He was about to give his standard Christianese quip, but it lodged in his larynx. "It…it was nice. Thanks. How was yours?"

"Fine. Say, how are you doing, buddy?"

Garreth looked from his VP to his manager and back. "Just fine, Ted. How are you?"

"Your job still suit you?"

"My job?"

"Right," Ted said. "Are you still enjoying working here?"

Garreth sat up straighter. "I love my job, Ted. You know that."

Ted nodded solemnly. "What would you think about a special assignment? You think you're up to it?"

Garreth's eyes widened. "Sure, Ted. Of course I'm up to it. I'm here to please, at your service, whatever you want. Just…you know, just so long as it's not like the 'special assignment' Kim Phillips got last month. It's not like that, right? I mean, as soon as she finished it, she was laid off."

No one spoke for a minute. Garreth noticed the golf photos all over Ted's office. He had an absurd clock with a golf-club second hand putting the seconds away. Through the door behind him, Garreth could hear his own phone ringing. He didn't move.

Dominic crossed his legs. "Garreth, we're just thinking that maybe you'd be happier somewhere else."

"Somewhere else?"

"Right. Like maybe over in marketing or sales?"

"I like it here, Dominic."

"Maybe you'd even like it in the Portland office," Dominic said. "Ever thought of that?"

Garreth laughed—at least he meant to laugh. "Are you kidding? Portland? Traffic and crime and gangs and homeless people. And all that…city?"

"The Blazers are there," Dominic said.

"And Portland has so much culture, Garreth," Ted said, managing to sound almost wistful. "I get back there whenever I can for the theater and the symphony."

"I really don't think I—"

"Here's what we have in mind," Dominic said. "Steve Purswell has an opening in admin over there. It's a spot we think you'd be great for. You'll be working in accounts receivable, helping Cascade's bottom line. And you know we can always use the help there, right?"

"Sure, but I—"

"The job's yours if you want it. You'd start September first."

"September first? That's in two weeks!"

"Your spot's in a nice quiet area," Ted said. "I was up there last week talking to Steve. It's ready for you."

"A cubicle?" Garreth folded his arms. "Well, there's my decision right there, then. I love my office. I worked hard for it and waited a long time. I don't really feel like going back into a cube."

Another silence, this one icier than before. Garreth felt an almost uncontrollable urge to bolt for the door. Finally Ted leaned forward, elbows on knees.

"Here's the deal, Gare. You don't have a whole lot of choice right now. Your attitude is…not what we like to see in a Christian company. Do you know how many people have told me things you've said about me and Dominic and the company? You're lucky I've stopped them where they were, because if they ever got up to Michael you'd be out of here so fast your head would spin."

A flush crept up Garreth's neck. He held his silence.

"Your work is suffering," Ted continued, "you're missing deadlines, you're getting to work late and leaving early, and taking long lunches almost every day."

"I didn't realize I was being watched." The words were out of his lips before he could stop them.

"You're not being watched," Dominic said. "But some things are hard to miss."

Ted went on. "I've actually had artists calling me telling me things you've said about Cascade Gifts. You can imagine my surprise—and my discomfort—as I tried to dig out of the holes I found myself in."

The phone on Ted's desk rang. He swiveled around and jabbed the button to consign the caller to voice mail.

"I'll lay it on the line for you, Mr. Adamson: I'm fed up with your attitude and your behavior. Do you know we almost lost Joy Leeman because of you? She was ready to sign with New Day because you told her Cascade was doomed to go bankrupt over all the poor decisions management was making. Why in the *world* would you say something like that?"

"I didn't s—"

"You know what? I don't even want to hear it. She didn't go to New Day. I salvaged it. But that was a conversation I never should've had to have."

Garreth looked at Dominic. "This is all coming from you, isn't it? You've been out to get me since I got here."

Dominic's eyes bulged, but it was Ted who answered. "You are so wrong, Garreth. I wanted to fire you two weeks ago, after that talk with Joy. But Dominic stood in the gap for you. He said you were a good employee when you tried hard. He suggested the transfer to Portland. When I was up there I found out who had an opening and got you in with Steve." Ted shook his head. "Don't burn your bridges, boy. One day you're going to find yourself on the wrong side of the river."

Garreth clenched his fists. "I…Dominic, I didn't know. I'm—"

"Forget it."

"So here's the deal, Gare," Ted said. "You can transfer to accounts receivable or you can walk. We'll give you a severance package and write you some letters. What's it gonna be?"

Something inside Garreth fell, like a weak table leg finally giving way. "I don't…I mean, could you…could I have another chance? I know I've been messing up at work. And it's not just at work; it's my whole life. I feel so out of control all the time and I know it has to do with my walk with God. I'm just…I've just gotten, I don't know, *bored* with God. But I know I can get it right.

"I'm sorry about the things I've said about everybody. I just…fall into it. And people like to listen. Certain people, I mean. And I guess it kind of poisons you. Anyway, what I'm trying to say is that…" He looked at his manager and his vice president. "I'm out of luck, aren't I?"

Ted rubbed his face. "Oh, Gare. It's not that we—"

Ruby, Ted's executive assistant, barged into the office. "I'm sorry to interrupt, Ted, but there's been an accident. Kent's car was hit coming back from a meeting."

Everybody stood, speaking at once. "What?" "How?" "Is he okay?"

"Kent and Donna and Bill and Esther were all in the car, too," Ruby said. "They're on the way to St. Charles' in two ambulances. They're CareFlighting Donna straight to Portland."

"Oh, no."

"Is everyone alive?"

Ruby sat down. "I think all of our people are alive. But the lady in the car that hit them…"

The entire company wanted to get in cars and drive the eighteen miles to Bend. But in the end the order came down that only top management would go.

Garreth was back in his office when Dominic came by. "Looks like you get your wish."

"What do you mean?"

"That lady just gave you your job back. With Kent and Donna out for six weeks, we can't afford to lose you right now."

Garreth shut his eyes. "I'm ashamed to say I thought of that, too." He looked up. "Dominic, I really am sorry for what I said to you in there."

Dominic smiled and shook his head. "What's gotten into you, Gare? You used to have the best attitude of anyone here. You'd always come in singing some worship song or telling me what God was teaching you. Where'd that guy go?"

"I have no idea. But I'm sure going to go looking for him."

"Well, don't look for him; look for *Him*," Dominic said, pointing up. "That's where you'll find what you're looking for." He touched Garreth on the shoulder. "Come back to us, Gare."

Garreth was the last one to leave that night. He set the alarm and locked up behind himself. When he stepped outside, he thought he'd never seen a bluer sky. It was this immaculate cerulean that seemed to declare what God's favorite color must be.

When he pulled up to the corner near Hotel Sisters, the evening sun was hitting it just right. It seemed to glow with a timeless light, a light it shared with the old buildings, the cars, the people thronging the little town's sidewalks and shops.

When he passed the last building on the edge of town, the mountains struck him almost bodily. Had he ever really seen them before? Not in months. Three snow-speckled peaks, lifting themselves in praise, cloaked in sunset pink, crying out for him to join them in worship.

Arcs of water from the sprinklers combed the verdant fields like silver feathers. Maybe green was God's favorite color instead. Majestic elk pranced to and fro, made noble by size, patience, and the shepherding mountains behind.

Garreth pulled off the road. He strode to the wooden fence and hung on it, staring in awe at God's creation. The mountains rose out of the clouds as if from the steam of creation. How could man not see God when all around him were views like this?

He hung his head, cut to the quick by his own thoughts. How had he strayed so far from God? From who he really was? He vowed to run back to Jesus if He would still have him. In his spirit, he knew that He would.

He suddenly noticed he was shoulder to shoulder with his fellow man, worshiping the Lord of the mountains. He took pictures for a group of tourists so everyone could be in the shot.

He drove through the deep forest, astounded by the massive ponderosa pines on either side. Their towering trunks glowed orange in the setting sun. Sunlight dappled the road and bathed his face a golden sheen.

Garreth pulled into his subdivision, lost in reverie. He waved at cars going the other direction, and the drivers waved back. He had to stop for a family of deer that was crossing the road—a buck still in the velvet, a doe, and two spotted fawns. Garreth watched in wonder.

When he pulled off the road onto his gravel drive, the sound was a mercy. He rolled along slowly, not wanting to raise a cloud of dust.

He shut the car off, opened the door, and slid out. The wind blew through the pines like heavenly strings, pure salve for his soul. The treetops were aflame with sunlight. He swayed there, eyes closed, breathing the pollen, feeling true earth beneath his feet—praising God for a second chance. Grateful for the tiny drops of liquid that fell on his face like angel tears.

Pine sap. Wonderful.

ABOUT THE AUTHOR

Jefferson Scott has lived most of his life in north Texas. But when he moved to the ponderosa forest around Sisters, Oregon, he knew he was home to stay (God willing!). Still, he knows that when we take our eyes off God, discontentment can creep in even if we live in the most beautiful spot on earth. "A Matter of Perspective" is a study of how one event can cause the things we take for granted to become precious once more.

Scott's Christian technothrillers include *Virtually Eliminated, Terminal Logic,* and *Fatal Defect.* Find more of his writing at www.nappaland.com.

THE DARKEST NIGHT

Lauraine Snelling

obby...Robby!"

My voice cracked. Tension crept over the top of my scalp and pulled at my eyes. Where had he gone? I had put my three-year-old, not-so-charming-today son to bed for his usual one o'clock nap. He and I both needed it after the fussy morning we'd had. Nothing had gone right. Panic was giving me the shakes.

It started off when Bob and I had an argument—no, not an argument, a fight. Money again—the fights were always over money. I hate to send my husband off to work with angry words. I guess everyone woke up in a cranky mood.

"Robby, where *are* you?" I looked in the beds, the closets, all over the house. Where would such a little tyke go?

I dialed my neighbor and best friend. "Marge!" My voice rose an octave. "Robby is gone. Have you seen him?"

"Now, calm down," Marge said in her soft-spoken way.

Who wants to be calm? I want to see Robby—now!

"How long has he been gone?"

"I don't know. I put him down at one like always, but I was still so tired from that flu that I had to lay down for a nap. I only meant to sleep for half an hour, but I didn't wake up. Now...he's gone."

"Where have you looked?"

"Everywhere...the house...the yard. He's never opened the gate by himself before."

"I'll get my coat. The kids will be home from school in a couple of minutes. They can help us look."

"Hurry!" I hung up, but my fingers clung to the phone.

Pulse racing, I glanced around my yellow and orange kitchen. The breakfast table not yet cleared, our tiger cat licking up the milk Robby had spilled at lunch. When would I get my act together? Morning fights made me feel like chucking it all, like I was completely worthless.

I shook my head. Who cares about that? Right now, Robby was all that mattered. *Think, Pat, think!*

A gust of late October chill blew in as Marge opened the back door. There's nothing like late fall in Washington state to put goosebumps on your arms.

"Brrr. Let's go." She paused. "Have you called Bob yet?"

"No, I'm afraid to. He left in such a huff this morning. He'll just think this is one more thing I can't do right."

"Call him. He needs to know."

"No, I can't. We'll find Robby any minute. It's no use worrying him for nothing." I tried to smile. That's all it would take, a few minutes. After all, a little guy like Robby couldn't have gone far.

Shrieks and hollers of "good-bye" and "see you tomorrow" rang from the long yellow school bus stopped in front of Marge's house. She dashed out the front door.

"You kids drop your stuff. Robby is gone. Help us look for him."

Bashful, sixteen-year-old Kevin was the first to run around to our back door. "Gosh, Pat, I—I'm sorry. Have you looked in the woods yet?"

"No, he's never gone outside the fence before."

"Where's Blacky?" Kevin glanced over at the empty chain in front of the doghouse.

"I don't know." I hadn't thought to check. "Wait, Blacky was in the house." I thought back. "I let him off the chain this morning so he and Robby could play inside. It was so cold out."

I started to shiver again. Marge put her arm around my shoulders.

"Kevin, go look in the woods, down by the creek. If Robby is with Blacky—well, you know how that dog loves water."

"Where do you want me to go, Mom?" asked Karen, Kevin's graceful blond twin. The twins took turns sitting for Robby on the rare nights we went out. Kevin had been teaching Robby how to catch a football. Karen read him stories by the hour. They both treated him like a much loved baby brother.

"Down the street, check at each of the houses. Maybe they went into someone else's back yard to play."

Both the kids took off. "Now, you go up the street that way," Marge said to me, "and I'll go over one block and cover Garfield." She waved as she jogged across the newly patched asphalt.

I nodded. It was all I could do. While the sun was shining, the late afternoon wind tugged at my sheepskin jacket. I wondered if Robby had on a jacket. I'd forgotten to check.

I mounted my bike with the youth carrier bolted on the back.

"Robby...*Robby!*" I called again and again. "Blacky!" I tried to whistle. My lips wouldn't pucker. Robby and Blacky *must* be together, or Blacky would have come by now. He never left Robby by himself. From the start, he had been Robby's self-appointed guardian.

I rang every doorbell.

"Have you seen a little boy, three years old with curly brown hair, blue eyes? He's with a large black lab." If no one answered, I looked in the backyard anyway. My voice sounded like I'd spent three hours cheering at a close basketball game.

What was he wearing? So hard to remember. *Blue jeans. He always wears those. I think I got out a red T-shirt for him this morning.*

At the end of the pavement the houses quit, too. A large, grassy field sloped down to tall evergreens.

I turned and pedaled for home. Maybe one of the others had had more luck than I. That's it. Robby would be sitting at the kitchen table. Kevin would be tickling him 'til he squirmed. And Marge would fix us all a cup of cocoa.

The three blocks back to the house seemed to take forever. No lights in the front room, they'd all be in the kitchen. I opened the door to silence. The mess was still there, but no Robby.

"Oh God, please watch over him. He's so little."

Marge and Karen came running in the back door.

"No sign of them," Marge panted. "I went up and down both sides of Garfield. No one had seen them."

"I went clear down to the shopping center," Karen added. "Nothing."

"Has Kevin come back yet?" Marge asked.

"Don't think so, but I just got back myself. How far can a little guy go?"

Karen shrugged, her lips quivering.

I grabbed Marge's hands. "You don't suppose someone kidnapped him?"

"No." She squeezed my cold hands. "No, Blacky wouldn't let that happen. No one touches Robby when he's around!" Marge, always the logical one. Thank you, God, for a friend like her.

"Where can I go next?" Karen's blue eyes filled with tears. Karen often came over to take Robby with her on walks.

"Why don't you hit the woods and help Kevin? There's a lot of ground to cover back there."

"Guess I'd better call Bob." I hunched my shoulders.

"Yes, and the police right after that. We've got to have more help."

I could hardly see the numbers as I dialed the phone.

"Can I speak to Bob Hansen, please?" I could hear the compressors in the background. The paint sprayers at Bob's body shop were always busy.

"Pat, you know I've asked you not to call me at work."

I interrupted him. "Bob, it's an emergency. Robby's gone."

"Gone? What do you mean gone?"

"I can't find him anywhere. Marge and the kids and I have been looking all over. We can't find him."

"Is Blacky with him?"

"Must be, he's not here either."

"Have you called the police?"

"No, I'm going to right away. Marge said to call you first. Bob, it's getting dark and cold…and…and I'm so scared." I started to cry.

"Calm down, Pat. Call the police. I'll be there as soon as I can."

I hung up the phone and leaned against the wall, trying to stop the tears that had turned into hiccups. Marge wrapped both arms around me. What if I had been all alone? I had never appreciated her calm assurance and good sense as much as now.

She shoved a cup of coffee into my hands. "Drink this and tell me what Bob said."

"He'll be home as soon as he can. Now I have to make sure about what Robby is wearing and call the police. I'll check his bedroom. You look in the living room. See if his blue jacket is anywhere."

I stopped at the door to Robby's room. The bedcover was rumpled, as if he had just climbed out of it, his white-tummied teddy bear thrown against the wall. The red fire truck—how I tired of hearing that clanging bell—was parked in the center of the Big Bird rug. No jacket anywhere. There were his tennis shoes…oh, dear heaven…his tennis shoes. What did he have on his feet?

I ran to the kitchen where jackets and boots lined one wall by the pantry. *Thank you, Jesus, his cowboy boots are gone. No jacket, so he must have that on, too.*

"No jacket in the other room." Marge had come back from her search. "I'll dial 9-1-1. You sit down for a minute." She handed me the telephone.

I slumped against the hard frame of a wooden chair. The wood pressing at the back of my neck helped me concentrate on what to tell the officer.

"Dispatch. How may I help you?"

I clutched the phone. "This is Pat Hansen. My little boy, Robby, is missing." I tried to stifle the sobs but failed.

"Easy now, ma'am. What is your address?"

"336 Hawthorne Lane."

"Phone number?"

"What has that got to do with it? We've got to find Robby!"

"Just give me your phone number," the reassuring voice continued. "I have to know how to get in touch with you. I'll need a lot of information."

"It's 480-3132. Please do something."

"Now tell me exactly what your little boy—"

"Robby."

"What Robby looks like and what he is wearing."

"He is three years old. He has light brown hair—it's curly—and blue eyes. He's wearing…" I continued with the description. It had nothing to do with hugs at bedtime, peanut-butter-and-jelly kisses and soapy giggles in the bathtub. I wondered vaguely how to describe Robby's look of wonder at a tiny tree frog's feet on the front window, his explosion of joy when Blacky puts one paw on Robby's tummy when they wrestle…and licks his face all over.

Robby, the child I get impatient with, but would die without….

I jerked my mind back. "He has on a blue jacket and cowboy boots. Our dog is with him."

"The dog, what does it look like?"

"Blacky is a large black Labrador with a red collar. His license is on the collar."

"Where are some of the places he likes to play?" The dispatcher continued the questions as I stuttered answers. "How long has he been gone?"

"I missed him at 3:30." The guilt rolled over me like huge breakers. If only I had been more careful, not gone to sleep. My father always said that I'd lose my head if it wasn't tacked on. He was right, only it wasn't my head I'd lost. It was his only grandson.

"Has he ever done this before?"

"No, of course not." What did he think? That Robby was a runaway?

"Now, I want you to stay there so someone is always by the phone in case he is found. We'll put officers on this immediately and contact you later."

"Th-th-thank you." Hanging up the wall phone felt like lifting an eighty-pound weight. Nothing on my body worked right. All my eyes wanted to do was run like downspouts in a storm. I wanted to hear a small voice call, "Mommy!" Was it only this morning that I had wanted to be left alone for a while? For a long while?

A car door slammed at the same time gravel sprayed from car wheels in the driveway. Bob burst through the back door.

"Have you found him?"

I shook my head as I ran to the comfort of his strong arms. Neither of us said anything for a moment. All of our morning anger disappeared in our need to hold each other.

"Tell me what's happened so far," Bob said.

I told him everything we had done. As I spoke, the tears refused to stay back.

"Bob, I want him home. You know how frightened he must be?"

"I know. Have the twins come back?"

"No." Marge handed Bob a cup of coffee. "I heard them calling him a while ago, but nothing lately."

"Kevin knows those woods as well as anyone. If Robby is with Blacky, that's probably where they are." Bob swallowed the rest of his coffee. "I'm going to find Kevin. You stay here like the officer said."

"But, Bob, I need to be doing something. I'm going out of my mind." Fear tore at my middle again.

Bob hugged me, then shrugged into his sheepskin jacket. "We'll find him, Pat. He's okay."

I looked at the clock: 5:30. Two hours had gone by and no Robby. I stepped out the back door. The sun was down, the woods beyond our cedar fence already darker than dusk. We'd bought this house because of the open fields and woods, such a perfect place for our future children to grow up. No close neighbors gawking in our back window.

Now the majestic evergreens and flaming vine maple were not the rustling friends of our many walks. The star-flung night was our enemy.

I turned and stumbled over the door frame. My feet didn't want to obey. Each minute hung around like an unwelcome salesman.

The doorbell rang. I hurried through the house, hoping to see…but it was only a blue uniform.

"Mrs. Hansen?"

"Yes, won't you come in?"

"We've looked all over the neighborhood. There's a unit out in the woods and the information has gone out to all the cars." The young officer paused. "I'm sorry, we're doing all we can."

"I know you are. Thank you."

"Is there any more information you can give us? Did he have any medical problems?"

"No, none. He was…is…perfectly healthy." What was my mind doing? *Was.* What an awful thing to think! *I know he is alive. Is. Is, not was.*

"The sheriff's patrol has a canine corps. The dog will be here pretty soon. Can you get some clothing your boy has worn recently that you haven't washed?"

My mind kept wandering away from the conversation. *Careless! You are always losing things: car keys, notes, W-2 forms. You are just careless! Now you've really done it!* The voice inside my head wouldn't stop.

"Mrs. Hansen, are you listening to me?" The officer touched my shaking arm.

"Um, I think so." I swallowed and wet my lips. "No, I'm sorry, what did you say?"

"Do you have someone here with you?"

"Yes, my neighbor."

He seemed relieved. "Good, we'll be back shortly." He turned to go. "I'm sorry, Mrs. Hansen. I have a little boy, too."

Sorry. How can people really know what sorry is? It's not their only baby who is missing.

"Pat…Pat." Marge shook me back to the moment. "The canine unit is here. Get something for the dog to smell."

I ran back to Robby's room: the toys were still in the same places. Grabbing his blue gingham baby quilt, I didn't stop to pick up the bereft brown teddy bear that had tumbled to the floor.

All of my friends had embroidered squares for this quilt and then sewn them together for this long-awaited child. Robby loved it and still slept with it, faded though it was. Whenever Robby needed a hug, he'd go get his quilt and pull at my leg until I picked him up. Then we'd sit down in the rocker to snuggle.

In the backyard stood several men in the beige uniforms of the local sheriff's department. A large black-and-tan hound with long ears and sad eyes was straining at a leash. Nose to the ground, he sniffed at all the places where Robby usually played—the sandbox with the red roof in the corner, the blue-and-white swing set. I handed the man the quilt.

"May I take this along?" he asked.

"Yes, it's Robby's." I prayed that the dog would be the one to find Robby.

The sheriff turned back. "By the way, if you hear one shot, it means we found him. A second shot will mean he's okay."

The dog's wet nose had left a streak of mud on the quilt. Dog pulling at the leash, nose to the ground, man and beast left the yard.

I turned back inside, shivering. Beyond chilly. The temperature was dropping fast. The weatherman's prediction for a temperature drop was coming true. Could such a little boy survive in cold like this?

"Pat, wake up." I jolted as Bob gently shook me.

"Have you found him? Where's Robby?" I jumped out of the rocker. I couldn't even remember sitting down.

"No, everyone is still looking. I came back for some coffee and something to eat. Have you eaten?"

Food. How could anyone eat at a time like this? My stomach heaved at the smell of chicken noodle soup wafting from the kitchen. I could hear the twins talking with Marge. I felt like I was drifting in another world, looking at this one from far, far away.

"Oh." I sank back into the chair. My legs refused to hold me up.

"Pat, come and have a cup of coffee with me." Bob took my hand

and pulled me into the comfort of his arms. I held on to his shoulders, wanting to cry—but all the tears had been used up.

"All right. What time is it?"

"Eleven o'clock."

"Eleven o'clock. Robby's been gone for over seven hours." It seemed more like seven days.

"I know. Come on."

"Well," said Marge as the door slammed behind the twins, whom she'd sent home to bed, "how about some coffee? Soup? I've got it all hot in case anyone comes back and needs it."

Practical Marge. Always caring for someone else. What a blessing. The kitchen, all clean and shiny, was proof that *she* hadn't been day-dreaming.

The night dragged on. Bob went out again about midnight. Each time people came back, I flew to let them in. But each time, no Robby. Where could one little boy have gone in such a short time? How far could he walk? Where was our dog? Blacky should be barking like crazy.

At 4 A.M. the sheriff came in, stamping his feet.

"It'll be dawn soon and easier to locate him. We keep hearing a dog bark every once in a while, but can't zero in on it. Might be one of the neighborhood animals barking at all the commotion." Marge handed him a steaming mug. "Thanks."

"How cold is it out there?" I asked.

"Thirty-five degrees, ma'am. But at least there's no wind or rain." The sheriff had a hard time looking me in the eye. I knew he was losing hope.

"We're giving the dog a rest. We'll take him back out at first light." The man turned to go. "We're doing our best, folks."

I hugged both my elbows with nearly numb hands. I felt so cold here in the house—what about Robby? Being frightened would lower his body temperature even more. I now understood the adage "scared to death."

At five o'clock Bob stumbled back in, face drawn and gray. As he collapsed into the nearest chair, I dished him up some soup.

"He's so little…" That's all Bob could say.

I rubbed the back of his neck, the cold from his jacket creeping into my hands. At least he hadn't accused me of carelessness. I was doing enough of that myself. *If only* was such a vicious accuser. It kept buzzing in my mind like a dentist's drill. *If only* I could turn it off.

The other side of my mind kept praying, *God, please bring him back. I'll be more careful. I'll never be impatient with him or anyone again.*

By six the sky had lightened outside the kitchen window. Slowly the fence became visible and then the trees. I heard the patrol head out with the dog in the lead.

A new day; what would it bring? I didn't think I could stand the agony much longer. They had to find him. He had to be *alive.* Death had already come to our house once before, taking our unborn baby girl. Surely it wouldn't happen again. We were much too young. Death was for old people, for other families.

"He's got to be alive!" I nearly screamed the words. Bob stared into his soup mug.

"Easy, Pat. Hang on." Marge hugged me. "Nobody's given up yet."

I clung to her. She stayed so positive. Surely God wouldn't let this happen to us.

I stepped out onto the back porch. To the east, pink and vermilion slashed the horizon. Shivers instantly started in my shoulders and engulfed me. It was so cold…so bone-chilling cold.

In the distance I heard the dog tracking. So different from a regular bark, his voice carried clearly on the early morning breeze.

In an instant the bugling changed, became more frenzied, then steadied to a deep repetition. Bob bounded to the open door.

"He's found something. That's his treeing call!" Bob hugged my shoulders, straining to catch any differences in tone.

Standing there shivering, afraid to breathe in case we might miss something, we heard a rifle fire once. They'd found him! I couldn't suck air past the granite boulder on my chest. *God, please, please.* Then another shot…

Robby was alive!

With tears cascading down my cheeks, I turned to Bob and his reassuring arms. Robby was alive; he was coming home to us again.

Half an hour later a beaming sheriff pushed open the gate, holding a grubby little boy in his arms and escorted closely by a black lab.

"Here you are, folks. One tired little fellow."

"Mommy!" Robby reached out to my waiting arms.

Mommy. What a wonderful word. I clutched him close, and Bob hugged us both. Blue eyes sparkled above tear-stained cheeks.

"Mommy, I'm hungry." Robby looked from face to face as we all burst out laughing.

"Leave it to a boy." Marge covered her tears with a chuckle.

Blacky leapt around our feet, not wanting to be left out. We all trooped into the kitchen. After changing his wet clothes, I set Robby in his high chair and took the cereal down from the cupboard.

"Excuse me, folks," the officer interrupted. "I have to file a report. I'll be right back."

The officer later told us that they had found Blacky and Robby curled up in a narrow ravine under thick huckleberry bushes. He figured Robby had slid down and couldn't climb back out. Robby was still asleep, but Blacky's barking had brought the searchers. Our faithful dog had curled around Robby's sleeping body, keeping him warm.

And alive.

"He probably wouldn't have made it without the dog," one of the rescue team members said. "He was lucky."

"That dog is a real protector," the sheriff added. "He wasn't going to let us touch your boy."

We felt blessed beyond belief. Our baby was back. No more resentment for me. Life and living were too precious. After that, when Bob and I would start picking at each other, we would only need to look at Robby playing with Blacky to realize that whatever was bugging us just wasn't as important. Money was still an issue, but not worth fighting over.

Now we try to hash things out together. I've been working on staying on top of things like housework and not forgetting stuff. It's as though those hours when Robby was lost were our trial by fire.

Nightmares haunted me for a long time. I'd wake up shaking and Bob would hold me. He has strong, comforting arms.

I told Marge about the nightmares one day. She said they'd go away eventually—and they did. Now I spend time each day thanking God and reminding myself how blessed we are, especially as we amble through the woods and fields and Robby grabs my knee.

"Gotcha, Mommy."

I swing my son up into my arms and we rub noses, both of us giggling. Ah, what a gift, the laughter of a small child. I am so blessed. I can never say this often enough.

ABOUT THE AUTHOR

Lauraine Snelling is an award winning author of forty novels for young adults and adults. She and her husband, Wayne, live in the mountains of California, where birds and wild critters make homes in their yard. Hummingbirds and California quail are her favorites. Lauraine loves reading, writing, gardening, and any kind of needlework. Her bassett, Woofer, makes sure the rug stays in place, and her cockatiel, Bidley, reminds the dog when visitors have arrived.

ON ACCOUNT OF
A SKUNK

Melody Carlson

Sisters, Oregon, 1896

ell me it ain't so, Sally Rose," pleaded Homer Griffin as he eased himself down on the wooden bench. With a dejected shake of his old, gray head he leaned his elbows onto the gingham-covered table and sighed. "I just been over to Sam's getting my horse shod and he says you're closing this place up—fer good, he says! Now just tell me it ain't so."

Sally Rose smiled at the old regular as she set a cool jar of water in front of him. "You having the special today, Homer?"

He looked up at her and nodded, then groaned. "I swear, Sally Rose, ain't nobody—not since my sweet Bess passed away—has ever made biscuits as tender and light as yours. Please, just tell me it ain't so."

"It's true," called out Ben Hill from the other side of the crowded little café. "She's shutting this place down, and ain't nothing any of us can say is making any difference to her."

"But why, Sally Rose?" moaned Homer. "Ain't because you don't get enough business. Land sakes, I'm in here near every day. I know you're making good money, girl. Please, just tell me why you're closing this place up."

Sally Rose chuckled as she set a small plate of hot biscuits in front of him, and then patted him gently on the shoulder. "Well, Homer, it's kind of a long story…"

"We got time," called out Betty Harrigan, who was already enjoying her supper of lamb stew. The rest of the patrons agreed, urging Sally Rose to tell them her woeful tale.

"Well, first let me get Homer his supper," she said, making her way back to the kitchen. She listened to their comments as she ladled out a generous helping of stew, careful to include plenty of the sweet, tender meat.

She set the steaming plate before Homer, then stepped back to lean against the nearby counter as she wondered how to begin…how to tell them exactly why she was closing the café. "All right, I reckon you could say it's all on account of a skunk," she finally began, pausing to laugh lightly.

"A *skunk?*" said Homer, his mouth still full of the savory stew.

She nodded. "Don't you all remember two years ago in the late spring when Jessie McPeters's horse startled that mother skunk?"

"You bet!" Betty laughed. "The horse threw that boy for a loop and took off, then poor Jessie come a-walkin' back into town a-smellin' to high heavens!"

"Yes, but he also broke his arm," Sally Rose reminded them as she headed over to fetch the coffee pot. "And as a result, my pa's outfit lost themselves a cook."

Homer nodded. "Yep, and that's when you signed on to cook for the sheepherders that summer. Afore that, no one ever knew what a fine cook you were."

"Well, no one but Pa." Sally Rose smiled as she filled Ben's empty cup.

Ben looked up at her. "But what about that young Adam Johnson? I'll bet he knew you were a fine cook."

Sally Rose winked at him. "That's true. Adam had tasted my cooking a time or two. But when I wouldn't change my mind about going out with the sheepherders that summer, Adam threw a real tizzy fit."

"Aha," said Betty. "So that's why he took off like that. We all thought you two were going to be hitched before the end of summer. And no one could ever figure what had set him off like that."

"So Adam didn't approve of his intended going off to live with the sheepherders for a summer," said Ben wryly. "Well, can't say as I blame the boy."

Sally Rose frowned at him. "Ben, you know as good as anyone that my pa was leading the outfit and he wouldn't have allowed me to go along if there was anything disrespectful about it. Besides, it turned out to be a fine summer. Those lovely green meadows and high mountain lakes." She sighed. "I'd been cooped up in town until then and I'd never realized how beautiful this area really was."

"Yeah, you and your pa had barely just moved to Sisters," said Ben. "I recall him telling me that he didn't expect you to stay long, neither. Said you'd dragged your heels all the way from California up here, and that you'd only stay long enough to see him settled, then move on."

She nodded. "That's right. When Pa told me he was moving to Sisters, Oregon, I thought he'd gone plum off his rocker. I promised to come up here with him and then I was heading for a city somewhere— Portland or maybe back to San Francisco. I thought I'd had enough of country living to last me a lifetime."

"I remember Adam talking that same way," added Betty. "No wonder you two hit it off like that, right from the start."

Sally Rose replaced the coffee pot. "Yes, we had some big plans to get ourselves out of here before snowfall."

"But then you lit off with them sheepherders." Homer chuckled. "Ya got a mind of yer own, Sally Rose, that's fer sure. But what's this about shutting down on account of a skunk?"

"Well, like I said, I spent the summer cooking for the sheepherders, and as a result I threw away my chances with Adam." She chuckled. "A blessing in disguise, really. And at the end of summer, Pa gave me a cut of his earnings. I got myself enough money and confidence to start up this little café."

"And we've sure been glad about that," said Betty's husband. "Some of us fellers need a break from all that—" he glanced at his wife—"uh, *good* home cooking upon occasion."

Betty jabbed him sharply with her elbow. "Hush, you! Let her finish the story."

Sally Rose moved a hot apple pie near the window to cool. "So, like I said, on account of the skunk I decided to stay on in this area." She closed her eyes and sighed. "After spending just one summer out there, breathing the smell of the pines and wildflowers and seeing those big beautiful mountains every day…well, I discovered I didn't want to leave this country after all."

"Well then, what's the problem?" complained Homer. "You love living here; we love your café; what's all this nonsense about shutting down on account of a skunk?"

"That's what I'm wondering," said Ben. "I'd say we should be right thankful for that varmint. If not for Jessie upsetting that mama polecat we wouldn't have had this fine place to eat these past two years."

"But that's not the end of the story," said Sally Rose.

"I figured as much," said Homer, pushing his empty plate away from him.

Just then a man who was new to town walked in, and everyone looked up as he removed his hat and nodded to Sally Rose. "Afternoon, everyone," he called out as he found a vacant table next to the wall. "I'll have the special, Sally Rose."

"Coming right up, John." She headed back to the kitchen, listening to their chatter as she filled another plate to heaping.

"You hear that? She called him by his first name," Betty whispered, loud enough for all to hear.

John laughed. "And I'd appreciate it if you all called me by my first name."

"Well then, *John,*" said old Homer as Sally Rose came out of the kitchen, "is it true that yer a preacher man?"

John laughed. "Word spreads fast in small towns."

"So it's true then?"

He nodded. "Yes, I felt God tugging on my heart to come out here and start up a church in Sisters. Our first meeting will be on Sunday at the Foster ranch."

"The Foster ranch?" said Ben, eyebrows raised. "You telling me Jim Foster agreed to doing church out at his place?"

John nodded. "That's right. He and my dad are old buddies."

The group seemed impressed. As she slipped back into the kitchen, Sally Rose hoped this might distract them from their previous conversation.

"Now just a minute, Sally Rose," called out Homer. "You never did finish telling us your story about how you're closing up this place on account of a skunk."

"On account of a *what?*" asked John, his fork clattering to his plate. "What's all this about, Sally Rose?"

She emerged from the kitchen with reddened cheeks and answered hastily. "Oh, I was just telling everyone that I'm going to be shutting down the restaurant soon."

"But on account of a skunk?" John frowned. "What's that all about?"

"Well, on account of the skunk that scared Jessie's horse and landed me a cook's job, and made me love living in this part of the country, and then opening the café, and then, well, other things…."

"What other things?" demanded Betty.

"Well…" Sally Rose glanced over at John.

He laughed. "Well, as long as *I'm* not the skunk, I think you should, by all means, finish the story, Sally Rose."

Everyone looked thoroughly confused now. "What are you talking about?" asked Homer, scratching his head.

"Well, on account of everything I already told you, I wound up staying in town long enough to meet the man who has finally stolen my heart," finished Sally Rose, setting a hand atop John's broad shoulder.

"That's right," said John, standing up to look her in the eyes. "Sally Rose and I plan to be wed on the last Saturday of this month—before her father heads out for summer with the sheep herds. And we'd both appreciate it if all you good folks would come to our wedding. It'll be held out at the Foster ranch."

"Well, I'll be," exclaimed Betty. "So *that's* why you're shutting down the café."

Sally Rose nodded, her face aglow with happiness.

Then John spoke up. "Now, I sure hope these good folks don't think it's because *I'm* making you, Sally Rose."

She laughed. "No, it was completely my decision. Although I must admit, after all this talk today, that I'm having some second thoughts. I just didn't realize how much you folks enjoyed this little place."

They enthusiastically reminded her how much they loved the café and didn't want to lose it.

"Well, maybe you should give this thing some more thought, Sally Rose," said John. "Maybe we can arrive at some sort of compromise, like not being open so many days a week, or perhaps just serving a midday meal—something along those lines."

"Yes!" agreed Ben heartily. "I'm liking this man's way of thinking already."

"I'll say," said Homer. "Why don't you think it over, Sally Rose? Now that everyone in town has heard you're closing up on account of a skunk, you wouldn't want them to be a saying it's on account of your *intended.*"

"That's right!" shrieked Betty. "People might go 'round saying that John Alberts, the new preacher, is a skunk!"

Sally Rose's eyes twinkled. "Not once they got to know him, they wouldn't." Then she went to retrieve the pie cooling by the window and turned to the crowd. "And today, dessert is on the house."

"Three cheers for Sally Rose!" called out Betty's husband.

When it quieted down again, old Homer, his forehead still slightly creased with concern, spoke up. "And you promise to give some more thought to keeping this place open, Sally Rose?"

"You bet I will, Homer." She wiped her hands on her calico apron. "So now, do you all understand how all this *really* was on account of a skunk?"

"Well, God bless that skunk!" called out John Alberts with a wide grin.

ABOUT THE AUTHOR

Melody Carlson is the award-winning author of over fifty books for children, teens, and adults. Her latest novel series, Whispering Pines (Harvest House Publishers), is set in a small tourist town very similar to the one in which she now lives with her husband, two grown sons, and chocolate lab, Bailey.

HOME IS THE SAILOR

Robert Elmer

*P*ull in that sheet a little more." Greg's father pointed at the rope leading to a corner of the small pointed sail at the front of the boat.

Small pointed sail? Greg knew better. That corner of the jib was the clew. And he held a jib sheet, not a rope.

He knew. His dad had made sure of it when he was only a kid. Back when his friends were learning shapes and colors from *Sesame Street,* he was crawling around inside the twenty-seven-foot *Annie B,* learning starboard tacks, baggywrinkles, and chainplates. Before he could walk he knew how to tie a bowline, two half-hitches, and a sheet bend. And by age three he could tell the difference between a ketch, a yawl, and a schooner—from three miles out in Bellingham Bay.

Only trouble was, he hated it all. Or maybe "strong dislike" would be a nicer way to say it. He *strongly disliked* the salt spray that dried on his skin, the nautical mumbo jumbo, the dead fish smells, the water.

Especially the water.

And the deeper it was in the middle of the bay, the more he hated it.

"Ninety-six feet under the keel." Dad checked their electronic depth finder and adjusted his silly canvas wide-brimmed hat. "And perfect sailing weather."

"Right, Dad." Greg closed his eyes and wondered why his father still didn't understand. He thought about what he had to tell his father. He'd rehearsed it for days. *This isn't going to be easy.*

But when had anything with Dad ever been easy? Maybe when he was a little kid, before... He rubbed once more at the scar on his bare foot. Even after ten years, he could still make out the teethmarks.

Sure, everyone had told him it was a one-in-a-million occurrence, a freak accident. He'd tried his best to believe it. But he'd also done a pretty good job of connecting the dots: Eight-year-old Greg Wright goes sailing with Dad. Dad tosses Greg off the boat to go swimming in Fossil Bay. Greg nearly loses his toe to a maniac wolf eel with *very* sharp teeth.

It didn't take much to work the equation backward either. To stay away from eels, stay away from sailing with Dad. Simple.

But he could never disappoint his father. *Who, me? Afraid? Not in Dad's navy.* So Greg had been drafted as first mate, since they could never drag Mom or Andrea out on the boat. After a few, uh, unpleasant encounters, the girls both said they'd had it with the evil Porta Potty.

Thinking he could change their minds, Greg's father had written out the instructions for using their little white pot. He'd even laminated the instructions on a three-by-five-inch card, entitling it "The Wright Way to Flush," and mounted it on the bulkhead above the seat.

Step A: Open valve. Step B: Open lid. Step C...

Never mind. The girls still refused to come sailing, which left reluctant Greg and oblivious Dad.

Greg sighed and cupped a hand over his eyes to shade the sharp afternoon sun as it glimmered off the water. Off to port he could make out the thickly-forested turtle humps of Lummi Island. And just ahead, the little flat-decked *Lummi Chief* scurried like a water bug across Hale Passage, from the mainland out to Lummi Island and back again. A handful of day-trippers and bicyclists crowded around three cars and a UPS van. A couple of young girls waved.

I have to tell him today, Greg reminded himself as he waved back. *No more waiting.*

"Ahhh." His dad took a deep breath. "Nothing smells better than saltwater, eh?"

Greg could imagine plenty of things that smelled better, like double cheeseburgers cooking at Grant's Drive-in on a Saturday night. Now *that* was a good smell. So was cotton candy at the Northwest Washington Fair on a hot August night. Even the grass in their backyard smelled better just after it was cut—as long as it was his sister Andrea's turn to mow.

But not saltwater. Anything but deep, blue-green saltwater.

"Dad, I—" Greg began, but he'd lost his courage. His dad raised one eyebrow.

"Yeah?"

"I…think it's time to turn east, isn't it?"

Greg had already glanced at the chart of Bellingham Bay and San Juan Islands, upon which his father had carefully penciled a course. After slipping through narrow Hale Passage on the slack tide, they would turn north-northwest around Point Migley to a heading of 210 degrees, tack across the Strait of Georgia, and drop anchor in three fathoms at Fossil Bay, Sucia Island.

And that's exactly the way it would happen, because everything always happened the way Dad planned it.

Except maybe this time.

"Pretty soon," replied his father. "Ready about?"

A set of waves surging around the island sent them into a rocking-horse motion. Foam gurgled by the lower railing and the rigging hummed softly in the gathering wind. Greg loosened the jib sheet at his father's command.

"Ready." Greg sighed. He would tell his father later.

Warren Henry Wright looked at his son and wondered how they had drifted so far apart so quickly.

College will do him good, he thought. *It'll sharpen his focus.*

And if anyone needed sharpening, it was Greg. Greg, who could have made straight A's if only he'd applied himself…Greg, who seemed to prefer wasting his evenings playing a whiny electric guitar with his garage band and getting away with B's and C's. That would change this fall. The University of Washington had a fine engineering program.

Not that Warren had ever pushed engineering. Not for a minute. But he didn't hide the fact that he expected his son to excel. What father didn't? As he'd always told his children, the world needed more committed Christians in every field. But the choice was Greg's.

Naturally, Warren had struggled with letting go. And maybe that was part of the problem. But who could blame him? Before he retired last year from the highway department, he'd made his living being in control. By planning for every detail. And then some.

That was good for bridges and overpasses. His projects had always turned out exactly as planned, on time, under budget. He could teach a freshman designer how to figure stress loads and compensate for foundation shift. And he could still do the equations with a slide rule, for heaven's sake.

But teach my own son to make the right decisions?

That was another matter entirely.

He'd thought things would be different once he took early retirement. He'd finally have more time for his wife, Annie. More time for sailing with the kids, a passion of his since he was young.

But somehow he hadn't managed to pass on that passion to them, especially not after the Porta Potty fiasco. Certainly not to his daughter Andrea, who at age fourteen had recently discovered boys in a big way—or rather, they had discovered her. He'd often considered unplugging the phone and posting a No Trespassing sign at the front door.

Greg was another matter. They had once been close, but in the last couple of years before his retirement their relationship had turned intense—or sour. Or something he couldn't quite put his finger on.

Well, it couldn't be helped. With meetings nearly every evening and a brutal travel schedule, he'd missed more of Greg's junior and senior years in high school than he'd liked. And then came all the time spent refurbishing the boat.

"It's okay, Dad," Greg had told him once. Greg had always been like that, easy-going and loyal. Even so, Warren had a nagging feeling that it had not been okay.

He looked at Greg now and wondered how much of the boy's life he had really missed. Too much. Who had taught Greg his values? Not his dad.

Or what about the faith Warren had promised to pass along to his children? That had been put on hold for the past few years, too.

"You know how busy I've been," he'd explained to Annie. She had understood that he couldn't start thinking now about what he had left behind. The calls from church friends he had never returned. The chances he had passed up to pray with Pastor Evans. Even the unkept promise to disciple his brother-in-law, Dave.

Lord, help me to pick up the pieces, he prayed quietly as they glided through Hale Passage. A Lummi Indian fishing boat piled with gillnets passed to starboard, but no one waved.

Greg sat in a corner of the open cockpit with his eyes closed and his headphones on. Warren didn't recognize the wild-looking CD at his son's feet. *Resurrection?* Of course, he didn't recognize very much about his son's world anymore. And whose fault was that?

Maybe tonight we can talk.

Talk. The thought made him bite his lip, because who knew where they would end up once they started? The problem with talk was that he couldn't control it or measure it—not in the way he could measure a good freeway interchange, anyway.

Meanwhile, Greg was off in his own high-decibel, rock-concert world. Only a few feet away physically, but miles away mentally.

Later that afternoon Greg settled into his perch on the foredeck and watched a jet's vapor trail far overhead.

That'll be me, on my way to Nashville. Five days and—he squinted at his watch—*four hours from now.*

Problem was, Greg knew his father didn't have a clue where his son was headed. Not a clue in the world.

He still thinks I'm going to the U.

He chewed on his nails and wondered how con men slept at night. Con men like him. At least his mother had promised not to say anything—though maybe it would have been easier if she had.

No. I have to tell him myself. Soon.

He patted the letters in his shirt pocket, just to be sure. The invitation from Bernie to play lead guitar for *Resurrection* was still there, right next to the college acceptance letter. He resisted the urge to pull out Bernie's note just once more, to reread it again. He would have liked to make sure he wasn't dreaming, that God wasn't pulling his leg.

Dad's never going to understand.

"Ready with the anchor?"

His dad's question broke into Greg's daydream as they neared Fossil Bay. Sandstone cliffs framed the long, narrow cove, giving shelter from the west swells.

"Been ready." Greg glanced back at his father.

"All right, then, on my mark, let it go, but don't—"

"I know." Greg gave his father a weak grin. "Don't let it splash."

Actually, anchoring in Fossil Bay wasn't hard. Just set the hook and back it down. And Warren had confidence in the oversized Bruce-style anchor he had bought for the *Annie B.* It would hold through a hurricane.

The main problems with this mooring were the other boats. Some of them paid out too much anchor chain, others not enough. He jerked his thumb at an obviously homemade purple cabin cruiser drifting nearby.

"Watch out for that one."

"Yeah." Greg slipped back to the cockpit. "But listen, Dad, I have to tell you something."

"Oh?" His father finished coiling a rope, then turned his head to the side, waiting.

"It's about…this fall."

"Greg, if it's about the money, I've already told you not to worry. Your mother and I want to help."

"No. It's not about tuition, Dad."

"Okay." Warren squinted and wondered. "Then what?"

Greg took a deep breath and seemed to study his tennis shoes.

"I'm not going to the U."

After a pregnant pause, Warren gathered his composure. He struggled to make sense of what Greg was telling him: Bernie's offer, doing something to honor God, the chance of a lifetime….

"…and we're going to do lots of praise concerts, get into some warm-up acts, maybe even on some secular stages, you know?"

Warren didn't know.

"It's a ministry, Dad. We're not just goofing around. We've got a bass player, a sweet drummer, and I'm going to play lead—"

"So let me get this straight." Warren stared at his son as if he'd just dropped out of the sky. "You're giving up college to play with your garage band buddies? After all you did to get accepted to college?"

"They're not my garage band, and I'm not giving up on college." Greg pulled out his letters. "See? I've even saved the U-Dub acceptance letter. I *want* to go to school and I *will* go, I promise. Just not now."

"Not now? What does that mean?"

"That means not this year, and maybe not next year, either. Bernie thinks we should go for it now. So do I. We've been praying a lot about it."

Warren tried not to frown, tried to keep from boiling over. He yanked off the knot Greg had just tied on an anchor line and retied it his way.

"So I feel like if I said no to God now, I might not get another chance, not like this. Do you know what I mean, Dad? Have you ever said no to God? I don't want to do that."

The question caught Warren off-guard. He opened his mouth to defend himself, to say the adult thing, but no words came out.

Have you ever said no to God?

"I don't mean to disappoint you and Mom. I just have to do what I think God would want me to do. And…I want your blessing."

Still Warren couldn't find his tongue. And for some reason all he could remember was the little play guitar Greg had always liked to strum as a kid. He'd played for the Sunday school pageant one year. He'd been…what? Ten years old? Everyone had thought it was cute, and it was. But surely it was the sort of thing Greg would grow out of.

"Dad?"

Warren turned away.

"Why don't you take the dinghy ashore?" His voice was husky when he finally spoke. "Stretch your legs. We can talk about it later."

Greg didn't reply, just stuffed the letters back in his pocket. He wrestled the inflatable boat from the cabin top and lowered it into the cove. A minute later he was gone.

By eight o'clock Warren had scrubbed the last of the noodles from the pan. He held it up for inspection to the evening light flickering through the porthole. Where was Greg? So much for father-son bonding. He frowned and looked around the compact cabin of his empty boat.

In the corner by the companionway ladder, his navigation station was filled with the latest aids: a little satellite navigation receiver, a high-power VHF radio, and a laptop loaded with West Coast charts from Ensenada to Anchorage.

So I know how to get there…alone.

His boat was nothing if not shipshape. He'd spent the better part of the past six months, evenings and weekends, organizing the interior of the *Annie B.* Every tool was labeled and double-secured with Velcro tie-downs, from emergency beacons to extra spark plugs for the small but efficient inboard. Each sail was labeled and neatly stowed in well-ventilated lockers, too. Just so.

But so what? He couldn't smile, couldn't feel the pleasure—especially not after what Greg had told him. It didn't matter that he'd finally equipped the *Annie B* just the way he'd wanted. Because as he looked around at the snug little boat, he was only reminded that the real Annie B—the one he'd married twenty-eight years ago—wasn't aboard.

And neither were his children.

How much could I get for this thing? His cheeks still burned from the shame he'd felt at his son's question.

Have you ever said no to God?

"Well yes, son," he said to the empty boat. "As a matter of fact, I tell him *no* all the time."

For just a moment he might have smashed his drinking glass down in disgust. Instead he climbed back upstairs into the cockpit to retrieve the other two dishes he'd left there.

"And to tell you the truth, I've become quite good at it."

He skipped a stair on the way back down into the cabin. Big mistake. Because as he reached to catch himself, the dishes flew out of his grasp. Even worse, his ankle turned and his toe caught between the rungs of the companionway ladder. Warren heard a sickening *snap* as he fell backward and down into the cabin.

"I'm going to U Dub next year."

She batted her eyes at Greg as they sat on the foredeck of her parents' motoryacht, nibbling on legs of barbecued chicken. Greg figured the new Bayliner 47 had *varoomed* out of the factory with every option—and a six-figure price tag to match. "My parents told me I could study whatever I wanted. Daddy's a doctor. I just *love* sushi. What about you?"

"Yeah." Greg nodded absently and took another sip of lemonade as they bobbed at anchor. After a short hike with him around the island, his new friend now chattered aimlessly about her friends, her college plans, her parties. All she needed to keep her going was a good nod once in a while, a smile, or an "uh-huh."

"And a friend of mine is in a sorority, so…"

Not that Greg minded spending time with someone like her. She was his age. The setting sun lit up her golden hair. And would he like more chicken?

No, thanks. From the commanding height of the new Bayliner, he could see where the trim hull of the navy-blue *Annie B* bobbed several hundred yards away. Maybe he had paid out a bit too much slack in the anchor chain.

Dad will be all over that, he predicted as the *Annie* swung to within a couple lengths of the homemade purple cabin cruiser. *In a minute, he's going to be ordering all hands on deck.*

For the first time in as long as he could remember, Warren felt utterly, completely helpless. Weather he could plan for; boats he could fix. But now, nothing he said or did made any difference. The pain in his broken leg had a mind of its own. Like Greg, it wouldn't listen. His head throbbed as well. For the next couple of hours Warren lay in an unceremonious heap on the floor, struggling to stay conscious.

As he did, every gasp for air only clinched his leg more tightly in a grip of searing pain. And every move made him want to scream in agony.

But no, that would not do.

No one's going to find me like this. Only Greg. But what's taking him so long?

Outside, he heard a thump and a scrape, then another scrape.

"Darn," he mumbled, "that old scow next to us has pulled loose."

He bit his bottom lip to take his mind off the pain, but nothing would dull the throbbing. And nothing could keep Greg's words from repeating, over and over, in his mind: *Have you ever said no to God?*

Warren knew the answer to his son's question. Still, all he could do was lay on his back in the middle of the well-polished teak floor, and pray, and wait. His mind faded in and out like a too-distant radio station. For a while he wasn't even quite sure what he was praying for.

For himself?

"For Greg, Lord," he whispered, "that he'd be happy serving You. And please…don't let me get in his way."

The thought of getting in the way seemed almost funny as Warren considered his position on the floor. And he couldn't stop praying…couldn't stop thinking of all the ways he'd said no.

No to the people at church. Would Dave still want to meet with him, after all this time?

No to Annie. Naturally, he'd been too busy working.

No to Greg and Andrea. The boat had come first.

And no to God.

But that was going to change…

"And they were like—" she giggled—"like, *begging* me to come to this party, and…"

"Uh-huh." By this time Greg had located a pair of binoculars for a better view of the *Annie B*. Though it was just a few hundred yards away, he could see in the windows as if he were on deck.

As far as he could tell, no one was aboard the purple cruiser. Like a has-been hockey player, it body-checked the trim little sailboat in the midsection.

"But my daddy, did I tell you he's a doctor? He *promised* he would pay for everything, so I thought—"

Greg didn't wait for her to finish. And he never took his eye off the two boats as he launched down the steps and dove into the inflatable.

"Sorry to run," he called over his shoulder as he yanked at the starter cord of the little outboard. "Thanks for the chicken."

"Oh!" She leaned over the railing to watch him zig-zag through the anchorage. "But, like, already? I thought we could—"

"Dad!" Greg cried as he rammed the inflatable against the hull of the *Annie B* like a bumper-boat and tumbled onto the deck. Never mind the old purple cruiser that now lurched dangerously close by. Never mind anything.

"Dad, are you here?"

Warren Wright's angel finally came tumbling in through the companionway, nearly falling over his father in the process. And he supposed it wasn't the way an angel was supposed to act, exactly, blubbering over him, telling him he was sorry—sorry for not staying with him, that this never would have happened if he hadn't left his father alone.

Some of it Warren heard, some he didn't. He wasn't quite sure. But he was sure that his leg still throbbed.

"I'm so sorry. I should've been here." Warren heard that part.

"I don't blame you, son." He pulled Greg closer. "But now, I've been thinking."

"Shh, Dad. Just relax. Help is on the way."

"No, listen!" Warren tried to lift himself up, but that hurt too much. Best he could do was grip Greg's hand. "I'm going to make you a deal."

"Dad, you don't need to—"

"Would you stop it? I've been laying here thinking for the past couple of hours. The Lord got my attention, understand? And now I'm trying to tell you something."

"All right, Dad, but—"

"The deal is this: I won't say no any more to God if you don't, either. Got it?"

Greg didn't answer right away.

"Did you hear me, Son? I say yes to God, you say yes to God. Deal?"

Greg didn't let go of his father's hand. And his whisper was soft but clear. "Okay, Dad. It's a deal."

"And one more thing." Warren groped for his son's shirt pocket. After a moment he pulled out the folded envelope with a University of Washington return address. "Is this the acceptance letter you were telling me about?"

"Yeah, Dad."

Warren ripped it in half and dropped the two pieces in his son's lap.

"I'll be in the front row for your first concert." He winked at Greg.

And Warren Wright smiled as he laid his head back on the floor of the *Annie B* to wait for the doctor.

ABOUT THE AUTHOR

Robert Elmer is the author of the new Promise of Zion historical fiction series for young readers, as well as *AstroKids,* the Young Underground series, and the Adventures Down Under series. He and his wife, Ronda, live with their three teenagers in the Pacific Northwest. His experience as a lifelong sailing enthusiast served as inspiration for this story, as well as his love for the beautiful Puget Sound waters near his home.

CICELY'S HATS

Janet Chester Bly

On the June morning that Neoma Hocking and her grandchildren left St. Joseph, Missouri, no one saw them off.

They loaded Hank's extended-cab truck and fifth wheeler with vacation gear and drove a determined route up Highway 29, past twisted hollers, rocky terraces, and thick forest fences…the familiar scenes of home to Neoma. Now home was a retreating landscape in her rear-view mirror—a shell of a house with all the furniture stored and only a phone still hooked up.

Neoma resisted the strong urge to call one more time before crossing the Missouri border…to check for messages, just in case. She chewed antacid tablets and stole a glimpse at the kids in the back seat. Twelve-year-old Becky met her gaze with a glum look. She crossed her eyes in that way of hers that said, "Don't you dare ask what I'm thinking." Becky's five-year-old brother, Pudge, strained like a caged puppy against the seat belt. *At least they're not fighting yet.*

Two thousand long miles of prairie, mountains, and desert to cross. The corn rows got smaller, dryer. The sky opened to a full, blazing sweep. Neoma refereed spats and navigated highway signs. Two delays for pickup repairs. A blown-out tire in Nebraska. A broken drive shaft in Wyoming when a semi sideswiped them. They flew through Utah. At nights she called the empty house to listen for a message that was never there, prayed for patience and guidance, then tossed and turned on her hard trailer bunk.

Her vehicle stalled in Winnemucca, Nevada, just one day short of the California coast.

She knew she should drive straight to the ocean and on to Disneyland. The kids were anxious to get there. And it's what Hank would want her to do.

"We're headed west," Hank had told Neoma and the whole church two months before he was to retire. "I'm going to be the first descendant of Theodore Hocking to stick my bare feet in the Pacific."

Hank had packed Theodore's gold panning supplies and Pony Express Bible in the fifth wheeler while Neoma envisioned long visits with her college chum in Utah, a side trip to Aunt Cee's in Idaho, long novels to read, and lazy evenings of pulling out new sable brushes and an old easel on California beaches.

Now Neoma studied a soiled and tattered map at the Winnemucca campground. The closer they got to the California state line, the harder her head pounded.

"Make Pudge sleep with you, Nana. It's too crowded. I can hardly breathe." Becky kicked dirt devils, her hair stringy over a sullen face and freckles.

She looks so much like Trish at that age. Neoma shuddered. *And just as prickly.*

Pudge rammed Matchbox cars down dirt lanes, his arms and legs caked with grime. "Are we almost to Disneyland?" he asked.

Neoma pushed her hand across the map trying to press the crinkles into smooth paths. Fatigue seeped into her bones. *The kids are beyond restless. I should keep to the route. There are duties to perform.* She glanced at the camper that held the urn. Ashes over the Pacific, that's what Hank wanted.

"Aunt Cee lives in Idaho," she said. "A place called Road's End. We might never get by this way again." She avoided the kids' eyes and braced herself against the barrage of complaints. *Just this once. Just for me.*

Neoma roused them early the next morning for the ten-hour trip detour north.

She had Aunt Cee on her mind when she edged up the rugged four-thousand-foot grind of White Bird Grade. Aunt Cee, her father's youngest sister and a prominent guest at all family funerals and weddings. She was a colorful memory in Neoma's gray world.

"If Aunt Cee comes, it's party time," Trish had always said.

Aunt Cee had also lost a daughter and three husbands. She would understand.

When the truck ground to the top of the mountain, Neoma eased it across the rolling hills of the Camas Prairie. Becky pushed her feet into the back of the driver's seat, pounding against Neoma's tense flesh. Pudge yelled, "Nana! Becky's pinching me."

Neoma stomped down on the brakes. She pulled to the side of the road and turned to the children. "Becky, you sit up here with me."

Pudge, raccoon eyes wide, cheeks smudged, sat white-faced and sucked his finger. When Becky got in the front she slammed the door and crossed her arms tight across her chest, face rigid. Neoma didn't know whether to hug the girl or slap her. Instead she ran a hand over her tangled red hair. Becky yanked her hair back, shaking it out.

By the time they reached the Road's End turnoff, the June sky was gray and overcast. The rough pavement curved between stands of aspens and groves of evergreens. Sunflowers and Indian paintbrush filled the meadow.

At Road's End, all the streets were dirt paths. Empty shacks marked nameless residents who had left, taking their stories with them. Every house that was lit up and inhabited proved Road's End still had a reason to exist. Neoma thought it looked like the sort of place to hide, to be left alone, to just exist or sort things out. Or it could be a restful stop on the way to somewhere else.

Neoma studied a handwritten chart of directions on the back of a Christmas card. She turned off on an ungravelled road and halted in front of an old clapboard house. Six weathered steps led to a large covered porch lined with wooden benches. The shades were all up. Angels and ivy were etched into the glass that topped the double front doors.

A breeze whipped around them as they eased out of the truck. Neoma inhaled the scent of sweet pine and stretched her stiff legs. She pulled jackets out of the trailer for the children.

"Does Aunt Cee know we're coming?" Becky asked.

"I wrote her that we were heading west. She invited us to stop by, but I didn't promise anything," Neoma admitted. "We'll stay an hour or two and head on down the road."

Dark clouds had begun to gather like a flock of dirty sheep.

The door opened right before Neoma knocked. The house smelled of fresh popped corn and hot caramel and chocolate. Neoma caught a glimpse of bleached white hair swept up into a wide brimmed black hat that was cocked to the side and tied under her chin. A black velvet ribbon circled Aunt Cee's neck, holding a white satin rose. Black leggings ended inches above four-inch spike heels.

Cicely James had the quick eyes of a canny mind—cat eyes. Her words came fast, like skipped stones. "Neoma, how delightful! You and the children *did* come."

"I'm sorry to intrude on you, Aunt Cee—" Neoma began.

"Nonsense. Your rooms are all ready. You can stay as long as you like." She hugged Becky, then Pudge, then Neoma. A heavenly scent of lilacs engulfed them.

"We've got a trailer. We're camping—"

"There's a squall coming in. It may even snow," Aunt Cee said. "It's very warm and snug in here."

Becky gave Neoma a look of panic. "But what is there to do?"

Cicely laughed. "You must come to the rec room." She fanned her fingers toward them, nails squared and red, all exactly the same long length.

They followed her past a large kitchen. A pot of morel mushrooms soaked in water on the stove, floating on the surface like sea anemones. "Just picked them out of the forest," she explained.

Becky gagged.

Cicely pretended not to notice as she led them to a room spilling over with books and games. The walls were egg-yolk yellow and bare. A window looked out on a large manicured yard with a wooden seat and rope swings and a basketball court. "The former owner had lots of children," she explained.

"We're going to Disneyland," Pudge announced as he danced around the room.

Becky glared at Neoma, her eyes scratching through to her heart, and bumped against a tower of blocks in the shape of a fortress. The pieces scattered across the shiny wood floor.

Neoma felt the emptiness of depression settling in. She could imagine Hank saying, *You've got to think before you commit, Neoma. Think of the children....*

At dinner Becky only picked at the mushroom fritters, fried chicken, and garlic mashed potatoes, but she perked up at the fudge sundaes for dessert. Cicely coaxed Becky to play with Pudge in the rec room, throwing a rubber ball at ten plastic pins. She brought them homemade Cracker Jacks in bright pink resin bowls for a snack.

"So you're moving." Cicely wound her pencil thin legs around a stool in the kitchen.

"We have an option on an apartment. But I don't know for sure." *Oh, why did I say that? Now she'll want me to explain.* "Why do they call this Road's End?" Maybe she could change the subject.

Cicely laughed. "Nothing special about it. It's because the only way to get out is to go back the way you came in."

The guest rooms had double beds lapped with brightly-colored quilts. The mattress was soft, the sheets white-cotton clean. After Neoma had tucked Pudge in and murmured a prayer, she made her nightly call to St. Joe. No messages. As usual.

Neoma slipped into sweatpants and a T-shirt for nightclothes. She wadded her pillow into a soft ball and propped it behind her neck.

That night she dreamed of climbing a hill to her favorite park above the Missouri River. Hank leaned into her, his skin warm and shower fresh, his eyes bright, his spicy shaving lotion strong. An old longing shivered through her—a silent waltz of memory.

A young woman with Trish's flowing auburn tresses stormed up the hill on horseback. She screamed something at them. Neoma couldn't understand the words. Hank shoved her away before she was crushed under the sharp hooves. Hank took the blow, bloody prints on his chest.

Neoma stirred awake, trembling, with Pudge's face peering over her. "Nana, get up! We already ate breakfast!"

Neoma winced with pain as she rolled out of bed. She took a quick shower and slipped into the same jeans and pullover she'd worn the day before. She could hear Becky and Pudge squealing in the backyard. She peered out the window. Cicely Bowers, dressed in bright yellow, swung high above them, her hat clasped tightly to the top of her head.

Neoma felt a moment of release. She embraced the brief elation as she hurried through the house to the rec room door. She stepped outside. Yellow daffodils and red tulips greeted her. The taunting scent of pines and raw earth reminded her of the day that they moved into the first home of their own.

The parsonage had resembled an old woman with arthritis, always cranky, always needing attention. And the yard was small. "Trish needs room to run," Neoma kept protesting. But Hank had covered the yard of the new house with black plastic and gravel and lined it with evergreen bushes.

"I just don't have time." His eyes were penitent, full of ministry guilt.

Cicely eased out of her flying swing, cherub cheeks flushed, and landed near Neoma.

"We've got to go," Neoma said. "The kids are itching for Anaheim."

"No you don't," Cicely replied in a voice that settled the matter. "We're going to try on hats."

Neoma followed the kids and Cicely upstairs to a dormer room. It was one huge walk-in closet filled with clothes in three colors: black, yellow, and red. Rows of hooks held flowered hats, ribboned hats, plain hats. In the middle of the room stood a large mahogany-framed mirror.

Cicely studied the hats, then pulled several down for Becky. She handed only one to Neoma, a satin floral with jacquard brim and sisal crown. It was trimmed with a gardenia blossom that looked so real Neoma could almost smell the flower's fragrance. It would have been appropriate for a model in a Renoir painting.

Neoma eased the hat on, then tilted it to the side. The grosgrain band felt soft, firm against her head. She expected the kids to laugh. But Becky was too busy trying on her own—a perky panama style held on with a chinstrap. Pudge had climbed up on a dresser to reach for a cotton ducking cap with a long, coffee-colored bill. Cicely pulled it down for him. He pranced around, looking like a young Hemingway.

Neoma peered into the mirror, startled at the spectacle of a grungy grandmother at the hat shop. *It's been so long since I did anything to my hair. Some auburn highlights, a little makeup would do wonders.* She reached up for the brim, tilted the hat, then sighed. *This would have been perfect for Trish's wedding.*

Everyone in the church had looked forward to Trish's marriage to Davis Stanton. The women sewed curtains for the social hall and cushioned the pews. The choir director wrote a song for the couple and sang it from the balcony. Trish Hocking, preacher's daughter, unwed mother, finally settling down. Davis Stanton, new believer in Christ, formerly into drugs and hard living, now prepared to be a husband. Becky Hocking, six years old, ecstatic to have a father.

The marriage lasted seven months. A bed of bitter roses.

"He doesn't know how to treat a woman," was Trish's remark.

"I can't keep up with her credit card spending," Davis had retorted.

Trish announced she was pregnant and took Becky with her to St. Louis, leaving no forwarding address. Neoma and Hank didn't see Pudge until he was three years old. Davis, meanwhile, had moved to southern California.

"Did you wear hats when you were my age?" Becky asked.

Cicely chuckled. "Oh no, I was an old lady of forty-three when I put on my first one. A woman I worked for asked me to do modeling for a client of ours at a charity fashion show. I didn't know until I got there that I would be modeling hats! Every time I sauntered down that runway, I became a different woman. I believed I could change the world. The client let me buy any hat I wanted at a discount rate. I bought them all, quit my job, and set up my own hat shop and made more money than I ever wanted."

"But how did you get to Road's End?" Neoma asked.

"One day I packed all my hats and aimed east. I wanted to see new sights. But my car heated up climbing the Winchester grade. I limped into Road's End, saw this house for sale, and never got any further. It's felt like home ever since."

Becky twirled once in front of the mirror. She clutched the sides of a panama and made a slight bow. "Mama likes hats," she said, her face as rosy as her hair. "I wore one at her wedding."

"Yes, I know. I was there," Cicely reminded them.

"You were at Grandpa's funeral, too." Becky stole glances at the panama as Cicely donned a green band and bow. "He had a heart attack. Mamma couldn't take it. She ran away."

Neoma's heart quickened. *That's the first time I've ever heard her refer to Trish.*

Cicely untied the yellow hat and slid on a black one with yellow polka dots. "Your mama couldn't deal with her sorrow. And some people don't know how to embrace joy." Cicely cocked her head toward Neoma. "In grief and in happiness, we're often quite alone."

"You've got a charmed kind of wisdom," Neoma remarked.

"All the better to soar above this little scene of things," Cicely replied.

Neoma was startled. "You know the old poets."

Cicely chuckled. "I've lots of time for reading here at Road's End—I've lots of time for anything I want. And you can keep the hats…my present."

That afternoon a white plague of hailstones salted the yard. Neoma groaned under the weight of a migraine and napped on the rec room couch. It seemed as though a herd of wild horses were stampeding on the roof. Cicely taught the kids to play Hearts and took them into the forest for a mushroom hunt when the storm had passed. They smelled of wet wood when they returned.

"Hank seemed so weary those last months," Neoma confided as she pushed a broom around the kitchen floor after dinner. "He went to bed exhausted and woke up tired. The morning of the heart attack he was on his way to Presbytery. He dreaded those meetings…the friction, the controversies. Hank always tried to be the peacemaker, but at a great price."

Neoma stopped to watch Cicely bang the dishwasher shut. "Hours later I was at his bedside when the deep lines in his face slowly etched out. He heaved a last shudder and was gone. A year ago…tomorrow."

Cicely lowered her head. The hat and its brim covered her countenance. "I was there when all three of my husbands left this earth. My daughter, too. Leukemia, you know, like her father." She raised her head, a spunky look in her eye. "Some folks think I wear these hats to attract a man. They're wrong. I wear them to declare my delight in living. It's who I am." She paused. "Who are you, Neoma?" She said it so softly that it was more like a prayer.

Neoma stared at this whimsical woman who resided in this conventional house in this curious little village. "No one has ever asked me that before," she said in a whisper. She cleared her throat. "I don't know. I can't relax and just be the kids' grandma. I've got to be both mother and father. I think I could have done it with Hank's help—" Neoma stopped a moment, offered a half grin. "Years ago I…used to paint."

"Paint?" Cicely perked up immediately. "What kind of painting?"

"Oils and water colors, mainly. I've got a dozen canvasses shut up in a storage shed—bowls of waxy fruit, sprays of brambly roses, that sort of thing—and one of Trish on her baptism day. That was the last painting I did."

"Sometimes life is like a cul-de-sac: The only way out is by retracing the way you got in." Cicely's eyes clouded in deep thought.

"My way is to keep plodding forward, one foot in front of the other," Neoma said as she scanned the rec room. Two rapt faces stared at a video screen. Pudge sucked his finger while Becky wound ringlets in her red hair.

"The day of the funeral," Neoma continued, "Trish divulged to one of the church elders that she owed a number of debts. She said she wanted a fresh break for her and the kids. The elder had some means. He was caught up in the emotion of losing his pastor, his good friend, and mindful of the Scriptures that say to give to those who ask. If he had come to me, I would have warned him, but—"

Neoma stood very small in the room. She frowned as the pain shot through her, sharp, unrelenting. "He bailed her out. And I don't blame him for it. But she took the money and…we haven't heard from her since."

Cicely paced the room, her thin arm rubbing her chin. "You've raised a lot of children."

"Yes. When Hank and I married, after I had lost my parents, I still had my sisters and brother to care for. Then there were the foster kids. And some nieces and nephews now and then. It took a long time to put Hank through seminary on my librarian's salary. Only had room for one of our own. It's just as well, I'd only have more grandkids to raise." Neoma grimaced. "I'm sorry, that was uncalled for. I do love the children."

"Some children take a long time to grow up," Cicely replied.

"I assumed children were born to become adults." Neoma leaned on the broom handle. "To care for their own."

"And give the older generation a break. What will you do after your pilgrimage to the Pacific?"

"I've got to find a place big enough for me and the kids, a place we all like, and a place where—" *A place where Trish could find us, if she wanted to.*

"Wasn't the house you had adequate?"

Neoma took a deep breath. "The elder who gave Trish the money found out he had cancer a month or two after. Medical bills are eating up their retirement savings. I sold the house to pay him back."

Cicely frowned, closed her eyes, and spread her hands on top of her hat.

That night Neoma tucked Pudge into bed and read him a chapter from C. S. Lewis' Narnia tales. Becky covered her head and pretended not to listen. When Neoma turned out the light, Becky called out through the wispy darkness, "Maybe Mom called today."

Neoma was glad that Becky couldn't see her face. The swell of emotion began rising from deep within her. Neoma closed the bedroom door and stole into the rec room. She lay for a long time in the lone, dark silence on the floor, her arms cradled around one of the black ottomans, her face wet, her legs cramped.

There had been no time to grieve Hank's loss. No place alone to weep. No moments to deal with past failure and future lost dreams. There were the children and their constant needs. There were long hours at the library, working a full schedule instead of part-time. Now she felt nothing but acceptance of duty. She kept retreating the windows of her soul. She couldn't stay there. Her thoughts always hit a dead end.

Until Aunt Cee and Becky had pried her open. "Lord, soothe this throbbing passion into peace," she pleaded. She thought of Trish in her white baptism dress, then in her wedding gown...so full of hope, full of promise. She thought of Hank in his pulpit robe, hands held high in benediction.

Some time later she slipped down the hall and picked up the receiver. She punched the numbers without hurry, her evening ritual. She listened to the rings, heard the click of the machine. It was Hank's voice again: "You have reached the Hocking residence. We cannot come to the phone right now. At the beep, give your name and number. We'll get back to you as soon as we can." No callers after that.

Neoma replaced the phone in its cradle. Someone was peering through the darkness. Neoma flipped on the light.

She realized at once that something was very different about the room. Three paintings hung on the wall in front of her. In the center was Aunt Cee's house with the fence. On the right was a close-up of the glass over the front doors with etched angels and ivy. The left painting wasn't yet complete. The backyard was peopled in an impressionistic style. Cicely's form was unmistakable on the wooden swing. Shadows ghosted the other shapes. There was a touch of Neoma's style in them, but a flair all the painter's own.

Cicely was dressed in red tights, barefoot, no hat, her hands behind her back. "Look at the signature."

Neoma stepped forward. She tried to read the scrawl of the autograph: *Patricia Rebecca Hocking.* Trish?

"I don't...understand..."

"Before I explain, I must ask you a question." Cicely studied her niece's face. "Do you want contact with your daughter?" Neoma felt faint.

"I call home every night. The children—" *Need her.*

"But are you ready to see her, to talk to her?"

Neoma rubbed her forehead. *She has disappointed me, humiliated me. She abandoned her marriage and her children. She abandoned me. Yes, that's it more than anything. She left me when I needed her most. She assumed I'd care for her kids and had no other life of my own. She presumed I had no needs.*

Neoma studied the pictures again. The house with the backyard meant for playing and swinging. The lady of the house with her enthusiasm for life. The glass angels—

A quiet rage began to grow, but before it could fully erupt, it died. Neoma was spent, used up. "I didn't know she could paint like this."

"Neither did she, until a few months ago." Cicely watched for Neoma's reaction.

"What do you mean? Did she send these to you? But we've never been here before. How could she—?" Neoma's head ached as she tried to understand.

"You haven't answered my question."

Neoma searched for some clear thought through the fog of her emotions. All she could remember was her dream from the previous night. Her words were slow, careful. "I want to know what she has to say. I want to listen to her. That's all."

Cicely sat on one of the black ottomans and pulled Neoma down next to her. "Trish was here several months this spring, doing chores for me. She vacuumed your rooms and changed your beds. She left a few weeks ago."

Neoma swung around and stared. "But why didn't you tell me? Why didn't you call right away?"

"She didn't want me to. She's so ashamed."

"Where is she now?"

"In Reno. She found a job there through a friend of mine. I have her phone number."

"Reno's a few hours west of Winnemucca."

"If you want me to, I'll tell her to leave a message for you at the St. Joe house. Perhaps you could all meet somewhere in Reno."

"I don't know. It doesn't matter. I don't expect her—" Neoma stopped. Her voice trailed away.

"She'll do it."

Neoma looked at her aunt. "How can you be so sure?"

"Because of the black beret she was wearing when she left."

The next morning the kids piled into the back of the truck, each wearing their Aunt Cee hats. Neoma fondled the gardenia hat with its vintage three-inch blossom. She eased it onto her head and tugged it into a snug fit. "They don't wear these in St. Joe," she said.

"You could wear that anywhere, anytime," Cicely said, "if you really wanted to. Even in front of two easels out on a California beach—with your daughter."

They backed the trailer up the way they had come in. Aunt Cee waved and ran after them, down the dirt road, until the truck hit pavement. Neoma and her grandkids were headed to Winnemucca and due west.

ABOUT THE AUTHOR

This story combines Janet Bly's fascination with modern-day pilgrimages west, in the steps of eastern ancestors, and her compassion for grandparents raising grandchildren through default. The setting of Road's End, Idaho, is much like the small town in which Janet lives. Cicely is the eccentric yet cherished "aunt" we all need to turn to in time of family crisis. Bly has two grandchildren of her own and has authored twenty-seven books (more than half coauthored with her husband, Stephen), including the Carson City Chronicles series, *God Is Good All the Time*, *Hope Lives Here*, and *The Heart of a Runaway*.

The West

CONNOR SAPP'S
BASEBALL SUMMER

Deborah Bedford

Connor Sapp was the sort of ten-year-old boy who stopped to pick up a penny when he found one on the sidewalk. He believed in good luck. He also believed in baseball.

Folks from all over town came to the baseball field on weeknights to swat mosquitoes and eat soggy hot dogs and shout advice to the players from the stands. For that matter, folks from all over the country did the same thing. The whole town stayed full of tourists stopping over for a breather after touring Yellowstone National Park. Here in Jackson Hole, baseball gave folks something cheap and interesting to do.

Connor never felt the game was quite so lucky as when that mongrel dog showed up at the field. That dog stood as big around as a coyote, with a muddy ruff of white around his neck and strands of dirt dangling from his black belly. Nobody knew where that dog had come from or to whom he belonged. But let those lights come on at Mateosky, let boys gather into teams wearing shirts that read Jedediah's House of Sourdough and Wyoming Woolens, and here that dog would come, ready to go for the ball.

"Your mama coming tonight?" someone always asked Connor as he leaned his bike against the chain-link fence and trotted toward the dugout. "Nope," he'd answer. "She had to work. But maybe next week." And Connor would scoot his bottom across the splintery bench, feeling the wood snag his hand-me-down pants in a hundred places, and he'd think, *I'm like that dog. Nobody knows who I belong to.*

From the first fastball pitch that went out—they all had to throw fastballs because Coach said it'd be bad for their arms to throw change-ups and knuckle balls while they were still in Little League—that dog barreled along the fence, eyes riveted, jowls open, tongue hanging out. When Neathery caught the pop fly in left field, that dog barreled toward third. When Hodges threw to first to catch somebody leading off, that dog ran toward first. When Ames made a diving catch and tagged the runner out at the plate, that dog stood behind home, his haunches quivering, wanting the ball.

Kids who had dads at the games got coaching from the stands: "Keep your head down—step into the ball!" Kids who had moms at the games got cheered: "Way to go down swinging." "Nice cut! You'll get it next time."

Because he had no one in the stands, everybody rooted for Connor. "Give it a ride," somebody hollered when he stepped to the plate.

"Base hit gets a run!"

He took one practice swing, then another.

"Elbow up, son. Swing like you mean it."

Connor tamped the dirt with the end of his bat. Dust whorls rose and danced. He couldn't quit thinking about those folks all expecting something from him while his mama checked in overnighters and gave out room keys at the Virginian Motel.

His knees started feeling a little wobbly.

The ball hurtled past Connor at chest height. He heard the *smack!* as it caught the catcher's glove. "Steeeee-*rike.*" The umpire gestured with his arm.

On the second pitch Connor connected. Hit it early and sent it flying high over his right shoulder, bouncing into the alley and pinging between two dented trashcans.

"Foul ball," the umpire yelled.

"Way to get his timing."

"Straighten it out, Sapp."

"Just a little poke."

Connor bit his bottom lip, leaned into the plate, hoisted up his elbow. His teammates rattled the dugout fence. "Connor!" yelled his best friend Dusty. "Smash it clean into Old Man Holtby's yard."

Old Man Holtby ran a fly and tackle shop in a house that hadn't seen paint since the Vietnam War. Handwritten signs posted at all angles on

Holtby's fence announced: Fish and Float Trips, Apply Within. Fifty Years in Jackson. Double and Single Humpies, Wholesale Prices by the Dozen.

Rumor had it that Holtby killed fish for the sheer pleasure. While the new Orvis store on Broadway and the fly-fishing instructors at Jack Dennis Outdoor Shop on the square extolled the virtues of catch-and-release, Holtby promised his customers to bring them back with their limits before noon. Holtby kept his favorite recipes hanging on a bulletin board: Trout in cornmeal batter. Trout over an open fire. Trout wrapped in bacon.

The pitcher hid the ball behind the small of his back, Connor knew, so each batter couldn't see the seams. The pitcher cocked his knee and peered out from under the brim of his cap with a sneer that would make Butch Cassidy look friendly. He started wind-up number three.

"Come on, Connor," Dusty yelled. "Belt it!"

Plenty of times, Holtby's window had been knocked out by base-balls. So many times, in fact, that Al Zuckerman down at Teton County Parks and Rec had told him to stop complaining and just send them the bills. Holtby kept an old fishing boat hidden in his garage, and Connor had heard that you could still read the words *Rip Them Lips* scrawled along one side in faded orange paint.

Connor didn't often pray when he played baseball. He figured God had people He loved standing on both sides of the plate. But today felt different. He lifted his elbow even higher. *Lord, don't really care if I hit this ball. Just wish something would happen that would make my mama start coming to the games.*

That's when the ball came right at him at a nice speed, full in the strike zone, a change-up that the pitcher must have supposed would reel him in. "Meatball!" somebody bellowed from the stands. Connor smashed it clear to kingdom come.

The ball sailed up over the shortstop's head…up, up, even higher as the left outfielder started to run, his arm stretched and his glove out-spread, his face upturned toward the sky. Folks in the bleachers went crazy. They clapped and screamed and rattled the stands.

Dusty hollered, "Told you to hit it back there, but I didn't think you'd *do* it!"

The left outfielder ran out of room too soon. The ball flew over his outstretched glove, over the fence, over the red sign tied to the scoreboard that read, Blue Spruce Car Wash. Leave Your Western Dirt in Our Drains.

Connor jogged his way around the bases. He lifted a fist in celebration as he rounded second and his teammates poured out onto the field to congratulate him. That's when he saw that dog still running. Past the trashcans and the alley, past the lawn where 4-H cloggers performed during the fair, past the rodeo grounds and Old Man Holtby's tackle shop, clear into the road.

Guess I can be proud of that. After all this trying, that dog's finally getting a baseball.

The dog ran with his tongue dangling, his fur rippling, his jowls in a broad smile. He caught the ball on a bounce, right between his teeth. Headlights from the oncoming car illuminated the whole thing.

Connor heard the screech of brakes, the thud of fender on flesh, the yelp of the dog. It took a full fifteen seconds for him to realize what had happened. That dog. That dog he'd come to think of as *his* dog. That dog, the one that he felt was just like him, was lying in the street.

"*No!*" Connor never made it past third base. He turned and shinned the fence instead, never looking back at his teammates or the collection of moms and dads, not one of which was his own. He knelt on the pavement in the street, buried his face deep into the stink of muddy dog fur. The driver, a lady with glasses hanging around her neck on a strap, clomped around to the front tires.

"That dog came out of nowhere. I'm not responsible. Why wasn't he on a leash?"

"He isn't mine."

"Where's his owner?"

Connor shook his head. "Nobody knows."

"He looks like he's badly hurt. But I'm not taking him to a vet. It isn't my responsibility. Read his collar. Look." The leather strap must've been buried in the dog's scraggly fur for months and nobody had known it. "This tag says this dog's name is King. It says he belongs to somebody named Calvin Holtby."

Not until he was carrying King over to Old Man Holtby's did Connor remember his prayer. He figured God thought this would be a good way to teach him a lesson.

Maybe he shouldn't have prayed about baseball.

Only Dusty, his best friend, volunteered to go with him. Together they traipsed past the barrel in Holtby's backyard, past the boat with its two ancient outboard motors—one missing a propeller—and past the wooden bench with the hand-whittled words, Have a Seat. Fishermen and Liars Only. King whined from the crook of Connor's elbow.

The man who opened the dilapidated screen door had rheumy eyes sunk deep into his head and two white thatches of hair protruding like deerbrush from his temples. "What do you boys want?" he asked in a voice that reminded Connor of a snorting bison. The way he said the word *boys,* he might as well have used the word *hoodlums* instead.

"Your dog got hit by a car. Think he must've broke his leg. He needs to get to the vet."

"Your dog went after a home run," Dusty chimed in. "Ran into the street after the ball and he got hit."

Old Man Holtby moved one of King's legs—a good leg—up and down like a pump handle. "Cotton-pickin' dog."

"It isn't his fault," Connor said. "He was just out chasing balls."

"Any idea who hit that homer?" Holtby glared over at the baseball field. "Somebody's got to pay to get my dog fixed up."

Connor dug the toe of his cleat into the dirt, and Dusty jumped in. "Not sure who hit that ball, mister. Maybe Parks and Rec can help you pay."

Connor spit into the dirt and scrubbed the wet spot away with his shoe. He reached one grubby hand around and scratched the stringy fur behind King's ears. "I'm the one that did it. Guess I'm the one who's got to take care of your dog."

When Connor's mother stomped into the vet's office, she was mad and ready to haggle. "This is ridiculous." She smacked her purse against the counter the same way she'd swat a fly with a swatter, and squared off with Holtby. "Connor shouldn't be responsible for your dog. *You're* the one lets that dog run wild."

"Better calm down, Missus Sapp." A receptionist steered her in the direction of a chair. "You'll scare the animals."

"I want to scare Calvin Holtby. Terrorizing a boy like that when he's got nobody else to stand up for him. While I'm out working at The Virginian twelve hours a day trying to make ends meet."

Holtby squinted at her. "Seems to me my dog and your boy are a lot alike."

Connor listened to them going back and forth while an odd feeling took hold in his breadbasket. Something spoke to him, a message that grew in his own heart from inside out and outside in, something he hadn't known a minute ago but now knew better than his own name.

Some of what Mama said was right; some of what Mr. Holtby said was right. But he, Connor Sapp, was the one who could see the truth.

Mr. Holtby hunched over in his chair. Connor remembered sitting just that way in the dugout when his team had gotten trounced. "I got this." Connor worked one hand inside his baseball-pants pocket and pulled out his penny. "Found it on the sidewalk just this morning."

"Won't do much good." Mr. Holtby lifted his chin and scratched.

"I could earn off this vet bill working for you. Digging nightcrawlers or selling flies or something."

"Connor—" His mother settled her hands on both hips—"we haven't even discussed this. This isn't your responsibility."

The laboratory door opened and in walked the vet carrying King, all cleaned up with a shaved leg and a splint fastened to his rear haunch. White tape spiraled around his leg like striped peppermint candy. "Got to keep him quiet for a few days, Cal. He's going to want to hobble around some, but you'll have to keep him from it."

Connor didn't give up with Mr. Holtby. "I could come over every day before baseball. Clean up the yard a bit maybe. Or fix the fence where it's broken and paint you some new signs."

"King's got to come in again in a few days," the vet said.

Connor's mom dusted off her palms, and he figured she'd just as soon dust off the whole problem. "I'm not paying one red cent to take care of some dog that's never been taken care of in the first place."

Holtby struggled up out of the chair, and King began licking his pale, twisted hand. He stared at the dog, but his words were for Connor. "Guess I'd be willing to take you on, boy. Guess I'd be willing to see what you're made of and let you earn off this bill."

The first afternoon Connor skidded his bike to a stop in front of the house, Old Man Holtby had everything set up so Connor could work. "Haven't fed the earthworms since April." He handed Connor an old, dented coffee can and pointed out past the shed. "There's a pile of coffee grounds I've been dumping back there. Need you to scoop them up and work them into the worm bed."

"How's King doing?"

"King's doing fine. But you don't got time to see him. Worm bed's out back by the fence."

"Okay."

"Got the hose going. Dirt ought to mush up real nice when you get to working those grounds in with your fingers."

"You want me to use a shovel or something?"

"Can't use a shovel. That'd cut the worms in half."

Connor started in on the job, kneeling on ground so muddy that wet soaked through the knees of his jeans. He kneaded fistfuls of coffee grounds deep into the dirt clods. Every so often he'd spy a nightcrawler yanking away into the soil, fleeing from daylight. Connor couldn't help liking the smell of the damp, mildewy loam, the cool water, the warm muck.

As he clawed the dirt with his fingers, a thought came to him…one that made him pause for a moment to think over. Seemed to him that people could be like dirt, all cloddy and hard. Kind of like Holtby. But what would happen if God mixed a little water in with the dirt and made something soft and mushy, like mud, out of somebody's heart? Maybe if they listened to God, people could get as workable as worm beds.

'Course, it'd take God to do that with someone as hard as Mr. Holtby.

Connor nodded. *Lord, I know You love Calvin Holtby. Help me love him, too.*

On the second day, after Connor had parked his bike beside the rickety shed in the backyard, Mr. Holtby led him into the basement where cardboard boxes were piled high. "Got fifty cases of trout bait in here." Old Man Holtby used a screwdriver to slice open the first box. "Count these and make sure everything's accounted for, would you?"

"How's King doing?"

"King's doing fine. But you don't got time to see him. There's two hundred jars of flame-orange Power Nuggets in here. The rest should be divided up between Pautzke's salmon eggs and Natura rainbow with glitter. Want to make sure I got everything I ordered."

Connor sat down on the floor and began clearing boxes. He sorted hundreds of bottles. Balls o' Fire, Soft But Satisfying. Uncle Josh's Natura, Stimulates Active Feeding. Hours later, Connor had them all counted around him. Before he returned them to their boxes, he opened a jar and sniffed it. *Phew!* He screwed the lid back on tight and started to set the jar down, when another one of those thoughts stopped him.

The jars had looked so appealing…but one whiff showed that what was inside was far from it. At least to human noses. *Guess things aren't always what they look like on the outside, Jesus. An' neither are people. Sometimes things are different when you smell what's in the jar.*

He stood to find Mr. Holtby watching him, but all the old man said was, "Plenty more work to do once that's finished. Those worms ought to be good and fat by now. Counting on you to help me carton up a few."

On Saturday, the third day, Connor showed up even though he didn't have baseball. On the steps in front of Calvin Holtby's house stood two kids from Miss Hecht's fourth-grade class. "Hey, Connor. You want to come fishing with us? We're getting worms and going down to Flat Creek."

"Can't do that. Got work to do."

"You work here?"

"Yep."

"Sweet."

He nodded. "My mom never did teach me how to fish."

"I'll bet Old Man Holtby would teach you if you asked."

Connor paused. "Maybe. But I'm not asking today."

His buddies tucked their cartons of nightcrawlers into their jackets. Beside the front door stood a new sign painted in smudged, shaky black letters: Fresh Worms, $1.99.

"'Bout time you showed up." Mr. Holtby met him at the door with a battered saltine-cracker tin in hand. "Been waiting all day. Me and King, we've got something to show you."

"King!" Connor knelt and scratched King's ruff. King greeted him with a slobbery lick and a lifted paw.

"You go sit by the fireplace. Just watch this! Something I'd forgotten about." Holtby pulled a dog biscuit from the tin. King waited in a sitting position, his splinted leg pointing out behind him like a crank on a fishing reel.

Holtby balanced the biscuit on King's nose and stared full bore into the dog's eyes. "Crazy dog'll sit here all day with that on his nose. Won't move until I tell him it's time." He waited a while before he clapped. "Get it, King."

King flipped his nose and tossed the biscuit into the air, then snapped it up before it had a chance to hit the floor.

"Don't that beat all?" Although Calvin Holtby asked the question, didn't seem he expected an answer. He was looking at a picture the whole time. A picture of a pretty lady with white hair and a straw hat that let dapples of sun through onto her face.

"Emma taught King that trick when King was just a pup. Been seven years since Emma died. How could a dog remember after so much time?"

Connor wiped his hands on his jeans. "You got work for me today, Mr. Holtby?"

"You betcha." Holtby took slow steps outside and lugged in a heap of bent fishing rods and rusty single-action reels, the lines all knotted together. "These things are so tied together, I could untangle for a week and still not be started." He dropped them on the floor beside Connor. "Reels'll need to come apart and be put back together."

"Would you help me? I don't know how to take a reel apart."

Holtby stared down at his knobby hands as if he were staring down at something he didn't know. "Used to be, I could put an engine together in one day. Used to do most anything with my hands." He splayed his fingers and stared at them. "Confounded things don't work anymore. Just about lost all the spare parts I can lose."

Connor started unraveling lines. At first it seemed impossible. But Calvin Holtby tinkered beside him and, for some reason, the job got easier. King lay near their feet; occasionally the dog would lift its head and watch them, as if to make sure they stayed right where they belonged.

"Sure was nice selling those nightcrawlers today. Bet you it's been a good three months since I've sold a worm."

Connor's fingers worked through the kinks and knots in the fishing line, and a picture formed in his mind…a picture of people all knotted up and tangled in something they didn't know how to change…

Connor frowned. What did *that* mean? What was the picture trying to tell him? *Lord, would You show me what You want me to do?*

As soon as he asked the question, that odd feeling from days before started in Connor's heart again. It grew, sitting heavy in his chest where he could feel the weight of it. A best friend whispering. He knew it from the inside out and the outside in. Heard it clearly. Couldn't believe it.

Me? You want me *to say something like that?*

Connor took a deep breath and trusted. "Mr. Holtby? You ever think about coming to one of my games? I'd sure like to have somebody cheering me on."

He looked up when Mr. Holtby didn't say anything. He found the old man staring at another picture beside his wood stove. He stared for a long time. "See that boy? That's my grandkid." He pointed with the screwdriver that always seemed to be in his hand. "Moved away from here when he was ten. Just after Emma died."

"Guess you miss him."

"Never even got the chance to teach him how to fish."

"Bet he could've caught lots of 'em."

"Yep, he could have." Mr. Holtby's gaze lingered there for a long time. "Don't know what happened. Only way I know to run this business is the way my father taught me. And somewhere along the way while I wasn't looking, things changed. Grandson didn't want to go fishing with me. He had other more important things to do."

Sadness flooded Connor's heart. "Maybe things haven't changed so much as all that. Maybe your grandson just didn't understand."

"Maybe so."

"Wish you'd come see me play baseball."

Calvin Holtby wiped the grease off a reel with a rag. He laid the polished reel beside Connor's knee. "Never had anybody invite me to a game before."

"Guess this is the first time, then."

Mr. Holtby stared at the reel for a long time. "Don't think I could do something like that."

"You don't?" Connor's hopes sank.

"Nope."

But Connor noticed the old man's eyes had started twinkling.

"Couldn't come to a ball game unless you'd agree to let me take you fishing in return."

Connor jumped to his feet. "Oh, *yeah!* I will!"

"Well," Mr. Holtby said, looking pleased with himself, "we've made a deal. We'd better shake on it."

"Yeah, we'd better." Connor reached out his hand and felt the old man's gnarled, rough fingers encasing his own. All of a sudden, Connor knew who he belonged to: a God who understood and loved and listened to everything that went on inside of people. He and the old man grinned at each other like new friends. All thanks to a mangy dog named King who needed to chase baseballs. And to a heavenly King who'd been beside them both while Connor sorted stinky bait, untangled impossible knots, worked water to make mud out of dirt—and hit a whale of a homer.

In that very moment, Connor decided it was okay to pray about baseball after all.

ABOUT THE AUTHOR

Bestselling author Deborah Bedford has excellent reasons for setting her story in Jackson Hole, Wyoming: "I was expecting a baby, my husband had lost his job, we lost our health insurance, and we had three days to find a new place in Wyoming to live. For over a year we had been hearing a call to move to Jackson Hole—I was already driving two hours on icy roads to be seen by a doctor there—but no rentals were available. We prayed, trusting the Father. Early the next morning, a new classified section rolled off the press at the *Jackson Hole News*. In it we found an ad for a beautiful little log cabin. Not just something adequate, but something *extraordinary,* with a pond and kestrel hawks and a view of the Sleeping Indian. Fifteen years, two children, three jobs, ten novels, and several dogs later, we are still in Jackson Hole.

"The only thing more fun than writing about Teton County is writing about baseball and boys. Baseball in Wyoming is not for the faint of heart. We have survived games in July in ski hats and mittens. We have slept outside during windstorms that earned our tent the nickname 'The Giant Lung.' But such, I believe, is a beautiful picture of life with the Lord. When we lay down our lives and trust Him, He always surprises us. He doesn't provide only what is adequate; He astounds us with His blessings."

I SEE THINGS DEEPLY

James Scott Bell

My Uncle Cecil was a failure.

I remember my father shouting at my mother one night when Uncle Cecil was on his way to stay with us.

"He's a failure!" my father shouted.

"He's my brother!" my mother shouted back.

"He comes here and freeloads! Why doesn't he get a job?"

"He can't hold a job, you know that."

I wondered why my uncle couldn't hold a job. I was twelve and I had a job cutting lawns in my neighborhood. I didn't have any trouble finding work. We lived on Canoga Avenue in Woodland Hills, at the west end of the San Fernando Valley. There were lots of houses and green lawns.

Canoga Avenue was a ribbon of road that ran past our house and stretched almost all the way across the valley. On both sides of the street stood magnificent old pepper trees. Big, green, and bushy, they shaded the road from the sun. When I rode my bike down the street, it was like traveling through a verdant tunnel into a fairy tale.

Back then the valley was the part of Los Angeles that moved at a leisurely pace. It was a place to raise a family and live, if not off the fat of the land, then at least close to a neighborhood market. In those days the folks who worked at the neighborhood markets knew your name.

A few blocks west of my street they were turning the big field into a shopping center. I was sad about that because I used to play there. That was the field where they'd have Easter egg hunts and bands sometimes. They were going to build a new Safeway store.

That summer I was looking forward to splashing around in our pool with the neighborhood kids and—unfortunately—my big sister Emily. Emily was sixteen and couldn't get enough of The Beatles. She'd lie on the pool deck with The Beatles blaring from a record player. I couldn't stand them. I preferred The Beach Boys, who sang about Southern California girls and beaches and cars. As far as I was concerned, The Beatles were aliens who had invaded our shores.

On those warm nights I liked to open the window in my room for any breeze that happened to blow and listen to Vin Scully call the Dodger games on the radio. He had a voice like honey, and more than once I fell asleep in bliss as the game stretched into the later innings.

But this summer routine was to be interrupted—and soon.

My father told my mother, "There'll be trouble if he comes here. There always is."

"Please try," Mom said. "Cecil is still trying to find his niche."

"Niche? I just wish he would find a job. And keep it. Or a wife. But who would want to live with that dreamer?"

"He's a good person, Sid."

"He's a failure. An absolute failure!"

So Uncle Cecil came to us that summer after getting fired from a job in Rancho Cucamonga. I didn't know what job it was, nor did I ask. I sensed that Uncle Cecil was tired of being asked and that he had come to our house so he could rest.

When Uncle Cecil wasn't around, my mother kept telling my father to just let him have some peace. But Dad spent most of that summer grumbling. More than once he told Uncle Cecil, "Keep out of my way."

Uncle Cecil was tall, with curly black hair that was beating a retreat from his forehead. He had deep-set eyes, like a couple of secrets hiding in his head. He also had a mouth with a smile like the Fourth of July.

That didn't help him with my dad, though. My dad didn't care what Uncle Cecil did with his mouth, as long as he kept it shut.

"I see things deeply," Uncle Cecil said to me one day as we walked down Canoga Avenue. I was going to the market for my mother, who wanted eggs, bread, and cooking oil. Uncle Cecil said he would walk with me and would buy me a roll of Necco Wafers. (He told me that Necco Wafers were "the greatest candy in the world," as if there had been a contest and it had won.)

"How deeply?" I asked.

"Aha!" Uncle Cecil said, smiling widely and sticking his finger in the air. "I knew you were a poet like me!"

"A poet?"

"Yes! When I told you I saw things deeply, you didn't ask me what that meant. You only asked me *how* deeply. Most people, when I tell them this, look at me like I'm crazy."

I remembered my dad's look whenever he saw Uncle Cecil, and it was exactly like that.

"We poets," he said, "see things deeply. God made us this way. Do you know the Psalms?"

"In the Bible?"

"It is poetry inspired by God! I tell you, David saw things more deeply than other people. That is why he was called a man after God's own heart."

We were getting close to Ventura Boulevard. The majestic pepper trees enfolded us. It was a hot day, but we were in a cool refuge of shade.

"Poems are made by fools like me," Uncle Cecil said. "But only God can make a tree." He stopped and put his hand on the gnarled trunk of a fat pepper tree. He patted it like a man would pat the hand of a dear friend. "Good old tree," he said.

"Yes," I said.

"And I know you are a poet because you never asked my why I can't hold a job."

I never had, but I *was* curious.

"I'll tell you, poet to poet. Once I was working on the freight dock at a big warehouse. I drove a forklift. I loaded big palettes and boxes and equipment onto trucks. It was hard work, but not brainy. So my brain was free to think about things. One day I was thinking about all of the junk I was loading and how we never ran out of it. When a supply of anything got low, *bingo!* Like magic we'd get more of it. We would keep shoveling junk out into the world, and on this particular day I began to wonder what would happen if we kept shoveling junk until it was everywhere. Until the whole world was covered with junk. Then what would we do?"

I waited for him to go on, but he was kind of staring into space. "But what about the job?" I asked.

"Oh yes. As I was thinking about junk I drove the forklift off the loading dock and almost killed myself. And that is why I can't seem to hold a job. Now, how about those Necco Wafers?"

That night we did what we always did in my house that summer— watched the evening news as we ate dinner. I think it was my dad's way of not having to make conversation with Uncle Cecil.

Emily wasn't there. She spent most of that summer with her friends, no doubt polluting her mind with The Beatles. On this particular night I remember Walter Cronkite on TV talking about war. There was something about a big push in Vietnam, near a place called Da Nang. Lots of our soldiers were being killed.

There was silence all around the table as we watched the news report. Images from a jungle, with soldiers in uniform running and shooting, flashed across the screen. Then there was an explosion. And voices screaming.

Suddenly Uncle Cecil threw his napkin down.

"I can't stand this war!" he shouted.

My father's face started turning red. He had been in the army during World War II, in Sicily. "You want the Communists to take over?"

"Our boys are being slaughtered! For nothing!"

My mother put her head in her hands.

"Nothing?" my dad shouted. "Communism is nothing?"

When my dad yelled, people all over the neighborhood could hear him. It was a force of nature, my dad's voice. Uncle Cecil was no match for it.

"Leave my table!" Dad yelled.

My mother started crying. "Sid, please."

Uncle Cecil stood up. "It's all right. I don't want to sit here quietly while boys are being slaughtered."

"Go on!" my father shouted.

I could see tears forming in Uncle Cecil's eyes. He tried hard to fight them back. His lower lip quivered like a scared dog. Then he turned and walked out our front door, closing it gently behind him.

On the television, Walter Cronkite was telling how many Americans the war had claimed this year.

We were having meatloaf and Brussels sprouts and mashed potatoes that night. Normally I loved that meal, but this time I couldn't finish.

After dinner I went outside to look for Uncle Cecil. The night was dark, but the moon was full and shining a pale orange through the haze of the day's smog.

I found Uncle Cecil sitting on our fence, looking up at the sky.

"I see things deeply," he said in a near whisper. "I wish I didn't sometimes."

"That's okay," I said, even though I didn't know if it was okay or not.

My uncle put his arm around me, and the next thing I knew he was pulling me into his chest. His other arm came around and hugged me. I could feel his body shaking a little. And he didn't say anything for a long time.

The next day my father left for work early. My mom fixed a big breakfast of pancakes and eggs and sausages. It was like a special occasion. She kept offering more to Uncle Cecil, and refilling his coffee cup every time it got half empty.

Finally my uncle said, "No more. I can't eat another bite."

"Sure you can," Mom said. "I have another short stack ready to go."

"I am leaving today, Jan."

My mother froze with the coffee pot in her hand. "You don't have to go."

"That's right," I said. "You don't have to go."

But I knew he did have to go.

After breakfast he packed his one suitcase—a beige leather affair with fraying corners—and started to walk out the door.

"Wait," Mom said. "I'll drive you to the bus stop."

"No," said Uncle Cecil. "I want to walk down Canoga Avenue one more time."

"I'll go with you," I said.

We walked under the trees that let in little shafts of light like a stained glass window. We walked mostly in silence because there were not many words to say.

When we got to the corner of Canoga and Ventura, where the bus stop was, Uncle Cecil came to a sudden halt. He dropped his suitcase and stared.

Across the street, a man wearing a hard hat and sporting the largest chain saw in the world was cutting down a pepper tree.

"No!" shouted Uncle Cecil, but his voice was drowned out by the sound of the saw.

Without waiting for the traffic signal to change, Uncle Cecil charged across Ventura. He was almost hit twice by cars, but he ran as if he didn't notice.

I waited for the light to change and then ran to join him.

Uncle Cecil was waving his arms in front of the man with the saw. When he looked up and saw my uncle, I thought he might run away the way people do when confronted by a crazy man. He shut off his saw and said, "What is it?"

"You stop that!" Uncle Cecil said. "What gives you the right to cut down this tree?"

"Huh?"

"You have no right! This tree was here long before you, and you just leave it alone."

"Hey, friend, I just do what I'm told."

"Only God can make a tree!"

The man with the saw shook his head. "They're all coming out." He jerked his thumb down the street.

Uncle Cecil looked. And his mouth fell open.

About half a dozen men with chain saws were starting in on the pepper trees. The air was suddenly alive with angry buzzing, like an attack of giant bees. This stretch of road would soon be treeless, making room for a wider street and big office buildings.

Uncle Cecil just stood there shaking his head. His shoulders slumped.

The man in the hard hat started his saw again.

I took Uncle Cecil by the arm and walked him back to the bus stop.

We sat on the bench together, saying nothing. Uncle Cecil just looked at his hands. Finally he said, "It will never be the same again."

We sat in silence for several minutes.

"Promise me something," Uncle Cecil said.

"Okay."

"Promise me that you will never stop looking at things, really looking at them, inside out and upside down, and finding the poetry. God makes trees and poets. Trees a man can cut down, but not a poet. Will you promise me?"

"Sure," I said.

The bus came, and Uncle Cecil got on. He paused on the step; just before the doors closed, he looked at me and smiled. It was like the Fourth of July.

I couldn't help smiling, too, though I knew that what Uncle Cecil said was true. Things would never be the same again. But I also knew something else, something I wanted to tell my father someday when I wasn't afraid of him. I wanted to tell him Uncle Cecil was not a failure.

I stood at the bus stop and waved until the bus was out of sight. Then I turned my back on the men cutting down the trees and right then I started looking deeply at everything, inside out and upside down, just like Uncle Cecil said.

And I still do.

ABOUT THE AUTHOR

James Scott Bell is a winner of the Christy award for Excellence in Christian fiction. He graduated with honors from the University of Southern California Law Center and has written over three hundred articles and numerous books for the legal profession. A former trial lawyer, he is the author of the Christian legal thrillers *Circumstantial Evidence, Final Witness* and *Blind Justice,* as well as the historical suspense novel *City of Angels* (coauthored with Tracie Peterson).

Fall in the Valley

Kristin Billerbeck

From the parking spot, Amy honked her horn continuously until nearly everyone at the shopping center turned. *Good, let them stare. I'm used to it. Only move that car!* Amy blasted the horn again until a manager finally came out of the grocery store.

"Can I help you with something? Our customers are complaining." His short white sleeves depicted every stereotype of a grocery store manager: close-cropped hair, boyish face, and an uncanny ability to overlook the obvious.

"Yes, you can find out who owns this car that's parked in the handicapped ramp and have them move it. Or better yet, you can call the police and have them ticketed and towed." Amy's shrewish tone startled her. Was that really her own voice? She drew a deep breath and started again. "Look, I'm sorry, but it's hard enough for me to get to the grocery store and I can't exactly get out of my car with the wheelchair when someone is parked in the ramp." She looked to the passenger's seat where her sporty black companion lay folded. *Stupid wheelchair.*

"I'm sure they'll just be parked there a minute." He shrugged.

"They may be back *soon,* as you say, but it's already been fifteen minutes, and I'm not exactly speedy when it comes to shopping." Amy's shrill tone was making its way back into her words, and again she breathed in deeply. She closed her eyes, muttering a prayer for patience. But it wasn't patience she really wanted; it was action. Even in her Ford

Aspire, a car she believed was aptly named because it made her aspire to drive something else, she couldn't open the door completely with the massive car illegally parked in the ramp. Amy was at the mercy of its owner.

"I'll see what I can do, ma'am. Only lighten up on the horn, okay?" The boy wonder sighed, rolled his eyes, and made his way back into the store.

Amy leaned her head on the steering wheel and eyed the European SUV. Silicon Valley was getting worse and worse. Too many rich, entitled, overly inflated, dot-com millionaires with more money than time. Or common courtesy. It showed in nearly every facet of life. People rushed by her at school without a moment's thought to help her and, worst of all, got angry when she blocked a walkway of any kind.

But this—parking in the handicapped ramp—was something that made her blood run cold. It stole her independence. "Let's face it, some-body in a wheelchair doesn't have anywhere to be, so I'll just park here," Amy sneered aloud.

A vision in black appeared, so real, yet so impossible that Amy rubbed her eyes. He whipped out a small metal clipboard and began writing. His silver badge glistened in the sunlight like an old Lone Ranger clip, and Amy felt the corners of her mouth turn up. *A ticket!* The SUV-driving, life-is-all-about-me prince was about to get a ticket. Amy slouched back into her driver's seat, crossing her arms, suddenly infi-nitely more patient. *I can wait for this.*

The officer continued to scribble, then stretched the overpriced windshield wiper and secured the ticket under it before snapping it back. He walked around the car, eventually stopping at Amy's window.

"Have you been waiting long, Miss?"

"About fifteen minutes. I appreciate the ticket, officer. Not that it will do much good."

"You're probably right about that. It's an expensive ticket though—nearly three hundred dollars—so at least it should hurt a bit."

"Three hundred? That's groceries for the month."

"Maybe for you and me. For most of this town, it's a day at the spa. Still, it's a day at the spa that person won't have. We're living in the fall of the Roman Empire here, so you have to be grateful for the little things." The officer shook his head, and Amy's eyes widened slightly.

"You've read *The Rise and Fall of the Roman Empire*?"

"Do you think that just because I'm a cop, I can't read?" His dark eyebrows raised and he winked. His sapphire blue eyes twinkled at her, and Amy found herself smiling back. "I'll have you know I graduated at the top of my class."

"No, I didn't mean anything like that. I teach World History at the local junior college. *The Fall* is one of my mandatory reads, though I don't think anybody understands why I have them read it. I'm praying for a discerning student who will someday understand."

"The breakdown of the family. It's the first sign. I'm Randy, by the way."

Amy took his proffered hand willingly. "Amy. Amy Watson."

Their conversation was halted suddenly by a raised voice and a series of curse words. An elegantly dressed woman, followed by a barrage of bag boys carrying groceries, led her son to the SUV. The woman's linen slacks were perfectly creased, her diamond jewelry reflecting the California sun's rays in a rash of color. The boy must have been about nine, and his mother's swearing left him wide-eyed in horror.

"Mom! Mom, *shhh*. There's a *policeman.*" The young boy, still dressed in a school uniform, tried to be discreet, but his mother's anger was clearly out of control.

"A *cop!* A cop who works for *my* tax dollars, and who has nothing better to do with his time than write ridiculous tickets!" She practically spat her words out. "Drug dealers roam free, there's probably a rapist or three down in San Jose, but *no,* they have to come to Los Altos and write a ticket!"

Randy gave a small smile and approached the still sputtering woman. "Good afternoon, Miss. I guess you missed the fact that you parked in a handicapped ramp?"

"No one ever uses these spaces anyway!"

Amy noted the way the woman avoided her eyes.

"Actually, ma'am, that's not true. These spaces are becoming more and more necessary, unfortunately. And when someone parks in them, folks like Amy here can't get their groceries. You can see how that might be a problem, now can't you?" Randy's soft tone sent a red wave of fresh fury over the woman's porcelain skin.

"Preston, get in the car!" She pressed a button to unlock her SUV's pearl white doors. "Just put those groceries in back," she ordered. A flurry of activity followed, and the woman made her way to Amy's car, pointing at Randy's badge. "Now listen to me. My husband works hard for our money. We have a right, as citizens of this city, to not be harassed by policemen who come in for the day."

Randy's jaw firmed. "You don't have a right to break the law. The law is the law. You break it, there are consequences. I'm just doing my job, ma'am. Amy here is a citizen, too."

Amy looked away as the woman focused on her, apparently readying to unleash herself on Amy when her eyes rested on the black wheelchair. "Do you really *need* that thing?"

Amy nodded, barely restraining what she wanted to say: *No, it's just a prop.* The woman grimaced and went back to her vehicle. She took the ticket and threw it into her front seat, then climbed in and backed the SUV out without another word. Her son stared with wide eyes through the back window.

Amy sighed. "I've lived here all my life, and I'm a stranger in my own hometown."

Randy shook his head. "All the money in this town, and there doesn't seem to be any real quality of life left. It used to be such a nice place, something for everyone: mountains, lakes, city life. Churches that taught the truth instead of self-realization garbage. Now it's too often just one little rat after another scurrying to the next event."

"At least you can afford to be here. I can't stay much longer. My salary at the junior college isn't enough to make the rent anymore. If I get one more rent increase, I'm out. It's hard enough to find something on the bottom floor." Amy hadn't verbalized her fears aloud before, but once she did, it didn't seem all that frightening anymore.

"I understand. My rent's ridiculous too. Well, maybe we're the lucky ones. Maybe being pushed out of this town is the best thing that could happen to us."

"I just wish I didn't have my buddy here." Amy pointed to the wheelchair. "I'd have a lot more options open to me."

"Nah, Amy, look at that woman there. She seems to have every-thing—her health, money, a nice son, a fancy car—and she doesn't seem to appreciate any of it. That wheelchair may slow your body down, but not your mind. You and me, we've got *time*…time to appreciate the per-fect weather today or talk with a new friend. I feel for people who drive themselves to the point of exhaustion for something meaningless. I mean, when does it end?"

Amy studied her wheelchair, its form etched into her mind. *When did it end?* She just wanted to teach her classes and read her books in the evenings. She didn't have—or ask for—much…and yet she *was* happy.

Quality of life. Throughout her years in the wheelchair she'd kept a positive attitude; but she had never thought of it as a blessing.

The Fall of the Roman Empire was happening before her very eyes, yet she was held sturdy by her wheelchair and faith. She contemplated it all, knowing it would take years of dedicated study to comprehend its fullness. She surveyed Randy and his good-hearted grin.

"How about dinner tonight?" Amy heard herself say, then jolted at the surprise of her own voice.

Randy's expression brightened even more. "Are you cooking?"

"You bet I am." Amy was actually anxious to maneuver her wheelchair from the vehicle and slide into place. "After all, I'm going grocery shopping, and if it takes me all afternoon, so what?"

She handed him her phone number, then rolled out her sporty chair with renewed vigor. Another expensive German car started to roll into the handicapped ramp when the driver spotted her—and then Randy in his uniform. The driver smiled sheepishly and backed away. Amy simply gave a friendly wave. She would not allow herself—or her anger—to be pushed again. God had created her to focus on Him, not on the irritations of the day. Or on her own limitations.

No, she wasn't going to get upset. She was going to take her time doing what she needed to do. And find things to be grateful for. Like an SUV parking in the wrong place and bringing her into contact with someone that she knew was going to become a friend.

"I'll see you tonight," Randy winked, and Amy grinned. Grocery shopping would never again be the same.

ABOUT THE AUTHOR

Kristin Billerbeck has written many inspirational romance novels and novellas. She lives in the Silicon Valley with her husband, three young sons, and infant daughter. She is currently involved in a start-up church near Stanford University, teaching kindergartners through second-graders. Visit Kristin on the web at www.KristinBillerbeck.com

THE DAY THE WIND STOPPED

Stephen Bly

Sina Marie peeked out through a crack in the unpainted back door. She gazed at the distant Wind River Range, just within view. The gray, predawn sky blued even before the sun rose high enough to break across the cloudless Wyoming sky. Dust swirled around the sage that lapped up on the bare backyard of the boarding house like the summer waves along Lake Michigan. The scattered, short-limbed junipers seemed to shiver even though the dusty air felt hot on Sina Marie's face and hands.

I've been in Wyoming for sixty-two days and sixteen hours and the wind hasn't ever stopped blowing. There can't be this much air in the whole world. Maybe it's gone all the way around the earth and is coming by a second time. If I had a pink feather I would toss it in the air and count how many days until it lapped the globe.

Sina Marie carried two long white stockings out onto the porch. Her white muslin dress, which had been bright and clean when they left Illinois, now looked dingy and gray.

I know, Mama…I should shake out my outer stocking every day and put the clean ones on next to my feet.

The rough wood of the unpainted back porch prodded her bare feet. She gripped the dirty socks and shook them in the wind. Her dark brown bangs fluttered in the breeze as she brushed her pigtails back over her shoulders. She squinted to keep the swirling dust from stinging her eyes, then spun around and ducked back inside. Sina Marie strolled across the house to the long entry hall, then pulled back a dusty lace curtain. She stared east at a tiny sliver of hesitant sun.

Lord, it is another beautiful Wyoming morning, except for the wind. Daddy said You created wind so all the clouds wouldn't get stuck in one place, and Wyoming is like a barn where You keep the wind until You need it somewhere else.

Sina Marie sat on the blue velvet settee and laced up her shoes. She chewed on her bottom lip when she stole into the kitchen. A heavyset, gray-haired woman smiled at her from beside the cast iron stove. "Good morning, young lady."

"Good morning, Mrs. Larson. What can I do to help you?"

"Honey, set the table for eleven. Use the rose china."

"Eleven? Did another boarder come in last night?"

"Yes, Mr. Griff Duncan arrived."

"Mr. Duncan? He came!" Sina Marie's brown eyes danced. "Why didn't you wake me up?"

"It was 2 A.M."

"Is he in room 6?" Sina Marie quizzed.

"Yes, but I will not have you disturb him. They rode all the way from Fort Laramie."

"I knew he'd be here."

The older lady dropped several eggshells into the huge coffeepot and replaced the tin lid. "He did mention a certain young lady's birthday."

Sina Marie ran her finger along the back of one of the oak chairs. "They all came, didn't they?"

"Yes. It isn't every thirteen-year-old that has a birthday party with so many handsome men in attendance." Mrs. Larson pointed toward the pantry door. "Set out the preserves, Sina Marie. We're having fried bread this morning."

Sina Marie Bennett set each china plate exactly two fingers from the edge of the table. To the right went a bread knife and a spoon. To the left on top the neatly-folded blue gingham napkin she set two forks.

Mr. Duncan will sit on one side of me, Young Mr. Scott on the other side at my party. I do hope they will behave themselves and not tease me too bad. Lord, I wouldn't mind if they did tease a little, but I will not marry either one of them no matter how much they beg. Mama told me I should not get married until I'm a least sixteen, like she was. Daddy said I shouldn't get married until

I'm twenty-one, but that's the way daddies are.

Sina Marie felt dwarfed next to the mahogany cabinet that stretched almost to the twelve-foot-high ceiling. She stared at a large box wrapped in white paper that was sitting on the hutch.

"Are you pining over that present Young Mr. Scott brought you?" Mrs. Larson asked.

Sina Marie jerked back from the hutch. "Of course not! Eh...did Mr. Duncan happen to...you know…"

"Bring you a present?"

Sina Marie dropped her head. "He said he would, not that it matters."

"He didn't mention a present."

"He didn't?" Sina Marie's shoulders sagged.

"No, but he said that a certain almost-thirteen-year-old girl was not to look in his saddlebags."

"I knew it! I knew he'd buy me a present." Sina Marie searched the large dining room.

"Are you looking for the saddlebags?"

"I want to know where they are so I can avoid them."

"Good, I thought you were going to peek."

"No, but if my brother were in the room I'd pay him a nickel to look inside."

"Hmm…a whole nickel?" Mrs. Larson grinned. "You are a rich young lady."

"I will be richer tomorrow. I will be wearing mama's gold necklace. She said I could have it when I turned thirteen."

"Yes, I heard her say that." Mrs. Larson strolled to the corner of the room and picked up a worn leather saddlebag. "Of course, he didn't say *I* couldn't peek at it."

"Yes, yes, Mrs. Larson…please do. What does it look like?"

"Yellow gingham."

"He bought me a bolt of yellow gingham?"

"No, he wrapped it in yellow gingham with a yellow ribbon."

"Yellow is my favorite color of all times. I wonder how he knew that?"

"I believe you mention it 'most every day."

"What shape is it?" Sina Marie pressed.

"It looks like a cigar box…" Mrs. Larson laughed. "I do believe he bought you a whole box of Cheroots."

"Mrs. Larson, I don't smoke cigars! Is it heavy?"

"Why yes, it is!"

"It's a book!"

"It's a heavy book."

"It's the complete works of William Shakespeare."

"How do you know that?"

"Because Mr. Duncan is from England and he once told me Shakespeare wrote a whole play just about me."

"Which one is that?"

"*Twelfth Night*…he said I was a lot like Viola."

"Oh, he did, did he?"

"Yes, except that I've never been shipwrecked, and don't have a twin brother, and I'm only twelve—*almost* thirteen—and I don't pretend to be a boy."

Mrs. Larson set down the saddlebags. "Yes, I can see the comparison."

The tall, thin man who entered was nearly bald and had a thick, black beard. "Good mornin', Mr. Carruthers!"

"Good morning, young Miss Bennett. But you know I will not let you drop your 'g's. Say it again."

"Good morning, Mr. Carruthers. How are you today?"

"I am very excited about a certain birthday tomorrow." He winked. "I believe everyone in town will be here."

"Mr. Carruthers, there aren't twenty people in all of Piñon City."

"You count tomorrow, young lady. I'll bet there are over twenty people here."

One by one the boarders filled the small dining room. Smelly Johnson was the last to be seated.

Mrs. Larson nodded at Sina Marie.

The girl folded her hands, dropped her chin, and closed her eyes.

"Dear Lord, this is Your Sina Marie. Please give us Your strength and blessing for the meal Mrs. Larson prepared for us even though the fire got too hot and the toast is burnt on the bottom side where no one can see it. Now, Lord Jesus, tomorrow is my birthday, and I think it would be very nice if the wind stopped blowing for one day. Thank you. Amen."

"That was quite a prayer, Miss Sina Marie." The voice of the man who had just entered was deep and gentle. Grif Duncan held a cup of steaming coffee in the doorway as his fingers stroked his long, drooping black mustache.

"Mr. Duncan!" She wanted to smile but bit her lip instead. "I thought you might be too tired for breakfast! How's Portagee?"

"He's as tired as I am. I rubbed him down and gave him grain and he's probably dreaming of how nice it would be if he was owned by a petite young lady, instead of a lumpy old Englishman."

"You are not that old, Mr. Duncan. Some people lead productive lives well into their thirties."

"Well, now, that's a comfort to me, Miss Bennett. Did you reserve that chair for me?"

"Yes, I knew you'd be here."

The tall man with small dark eyes and thick eyebrows slipped into the oak chair beside her. "Now, Sina Marie, what's this prayer about?"

"You mean the burnt toast?"

"No, I mean the wind."

"I thought I should ask the Lord for a day without wind. Wouldn't that be simply wonderful? Daddy told me I shouldn't pray for things like that."

"But you do anyway?"

"Do you think it's wrong for me to pray that way?"

Duncan turned over his fried bread and studied the blackened bottom side. "Miss Bennett, with a heart like yours, you can pray for anything you want. Of course, the Lord can answer it any way He wants to."

"I believe it's fair for me to ask that because He's allowed it to blow for two months now."

"Yes, but consider this." Duncan pushed the toast aside and forked into a ham slice. "Suppose there is a twelve-year-old girl across the street who is also going to have a birthday tomorrow. And what if she is very sick and not expected to live much longer, and the one thing she wants for a birthday present is to see her father fly a kite as she peeks out the window? Now, the Lord has two requests: one for wind, one for no wind. How will He know which one to grant?"

"That's easy. He will answer my prayer," she insisted.

"Why do you say that?"

"Because I'm here and there isn't any girl living across the street. There isn't even a building across the street. I'm the only girl in this town, remember?"

"Yes, but just pretend that there was someone there, then what would the Lord do?"

"Mr. Duncan, you simply can't spend all your life in a make-believe world. You remind me of my brother Richard. When he was young he would run around and pretend to be a pirate."

"Lots of children go through that stage."

"Richard did it for three years. Mother finally made him take off the eye patch. She was afraid it would ruin his vision." Sina Marie carefully sliced the blackened portion off the bottom of her fried bread.

"Do you have special activities planned for after your party?" he asked.

"I thought that since it won't be windy I would go for a walk up to the cedars and have a quiet afternoon with mother, father, and Richard. Don't you think that sounds very mature?"

"Thirteen is a very mature age." Duncan grinned. "I suppose you'll be thinking of getting married soon."

She bit her lip and tugged at the tiny jade earring. "Now, don't you start pining for me again. I have absolutely no intention of marriage for several years, and it will certainly not be to a man of advanced years."

"Oh, Miss Sina Marie, how you break my heart."

"But the Lord can use that to build character. Isn't that right, Mrs. Larson?"

"Darlin'—" the gray-haired hostess laughed—"the good Lord's been workin' overtime buildin' character in some of these men."

Sina Marie was licking molasses off her spoon when the delicate china cups on the shelf above the chair pegs began to rattle.

She glanced at all the men around the table as they rose to their feet and scurried to the front porch of the boarding house.

"The Bozeman stage!" Sina Marie called out. "It *did* come this week! Oh, I wonder what's on it?"

"I wonder *who's* on it?" Mrs. Larson added as she followed the twelve-year-old out onto the porch.

A blast of swirling dirt and sand greeted them as they huddled around the six-up team that rolled the stage to a stop in front of the unpainted boarding house.

"It's Tobias Horn!" Young Bill Scott declared.

"Toby, you old rattlesnake, what are you doing down here?" Mr. Carruthers shouted.

The short man, his gray beard halfway down his stained wool vest, grinned and revealed full pink lips and tongue. "Shoot, boys, it's a special lady's birthday, and I weren't about to miss it!"

"You came just for my party?" Sina Marie giggled. "But I'm only a girl."

"Until tomorrow, darlin'," the old man added. "Now boys, unload that small crate mighty careful."

"What's in it?" Mrs. Larson probed.

"Someone's birthday present."

"My word, it looks like a bundle of wet burlap," Grif Duncan said.

"That's because the burlap is protectin' somethin' special," Horn insisted. "Don' suppose there's any breakfast left?"

"There seems to be quite a few pieces of fried bread remaining," Mrs. Larson announced as they scooted back into the house.

Sina Marie waited at the porch and surveyed the dust-swirled street. Mrs. Greene's little brown dog with no name chased a scrap of red ribbon that was kept suspended in the air by the stiff breeze.

Lord, Piñon City is a funny town. There is one street and only buildings on one side of that street, because everyone wants their front door away from the wind. It has no mines, no trains, no farm ground, no reason for its existence. We stumbled in here because Richard was sick and Daddy took a wrong turn. Maybe there are some places on earth that You had no intention for people to live in. If so, then this might be one of them. It was a strange place the day we arrived. The buildings, the people, even the dogs lean into the wind. No one paints their house. No one plants a garden or a tree, let alone any grass. Not many even unpack their suitcases. That's what mama said the day we came here: "Don't unpack, honey, because we won't stay here long."

I guess we will stay here a while now.

It's still a strange place.

Like an ugly dog that loves you dearly, you have to apologize for it every day, but wouldn't trade it for a pen full of pretty-faced hounds.

After Sina Marie helped Mrs. Larson with the breakfast dishes, she scurried to her room and pulled out a dark green leather book. With a flour-sack towel she wiped the dust off the rawhide covered stool that served as her desk. Slowly she opened the bottle of India ink and dipped in the nib of the pen, then carefully printed the words "August 16, 1869" across the top of the page.

It is the day before my thirteenth birthday and this is my last day for being childish. So therefore I do hereby resolve the following:
   1. I will keep myself pure in thought and deed.

She stared at the line. *All right, Daddy, I can hear your lecture! I'll make you proud of me.*
She pressed the pen to the page again.

   2. I will say my prayers and read my Bible daily, just as I have since we started out from Illinois.

Mama, I didn't even tell you I read the entire book of Leviticus!

   3. I will make myself useful, without getting in other people's way.

She stared at the list for several minutes, then added another point.

   4. I will wear my mother's necklace at all times.

She thumbed through the journal to the first page. *April 10, 1869. The Great Adventure Begins.* She began to read. Somewhere in early May, she fell asleep.

That afternoon she and Mrs. Larson washed the cotton bedding and shook it dry in the backyard. She sliced apples, mended her yellow dress and drew a careful picture of the stagecoach pulled by six dark horses.

Supper was her favorite meal at the boarding house because all the men wore suits and ties. Young Bill Scott sat beside her.

"I bought you the prettiest present in Wyoming."

"Don't you tell me, Young Bill." She covered her ears.

"Bought it at the finest store in Cheyenne."

"Shhh! I'm not listening."

"It was the last one they had."

"If you say another word, I'll pour gravy in your lap."

"Are you that type of girl?"

"Only when Mama's not looking. And she's not looking now."

"Okay, I won't tell you. But I will say that a very fancy lady saw your present and tried to buy it off me. But I told her it was for my girl up at Piñon City."

"Young Bill, I am not your girl. Don't you go around tellin' people that."

"You're breakin' my heart, darlin'."

"Perhaps the Lord is teachin' you a lesson, Young Bill. Daddy told me that when we don't get what we want it is the Lord's way of teaching us to trust Him."

Sina Marie combed her hair out at 8 P.M. At 8:10 she laid out her yellow dress and brushed it clean. Then she opened the small hand-carved cedar box and lifted out her mother's gold necklace. She placed it on a rawhide-covered stool. At 8:20 she pulled back the quilted comforter on the long narrow bed and, out of habit, checked to see if Richard had put any crawly things between the sheets. At 8:30 she stood at her narrow window to stare out at the dark night.

Lord, this is Your Sina Marie. I'm goin' to be a young lady tomorrow. And I'm not sure how I'm supposed to behave. I've wanted to be thirteen ever since I was a little girl. But it's kind of scary. I'm not really as pretty as the men tease me to be. I mean, I'm not complainin' about the way You made me, but I'll never be as beautiful as Mama. That's okay. I never met any woman in the world that was as beautiful as Mama. Except, of course…when she's sick.

Sina Marie brushed the corner of her eyes. She let out a deep sigh.

Now, about the wind…I don't want to sound like Mrs. Cranshaw nagging Hubert to go to church, but I did ask for the wind to stop.

She peered out at the dark night.

Lord, if there's a girl who wants the wind to lift her kite…well…well… perhaps You could grant her the patience and health to wait an extra day.

The sand blew against the cedar siding. She tossed and turned. Several times during the night, she hiked down the stairs and out to the front porch. Each time she opened the door, she caught a blast of Wyoming wind.

Around 4 A.M. she crawled back onto the bed on top of the quilt. She tucked her knees up to her chest and fell asleep.

"Sina Marie!"

She sat straight up. Bright sunlight filtered through the window, making the suspended dust look like tiny flakes of angel rain. "I'm sorry, Mrs. Larson, I slept in. I'll be right down and set the table!"

The gray-haired lady stuck her head in the door. "Not today, darlin'. Happy birthday! I figured you'd want to come out on the porch and see your present."

"On the porch?"

"It's too big to get it all indoors."

"What is it?"

"Pull on your robe and come on."

Sina Marie ran several steps ahead of Mrs. Larson across the sitting room and slung open the door. Men filled the covered porch, some with pipes in their mouths, several with cups of coffee, some still barefoot. All stared out at the prairie. For the first time in anyone's memory, the Big Horn Mountains were in view.

Her eyes grew wide.

"What do you think, Miss Bennett?" Grif Duncan pressed.

"I ain't never seen anything like this," Young Bill Scott declared.

"It is magnificent," Mr. Carruthers added.

Sina Marie ran out in the street and spun around as if wearing a satin gown at the General's Ball. "See? See? What did I tell you? It's beautiful! It's the most wonderful present any girl ever got in her life."

"You mean, any young lady," Mr. Duncan corrected.

"Yes…Yes!" she shouted. "Oh, thank You, Lord! There isn't a bit of wind, is there?"

"Darlin', the only breeze today is from your gown twirling around the street," Mrs. Larson called out.

"What do you say now, Mr. Duncan? The Lord did answer my prayer."

"I do believe you're right. That little girl across the street must have recovered quickly and decided to fly the kite another day."

Still barefoot and in her flannel robe, Sina Marie rushed up the street toward several men on the front porch of the mercantile.

"Isn't this a marvelous day? I prayed for the wind to stop and the Lord answered my prayer!"

A tall man tipped his black, beaver felt hat. "Yes, ma'am, I reckon He did."

She stopped and stared into his narrow gray eyes. "Are you new in town?"

"I jist rode in this morning."

"You're invited to my birthday party at noon at Mrs. Duncan's boarding house. Don't be late; and you don't have to buy me a present unless you really want to."

Sina Marie counted twenty-one men, four women, two young boys, and three dogs at her party. It was almost 3 P.M. when she said her last thank you, crammed the big basket with her gifts, and hiked up the hill toward the cedars. Her long brown hair flowed down her back to her waist. A yellow ribbon kept her bangs in place. When she reached the clearing, she spread out the blanket and set down the loaded basket.

Lord, this is the first time I've been up here when I could set a blanket out on the ground without it blowing away. Thank You very much. I'm sorry I'm such a bother at times. Daddy says I can be very, very fussy.

She stared at the wooden headboard that read "Andrew Peter Bennett, born April 1, 1835, South Bend, Indiana. Died of cholera June 18, 1869, Piñon City, Wyoming Territory."

"Daddy, look at this beautiful book of Shakespeare that Mr. Duncan gave me. Next to my Bible it is the most wonderful book in the world. I'm glad you taught me how to read when I was quite young."

She brushed a tear from her eye. "I bet it's never, ever windy in heaven. Today is like heaven to me. I'm glad you brought us West, Daddy. It's a beautiful land. I was wrong to cry and fuss that night you took sick and tell you I hated Wyoming and wanted you to take us back home. I was just a little girl then. I think I've grown up some this summer."

Sina Marie took a deep breath and glanced to her left. Written in black paint on a flat rock were the words, "Richard Andrew Bennett, born September 21, 1859. Died of cholera June 16, 1869, Piñon City, Wyoming Territory." She reached into her basket. "Look, Richard, my very own folding knife! Isn't it wonderful? That's a real abalone shell handle and two blades! I believe it's the nicest one I've ever seen in my life…next to yours, of course. Yours was the best. And look—" she pulled up her faded yellow hem—"I got new yellow stockings from

Cheyenne. All the women wanted them, but I got them. And I got a sewing basket of my very own, and a tin of cookies all the way from Denver, and a pair of reading spectacles that I don't need, but they make me look very mature, and…"

She bit her lip as she stared at her brother's gravestone. "Are you older than me in heaven, Richard? Someone said that everyone was about thirty years old in heaven. If so, then you're already older. Don't let Daddy get so busy that he forgets about me, Richard."

She started to turn to her right, but found she couldn't force her head around. Finally, chin down and eyes focused on the basket, Sina Marie plucked up the damp burlap sack. She slowly unwrapped an armful of white daisies and red carnations and blue lupine and began to arrange them on the mound of packed dirt in front of the wooden sign that read, "Lucille Paine Bennett, born December 26, 1836, Rockport, Illinois. Died of cholera June 19, 1869, Piñon City, Wyoming Territory."

"Mama, these are the most beautiful flowers in all of Wyoming! And they are just for you. You always told Daddy you'd move anywhere he wanted to go so long as you could have your flowers. Aren't they beautiful? And your necklace, it feels so good around my neck. I feel very mature. Remember all those times I wanted to be old, and you always said, 'In the Lord's good time, baby, in the Lord's good time.' Well, Mama, I guess this was His time."

Tears tumbled down Sina Marie's cheeks and onto the cover of the Shakespeare book. "Oh, Mama, I miss our talks, and the long walk out from the wagon every night when you'd hold my hand and we'd look at the stars and you'd tell me about when you were my age. Do you take long walks in heaven, Mama?

"I had a dream the other night that the wind stopped blowing for one day, and I went for a long walk. Jesus was holding my hand, and I told Him how much I miss you. He said you and Him walked together every day.

"When I woke up I decided that if I walk with Him every day down here on earth and you walk with Him every day in heaven…well, it's almost like us walkin' together, isn't it? Except I don't get to feel your hand.

"Remember how windy it was every time we went for a walk? And you told me it's all those angels rushin' to and fro lookin' after little girls like me? I'm not a little girl anymore, Mama. So I guess that's why the wind stopped."

Sina Marie lay back on the blanket to gaze at the cloudless Wyoming sky. Biting gnats buzzed around her head. She covered her face with a linen hanky.

Finally, a slight drift of warm wind caused her to open her eyes and sit up. She could feel dried tears on her cheeks. She sighed and glanced once more at all three markers, then tucked the items from the blanket, all except the flowers, back into the basket.

"Daddy and Mama and Richard, it is time for me to go home. Not home to Indiana, not home to Illinois, not on out to Oregon. I'm going home to Piñon City. It's my place now. They need me. They like me. They treat me good. They treat me better than I deserve."

The sun hovered above the western horizon as she hiked down the hill. The wind picked up and flagged her skirt. Her head was raised, her chin out, her shoulders back, and each step seemed more confident than the last.

Lord, I think I miss the wind.

It might just have been the reflection of the dying Wyoming sun, but Sina Marie thought she spied a pink feather float above a distant gray-green sage.

"That's one lap!" she shouted into the stiffening breeze. Then, from deep inside her heart, she began to laugh.

Really laugh.

ABOUT THE AUTHOR

Stephen Bly has spent his life in rural areas and ranches of the West, which explains why most of his seventy books are western and historical fiction. According to Steve, "None of us gets to choose our hometown, but we do get to choose whether a place feels like home." Sina Marie Bennett makes that discovery on her thirteenth birthday in Piñon City, Wyoming Territory, 1869. Some of Steve's latest books include The Skinners of Goldfield series, The Belles of Lordsburg series, and The Fortunes of the Black Hills series. He and his wife, Janet, have three sons and two grandchildren.

WHEN YOU WISH UPON A STAR

Dave Jackson

*W*hen Barry Matson wished upon a star, it made no difference that he was four years older and twice as big as his sixth-grade classmates or that they called him Raspberry. He had wished *real hard* on that star.

And sure enough, one Sunday night Barry got his wish. Greg and Kathy Parker announced that they were taking the junior high youth group to Disneyland.

"Everyone?" asked Linda Parker.

"Everyone who gets a parent to sign this note." Linda's dad held up some pink sheets with a purple dittoed message on them and began passing them out. "Here it is," he began to read, "'Disneyland Trip, August 15, 1959. I hereby give permission for my son/daughter…'"

"Well, *I* don't need one of those," interrupted Linda, "'cause you already know I'm going."

Someone in the back snickered. "Neither does Raspberry, 'cause he's too big and dumb to go."

"No I'm not." Barry straightened in his chair. "I'm goin'—" his fifteen-year-old voice cracked, and he finished an octave higher—"'cause I wished on a star."

The snickering spread.

"That's enough, kids," said Mr. Parker. "Barry, don't you think prayer might have done more?"

"Oh, I did that, too." Barry stood up to reach over the other kids for his pink sheet. Ricky Seymour was in the way, so Barry moved him aside with one hand like he was lifting a three-year-old by the arm.

"Hey, take it easy, you big ape. That's my pitchin' shoulder."

But Barry got his pink sheet, and the following Saturday he was the first one off the church bus in the Disneyland parking lot.

Ticket books in hand, the kids walked under the Santa Fe & Disneyland Railroad sign and into the Magic Kingdom. Barry looked at the quaint storefronts that lined Main Street. "Is this really where the Mouseketeers live?"

"Oh, Raspberry," Linda Parker sneered.

"Quit callin' me that." Barry's voice rose. "You've called me that ever since the swim party, and it ain't nice!"

"Don't be so touchy...*Raspberry.*" Linda giggled and other kids joined in.

Mr. Parker ignored them. "All right, everybody, gather round...no, come back here, girls. I want everyone to stick together."

A groan rose like a Greek chorus. Then the kids all began clamoring about where they wanted to go first—the Explorers' Boat Ride through the jungle, sports cars in Autopia.

"I'm riding the bobsled down the Matterhorn," declared Ricky Seymour.

"No, you're not," scoffed Linda.

"You just wait and see!"

"You won't 'cause you can't." She flipped her ponytail with a snap of her head. "The Matterhorn won't be finished till next month." Then she turned to her father. "How come we have to stay together? I don't want to drive those stupid little cars. I want to be first in line for the TWA Rocket to the Moon! Please, Dad...Daddy."

Greg Parker turned to his wife, who shrugged. Linda jumped between them. "Come on, Dad. We won't get lost. *Everybody's* been here before."

"I haven't," said Barry.

Mr. Parker looked around at the rest of the group. "Well, all right. But use the buddy system and meet back at the ice cream parlor for lunch. Does everyone know where that is? And I want—" the group quickly dispersed, and his voice trailed after them—"everyone to have a watch. Okay?"

Barry held out his arm, thick as a limb on an oak tree. "I got a watch, Mr. Parker."

The youth leader smiled at his wife and then looked up at Barry. "That's good, Barry. Guess you can come with us."

"You ever been to a penny arcade, Barry?" Mrs. Parker sounded like an older version of her daughter. "We just love Main Street. Don't we, dear?" She grabbed her husband's arm, and Barry followed along behind like an awkward puppy.

Barry frowned. He still hadn't seen Mickey and Annette or the Mouseketeers.

"Look here, Barry," said Mr. Parker. "This is the ice-cream parlor I was talking about. It's got marble-topped tables and wrought iron chairs. They serve real ice cream—"

"Oh, Greg, look, the glass blower is in." Mrs. Parker pulled her husband toward the window of a small shop. "He's making a little dove. Oh, Greg, I want one of those. I want that one—the one he's working on right now—so I can wear it on a chain around my neck and say we saw him making it."

"Well, it's a little hot right now, dear. Try wearing that and you'll end up with a raspberry on your neck."

Barry stepped back and checked the button at the top of his heavy corduroy shirt. *Raspberry?* Why hadn't Mr. Parker said cherry or plum? Was he making fun of him? But the couple wasn't even paying attention to him. They were walking into the glassblower's shop, hand in hand like two lovebirds.

Don't be so touchy, Linda had said. It made Barry angry. Maybe Mr. Parker hadn't meant anything, but Linda always did. She was mean.

He stood on the sidewalk, looking up and down Main Street. So many people, but no Disney friends…no friends at all.

Wait. What was that? A huge brown… Barry's jaw dropped. It was Pluto, getting his picture taken with some children. Barry grinned and drifted toward them. This was the real Disneyland, just like on TV.

But the moment he got near, Pluto waved at the children and walked away. Barry followed. Pluto walked faster. Barry hurried. Then Pluto turned down a little alley between two buildings. Barry peeked around the corner.

Pluto stood there pulling at one paw with the other. Suddenly it came off like a glove. Barry's eyes widened. Pluto had nothing but a human hand inside.

Barry stepped into the gangway and approached Pluto. "What's the matter with your paw...uh, your hand?" He leaned down a little so he was at eye level with the big dog. "Are you pretend?"

"No more than you are, buddy," said the dog head. "But I don't know how they expect us to stay in these hot suits all day." Pluto grabbed his head with one paw and the hand and lifted it up.

"You *are* pretend!"

"No kidding." The Pluto person tucked his dog head under one arm and raked his other sleeve across his sweaty forehead.

Barry giggled, deep-throated and open-mouthed. "I sure did think you was real!" He nervously rubbed his upper lip, where a faint mustache grew.

"Yeah, yeah," said the dog suit. "Just give me a break, okay? And get outta here before some little kid follows you in here and sees me."

Reluctantly, Barry turned and merged back into the crowd as they pushed deeper into the heart of the Magic Kingdom, past a horse-drawn trolley, popcorn vendors, and a surrey with a fringe on top. *Putt, putt, putt* came an old car. Barry started to hum "When You Wish upon a Star." But he stopped at the second line. Did it really make no difference who you were?

Up ahead he saw a huge fort, just like Davy Crockett's, with log blockhouses on either side of the gate. Over it hung a sign— F-R-O-N-T-I-E-R-L-A-N-D. Barry grinned. *Frontierland!* This was more like it.

As he walked through the gates, Barry heard a steam whistle blowing in the distance. "Excuse me! 'Scuse me!" he said, pushing his way forward. He checked his shirt pocket to be sure he still had his ticket book for the paddle wheel riverboat.

"Stop in the name of the law!" *Bam! Bam! Bam!*

Barry froze. What had he done now?

He turned slowly. In one hand, a Matt Dillon-like sheriff held a still-smoking pistol. With his other hand he gripped the collar of an unshaven man sporting an ace of spades in his hatband.

"Black Bart," yelled the sheriff, "I arrest you in the name of the law for cheating at cards, disrupting the peace, and—oh, yes—robbin' the bank." Then he hustled Black Bart away.

Barry's heart slowed. Boy, that was something! The families and kids around Barry were nodding and talking. He grinned at no one in particular as they wandered away.

Suddenly he had to leap out of the way for a stagecoach that rolled to a stop right in front of him. Several people got out and went into what looked like an old hotel. A large ornate sign reading The Golden Horseshoe hung from the balcony over the porch. A poster beside the door said Pepsi-Cola Presents the Golden Horseshoe Revue. Come One, Come All.

"Well, don't just stand there, pardner." A beautiful young woman in a dazzling green dress touched Barry's arm and winked. "Come on in and see the show."

Forgetting about the paddle wheeler, Barry followed her through the double swinging doors. Her auburn hair was pulled back, and little ringlets cascaded down, brushing her ivory shoulders. Just before she disappeared into a side hallway, she flashed Barry a smile as warm and bright as sunshine in May.

"Please find a seat," said a little man in a white shirt with a red vest. "The show is about to begin."

Barry looked around. The room was filled with tables and chairs, and a bar ran along one side. Below the gilded stage at the front of the room was an orchestra pit with a piano and several musicians. Box seats behind little white fences hung from the side walls like oversized picture frames.

Barry edged toward a table near the front where three men already sat drinking from dark mugs and eating peanuts from a basket in the center of the table. The men were all older, balding, and fat. One glanced at Barry through pale, watery eyes, and then turned away.

"What can I get for you?" It was the little man in his white shirt and red vest. This time Barry noticed little black garters around his sleeves.

"Uh…"

"What would you like to order? Sarsaparilla, root beer, Pepsi-Cola?"

"I like root beer."

The man brought a frosty mug of root beer as the room lights dimmed. Barry grabbed the edge of the table. "What's happening?"

"That'll be a dime," said the man.

The orchestra burst into a twangy rendition of "Buffalo Gals, Won't You Come out Tonight?"

"That'll be a dime…please."

"Pay him!" The fat man with the watery eyes glared at Barry. "He needs a dime for your drink."

Barry dug in first one pocket and then another. He stood up so he could reach all the corners of his pockets. Ah, there it was. He dropped a dime on the table as the watery-eyed man scowled at him. "Sit down!"

The red velvet stage curtain parted, the limelights rose, and four girls came out dancing. Except for the colors, their dresses were the same—cut low in front with full skirts held out by frilly petticoats. The blonde wore red, the girl with black hair had on yellow, the brunette wore blue, and the green dress... Barry sucked in his breath, coughing on his root beer. The girl in the green dress was the same one who had invited him into the saloon!

"Ladies and gentlemen," shouted the piano player from the orchestra pit. "Won't you welcome the Golden Horseshoe's famous cancan girls!"

Everyone applauded, and the girls began to dance across the stage, kicking high and swinging their skirts. When they were lined up in the golden glow of the footlights, the piano player said, "On your left is our dear Cricket McGruder." Everyone clapped. Barry joined in.

"And in the blue, please welcome Miss Kate Duncan." More clapping.

"Next is the blond bombshell, Trixie...Fremont." He strung out her name as the audience cheered with whistles and catcalls.

"And finally, the newest addition to our Golden Horseshoe Revue, Miss Misty Moore!"

Barry clapped as hard as he could. The watery-eyed man said, "Misty Moore, huh? You like Misty?" He turned to the other men and jerked his thumb. "Kid likes Misty." Their deep laughs sounded like sticks being dragged along a picket fence.

Barry stopped clapping. "Misty..." He whispered the name. "Misty." Her green dress was like a forest morning, setting off the rosy flush on her cheeks. But...why were those men laughing like that? It didn't sound right.

All four girls linked arms and danced so that their line turned like a pinwheel until their backs were to the audience. Misty glanced over her shoulder and smiled—right at him, Barry thought, just as she had done after inviting him into the Golden Horseshoe. Then they all flipped up their dresses, showing off long legs in black-knit mesh stockings.

Everyone roared...except Barry. He was thinking about Misty. She looked familiar. Had he seen her before? He closed his eyes and tried to think. He opened them when the music stopped. Each girl stepped forward and made a deep curtsy as the audience hooted and howled. Misty was last, and as she bowed revealingly low, Barry suddenly remembered the calendar girl pinned high on the wall in Arnie's Auto Repair. Could *that* have been Misty? Had some Peeping Tom—someone like that fat old man sitting next to him—taken a picture of her? Barry had never dared look very closely at the calendar, just a glance or two. But the vague image he carried in his mind sure looked like Misty.

Barry scowled at the men near him. "Come on, Misty! Yeah, Misty!" The watery-eyed man was whistling and clapping.

Barry's face grew hot. Was that man thinking about the calendar, too?

The curtains began closing, and the girls sashayed back through the narrowing gap, each one flipping up her dress before disappearing.

The men guffawed and slapped the table.

Barry stood, clenching his big hands. He wanted to hit the watery-eyed man for leering at Misty. He knew what it felt like to have people make fun of him. But he turned away and stomped to the back of the saloon. He followed the dark hallway down which Misty had gone earlier. Still able to hear the cheering crowd in the saloon, he looked ahead. There, in the glare of a single bare light bulb, the dancehall girls jockeyed for position around a small wall mirror to repair their makeup.

Except Misty. She was leaning back against the wall, her shoulders slumped, head down. Barry squinted and moved a little closer.

"What's the matter? You sick or something, honey?" he heard the black-haired girl say.

"Nah, I just hate this job. The old man won't even give me a day off. Frankly, I want outta here."

In the shadows, Barry's eyes widened. That must be the same old man out there at the table! Was…was Misty some kind of a slave? Having to dance so he and his mean friends could laugh at her? Maybe forcing her to take pictures without any…. Barry couldn't stand the idea.

He took the last few steps into the circle of light. "Hi, Misty. Don't worry anymore about that old man. I'll get you out of here." He grabbed her hand and fled back down the hallway, pulling her after him.

"Hey, kid!" she sputtered with a nervous little laugh as they ran out into the daylight in front of the Golden Horseshoe. "What do you think you're doing? I've still got a show to do."

Barry looked up and down the street. "It's okay, Misty. You don't have to do any more shows if you don't want to! I'll help you get away." Half-running, half-walking, he headed toward the stockade gate at the entrance to Frontierland.

Misty gave a short laugh as she stumbled along. "'Help me get away'? What are you talking about—? Hey, slow down! I can't run in these shoes."

Barry just kept going. Outside the stockade gate, he turned toward Main Street.

"Hey, Raspberry…. Over here! It's time for lunch."

Barry jerked his head around and moaned as he spotted Linda Parker and some of the other girls headed toward the ice cream parlor. He couldn't let Misty hear that name! He hesitated. Maybe Linda and the other girls would be impressed when they realized what he was doing for Misty.

"Who are they?" asked Misty, finally jerking her hand away and shaking it to restore circulation. "You sure got a strong grip."

"Sorry." Barry wiped his sweaty hand on his shirt. "Uh—that's my church youth group." He grinned.

"What?" Misty looked at him more closely. "Aren't you kind of young to be a youth leader? Look, Raspberry…"

"My name's not *Raspberry.*" He spat out the loathsome name and grabbed her wrist again. "I'm just Barry."

"Okay, *just* Barry. Ouch! Don't squeeze so hard. This little game has gone far enough. Look, I've lost my shoes and I've got to get back to the show or I'll get fired. Okay? Thanks for trying to help me out, but—"

"Hey, Raspberry," called Linda Parker. "Who's that? You playin' Beauty and the Beast?"

Barry eyed the girls coming toward them. He took a step back. No! They wouldn't understand, and…and he didn't have time to explain to Misty, either. He gave her a pull and began running across the plaza.

"Barry, stop! Let me go!" Misty shouted.

Behind him, Barry heard Linda's shrill voice. "Hey! Help, somebody! Raspberry's kidnapping that woman! Help! Call the police!"

Police? Kidnapped? The words tumbled through Barry's mind as they ran. He would never *kidnap* anyone. What was Linda talking about? But he had no time to worry about her. She was just mean, anyway.

"Stop in the name of the law!"

Barry glanced over his shoulder. The sheriff from Frontierland was running out of the gate. Barry felt a stab of panic. He sure hoped Matt Dillon wouldn't start shooting like he had at Black Bart.

Still holding tightly to Misty's wrist, he took off toward...toward... where was he going? He ran past a huge white rocket ship standing on its tail and headed deeper into Tomorrowland. Just beyond the Autopia track, he could see a large mountain, the top half covered with snow. He headed toward it. Maybe they could hide there or get away in the hills beyond.

He could hear Misty making strange noises as she staggered along behind him. Was she laughing...or crying? He wanted to stop and tell her it would be okay, but one glance over his shoulder told him he couldn't stop. The sheriff, some policemen, several people in uniform, and some of the kids from his youth group were running after them. They had to hurry. He dragged Misty around a corner but was stopped by a gate posted with a sign that read Coming Soon! Matterhorn Bobsled Ride.

The gate was locked with a chain. Barry looked up. He could climb over, but what about Misty? "We gotta find a way."

Misty's breath came in ragged gasps. "Barry, *please*. Don't do this.... You're going to get into big trouble. Just let me go, and I'll—"

"Oh, don't worry 'bout me, Misty. C'mon, I think we can get through over there."

He pulled her through a gap in the fence and ran for the mountain. At its base he found an opening—*like a cave*, he thought. But inside were huge timbers and tracks. It looked more like the inside of a warehouse. Light came through holes high up on the walls—or were they windows? And then Barry saw some stairs.

After two flights up the steep steps at Barry's fast pace, Misty was nearly collapsing. "Here...I'll carry you," he said gently. "They won't get us." He swung her up onto his shoulder and continued.

"No! Put me down, Barry. You've got to stop this!" Her voice had changed, and Barry could feel her fists pounding his back. "Put me down!"

He paused. "Misty, what's the matter? Am I hurting you?" But just then he heard their pursuers enter the mountain. "Go away," he yelled. "Leave us alone." He pushed Misty's green dress out of his face and leaned over the railing to look below.

"Look out!" she screeched. "Hey, you're gonna drop me."

Suddenly it became silent below, and all Barry could hear were soft sobs from Misty. Then someone yelled, "Everyone out! He's threatening to drop her!"

Barry turned and continued up the steps, but more slowly now. "It's…okay…Misty," he puffed. "I won't…drop you."

"Barry, listen," Misty pleaded. "I appreciate what you're trying to do, but you've got to put me down."

But Barry couldn't stop now. Up he went, slower and slower, with the most beautiful girl in the world over his shoulder. Finally he reached the top—a small room with open windows on opposite sides—and put Misty down. She sank to the floor in a heap, and Barry watched in horror as he realized that she *was* crying.

Somehow it had gone wrong, terribly wrong.

"Oh, Misty. I'm sorry. Are you hurt?"

She took a deep sobbing breath. "No. I'm not hurt. It's just the… Oh, this is ridiculous!"

"I didn't mean to…I would never…"

Misty wiped her eyes with the back of her hands and gave Barry a red-faced smile. She was still half-crying. "I know, Barry, but this is really stupid, carrying me up here to the top of the Matterhorn. You could get hurt. What do you think they're doing down there? We both could get hurt." She stood up and took a step toward the stairs. "I'm getting out of here."

"No. Wait!" Barry held his hand out to her. "I just wanted to help you."

Misty rolled her eyes impatiently. "I know, Barry, but this isn't help."

Barry stared at her. He wasn't helping? Was he just…being stupid, like she said?

He turned to look out the window by the stairs, his bulk still barricading her way to the steps. A hundred and forty feet below spread the Magic Kingdom.

"I always wanted to come to Disneyland, but…but it's not like on TV. It don't seem magic anymore." He watched the tiny people below scurrying around between the trees and buildings. Then he frowned and leaned out the window a little. "Hey, they got guns down there, Misty. They got guns. Why do they have those guns, Misty?"

But there was only silence behind him.

"Misty…Misty?" He turned. She was gone. He looked down the stairs and listened but heard nothing. He looked around frantically. Where was she?

Suddenly, a scream shattered the mountain's quiet. "Misty!" He ran to the other window and looked down. She clung to a handhold several feet below. "Misty! How'd you get down there?"

"I thought I could…. Just help me, Barry! I can't hang on anymore!"

"But how?" Even as he asked, Barry was climbing out the window onto a workman's ledge about four feet below the window. Still gripping the window with one hand, he tried to lean down. "I can't reach you, Misty."

He looked below. Like little cartoon characters, the police came running to this side of the mountain, their guns drawn. He could hear them yelling for him to surrender or they would shoot.

Then he heard Linda Parker's shrill voice. "Leave her alone, Raspberry! She didn't do nothin' to you."

He gritted his teeth. *No…and she doesn't call me Raspberry, either.* But what if she saw—? He licked his lips, watched the crowd of onlookers and the ones with guns, and fought down panic.

"Don't worry about them, Barry," Misty pleaded. "I can't hang on anymore. Try reaching down with one leg."

He swallowed and did as instructed, stooping on the ledge, clinging to the window above, and stretching one foot down as far as he could.

"It's not enough, Barry! Use your shirt. Take it off and roll it up like a rope. Reach one end down to me. Hurry!"

Barry just clung there to the side of the mountain.

"Barry! What are you waiting for? Take your shirt off!"

"Oh, Misty! Oh, Misty, Misty. I can't! You'd *see…*" He felt desperate. "O God, I don't think wishin' on a star works. Please, Lord, what should I do?"

If he took his shirt off, she would see. Would Misty laugh at him too and call him Raspberry?

"Barry, *please—*"

With a choked wail, Barry peeled off his heavy corduroy shirt, rolled it up, and reached down.

He knew that Misty and the whole world could see the large raspberry birthmark that covered half his chest and one shoulder, but he lowered his shirt until the end brushed Misty's white knuckles. With a weak cry, she released her grip with one hand and grabbed the dangling shirt, then did the same with the other. When he felt her weight, Barry hoisted her up as smooth as a derrick until her feet came to rest on the ledge beside him. Putting his arm around her slender waist, he helped her climb through the window.

Finally he crawled in behind her.

She stood there breathing hard and looking at him…without his shirt.

Barry's face colored, and he quickly unrolled his shirt. But before he could slip into it, Misty stepped forward and gave him a hug, a hug that would hold him for life. "Thank you, Barry. You know…you saved my life."

She drew back and smiled sheepishly as he slipped into his shirt. "Guess what I did was pretty stupid, too, huh?" She extended her hand. "*Now* can we go down?"

Shyly, he placed his hand in hers. "Okay, Misty."

Her smile widened; it was like sunshine in May.

ABOUT THE AUTHOR

Dave Jackson remembers visiting Disneyland shortly after it opened in 1955. He has since returned with his wife-to-be, Neta (to buy a glass dove), later with their infant son, Julian, and most recently with their granddaughter, Havah. However, he neglected to take his own daughter, Rachel, and hopes she's not been wishing upon a star ever since.

The Jacksons are the authors of Hero Tales I, II, III, and IV, and the historical fiction series of thirty-four Trailblazer Books (Bethany), introducing young readers to great Christian heroes. They have also written numerous books for adults. They make their home in Evanston, Illinois, where they attend The Worship Center, a multiracial congregation.

The Southwest

GRAPES WITHOUT SEEDS

Jane Orcutt

Like most old folks, I can't rightly say that I enjoy change. Which is probably why I've lived in this same house now, here in Fort Worth, for nearly sixty-five years. Oh, every once in a while I might get a hankerin' to shake up the routine, like move the silverware to a different drawer or have my grandson move my easy chair away from the window instead of in front of it. But all in all, I cotton to things pretty much staying the way they are.

I'm sitting on the front porch of this old house, watching, waiting—suitcase beside me—as I hold a bowl of red grapes I bought down at Albertson's earlier this week. Everything I purchased seemed special because I knew it was the last time I'd get to enjoy them here in my house. Knew it even as I shuffled behind the large metal shopping cart I didn't need for groceries, just for hanging on to. I guess there's still too much Simpson pride in me to finagle one of those motorized carts the grocery stores provide for us old folks.

"A go-devil," my Simpson daddy would have called one of those contraptions. He hated just about everything motorized. I remember as a kid growing up how our neighbors bought a used Packard back in 1925. We Simpson kids were so jealous, but Daddy refused to have anything to do with cars. Our bare, dusty feet did just fine for tramping the flat prairie earth that stretches from one blue side of the sky to another.

No sir, I couldn't lay claim to any sort of automobile until I married my Bill. What a fine day it was when he returned to the old neighbor-hood with a spit-shined Ford after graduating from A&M. I think what made me want to marry him wasn't the automobile itself but his pride in ownership. He not only could drive that contraption, he could fix it too.

Bill and I'd known each other since we were younguns, been friends as long as we could remember. We grew up on farms just east of here, back when a trip to Dallas seemed like a trip to the moon, not just down the road as it is now. It seems like we were always teasing each other, egging ourselves into more mischief than our mamas had patience for. These grapes I'm holding now are smooth and cool, but I remember a time when Bill dared me to eat a bunch of wild mustang grapes. Shoot, everybody knew they made great jam, but were the tartest bunch of fruit God ever made. Why, just holding them would make your hands sting!

But I was ornery and young and certainly not willing for ol' Bill Bender to get the best of me, so I shoved those thick-skinned, rough grapes in my mouth and chewed 'em up good.

All the time I was trying hard not to make a pucker face at those nasty-tasting things, Bill was laughing. "What are you going to do with the seeds, huh, Grace? You gonna swallow them too?"

Well, just to show him, I did. I managed to spit one out at him—caught him right smack in his face, which knocked the sass out of him for a moment. Then he whooped louder than ever. On our wedding night, nine years later, he whispered that that was when he knew for sure he loved me. He figured that any girl fiery enough to do that would grow into a woman who could handle just about anything life threw her way.

Some folks would say it's God that does the throwing of the bad stuff as well as the good. Like when our first baby was born, a little boy hardly bigger than my fist, he was born so early. Bill was off somewhere in northern Italy, fighting with most of the other boys from around here, so I had nobody to grieve with except the wives who were left behind. Some of them just laid their heads beside me on the pillow and let the tears run down the eyelet cover, while others stood straight and tall by my bedside and clearly assured me of the Lord's will and mysterious ways.

I didn't much think it was the Lord's will to whisk my little baby away like a pound cake that didn't quite rise proper. But He did see fit to bring Bill home safe from the war and to later give us two healthy sons and a daughter, to boot.

As I look around this wide old porch, I think about all the feet that have pounded up and down these crumbling concrete stairs and across these paint-peeled wooden planks. I can hear that screen door banging as the kids stampede out of the August heat to watch Howdy Doody or the Mickey Mouse Club. I remember the countless Easter photos posed on these old steps—for years, me with a babe in arms and a toddler or two to keep still, then later with three squirmy kids and a husband whose solemn "Now, children" was enough to keep them in line while a neighbor snapped a shot with our old Brownie camera.

Then things seemed to change faster than I can scarcely recollect. School started, then junior high, and before I knew it, there were dates and proms—corsages in the refrigerator that smelled of sweet promise but would crinkle and brown at the edges after the dance was over. Through the years I packed lunches and kissed boo-boos, held small hands as we walked solemnly through the doors of South Hi Mount Elementary for the first day of school, and the next thing I knew, my kids were breaking free to run down the sidewalk toward college and lives of their own.

To a mother it's a bitter taste, like those mustang grapes, when your kids leave home. In my day women's lives revolved around raising those children, and when they took wing from the nest, it was like a chunk of yourself went too. Maybe all that women's lib talk about getting jobs just like men wasn't so we could have our own money, but so we could protect our hearts just a tiny bit when our kids went away. Maybe a job gives some women a safety net to fall into when the heartbreak's too much.

Me, I fell back on my Bill, who'd been there all along, who pledged to stay beside me till death parted us. Which sadly was just a few years after the last child, our Daisy, graduated from A&M. Bill and I were sitting out on this very porch, right over yonder where we used to have two identical rocking chairs and sit on occasion. I was cross-stitching a Baby's First Christmas for our first grandchild, and Bill was reading the sports page, like most every other evening. Suddenly he put down the paper and said, "I'm feeling kinda tired tonight, old girl. Think I'll head to bed early."

I didn't think much of it. He'd grown more tired lately, but the doctor said it was just old age finally settling in his bones. But the next morning, my Bill didn't wake up. A heart attack, the doctor said, though

I've always thought with something named so strongly as an *attack,* Bill should have woken up at least once. But there he was with that same sweet smile on his face that he always got when he slept, so I knew when the angels had come down from heaven to carry him away, he was at peace with the whole notion.

After nearly thirty years, I couldn't always say the same for myself. I've missed him every blessed day he's been gone. But as old age has taken up residence in this body instead of settling for being a chairside companion, I've had a taste of the sweetness that bitter can turn into. I'm nearing eighty-seven now, and every day that mansion in the sky looks prettier and more like home. And after I get up off my face from bowing to the Lord, I want to make a beeline for my Bill, who I just know will be holding the hand of that little child we lost so long ago, both of them waiting for me.

Till then, I have to live in this tired old woman's body, with this tired old woman's memory. Oh, there's still plenty I want to see and do. I want to hold my first great-grandchild that's due in a few months, and I want to be with my kids and their kids as much as possible. Maybe my son's right in moving me to Houston to be closer to him and his family. "Now, Mama," he said, "it's just a retirement home. You'll have as much free-dom as you want and people to help you if you need it."

I know what he really means. He thinks I can't negotiate these old stairs anymore or get around very well now that my eyes are too dim to drive. Well, he's probably right about needing some help now and again, but I'll be dadgummed if I'll refer to myself as *retired.* That sounds like someone who's given up on life.

It's a little early for Texas grapes and too expensive for California ones. The sign at Albertson's said these grapes are from Chile. Seedless. I pinch one off from the bunch, knowing that if I picked well, the first taste will be the best. I take a bite, anticipating sweet and slow…and hit several small seeds. My weak eyes must have tricked me again.

Remembering, I laugh. The seeds don't bother me—the grapes still taste good. I'll savor every bit while I wait for my son to arrive.

ABOUT THE AUTHOR

Award-winning author Jane Orcutt's latest release is *The Living Stone*. Her next release will be "Don't Look Back" in this fall's *Restoration & Romance* anthology. Her previous novels include *The Hidden Heart* and *The Fugitive Heart,* both past finalists for the Romance Writers of America RITA award. *The Hidden Heart* was also a past finalist for a Reviewer's Choice award. Jane lives in Texas with her husband their two sons.

FRAGMENTS OF TRUTH

Carol Cox

Allie Monroe squinted through her windshield against the late afternoon sun and pulled to the curb in front of the QuikStop mini-mart. She checked her watch—time to spare before she had to cover the town council meeting. Hopefully it wouldn't be another snooze. Being the community correspondent for the *Northland Sentinel*—the only newspaper serving this part of northern Arizona—kept her in touch with local happenings, but didn't provide much challenge.

"Allie!" A slight figure waved from the other side of the street and hurried across.

Stepping out of her Sentra, Allie waved back to Marlys Kendrick. She had done a brief article on Marlys and her husband when they moved to Colton eight months before, after his retirement from the English department at a Michigan university. She'd seen Stewart only once or twice since then, but Marlys now considered Allie her best—her only—friend.

Marlys peered out from under the brim of her straw hat, her timid face contorted. "I need your help." She rested her hand on Allie's arm. "It's Stewart. The police are after him."

"Stewart?" A more *unlikely* prospect for police pursuit than Marlys's stuffy husband would be hard to imagine. "What did he do? Burn trash without a permit?"

Marlys tightened her grip. "I'm serious. Matt Collins and another deputy came out to question him today. An archaeological site on Holden Mesa was looted last week. They think Stewart was involved."

Allie recalled mentioning Stewart's standing as an amateur archaeologist in her article, along with the fact that he'd planned to spend his retirement pursuing his hobby.

Marlys's voice brought her back to the present. "We still don't know many people here. You're a journalist. I thought you'd know how to go about getting the facts." Her lower lip quivered. "Please, help me find out what really happened."

Allie flinched. Covering ice-cream socials hardly qualified as investigative reporting. She patted Marlys's shoulder. "It's just routine. They're checking every lead and Stewart's name came up. It doesn't mean he's their number-one suspect."

"I'm not so sure. They asked a lot of questions, and Stewart…well, you remember how distant he can be. I don't think he helped himself a bit."

Distant was not the word Allie would have used. Stewart seemed like a man firmly convinced of his own superiority. Not exactly an attitude that endeared him to the local populace—or to the authorities. Maybe she could help both Marlys and herself. What a coup it would be if she managed to uncover the culprit and write the *Sentinel's* best story of the year.

"I'll see what I can do." So promising, she ducked inside the QuikStop for a soda. Back on the sidewalk, she tipped the bubbly coolness down her throat, studying the sky. June usually brought heavy clouds and the monsoon rains. Only a few isolated clouds floated overhead today, holding the tantalizing promise of moisture.

Allie drove past a row of red rock houses—built for railroad workers back when Colton got its start as one of the end-of-the-tracks towns marking the progress of the Santa Fe line—and pulled into the community center's gravel parking lot.

Ed Jernigan wielded his gavel with a beefy arm and beat a tattoo on the Formica tabletop, calling the council meeting to order. Allie pulled out her pen and prepared to take notes. No surprises tonight; not even a good argument to spice up the evening. Lyman Rogers, manager of Yavapai Stone, thanked the council for their help in obtaining a conditional-use permit to expand his operation. Matt Collins gave his report on derelict vehicles and breaking up an underage drinking party out by the cemetery.

When the meeting ended, Allie intercepted Matt before he could climb into the pickup bearing the Yavapai County Sheriff's decal. "I noticed you didn't say anything about the theft on Holden Mesa."

Matt hooked his thumbs behind his belt and glared. "How'd you hear about that?"

Allie grinned. "Word gets around. Who discovered the theft?"

"An NAU student went out to finish cataloguing the site. When he realized the place had been looted, he called us."

"He had a list of what was there? Then you know what's missing?"

Matt grunted. "According to the experts, this is one rich site. Potshards, tools, hunting points, you name it. Whoever took them got quite a haul."

"Why are you focusing on Stewart Kendrick?"

"Forget it, Allie. I can't reveal sensitive information."

"Give me a break. Archaeological thefts don't happen every day. You want to blow my chance to cover the biggest story of my career?"

Matt rolled his eyes. "The *Sentinel* isn't exactly the *Washington Post*. Go write a nice story about the 4-H kids. Leave the heavy-duty stuff to someone who knows what he's doing."

Next morning, Allie wrote her story on the meeting and a sketchy account of the looting, knowing she had only a few more details than most locals would already have gleaned through the grapevine.

She unplugged her computer in an act of optimism that the monsoons and their accompanying thunderstorms might arrive while she was out, and headed up I-40 toward Flagstaff. If Stewart Kendrick hadn't looted the site, who had? Allie ran through the names of everyone in town, then started on people in the outlying areas. No one stood out as a possible suspect. A person would have to know what to look for and where to dispose of it, and that implied expert knowledge. Which eliminated every local she could think of.

Except Stewart Kendrick.

Her visit with Professor Miles Jordan at Northern Arizona University informed her of the existence of a thriving black market in artifacts. Peering over his half-glasses, Jordan intoned, "People who raid these sites are making a tremendous profit at the expense of preserving Native American heritage."

Armed with a copy of the Archaeological Resources Protection Act, courtesy of Professor Jordan, Allie started home. She glanced at the clouds. Larger and more numerous than yesterday, they formed knotted clusters across the sky, but no rain trails appeared underneath.

The flashing light on her answering machine signaled one message when she walked in the door. She pressed Play and heard Marlys's quavering voice: "Please call me as soon as you get in."

She wasn't surprised when Marlys picked up on the first ring. "It's Allie. What's going on?"

"They came to talk to Stewart again. I think he needs a lawyer, but he won't listen to me. Have you found anything?"

Nothing that didn't point to her husband as a likely suspect, Allie thought. She sidestepped the question. "Was it Matt again, or a different deputy this time?"

"They weren't deputies. They were federal investigators."

Allie's stomach clenched. They meant business.

"Could you come out here? I need to talk."

Allie glanced at her watch. "Sure. I'm on my way."

The Kendricks lived on five acres north of town. Red dust from the cinder-covered road rose in a plume behind Allie's Sentra. The *brrmmp* of her tires on the cattle guard announced the entrance into open range. She slowed, not wanting to hit a wandering cow.

Marlys came out the moment Allie turned into the driveway, nearly hidden behind an armload of wadded wallpaper. "I'd just finished stripping this off the wall when they came."

Allie raised her eyebrows. "Red and aqua checks? I don't blame you for getting rid of it." She helped carry the long strips to the trash barrel.

"Thanks for coming." Marlys shoved the heap down and tried to fit the metal lid on tight. "We don't get many visitors." Her evident loneliness gave Allie a twinge of guilt. She'd interviewed the Kendricks for the newcomers' column, but had she bothered to do something as basic as invite them to church or do anything to help them assimilate into the community?

"So tell me what happened," she said after Marlys had settled her into a comfortable chair with a tall glass of iced tea.

The older woman's face clouded. "It was terrible. They kept asking the same things over and over. What was Stewart doing the night the site was looted? How much did he know about the black market? They kept looking at his collection." She waved toward a spot behind Allie. "They wanted to know whether he could prove where each piece came from."

Allie swiveled to look and nearly dropped her glass. Framed displays covered the wall and filled a glass-topped case. Closer inspection showed an amazing array of arrowheads, spear points, potshards and beads. No wonder they were interested. Stewart had a collection worthy of a museum.

"They're all from private property," Marlys insisted. "But they didn't seem to believe that. I don't think they *wanted* to believe it."

"Is Stewart worried?"

"He seems bored by the whole thing, answering questions in the briefest manner possible, and not bothering to defend himself at all."

Not good, Allie thought. Investigators might consider such behavior evasive.

Marlys twisted her hands in her lap, her loneliness a palpable thing. "When we moved here, I thought we'd found the epitome of small-town life. I was wrong."

"Not exactly Mayberry, you mean?"

Marlys managed a weak grin. "That's about it. I'd always dreamed about living somewhere with that sense of community and friendliness. People here aren't what I expected."

Allie shook her head slowly. "I think you've only looked at the packaging. People here may not have the polish you'll find back east, but check out what's underneath instead of the veneer." She knew Colton had the warmth and neighborliness Marlys longed for. People supported one another even when they didn't see eye-to-eye. Even as newcomers, Stewart and Marlys could have expected that same sense of solidarity—if Stewart hadn't alienated everyone with his arrogance.

She laid a hand on Marlys's forearm. "Give them the chance to give *you* a chance."

"Back for another interview?" Stewart's unexpected appearance made Allie jump. "An exclusive story from the prime suspect, perhaps?"

Allie looked at him coolly. Tall, with patrician features, he wasn't bad looking, but his manner affected her like fingernails scraping a chalkboard. "Actually, I came to visit Marlys."

"I need her now for something more important than chitchat. If you'll excuse us?"

Allie fumed. No wonder the Kendricks hadn't been swamped by well wishers. Even the Welcome Wagon wouldn't be likely to drop in on Stewart. Run over him, maybe.

Guilt over her attitude flooded her. "I'll be praying for you," she managed.

"I hardly think platitudes spoken to the air will have any effect on my life."

Allie gaped; Stewart smiled condescendingly. "I don't need a myth to sustain me. I have yet to find anything in that collection of fables that applies to me."

"Have you ever read Psalm 14:1?" Allie called over her shoulder as she walked to her car. She paused to peel off a wayward scrap of wallpaper that had wrapped itself around her front tire, and then drove back to town, already ashamed of giving in to the impulse to fling the verse at him in anger. Would he bother to look it up? She speculated moodily on his probable reaction to "The fool says in his heart, 'There is no God.'"

She parked in front of the QuikStop and went inside to make a dent in the snack section. Emerging from the store sucking a frozen juice bar, she heard a strident shout of "Wrong way!" and grinned. Tommy Woodruff stood across the street, flailing skinny eight-year-old arms at a car heading east on the westbound one-way street, a holdover from the days when Route 66 ran through the middle of town. He glanced up, and Allie wiped the smile off her face.

"That's another one with California plates." The little boy shook his head. "Don't they teach 'em to read there?"

Allie stifled a grin. "That's why we need you."

The little boy threw out his chest and went back to his self-imposed traffic watch. Allie turned to find Lyman Rogers leaning against her car.

"I thought I'd check with you instead of the rumor mill. Is it true they think Stewart Kendrick took those artifacts?"

Allie nodded. "It looks like it."

"That's a shame." Lyman's eyes shone with sympathy. "It'll be hard on his wife."

"It isn't a done deal yet. I'm not convinced he did it." She drove off, wondering at her sudden conviction of Stewart's innocence. Unappealing as he was, she found it hard to picture him as a thief.

A line had formed at the water station. People who lived outside town visited while waiting to pump water into barrels to be hauled home. Allie parked nearby. It might be a good opportunity to pick up an idea for a line of investigation.

By the time she had worked her way through the crowd, it appeared the community's opinion was unanimous: Stewart Kendrick was guilty as sin.

Ben Vega echoed the general consensus. "The man keeps to himself and never has time for the likes of us unless he's looking for information on where to find a place to dig. Far as I can see, he's been using us. About time someone caught up with him." He positioned the two-inch hose and fed quarters into the coin-op dispenser. Water gushed from the hose and drummed on the bottom of the barrel. Pushing his feed cap back on his balding head, Ben squinted at the cloudless sky. "I'm telling you, we'd better see some rain soon or it's going to be one bad year."

After a fruitless morning chasing investigative leads into dead ends, Allie spent the afternoon and evening interviewing a TV crew that was shooting a documentary at the flagstone quarries. When the sunset faded, she started back to town, reviewing her knowledge of the theft. She was missing one basic piece of information: Where was Stewart when the site was looted? Marlys's home wasn't far out of her way. It would be easy to check.

The house was dark, and no cars were in the driveway. Chagrined, Allie turned back toward town. A dark shape loomed just outside her window, and she swerved, fighting to maintain control while the Sentra slewed wildly on the gravel shoulder.

The other vehicle sped off toward town, its bulky form soon swallowed up by the darkness. Allie flashed her lights angrily, even while realizing the futility of the gesture.

Allie crept through town, thoroughly unnerved by the near miss. The small sentry at the corner of Third and Center waved, giving her an excuse to stop.

"Hi, Tommy," she said weakly. "Getting much action tonight?"

"You wouldn't believe it. I just got one going the wrong way, and with his lights off, too." He shook his head. "He knows better."

Goose pimples prickled Allie's arms. "Who knows better?"

"J. D. Cochran. You know that silver Blazer he drives? He went by here just a couple of minutes before you did. Blew the stop sign at Fifth, too."

Allie made a mental note to have a chat with J. D. once her blood pressure returned to normal.

Sleep eluded her until dawn, only a couple of hours before the ringing phone shattered her dreams.

"Hello?"

Racking sobs were the only response.

Allie fumbled for her Caller ID. "Marlys?"

"They've arrested him. They came out with a search warrant early this morning."

"And found…?"

The sobs increased in intensity. "I'm not sure. They searched our shed, then they handcuffed Stewart and read him his rights." She drew a shuddering breath. "It looks bad."

Allie sat up, fully awake. "Do you have a lawyer?"

"I'll try to find one as soon as I hang up. I wanted to talk to you first. What am I going to do? Everyone around here thinks he did it. A lawyer can protect his rights, but I need someone who'll look for the truth." Marlys's voice caught on a ragged breath. "If he goes to jail, it'll kill him."

"Don't borrow trouble. You said he's innocent."

"Innocent people can be convicted." She started to sob again.

Allie sighed. "Okay, let's take that as the worst-case scenario. We're still not talking about life imprisonment. The absolute worst he could get is a year plus a fine."

"That'll be enough. Stewart is a proud man. If he's publicly branded a criminal, it will crush his spirit. He'll never recover."

Allie found Matt Collins coming out of the QuikStop carrying a steaming cup of coffee. "We need to talk. What made you decide to arrest Stewart Kendrick?"

Matt sipped his coffee and avoided eye contact. "We got a call about that shed back of his place. The guy has a whole restoration setup out there."

"So he reconstructs pots. That's not enough to hang him."

"No, but we found a zip-lock bag containing shards that match the type found at the site. We also found a topo map with a neat little X marking the spot on Holden Mesa. Satisfied?"

"Who made the call?"

Matt shuffled his feet and stared into the distance.

"An anonymous tip? Come on, Matt. Doesn't this sound like a setup to you?"

"Get off my back, Allie. I'm just doing my job. Tell you what. If you want a breaking story, I just took a report from Lyman Rogers about kids messing around in his stoneyard. Why don't you go check that one out if you want to play Girl Wonder?"

Allie stomped back to her car. The stoneyard story wasn't much, but it was news. She parked on the street and made her way to the office through a maze of pallets loaded with flagstone. The stone slabs stood upright, their jagged edges reminding her of broken giant's teeth.

"They sneaked in over the weekend and knocked over a slab of wall rock," Lyman told her. "Someone's going to get hurt if it doesn't stop."

"Can I get a photo of the rock? It'll give the story more impact."

Lyman ushered her toward the back of the yard. Next to his gray Bronco, Allie slid on some loose gravel and fell to the ground, one foot making painful contact with the back tire. Fussing like a mother hen, Lyman picked her up and dusted her off, apologizing profusely.

Allie shot several photos and drove east toward home, her mind on Stewart's arrest. Headlights flashed impatiently, and she braked, watching the oncoming car stop only a few feet from her bumper. The other driver opened his door and put one foot on the pavement.

"Wrong way!" The man's head swiveled toward the shrill voice.

Tommy Woodruff had moved his base of operations one block south to monitor the eastbound traffic. He pointed a finger at the overhead sign. "You're going the wrong way, mister!"

The driver glared at Tommy, Allie, and the sign, whipped a U-turn, and roared back the way he had come.

Allie pulled up next to Tommy and gave him a thumbs-up. "Maybe the town should buy you a uniform and make you a junior deputy."

Tommy beamed. "If I hadn't yelled, that Mustang might've creamed you."

"It was a Camaro," Allie corrected, grinning, "but you're right. You saved me."

Allie propped her elbows on her knees and leaned forward on the bleacher seat. The home team led by eight points. With only one loss this season, chances looked good for the Colton Cougars to be league champs again. The pitcher went into his windup.

"Allie!" Insistent fingers prodded her shoulder and she turned to see Ben Vega beside her.

"Strike one!"

Her head swiveled back to the game.

"Allie!" Ben recaptured her reluctant attention. "I just picked it up on my scanner. There's been an accident out on the highway. Somebody hit an elk. It could be a bad one. I thought you'd want to know."

Crack! Her head whipped back in time to see the ball clear the fence. Andy Jernigan had brought in a grand slam, and she'd missed it.

Sighing, she tucked her notebook into her pocket and headed for her car.

Flashing lights pulsed in the twilight. Allie pulled off the road well away from the emergency vehicles and took a moment to assess the scene. Her mouth tightened, recognizing what was left of J. D. Cochran's Blazer.

She strode across the highway, glad to see its driver standing upright and talking to the paramedics. He glanced up when she planted herself in front of him.

"Living dangerously these days, aren't you, J. D.?"

J. D. shook his head, and then winced. "I wasn't speeding, if that's what you mean. She jumped right out in front of me. I couldn't do a thing about it. Thank goodness she only caught my fender."

"I was thinking about last night." At his baffled look, she added, "You remember. When you nearly ran me off the road, driving with your lights off? Tommy Woodruff saw you."

He started to shake his head again, but caught himself this time. "Wasn't me, Allie. I'm just on my way back from Phoenix. I've been down there all week."

Allie decided to let it go for now. She went through the motions of getting the information she needed for her story, then drove away, pondering the difference between J. D.'s version and Tommy's.

Back home, she stepped out of her sandals and bent to pull off a wad of paper stuck to the sole of one. She frowned at the gaudy pattern. Where had she seen those checks before? She smiled, remembering Marlys's wallpaper. She must have stepped on this piece in the driveway.

She tossed the sandals in her closet and froze. She had been wearing running shoes the day she visited Marlys. How had this piece gotten on her sandal?

Pictures formed in her mind. She saw herself talking to Matt, visiting Lyman. Then the Little Leauge game and her encounter with J. D. Where had she gotten the wallpaper?

She remembered slipping, falling, her foot jamming against the Bronco's tire. Could the paper have stuck to her shoe then? But that paper had no business being at the stoneyard or on Lyman's vehicle.

Unless…

Allie parked well off the road a block from the stoneyard and walked the rest of the way in the darkness. Not even the moonlight penetrated the heavy cloud cover. She halted a moment at the edge of the yard, eyes straining to catch any sign of movement. Satisfied, she slipped behind the front row of pallets and switched on her flashlight, keeping the beam pointed down. She made her way slowly through the maze, hoping she was heading for the spot where Lyman's Bronco had been parked earlier.

Gravel rattled, and Allie froze, flipping the flashlight off with her thumb. The sound was not repeated, and she breathed again. More than likely she had disturbed a cat. Turning the light on again, she found that she had reached the place she was looking for. She swept the light along the ground.

The light stopped, focusing on a fragment of checkered paper caught under the corner of a pallet. Allie stooped and grasped the paper between two fingers.

A hand snaked around the far edge of the pallet and caught her wrist in a steely grip. "What are you doing here?" Lyman Rogers stood, pulling Allie upright.

Allie tried to pull away, but Lyman tightened his grip until she cried out. "Why were you out at the Kendricks'?"

Lyman looked grim. "I thought you saw me the night I left the stuff in his shed. Running you off the road was supposed to scare you off, but you just couldn't leave it alone, could you?"

Allie swung her flashlight hard against Lyman's arm. He yelped in pain and released her. The flashlight flew from her hand and they were instantly plunged into darkness. Allie scuttled backward and slammed into a pallet of stone.

"I can find you without a light." His arm swept along the stone, working its way toward her.

Allie dodged, hands outstretched, trying to find a way out. Slipping between two pallets, she crouched, trying to control her breathing. She groped for something, anything, to use as a weapon.

"Why did you care about Kendrick, anyway? He isn't one of us. It was a nice little trap." His foot scraped on the gravel, all too close to her. "But now you're the one who's trapped, aren't you?"

Allie's frantic fingers found a loose board on a pallet. She wiggled it back and forth, trying to pull it free.

A large rock struck the slab of stone next to her head. Tiny chips of flagstone flew off, stinging her cheek. "Missed. I won't next time."

A gap in the clouds appeared, releasing a faint ray of moonlight. Allie spotted the rock Lyman had thrown and clutched it in one hand, still tugging at the board with the other.

"There you are." He smiled.

Allie drew back her arm and threw the rock. Lyman's head snapped back and he slumped to the ground. With a final wrench, she pulled the broken board free and stood over him, gripping it like a baseball bat.

A beam of light flashed around her. She whirled, still clutching the board.

"Whoa, Allie. You don't need that." Matt Collins relieved her of her weapon and knelt beside Lyman, then radioed for an ambulance. "Your buddy Tommy told me he thought it was funny you parked back there and then came skulking down here. When I saw Lyman parked behind you, I decided to check it out."

Allie hugged herself, trying to stop trembling. "He took the artifacts and framed Kendrick. He thought I'd figured it out, but I was still piecing it together."

Matt wrapped an arm around her shoulder. "Relax, it's over. Not bad, Girl Wonder. Not bad at all."

Allie scraped the last bite of ice cream from the plastic bowl and set it beside her on the park bench. She turned to Marlys. "I'm glad you came to the social." She nodded toward Stewart, who was standing near the park fence. "How hard did you have to twist his arm to get him here?"

"Not as hard as I'd have had to a couple of weeks ago." Marlys smiled. "I think he's coming around." Stewart walked toward them and she continued, "How did you find out Lyman was guilty?"

Allie grimaced. "I didn't. I was just trying to figure out why he'd been to your place. He thought I'd seen him out there and panicked. It was a perfect case of 'The wicked man flees though no one pursues.' I might have figured it out sooner if Tommy hadn't confused Lyman's gray Bronco with J. D.'s silver Blazer."

Stewart cleared his throat. "I understand they found the missing artifacts at Lyman's home."

Allie nodded. "According to Matt, Lyman had developed a nice sideline in the black market over the past couple of years. He'd gone pot hunting with his grandfather when he was younger, so he had some background for it."

"I can understand why he tried to implicate Stewart," Marlys said. "Having someone so convenient to blame must have been too tempting to pass up. But why did he try to hurt you? He didn't have to risk an assault charge."

Allie shrugged. "As it turns out, the artifacts weren't his only extra income. He also did some creative bookkeeping at the stoneyard. He knew that if he was caught for the theft his boss would be taking a close look at his business activities. He was afraid of losing everything."

"How sad," Marlys said. "I can't tell you how much I appreciate what you've done. We both do." She turned to Stewart for confirmation.

His gaze challenged Allie. "I looked up that verse."

She looked at him steadily.

"What does your book of pleasant homilies have that would apply to someone who has been wrongfully incarcerated?"

"How about 'The truth will set you free'? It applies in more ways than one." She watched Stewart's smug look waver for an instant, and she smiled inwardly.

Overhead, thunder rumbled, and a sudden wind blew her bowl across the park. Allie chased it, laughing when raindrops spattered her face. The hope for rain had finally been realized. There might just be hope for Stewart, too.

ABOUT THE AUTHOR

Carol Cox can't remember a time when she didn't love stories and story-telling. She has published three Christian romance novels and six novellas. Like the characters in this story, she enjoys small-town life in northern Arizona, where she lives with her pastor-husband, Dave, their teenage son and preschool daughter, one dog, and a growing number of rabbits.

JESSICA'S GIFT

Karen Kingsbury

Dedicated to all the Jessicas who live in our hearts…

Nestled in the heart of the town of Cottonwood, Arizona, behind the post office, in an unassuming house, lived a little girl named Jessica Warner. In many ways there was nothing unusual about Jessica. She was five years old, with naturally curly, golden-blond hair and blue eyes that shone with unfettered joy. She had a smile that brightened any room—even in a town where the sun shone almost every day of the year. And she had a favorite doll named Molly that was tattered and smudged and loved into a raggedy state.

The Warner family loved everything about living in Cottonwood. It was a town where parents visited during weekend soccer games and people waved at passersby on Main Street whether they knew one another or not. Joe Biggs, the barber, and Steven Simmons, the paint store manager, hung Mingus Rocks! signs in their windows. This was their way of cheering on the Mingus High School football team, which every year toyed with the idea of a state title. Cottonwood was a town where doors went unlocked, children played safely in their rock-garden front yards, and teens complained about having nothing to do.

Although the seasons didn't leave their mark on Cottonwood the way they might in a midwestern town or a seaport along the Atlantic Ocean, the Warners savored the subtle changes: the sparkling spring days, when the sun played on the distant red rocks of Sedona; the heat of summer, when great monsoons would sweep into the Verde Valley; and the fall, when the wind kicked up and Yavapai County Fairgrounds played host to the annual Harvest Festival.

Really, the months were like a yearlong crescendo building their way to the Warners' favorite time of all: the Christmas season. For that was when the high-desert town of Cottonwood came to life as miraculously, the townspeople suspected, as Bethlehem had some two thousand years earlier.

The official arrival of the Christmas season was inducted each year when the city manager and his deputy climbed the ladder on Ernie Gray's fire truck and strung the Happy Holidays garland across Main Street. Between then and the morning of the Christmas parade, home-owners partook in a competitive house decorating contest that was usually won by residents living at the top of Highway 269, not far from Quail Springs, at the base of Mingus Mountain.

Jessica's mother Cindy knew they'd never have enough money to live in Quail Springs, but they decorated all the same.

Or at least, they used to.

As Christmas 2001 drew near, it was clear to everyone in the Warner home that this year would be different. And when the garland was strung up along Main Street, Jessica began to pray a special prayer out loud in her bed at night. Long after saying good night and being tucked into bed separately by her parents, Jessica would close her eyes and raise one hand high above her head, reaching out to God.

"Dear Jesus," she would whisper, "I'm not telling Mommy and Daddy about this, so please listen good. It's Christmastime, and that's when You listen really hard to little girls' prayers. My teacher told me so. My prayer is this, God: Please make Mommy and Daddy love each other again."

Jessica knew they hadn't gone to church for a long time. And prayer seemed to have been forgotten in the Warner home. Still she prayed the same prayer every night that season.

In that way, she was like boys and girls in many homes across the country. But Jessica was also very different. She could neither run nor skip nor play hopscotch with her girlfriends. She could not jump rope or play hide-and-seek or run three-legged races.

She couldn't even walk.

Jessica had cerebral palsy.

It was something the townspeople of Cottonwood both knew and understood, something that made them protective of little Jessica and caused them to go out of their way to wave at her in the aisles of Smith's Market, or to tousle her beautiful blond curls as they passed, or to remind her that only angels were as pretty as she was.

And when they said such things, when they touched her hair in that gentle way, Jessica didn't mind at all that she was different.

Jessica Warner was something of a fixture around Cottonwood, and the people who lived there felt richer for her presence. She was too young to understand all of that, but Cottonwood was her hometown. And Steve and Cindy Warner knew their daughter wouldn't want to live anywhere else for all the world.

That year, sometime after the garland was hung, Jessica asked her mother why her legs didn't work the same as those of other children. Cindy bent down and hugged her daughter close, her chest trembling as she tried to control the tears that welled up at the question. Gently she helped Jessica to the living room sofa.

"I'd like to tell you a story, okay, honey?" Cindy ran her hand over Jessica's silky hair.

The little girl nodded and clung more tightly to her Molly doll. "A story about me, Mommy?"

Cindy blinked back tears. "Yes, Jessie, a story about you. About what happened when you were born."

Then Cindy told her daughter how she had been born a little too soon, before she was ready. Doctors tried to stop Cindy from delivering, but it was no use, and Jessica Marie was born ten weeks early, fighting for every breath. Three months later, when she had gained enough weight to go home, it was with this warning from her doctor:

"I'm quite certain Jessica has some cerebral palsy," he explained. "This is not something she will outgrow; but it is something that can be worked with."

Cindy paused in the story. "You're very special, Jessica. God told me so Himself the day He gave you to me."

The rest of the story Cindy kept to herself... How for that first year,

Steve and Cindy refused to talk about their fears; how they attributed Jessica's low birth weight to the fact that she didn't roll over or sit up or crawl like other babies her age; how in the days and months and years since then they'd each anchored on opposite sides of Jessica's health issues.

They had stopped taking Jessica to church after her first birthday. It was just too hard to face the curious comments and questions from their friends.

That was the year Steve purchased a pair of pink ballet slippers and hung them on a hook above Jessica's crib. "You're my perfect little princess," he whispered to the sleeping child. "And one day you'll dance across the room for me, won't you, honey?"

But doctors told the Warners that there would be no dancing for Jessica. The cerebral palsy did not affect her mind, but her motor skills were severely lacking. She would be doing well to be using a walker by the time she entered kindergarten.

When it became clear how great Jessica's handicap was, Cindy quit her job to stay home and work with her daughter. She helped the child through hours of stretching routines and exercises that often left both mother and child exhausted by the end of the day.

"You're wasting your time," Steve would tell her. "She doesn't need all that work, Cindy. She's going to outgrow this thing. Wait and see."

And so Cindy's days were spent helping Jessica live with cerebral palsy, while Steve's were spent denying she had it. Worst of all was the fact that in the midst of their miserable situation, their love for God grew cold and distant.

And Cindy told herself that it didn't matter that the only member of the Warner household who listened any longer to Bible stories and prayed to Jesus was Jessica, who after her second birthday went to church each Sunday with her grandparents.

The years passed slowly, and Jessica made little improvement. Days before her fifth birthday she learned to spread her knees wide and crawl across the floor in a series of short, jerky motions. It was a victory, no matter how small, and Steve and Cindy shared their little girl's excitement.

"That's my girl!" Steve told her. "One day you'll outgrow that cerebral palsy and wear those ballet slippers."

But that night after Jessica was asleep Cindy broke down. "Her progress is so slow! I've done all the exercises, all the stretches. I've monitored her diet and read every book on the subject. I've done everything I can. Why isn't she making more improvements?"

"I've told you, Cindy. You have to be patient. She'll outgrow this thing when she gets older."

"She'll never outgrow it, Steve!" Cindy was screaming and didn't care. "If we work with her she can make progress. But you're never going to come through that door one night and find her dancing in those silly ballet slippers. Don't you understand?"

After that their lives grew even more separate. They communicated only when necessary and began socializing in separate circles. Cindy joined a cerebral palsy support group and finally found the understanding she'd been missing. The members of the support group did not deny Jessica's problems; rather, they brainstormed with her for solutions.

Meanwhile Steve had been given a promotion, and with it came the task of organizing after-work events. His office friends were cheerful and upbeat, and Steve was often the life of the party. He liked them because they did not know about Jessica's cerebral palsy, and so they never talked about muscle coordination or support groups or daily exercises.

Often, entire weeks went by in which Steve and Cindy saw each other for only minutes at a time, passing silently like strangers in the hallways of the Warner home.

Finally, two weeks before Christmas, Steve took Cindy's hand gently in his own and studied her eyes. "It isn't working between us, is it?" Tears sprang to Cindy's eyes, but her gaze remained fixed on Steve's. "No, I guess it isn't."

"I'll talk to a divorce lawyer." His voice was gentle, sad. "But let's wait until after Christmas. For Jessica's sake."

Jessica could tell that things had, for some reason, grown worse between her parents. She talked it over with Molly, her beloved dolly. "I'm asking Jesus to make them love each other. But they aren't very nice to each other anymore. I'm scared, Molly. Really scared."

Molly didn't answer, but Jessica knew her friend understood. And she clutched the doll to her heart as she whispered her prayers once more.

Cindy hated dinnertime. It was cold and silent and hopeless. But one night Jessica broke the silence. "Please, can we all go to church together this Sunday? Preacher's going to tell the Christmas story and he said the whole family's invited."

Steve and Cindy exchanged cool glances, then looked away. Seemingly embarrassed, Steve cleared his throat. "Yes, sweetheart, that'll be fine. We'll all go to church together this Sunday. Like a family."

When Sunday came they dressed Jessica in a white satin dress and sat beside her in the pew for the first time in years. As happened each year at that time, the service was put on by all the Christian churches in town and held at the high-school auditorium. The message was one of hope and joy, the story of the Christ child born to a weary world so that men might live forevermore. It was a message that was tried and true, and in their private prisons of pain Steve and Cindy quietly realized the mistake they'd made by walking away from their faith.

"God gave the greatest gift of all, the gift of pure love wrapped in flesh and bones, the gift of His Son," the minister's voice rang out. "But what of you? What will you give to the Savior this year?"

There was silence in the auditorium.

Tentatively, Steve ran a single finger along Jessica's stiff legs.

"I urge you," the pastor added quietly, "to take time these next few days and lay something at the Savior's feet. Something you love…or something you need to leave behind. Perhaps something that should have been laid there a long time ago."

On the way home that morning Jessica turned to her father. "Did you hear him, Daddy? He said love is the greatest gift of all."

"Sure, honey," Steve said, staring straight ahead at the road in front of him.

"That's what I'm getting for you and Mommy this year. A whole lot of love." Jessica fell silent a moment, then continued. "Preacher also said to give something to Jesus, something you love very much. Isn't that right, Mommy?"

"That's right, honey."

Again the child said nothing, but the look on her face was one of serious pondering.

Cindy forgot about Jessica's comments until the next morning. As they were getting ready for the day, Steve and Cindy spotted something near the nativity scene they'd set up on the living room floor. A soft cry came from Cindy, and she clutched her hand to her mouth as tears filled her eyes. She slowly made her way to the manger. What she saw touched her heart more than a thousand sermons on love ever could.

It was Molly, Jessica's precious baby doll. She had laid it at the feet of Jesus.

That afternoon while Steve was at his office, Cindy studied Jessica as she napped. What was the point of the pastor's message? If love was such a great gift, why was her marriage dissolving? How come Jessica had cerebral palsy? The child loved God enough to give Him her Molly doll, but what had God ever done for her, for any of them?

Cindy returned to the living room and sat alone, listening to the haunting sounds of Christmas carols on the radio. She wanted to believe, but still the question haunted her: What had the Christ child ever done for them?

When Steve returned late that night Cindy was already in bed. But before he slipped under the sheets next to her she felt him do something he hadn't done in months. He leaned over and gently kissed her good night.

The next day was Christmas eve, and Steve had already left for work when Cindy awoke. She climbed out of bed, fixed breakfast for Jessica, and coaxed her through two hours of stretches and exercises. Only then, just before lunchtime, did she again notice something unusual about the nativity scene. Molly's doll was gone, and a manila envelope now lay at the feet of baby Jesus.

Curiously, Cindy approached and took the envelope in her hands. There on the outside were these words scribbled in Steve's handwriting:

Lord, I have something to lay at Your feet, something I love very much. I give You my word: From now on I will accept Jessica as she is. I have been horribly unfair to my family by pretending she will one day be different than who You made her to be. I understand now. Jessica can only learn to live with her cerebral palsy if I learn to live with it first.

Cindy opened the package. There, inside, were the unused pink ballet slippers.

Cindy slipped her fingers around the slippers and allowed the tears to come. She cried because her little girl would never wear them, would never dance as her father had once dreamed. She cried because if Steve was finally ready to accept the truth, then maybe he was ready to work with her and not against her.

Maybe there was hope after all.

She wiped her eyes and looked at the carved figurine of the Christ child and suddenly the answer to her question was clear: Jesus had given them Himself. Because of Him they could learn to love again; with Him, they could survive as a family; through Him, they could live eternally in a place where Jessica would run and play and jump with other children.

Cindy fell to her knees and hung her head. "Forgive me, Lord." As she stayed there she began to wonder what a flawed woman like herself could give to One so holy.

Her tears slowed, and she tiptoed into Jessica's room and watched her sleeping. This time she felt no bitterness toward God as she studied the small girl. Golden ringlets softly framed her face, and Cindy saw only peace and contentment there as, deep in her own heart, a light dawned. In that moment she knew with absolute certainty what she should give to Jesus.

That night when Steve came home the house was dark but for the lights around the nativity scene. He studied the figurines standing around the Christ child and saw that his envelope was gone. In its place was a smaller white one. Steve crossed the room, set down his overcoat and briefcase, and slid a finger under the flap. Inside was a single sheet of paper and something small wrapped in tissue paper. Steve read the handwritten note with tears in his eyes.

Dear Lord, I give back to You what You, five years ago, gave to me. I have held on too tightly, Lord, forgotten that this precious gift was never really mine. I let another child take the place of the One that lay in a hay-filled manger that cold night in Bethlehem. And now love has all but died in our home. I'm sorry, Lord. I've tried to make her something other than what

You made her, but no more. I'll love her always, but I understand now that she doesn't belong to me. She belongs to You. Now and forevermore.

Steve unwrapped the tissue paper. There, inside, lay a single small picture of Jessica.

Steve heard something and he turned. With Jessica perched on her hip, Cindy was watching him from the doorway. Her eyes glistened with unshed tears as he went to her, hugging her tightly. Jessica wrapped her arms around them both.

"We can't throw it all away. Not when we haven't even tried," he whispered. "I'm ready to work with you, Cindy."

She nodded, choking back a sob. "All my efforts and all your denial and we almost missed the truth. When Jessie put Molly at Jesus' feet…Steve, she's perfect just the way she is. She loves more perfectly than either of us ever have. She reminded me of all God has done for me, for all of us."

"That's her Christmas gift to us, right, sweetheart?" Steve lifted Jessica's chin and kissed her forehead.

Jessica nodded and grinned—first at her daddy and then at the tiny statue of baby Jesus in the nativity scene. She did not understand everything that had happened between her parents and the Lord that Christmas week. All she knew for sure was that the town of Cottonwood felt a little like heaven that week because her prayers had been answered. The preacher had been right.

Love really was the best Christmas gift of all.

ABOUT THE AUTHOR

Karen Kingsbury is the bestselling author of several titles, including *Waiting for Morning, A Moment of Weakness, When Joy Came to Stay,* and *A Time to Dance.* One of her earlier books was made into a CBS Television Movie of the Week in 1997, and several of her current fiction titles are being considered for feature films. There are more than 1.2 million copies of her books in print. Karen lives in the Pacific Northwest with her husband and five children.

The Midwest

LIME AROUND THE OUTHOUSE

A FABLE OF THE 1950s

Jane Kirkpatrick

Jennie Jacobs pretended. Her friends all called her brave because she tried new things, things she knew she couldn't do well like kicking at the football while the boys laughed or riding the yearling calves in the back pasture when the hired man wasn't looking. Sometimes she pretended to be an adventurer by doing dangerous things. Once she had asked her father over dinner why she couldn't play inside the hogs' feeder. He'd raised one eyebrow over the steaming pork roast and told her, "Because I said so." Her little sister had kicked at her knees beneath the table and lowered her eyes.

The next day she challenged herself. Into the hogs' pen she led her little sister and a friend who had been allowed to spend the afternoon. Whispering, she moved the girls quickly through the sleeping pigs to the metal feeder—a tube rising like a stubby chimney in the center. Together they hefted off the metal cover. The bin stood taller than any one of the girls, so Jennie helped the two over the sides. They coughed at the cloud that rose from the soft grain inside, and then squatted on the cross bars.

"All set?" When Jennie heard them echo affirmatively, she stood up in the pen and began rotating the bin, turning the girls inside like squatters on a merry-go-round. The turning of the metal feeder ground the grain, which spun out like Rumpelstiltzkin's gold, filling the air with a dusty mist as the grain pressed into the hogs' feeders. The little girls inside giggled.

"Faster! Faster!" At their shouts, Jennie complied, her heart pounding, her bare toes gripping, wondering if the hogs would wake too soon, would smell the scent of fresh grain and snort their way to where she ran hanging on and spinning, too, her bare legs beneath her dress flying through the air.

Then, sure enough, the hogs awoke. Jennie's heart pounded as she worked to stop the bin from spinning. Yanking, aching, slowing the heavy tube, she pulled the giggling girls out and helped them slip between the rough backs of the hungry hogs that were pushing at the newly ground feed. Jennie felt such triumph as they raced the hogs and time and summer heat and felt such quiet later as the girls splashed through puddles, washing their feet clean of the soft manure, laughing their way to fall in a heap on the newly mown lawn. She pretended to do it for the girls' pleasure, but she really did it for her own.

Jennie whistled and sang—that was part of her act. Everyone at school thought of her as happy. They didn't know that at night she slept with the covers over her head to protect herself from dwarfs marching to the mines in search of diamonds for Snow White—she was sure she could hear them tromping outside her window. She tried to pretend she wasn't afraid, but she was.

Jennie watched people, like the older boys in the upper classes who shared the one-room schoolhouse. She looked to see how they did it, how they lived grown up. When she saw a boy swing from the high oak branch and let loose of the rope, falling into the pond, she wondered if he did it to conquer a fear or just to feel the wind on his face.

Older people, too, she watched…wiser people, like her Sunday school teachers and her parents. She wondered which of them pretended.

Then one day her acting changed. It began during story time. Jennie didn't pretend then, just imagined how the characters felt. She drifted away and became not Cinderella, but the ugly stepsisters. She knew what they all feared. She found more interest in Rumpelstiltzkin, too, who lied and made impossible demands just to keep from being left alone. And even Rapunzel's witch carried concern for Jennie—how the old hag must have felt betrayed after sharing her meals and climbing up the long-haired girl's tresses all those years. Yet when the prince came to steal Rapunzel away, all the witch wanted was their child so as not to grow old alone. Why, Jennie knew some people just like that who lived down the road. The grandma now raised up the daughter's child—though the woman was hardly a witch.

"We often fear what we don't know," Miss Potsner told Jennie's second-grade class as they sat around her on smooth wooden chairs. The teacher held a book up high so the children could see the large colorful pictures of a darkened forest, the red-caped child, a basket of cakes. It was one of Jennie's favorite stories, and she noticed that even the upper-grade students leaned over their inkwells as though busy, not wanting the younger children to see that they still cared about fairy tales. "Fears can be made smaller with information. That's why it's important to ask questions, to learn new things, to not be afraid of letting someone find out that you don't know something. No one needs to be afraid to say, 'I'm afraid.'"

"But Little Red Riding Hood wasn't afraid until she found out that the wolf wasn't her grandma," Jennie called out, her hand held high but not waiting for her teacher's nod before speaking. "That's when she finally ran, when she knew. Up until then, she was fine."

"She wasn't paying no 'ttention," Bobby Munson said, turning to Jennie. "Anyone could see her grandma didn't have no eyes or mouth or beard like that wolf. She shoulda been afraid before that and got herself out of there."

"My daddy's making a beard," Margie Olson offered. "And my mommy don't like it. She's afraid he'll look old."

"Maybe Little Red Riding Hood was pretending," Marcia Goetz said.

"How?" Jennie asked.

"To be brave, even though she wasn't."

"She got help, though," Sandra Anderson added. "She went for the woodcutter, and he came back and rescued them."

"That's what a man does," Joe Parker said, sitting up straighter. "My dad says my ma's got to be rescued from her addled mind most days, and for me to get used to it 'cause I'll be doing it for some woman the rest of my life."

"Her papa shouldn't a let her mama send her to the woods like that," Sady Thompson said with a scowl. "That wolf was waiting in the trees just to trick her."

"She wasn't paying no 'ttention, I tell you," Bobby repeated, his missing front teeth making some letters hiss against his gums. "She shoulda stayed home."

"But you sometimes have to do things that're scary," Jennie said. "Don't you? Otherwise…her grandma wouldn't have had anything to eat. She was going through the woods to help someone else."

"Addled thinking for sure," Joe Parker nodded.

"Don't mean nothing if you end up as the wolf's dinner," Bobby insisted.

"It does so." Jenny looked at their teacher. "It means something, doesn't it, Miss Potsner?"

"We were discussing the importance of asking questions and finding things out as a way to counter our fears," Miss Potsner said. "Fears are often signs that we are learning something new, or need to. And yes, Jennie, I do believe that doing something even though it's scary is important. But not *just* because it's scary." She looked over her glasses at Jennie, who wondered if her sister had told about the hog bin ride. "It's the why of what we do that matters. Helping someone else, especially when we're fearful. That's what's important. Even brave men say they've been fearful—in war times, for example, in faraway Korea, like we have now. They have chosen to leave home for a reason. What matters is that they do what's asked of them to help another. Just as Little Red Riding Hood did. And there was someone else willing to help her, as Sandra pointed out. There often are people willing to help. We have to learn to ask."

"Shouldn'ta been there at all," Bobby insisted. "Just stupid."

"And if people do stupid things, as you say, Bobby, does that mean they shouldn't be helped?"

"Huh?" He frowned, clearly confused.

"Even if we make poor choices, do things that get us into difficulty, don't we still deserve help?"

"I guess…" He took a sudden interest in his Roy Rogers shoelaces. "She still just shoulda stayed home. Can't nothing bad happen to you at home."

"That's not always true either, Bobby. Nor can we always stay in a safe harbor. What do the rest of you think?" Miss Potsner pushed her glasses up on her nose and lowered the book. "Who is braver? The one who has no fear, or the one who helps others despite her fears?"

Jennie kept her hand down and didn't answer. Ideas kept bouncing in her head like corn popping, keeping her tongue from talking.

She walked the half-mile home from the one-room schoolhouse slowly, her black lunch box strapped by a belt slung over her back. Were people who went to war actually afraid but pretending to be brave? She worried about her father going off to Korea, though he said farming was an "an essential occupation," whatever that meant. When she pretended to be adventurous, did it just mean she was learning something new or should be? And what about this idea that there would be others there to help you. Could that really be true?

"Where's Papa?" she asked her mother.

"At the outhouse, putting down the lime." Her mother wiped her hands on her apron. "What's the scowl for, sweetie?"

"Just thinking, Mama." Jennie put on her perky face and slipped through to the back door. She made her way past the lilac bushes to the little white-framed house with a dog carved into the door. She watched quietly while her father dropped a scoopful of white lime down each of the two holes. It kept the flies down, kept the smell from reaching up to choke them on the hot days. For all she knew, it must have kept the bees out too for she seldom saw any, not like at her friend Julie's house where the hornets nested and had to be taken away each spring by men braver than most.

"Whatcha doing?" She asked the question even though she knew.

Her father turned with a start. "You scared me, sweetie! Didn't know you were there." He nodded. "About done here. Then we can lime around. Want to help?"

Jennie nodded. With her little hands, she scooped into the white granules that were coarser than sand and dropped handfuls where her father showed her. They performed the task until there was a perfect circle. They would repeat the job after a heavy rain or when the whitish line had sunk into the grass. It was a common thing, and Jennie had never thought to ask its purpose. Until today.

"It's to hesitate the snakes," her father told her.

"Snakes?" Jenny looked around.

"Snakes don't like the lime. Oh, they may cross it to find the mice around the privy, but not more than once or twice because the lime eats away at their skin, and eventually they find someplace else to hunt. What's the matter?" He looked at her then. "You're not scared, are you? Those snakes aren't after you, Jennie. You're too big to eat."

"I ain't scared." Jennie straightened her shoulders. "I just never knew that's what the lime was for. I didn't know it was to keep bad things from happening."

"We do lots of things to keep bad things from happening," he said. "Your mother rinses the dishes so you won't get sick from the soap. There's a cover on the firebox so the house won't catch aflame from the sparks. It's…like saying your prayers, sweetie. Doing it every day, asking and thanking, doesn't mean you won't have troubles or things won't go wrong, but it's a reminder. You've done what you could and then you can trust that you're not all alone. So you can enjoy the warmth of that firebox and can roll your Mama's cooking around in your mouth without worrying over getting sick. And you can head to the outhouse here when you need to and watch the birds build their nest there in the tree instead of thinking about snakes. Nothing to fear, sweetie. The Bible tells us so." He patted her shoulder. "Want to go to town with me later? I've got to pick up some more feed for the pigs. We're sure going through it fast."

Jennie nodded her assent, her head filled with the possibilities of what she could be thinking of and doing if she weren't always riding fear and pretending that she wasn't.

Just before dusk, her father picked Jennie up and set her in the front seat of the old Jeep pickup truck and closed the door. "We're running a little late," he told her. "I just hope the mill's still open." They drove down the dusty lane, past three neighboring farms, past the Widow Marks with her yardful of geese. He turned to look at Jennie and she smiled. Her father smiled back and patted her hand. "Good to have your company," he said. As he spoke, his eyes drifted past her to the Parkers' barn.

It was a long building, the biggest and newest in the valley, with thirty dairy cows milked morning and night on the lower level along with calf pens and hay stored in the long loft above. A cupola like a doll's house sat on top, spearing the sunset. Pigeons lifted from it as they drove by.

"That's odd…" Her father frowned.

Jennie turned to look through the plastic windows that marked the side doors of the old Jeep. "What?"

"I don't remember George having a light up there. Must have just put it in. Forgot to turn it off."

They drove on past when suddenly her father braked.

"Something's wrong!"

Jennie heard fear in her father's voice. Fear from this strong man with hands like rope that gripped the steering wheel and turned the truck, racing full speed back toward Parkers' barn. Jennie felt her heart start to pound. Her hands grew sweaty, and she gasped for breath. Her head felt light.

The light was brighter now, but Jennie thought it shone because the dusk was darker. Light was always brighter against the dark.

"I thought so. Fire!" her father said.

Fire? Jennie saw no smoke, not even a tendril lifting toward the sky. Nothing seemed out of the ordinary to her, but her father had already stopped the truck and flung himself out, leaving the door open. He headed toward the barn, then turned back and shouted, "Go to the house! Tell Mrs. Parker to call Central. Now! Tell her the barn's on fire."

"Where are you going?" Tears were beginning to form in Jennie's eyes.

"To tell George! To help him get the cows out. Go now. Now!"

Jennie sat, confusion pressing against her head as she watched her father hesitate as though deciding whether to run up to the house himself. "Don't be afraid, sweetie." He took one last look at Jennie, then turned and disappeared inside the barn.

Flames exploded in the hayloft, shooting gold and red into the sky and raining arcs of fire.

"Papa!" Jennie wailed, too paralyzed to move. "Papa!" She waited for him to come back out and when he didn't, she knew there was no pretending bravery here, no pretending at all. Something pushed at her now and she raced up the hill to the Parker porch. Panting, she ran through the front door, her feet slipping on the shiny wood floor. "Mrs. Parker! Your barn! It's on fire! Call Central, Papa said. Call Central and get help! He went inside!"

Mrs. Parker stared at her. *Addled,* her son had called her that very morning, but right then she acted not addled, but able. She glanced once in the direction of the barn, gasped, then charged to the phone, the flesh of her arms swinging as she turned the knob. She rang a series of longs and shorts and longs, and then she stopped. Breathing heavily, she put the black receiver to her ear and into the mouthpiece she said, "I know you're all on the line wondering whose ring that was. This is Mary Parker. Our barn's afire. Bring buckets, hoses, whatever you've got. Please help us!"

While she rang Central, her son Joe walked out sleepily.

"Get your boots on!" his mother ordered. "The barn's afire."

"It is? How?"

"Green hay, I suspect." She grabbed a bucket and emptied out the eggs. "Got hot and combusted. Too much in a hurry, we always are. Come on, now. Let's see what we can do to help. You father'll be a wreck."

That night drew a long finger in the sand of Jennie's life. She worried for her father's life, for the safety of the men working to save a neighbor's barn. Every God-given sense was alert to sound and smell and touch and taste. She remembered how racing the hogs for the feed bin carried excitement with it, a taste of something that she relished. But too much of it, like this night, made her heart pound and ache in ways she didn't want.

She wanted her father to come out of the smoky barn, wanted to go home and spend the evening at the radio listening. Home with her mother and sister. Home to the calves in the back pasture and the sleeping hogs and to their own white privy in the backyard.

She thought of the lime around the outhouse, a prevention that sometimes worked but always gave a reason to let fear go. She breathed a prayer, and with it felt a calming. She stood a distance from the flames. Her mother and sister joined the others from the valley, bringing sandwiches and sun tea to cool the men's throats. Burning wood dropped from the rooftop like a hundred shooting stars. Men moved horses beyond the draw of the fire, pushed at cows ambling out from the smoke. The stench of flaming hay caused her to cough and she wondered if more than wood and hay burned inside.

"When's Papa coming out?" Jennie clenched her hands in front of her.

"I don't know," her mother said, both girls held tight against her apron. "I just hope they've sense enough to get out before the roof collapses."

Word came to Mrs. Parker, who stood beside them now, that a man who looked like her husband had been seen inside, still pulling on machines, pushing at cows to get out.

"No word of Charles?" Jennie's mother asked anxiously. The men just shook their heads.

They stood in clusters then, the women watching the volunteer fire department and their husbands pump and push and spray water that stopped short of the high pitch of the valley's highest roof but kept the walls wet and gave those inside more time.

Rafters creaked and crashed then, and Jennie stared up at her mother, wondering at the bravery she saw in that face. "God'll see us through," her mother said, and gently wiped away the tears from her daughter's cheeks.

Jennie felt a twinge of fear, but she stepped beyond it. There was nothing she could do. The tightness in her chest said, "Do what you must do." She had. She'd overcome her fear and sounded the alarm. She had put her lime around the outhouse—now she had to trust God to see them through.

It seemed like hours had passed when George Parker stumbled out through the black, billowing smoke that had been his barn. Other men dropped buckets and moved forward to help him, then pulled him away, blackened milking machines hanging like heavy irons from each of Mr. Parker's shoulders. Jennie heard the crash and crack of timbers as Mrs. Parker rushed to her husband.

And then, bent low behind him in the smoke, carrying a calf across his chest, came Jennie's father—just as the barn collapsed behind him.

Jennie ran to him, her heart again pounding—not from fear now but from joy. "Oh, Papa, Papa!" She grabbed at his legs.

"It's all right now, Jennie. It's all right." Her father set the trembling calf down. It licked at Jennie's arm, the rough tongue seeking reassurance while Jennie cried. "You did right," her father said. He coughed. "Got us good help." Jennie's father squatted low then, and lifted her up above the fray. With his other arm he held her mother, while Jennie's little sister grabbed at his knees.

Jennie stopped pretending after that. She saved it for school plays. She still made people laugh, they still called her happy and she still tried new things that were hard for her to do, but she didn't need to pretend to be brave to do them. Being afraid just took too much time and robbed her of the pleasure. As long as she did what she could, there was no reason to waste the pleasure of living on worry.

On the day she noticed her little sister's feet were as small and pale as a cob of corn, she realized how lucky they'd been in that hog pen, time after time. She stopped the merry-go-round after that. Instead she pumped herself up high on a swing that she'd asked her father to hang in the maple tree, to feel the rush of wind in her face. And she taught the calves to be led by a rope—even better excitement than riding them in the back pasture. She stopped watching others quite so closely—except for her parents.

She made sure that she still took time to put lime around the out-house. And she trusted God for the rest.

ABOUT THE AUTHOR

Jane Kirkpatrick, a Wisconsin native, lives in Oregon with her husband, Jerry, on their 160-acre ranch along the John Day River. A licensed clinical social worker, she works as a mental health consultant with families and children, primarily on an Indian reservation, where fables offer both healing and hope. Jane is the author of two non-fiction books: *Homestead,* her memoir, and *A Burden Shared,* a book of encouragement. Her six historical fiction titles include the Wrangler Award winner *A Sweetness to the Soul* (Multnomah) and her historical series Kinship and Courage (WaterBrook). Her award-winning essays have appeared in such magazines as *Decision, Focus on the Family,* and *Private Pilot.*

On her website (www.jkbooks.com) Jane shares monthly inspiration from the homestead. She is a frequent retreat and keynote speaker who encourages participants to seek the power of fables in their lives. Jane's own experience of discovering home includes a hog bin feeder, riding calves in the back pasture, watching her father enter a burning barn, and learning that fear conquered is indeed a blessing from God.

HOME TO SOUTHFIELD, MOURNING

Carole Gift Page

They were driving from Muncie, Indiana, to Southfield, Michigan, returning home after a week of mourning, attending to familial tasks and obligations, and enduring grief's bleak distraction.

At Anna's request, they had taken the back roads, passing through Bluffton and around Fort Wayne to Auburn, heading toward Somerset Center. They had turned onto U.S. 12, a rustic, winding, two-lane highway through the Irish Hills with their lush abundance of lakes and woods. It had stormed that morning and the humidity was high, the air still pungent with rain. The weeping willow trees were a vivid yellow-green and the redbud trees were starting to blossom a lovely violet-pink. It had been a long, late winter with snow in April, so the flowers—tulips, hyacinths, and daffodils—were just now blooming in mid-May.

At any other time Anna would have delighted in the profusion of late spring flowers and fields yellow with dandelions.

But not today. Not when the taste of death was still fresh in her mouth.

The truth still eluded her like a dream that evaporates with the dawn. It didn't seem possible that Anna's father was dead and buried.

During the final days of his illness, his children and their families had swarmed back to his side like stunned but dutiful bees, unwittingly enmeshing themselves in one another's lives, bumping abrasively as each sought to cope with death and the tedium of everyday living.

During that week rituals and habits clashed unmercifully. Silence loomed, the TV blared, and conversations were cliché-ridden, unfulfilling. Now, with the week over, friends and relatives poured out of the old southern Michigan homestead back to their separate, anonymous lives. Anna, exhausted but intact, could finally reflect on the significance of the past seven days.

It was perhaps too soon to analyze events and feelings. Anna still felt shell-shocked, her reactions anesthetized by incredulity and pain. But riding over familiar ground—the rural landscape somehow reassuring— and with Gil comfortably beside her in the driver's seat, Anna could afford to breathe again. Needed to breathe. Needed to reaffirm her life. And Gil's.

Gil had said little all week. But Anna had felt his presence, his quiet support as she sat paralyzed and tearless by her father's deathbed. Gil had demonstrated amazing efficiency in helping with the funeral arrangements, gathering information for the obituary, and handling a hundred unexpected details. Still, he remained somehow at a distance, remote.

It had not mattered until now. Anna had been too busy, too preoccupied. She had spent herself on the demands of a dozen others—first her father, afterward her mother and her younger brother and sisters and their families. The list seemed endless, the responsibilities exhausting. Why had she found no comfort, not from her family—and not even, she realized now, from Gil? Despite their twenty years of marriage, he had been as much a stranger as anyone in her father's house. The realization was disturbing.

Anna glanced at her husband from the corner of her eye. *Thoughts are skimming through his mind a mile a minute, and yet I can't read one of them.* She forced her eyes back to the road. *There's no one on earth I really know.* The realization astonished her. *Not my parents, not my brother and sisters. Not even my own husband!*

To distill the terrifying implications of this sudden insight, Anna blurted a banality she immediately regretted: "It's a beautiful afternoon for driving, don't you think, Gil? Look, the lilacs are starting to bloom."

He nodded absently, and she wondered if he had really heard her. She tried again. "Even taking the back roads, we're making good time, aren't we?" Another absurd remark. Could she say nothing worthwhile?

She had spent a week politely receiving the condolences of others, answering with the proper phrases, maintaining an acceptable balance of grief and control. She had succeeded in camouflaging her real emotions and reactions, the irritations and negative impulses. She had kept the mask of propriety in place against her will.

Soberly she recalled some of the incidents of the past week. When her brother and sisters argued over who would keep their father's valuable coin collection, she remained silent. When, on the night of her father's burial, her sister's children played the TV at full blast, Anna swallowed her anger and said nothing. When thoughtless friends and relatives dropped by at all hours expecting to be fed and then remaining to chat, Anna did what she could to feed them, though both the food and conversation were sometimes sparse. Anna's mother flitted about like a wounded bird, helpless and confused but still fluttering. Anna squelched her impatience (most of the time) and strove to assist the broken, baffled woman who had borne her.

Anna rationalized now that she had done well. No one could criticize her. And yet had she really communicated with anyone, even once? After a week of such meaningless verbal exchanges, she ached for real words.

"Hungry?" Gil's gravelly voice shattered the silence.

"No," she said without thinking, then added, "but it's time to eat, isn't it?"

He nodded. "It's dinnertime, and we're just outside Somerset. Still a couple of hours to Southfield."

"And the traffic will be bumper to bumper around Detroit, so go ahead and stop if you see a nice place."

It occurred to Anna that a pleasant atmosphere and good food might be just what she and Gil needed. What a welcome change to be served a delectable meal, to be free to smile again, to reaffirm their lives. After all, she and Gil were survivors. Thank God for that!

"How about Tom's Grill?" suggested Gil, slowing down and pointing across the road.

"Is their food good?"

"Truck drivers apparently like it. Won't hurt to try it, I guess."

"All right," she said, wanting to say no.

The place was just what she had expected, what she dreaded. A hole in the wall, a dreary, run-down truck stop. Anna felt irritated with Gil for even choosing it. Was he so insensitive to her needs that he failed to see she desired a bright, attractive atmosphere tonight, something to confirm that life was indeed still beautiful?

Tom's Grill. The screen door was full of holes and the walls were gray with grease and grime. Torn posters of long-dead movie stars—John Wayne, Clark Gable, James Dean—were tacked over cracked plaster, along with dog-eared signs advertising the special of the week. The place was stifling, lacking air conditioning, and the little air that could be had was tainted with onions and garlic. On the jukebox Waylon Jennings was crooning something about a love gone wrong.

"I didn't know it would be this bad," murmured Gil as they sat down opposite each other in a narrow booth.

"It's okay," she said, kicking herself because it wasn't. She realized this was the story of her life. She never said what she really felt. Did Gil?

"This heat—" he muttered, wiping his forehead. She nodded. Already she could feel perspiration beading her upper lip. Gil pushed a menu her way. She glanced at it halfheartedly, feeling snobbish, reluctant to accept anything the place had to offer.

A heavyset woman in a tight red dress came to take their order. Gil waited for Anna to order first, so she said, "Iced tea. And the roast beef sandwich." Gil ordered a steak sandwich and fries. *It'll be tough,* she predicted silently.

When they were alone again, she caught Gil's gaze and held it momentarily. She couldn't get beyond his eyes, though. Had she ever really tried? She loved him, but how often had she risked the pain of really knowing him and exposing her inner self as well?

"Are you all right?" Gil looked puzzled.

"Yes. I was just wondering—about my mother, how she'll get along now."

"She's always had a life of her own. She'll manage better than you think."

It was true. Anna understood that her mother had never really been close to her father. They had gone their separate ways, been involved in their own interests and activities for years. They had shared little more than a house and a bed. And yet now her mother seemed so devastated, as if the hub of her life had been removed.

"We're a lot like them, aren't we?" Anna murmured, momentarily bold.

"Like who?"

"My folks. We have our own lives, come and go as we please, just like they did."

"I suppose," Gil said noncommittally. At that moment the waitress brought their food, so for a time they ate in self-absorbed silence. The mashed potatoes were instant and the roast beef tough and dry; Anna pushed her food aside half-eaten. In doing so, she caught Gil's glance. His expression told her that he took the rejection personally.

"I wasn't hungry after all," she said defensively. But she *was* hungry; she was suddenly starving for something that had no name, for a closeness with Gil that did not exist, an intimacy between them that might give meaning to her grief—or at least make it more tolerable.

Not once this past week had she genuinely touched anyone she loved, nor had anyone touched her. *Why? Are we too selfish to spend ourselves on one another, too proud to risk being vulnerable? Instead of caring, we build up grievances. If it's that way in a family, what chance is there for the rest of the world?*

Someone was playing a Johnny Cash song on the jukebox, and the music jarred Anna out of her reverie. Gil was finishing his sandwich. Anna noticed with distaste that the salt and pepper shakers were greasy and that flies were already hovering over the gravy on her discarded plate. Her stomach turned, and she made a gesture of revulsion.

"What is it?" Gil sounded mildly irritated.

"Nothing." He was moving out and away from her, further and further away. Panic rose within her. She could be dying just as her father had died, and still Gil would not know how to reach her. Just as she had not known how to reach her father.

"Do you know what my father and I talked about before he died?" she said aloud, abruptly.

Gil looked up quizzically.

"The weather." She gave a short, ironic laugh. "We both knew he was dying. It was the most terrible and the most significant moment we had ever faced together, and all we did was try to kill time—like two strangers waiting for a bus."

Gil nodded. "It's always hard at a time like that."

"And my mother," persisted Anna, fighting a growing desperation. "I should have been able to help her more. We never talked. All I did was get impatient when she fluttered around so much."

"That doesn't mean anything," Gil murmured, glancing around and signaling the waitress for the check—his way of ending this conversation.

"It was the same with my brother and sisters," Anna rushed on, pinning Gil with her gaze. "We went right back to being bickering children under the same roof. We took one another for granted. We weren't available to comfort or share." Anna shredded her paper napkin into tattered snakes. "What's more, even their children irritated the life out of me."

"Their kids are spoiled brats," Gil noted dryly.

"That's not the point."

"Then what is?"

"Nothing," replied Anna shortly. *What's the use?* She slid out of the booth, stood up, and said politely, "I'm going to the restroom. Be right back."

The restroom was a drab, airless, foul-smelling closet. The walls were scarred with lipstick and ink. Anna glanced into the mirror and was stunned by her image. The heat had wilted her. Her face appeared puffy, unsettled, unattractive, and her gray-streaked hair fluttered about her head as if befuddled. She looked as distraught as she felt.

Impulsively she pulled open the door and fled. Back to Gil. Back to their table. Back where there was at least a sanctuary of sorts and the possibility of—something.

Anna stared at the booth where she and Gil had sat. The table had been cleared of dishes and wiped clean. Everything was gone. Even Gil. He was gone.

It's as if we never even existed, she thought, horror-struck. *As if our meal together, our words, our glances were simply erased. Will our lives be that way too—erased as swiftly, as senselessly, as my father's?*

Blindly she ran out of the grill, an irrational panic coursing through her veins. She ran. Breathless. Past incoming customers. Out into air, elusive salvation. The door slammed shut behind her. Late afternoon sunlight burst her vision, sent her mind pinwheeling.

She collided with Gil. He was coming back into the restaurant and caught the weight of her body full force. Recognizing him, she sank instinctively against his chest. He slipped his arm around her and led her gently toward the car.

"You were gone," she murmured weakly.

"I just came out to look at the tires before we hit the road again."

He helped her into the car and climbed in behind the wheel. She began to cry. "I haven't cried all week," she said, hiding her tears in her handkerchief.

Gil looked down the road. She could tell he wanted to get going. "Go ahead and cry. They say it's good for you."

"I was no help at all to my mother," she confessed miserably, knowing he didn't want to hear it again. "And I was so inadequate saying good-bye to my father—"

"You did the best you could, Anna."

"*Did* I? By talking stupidly about the weather?"

"What did you want to say?"

"I—I should have told my father...that I loved him."

"Why didn't you?"

Anna twisted her handkerchief in a gesture of futility. "I didn't know how. Our family has never been good at putting our feelings into words."

Gil's voice was mildly scolding. "Anna, you've got to stop torturing yourself like this."

There was a moment of silence before she blurted, "Gil, it's not just my father I grieve for. It's us."

"Us?" he echoed in obvious disbelief.

"How long has it been since we really said anything to each other? How long since I really wanted to know what you thought or felt? Or since you truly wanted to know me?"

Gil glanced down self-consciously. "Anna, it can't happen just like that—I mean, suddenly we tell each other our deepest thoughts? It doesn't come that way."

He stuck the key in the ignition and turned it. The engine flared, then began to hum rhythmically. Anna spoke over the drone of the motor. "Then how, Gil? What can I do? There's an emptiness yawning inside me like a gulf. I don't have enough tears to fill it."

"We'll talk," he assured her, putting the engine in reverse and glancing out the back window. "We'll talk, just give us time."

"Time is a thief. How much do we have left?"

"I guess there's never enough, is there?" He patted her knee, as if she were a child threatening a tantrum. "Remind me to have some air put in that left front tire tomorrow."

"Tomorrow is your appointment to pick up your new glasses."

"That's right. I nearly forgot."

"Me too."

In the early evening dusk she stared long and hard at her husband, seeing him anew all over again, storing his features in her memory. She would begin now to collect such treasures, preserving them like precious gems against the day...*someday*....

Instead of pulling out into traffic, Gil stopped and looked at her. Then he smiled. Their eyes held. He reached for her hand.

"I hurt, Gil," she whispered around the painful lump in her throat.

"Yes, Anna, I know," he whispered back. "I hurt too."

"You, Gil?"

He nodded. "I'm going to be an old fool and tell you something I haven't admitted before. When we were at your father's house, I hoped you would need me. I don't mean just to run errands or make arrangements. I mean, really need *me*. But you never once turned to me, Anna. I felt useless, unnecessary."

She stared at him in surprise. "Oh, Gil, all I really wanted was your touch, your understanding. I wanted you to hold me, to comfort me. But you kept your distance like the rest of my family. Sometimes I felt like screaming. We all sat there insulated against one another, staring forever at that hideous TV screen. We fixed meals and ate and washed dishes in silence. Gil, if we were all hurting so much, why didn't we ever talk? Why didn't you and I talk?"

"Maybe we were afraid."

"Afraid?"

"Afraid of revealing ourselves, exposing too much...risking rejection."

"But why, Gil? Why couldn't we just be honest?"

He shrugged. "Maybe we're afraid of what other people will see in us—the weaknesses, the imperfections. So we erect barriers. Hide behind walls until we feel safe. Our isolation becomes a habit, a selfish, comfortable indulgence."

Anna nodded. "But we miss so much behind those walls. I see that now. I suppose I was so afraid of tarnishing my self-sufficient image that I couldn't admit I needed anyone, even you."

He gazed tenderly at her. "You don't have to be afraid, Anna. I love you."

"I love you too, Gil. It's not too late to tear down those walls, is it?"

He smiled at her with his eyes. A warm, lingering smile as his hand tightened on hers. "Know what, Anna, my girl? I think that's what we've just been doing."

ABOUT THE AUTHOR

In many of her novels and short stories, Carole Gift Page has tapped into fond memories of her small-town, Midwestern childhood in Jackson, Michigan. But it was her Grandmother Gift's quaint hometown of Marion, Indiana, that inspired Carole's six-book Heartland Memories series of historical romances with Thomas Nelson. Carole's contemporary novels include *In Search of Her Own*, *Decidedly Married*, *Rachel's Hope*, *A Family to Cherish*, *Cassandra's Song*, *A Child Shall Lead Them*, and *A Bungalow for Two* with Steeple Hill, and *Kara* and *Carrie* with Bethany House.

Author of over forty books and eight hundred stories and articles, Carole has published both fiction and nonfiction. An award-winning novelist, Carole has received the C. S. Lewis Honor Book Award and been a finalist several times for the prestigious Gold Medallion Award and the Campus Life Book of the Year Award.

Carole speaks around the country on Becoming a Woman of Passion, based on her book by Fleming Revell, and has taught creative writing at Biola University. *Misty* (Spire Books) chronicles her family's journey through grief at the death of Carole's fourth child, a newborn.

She and her husband, Bill, live in southern California. They have three children (besides Misty in heaven) and three grandchildren.

THE PRIDE OF FREEDOM

Tracie Peterson

When June of 1944 rolled around, I was fourteen and just out of junior high. I was proud of that accomplishment, partly because it meant that next year I'd be starting high school, but even more so, it meant I'd be sitting at the adult tables for the Fourth of July celebration and every celebration, funeral, or supper after that. I'd grown up and I was just about to bust a button.

Fourth of July was just about the best time of year, as far as I was concerned. I mean, who could ask for a day with more fun packed into it? The only thing I would have wished for that summer was that Uncle John could have been home to share in my enthusiasm. But this year Uncle John was a private in the army, serving somewhere in France or England, as his letters home always noted. The war had taken my favorite uncle far away, and in spite of the sacrifices of rationing and doing without, it was Uncle John I missed the most.

Uncle John had given me an enthusiasm for the Fourth that found deep roots in patriotism and history. He was proud to be an American, and when his draft notice came, it didn't matter that it was for another John Williams who lived ten miles south. He took up that paper in the proudest order and went to serve his country.

"It's our duty to serve," he had said. "We're free because others have gone before us. Never forget that."

I remember sitting for hours listening to him on balmy summer nights before he shipped off to boot camp. Nights when the fireflies were so thick they were nearly lighting the yard well enough to read by.

At times like that, we would gather after chores and generally cast our lots together for supper. My Aunt Ida and Uncle Bob lived with their five kids on the farm adjoining Grandma and Grandpa's, and my family had the farm to the south. Uncle John had just recently bought the smaller property to the east, but he was still working his folks' land as well as his own. That just left my Aunt Doris, a war widow with four strapping boys—all under the age of sixteen—who worked the farm to the north. We were like a community unto ourselves, and summers were the best.

Summers meant hard work because of the farms, but they also meant a time of laughter and games, of stories and tales of family exploits. We would go outside because the house was always too hot, especially after the women had been cooking. We'd lay out two or three tables with food and pitchers of ice water. We kids were in charge of rounding up tables and chairs, and when the men came in from the fields we knew the fun would soon begin.

My grandma would almost always start by chiding the men to wash up, even though they were headed out of routine to the pump. She loved to give my grandpa a hard time, telling him that she hadn't seen him really clean since their wedding. Grandpa would always tease her back, saying that if he washed up too good, there just might not be much left of him. He always figured himself to be made up of mostly good old Kansas dirt and sweat.

Those times together were always special, but celebrations were even more of an occasion. Fourth of July meant the summer was half over—the wheat was harvested, the risk of hail was pretty much past. The Fourth was also a time of taking pride in our freedom. A freedom hard earned and often fought for, as my grandpa was fond of saying. This year it seemed even more real to me, because of Uncle John. So as June drifted by and word came of the allied troops taking Normandy Beach under heavy loss, we were a mighty proud gathering.

That was, until the telegram came the last week of June, telling us that Uncle John was missing in action.

I was pretty angry about that. I heard my aunts whispering in the kitchen that this was "how it began." They knew enough people from the community, my Aunt Doris included, who'd received those ominous telegrams. First they told you your loved one was missing—that sort of prepared you for the worst, Mom said. Then, as in my aunt's case, the second telegram came. Boy, you hoped never to see that second telegram. You always knew what it meant.

"We're gonna have hope," Grandma told her girls. "We're gonna trust the good Lord to have John in His care."

There were tears and nods, but very few words. I remember feeling pretty angry. I went outside and found Uncle John's dog, Buddy. We walked down to the creek and sat there for a long time—just Buddy and me. I wanted to pray, but at the same time, I didn't want to pray. I figured God was being just plain mean. If Uncle John was missing in action, God knew where he was, and it seemed kind of cruel to keep that news from us.

But in spite of the news, life went on. Grandpa got help from Uncle Bob and some friends and harvested the last of the wheat on the thirtieth of June. July first, my Aunt Ida had her sixth baby—a girl—and on July second, their dog had pups. Compliments of Buddy.

By the third of July our kitchen was filled with the aroma of special foods we'd gone without the rest of the year. My mom had taken up precious apple preserves and made pies. Sugar that had been set aside for just such an occasion was pulled out and made into cakes and cookies and Grandpa's favorite homemade mulberry ice cream.

Being a farm family, we were luckier than city folks. We had cows and chickens, mulberries and raspberries galore. We had orchards that always bore enough fruit to can and dry for all four families and then some. But more important, Mom said we had a sense of family that some city people had forgotten.

"When you leave the farm," Mom had said, "you sometimes forget how important it is to help one another—you get used to doing things on your own and forget that God gave us one another to help lessen the burdens of life."

I guess that's why, when the second telegram came the afternoon of the third, telling us that Uncle John had been killed, I felt a real sense of loss. How could he be gone? How could I have not known he was gone all this time?

I wasn't going to cry, because I was just plain mad. But then I saw Grandpa and Pop take out their dirt-smudged handkerchiefs and wipe their eyes. That did it. I'd never seen my dad cry, and there was something so very terrible and frightening in that moment.

I ran off to the creek, blinded by my tears. I didn't want to be with the others. I didn't want them lessening my burden. I wanted to be alone.

But Buddy saw it different.

He followed me to the creek as if understanding the moment. He didn't impose himself. He just plopped down on the bank beside me and put his head down on his paws like he always did. He looked up at me with big mournful eyes that seemed to know.

I told him to go home. Told him that I didn't want him there. It was just too painful. It was like—well, it was like he was teasing me: Buddy was there and Uncle John wasn't. That just wasn't fair. But Buddy didn't go, and eventually I found myself stroking his fur, then hugging him close. I bathed that dog in my tears, but Buddy didn't seem to mind.

That night I couldn't sleep. I knew life was never again going to be the same and it frightened me more than I wanted to admit. I took out a picture of me, my Uncle John, and Buddy—the one taken right before John had gone off to war. Pop, something of an amateur photographer, had taken the picture and offered it to me for a keepsake. I'd put it in the scrapbook for a long time and then when the first telegram had come, I'd taken it out and put it in my Bible. I thought—really hoped—that somehow it might keep Uncle John safe.

Taking the picture and the Bible with me, I crawled back into bed and cried myself to sleep. He wasn't coming home. For all the times I had pretended how it would be, nothing would ever be the same. Uncle John had given his life for our freedom—my freedom. I just wasn't sure it was worth the price.

Fourth of July dawned bright and clear, not that it mattered any-more. The family kind of moved around in a strange sense of routine. I got out of bed just like I did every morning and went down to the barn to help with the milking. We had devotions at breakfast, but nobody really said much about Uncle John. I think we were afraid to. I know I figured if nobody said anything, I could go on pretending it'd all been a bad dream.

That afternoon I helped with the grain truck and by the time the sun was setting in the west, I was back in my grandparents' yard, waiting my turn at the pump. My cousins were there too. Aunt Doris' boys teased me and talked of joining the army. That made Aunt Doris cry and go running for the house. Mom gave them a lecture about saving such talk for another time. My Aunt Ida's kids ran circles around Mom and begged for cookies. Mom was watching the kids for her sister, and I knew that meant that later I'd be helping with them as well.

You would have thought with no fewer than twenty people milling around that old farmyard, that a person couldn't have gotten lonely. But I was. I mean, I knew Uncle John wouldn't have been there for the celebration anyway, but at least he would have been alive. Now the events of the day before were leaving me mopey and disinterested. There was no reason to celebrate.

That was about the time Grandpa came out and told everybody we needed to hop to work and help get the tables and chairs up. Folks from the church had been bringing food all day in honor of my uncle, and it seemed that Grandpa had invited them all to come by that evening.

I can't say I had any heart for the gathering. I just wanted to go back to my room and hide away. I wanted to be left alone to think about how awful it all was, but instead I had to join my cousins in preparing for the evening's events.

By seven o'clock, the yard was so full of people you would have thought we were having a tent revival. The entire church had shown up, and that was when I learned that in addition to my Uncle John dying, two other families in the church had received similar telegrams. We weren't bearing our pain alone.

After everyone had eaten, Grandpa surprised us all by calling the group to order. He stood up on an overturned crate and waited until everyone had quieted down before uttering a single word. You could have heard a pin drop. My grandpa was a most impressive man—tall and big at the shoulders—but with a gentleness of spirit that drew people to him like a circuit preacher.

"I know we have reason to be upset," he began. "Our boys have taken up arms and are now far from home. Some have given their lives, like my son John or my son-in-law Dave. We're all hurtin' pretty bad over it. It's not the kind of news anyone wants to deal with."

I sat down on the grass, wondering why Grandpa was making this speech. I didn't want to hear it, whatever it was. I didn't want to think about Uncle John or even Uncle Dave. I just wanted the day to be over. Fourth of July would never be the same for me, and I would just as soon have not celebrated.

"Now some of you are feeling like the sacrifice wasn't worth it," my grandpa continued, almost as if he could read my mind. "Some of you came here for a funeral dinner instead of a Fourth of July celebration. But I want you to know that my boy, for one, loved this holiday. He loved what it represented—the freedom that it offered."

Some folks were crying by now and others were nodding in agreement. I couldn't understand why Grandpa would do this to us. Grandma was crying softly into her apron not three feet away from where he stood. Surely he had to know how painful this was for her…for the others…for me.

But he went on. "Freedom comes at a high price. John knew that. He spoke of it often. From the time that boy was born, he knew enough to recognize the value of freedom. Partly because we told him about those who had gone before us—who had given their all so that we might be here today enjoying the things we do. But partly he knew it because of who he was inside.

"John loved God—accepted Jesus as his Savior at a young age. He joined the Boy Scouts when he was eleven years old and a prouder man in uniform you have never met." Grandpa smiled then, even as he drew out his handkerchief to wipe his eyes.

"I'll never forget when John learned the story of Francis Scott Key and how he wrote our national anthem. John came home and gave the story to us—just like he was the first one to hear the news, to know what had really happened. He was just plain excited by the thought of that man waiting out on the ship, waiting to see if the war would give the land over to the enemy. Waiting to see if the flag, *our* flag, was still there."

I sat up a little straighter and found myself caught up in Grandpa's words. I remembered John relaying the story to me. I remember his enthusiasm for the moment. He had a way of bringing the story alive for me. I could almost feel Uncle John sitting right there beside me, smiling and nodding at the words Grandpa spoke.

"I know," Grandpa continued, "that my boy was looking to our flag when he fell. He was proud of this country. Proud to serve and give what others had given before him. John always used to say something he'd heard his great-grandfather say: 'We're free because others have gone before us.' Now John has joined them, and I know my boy well enough to know that he wouldn't want us to mourn his passing. He'd want us to celebrate his love of this country. He'd want us to celebrate our freedom and never forget the price."

I wiped the tears from my eyes and felt ashamed of my attitude. I'd been so lost in my own feelings and sorrow that I'd lost sight of what Uncle John's death was really all about.

Grandpa climbed down from the crate just about the time someone in the crowd began to sing "The Star Spangled Banner." One by one, folks got to their feet. I stood quickly, remembering Uncle John's admonishment: "When you see the flag pass by or you hear our nation's song, don't be slow about standing in respect. That flag has led many a weary soldier home."

I sang along and thought of Uncle John. I thought of heaven and how it must be for all those soldiers sitting around waiting for their loved ones to join them. I sang with particular pride as the tiny American flag we had put as a centerpiece on the main table fluttered ever so slightly in the breeze. It was a precious symbol, I thought. The day was a precious day. Uncle John had given his life so that I might sing this song, fly the American flag, be whatever I wanted to be.

I smiled then and suddenly knew everything would be all right. The war. Our country. My family. The flag had led another weary soldier home—the flag still waved...o'er the land of the free and the home of the brave.

ABOUT THE AUTHOR

Tracie Peterson, bestselling author of one non-fiction and over forty fiction titles, lives and works in Topeka, Kansas. As a Christian, wife, mother, writer, editor, and speaker (in order of importance), Tracie finds her slate quite full. Her story "The Pride Of Freedom" was developed around some factual and not-so-factual accounts of a beloved great-uncle who lived in a small rural Kansas town and died on a battlefield in France. The story is written in hopes that no one forget there is a price for freedom, as well as a pride that we should take in our country and those who have served her so well and have given so much.

THE WEDDING

Denise Hunter

*I*t was not the first wedding in Dorothy Stuart's backyard. With four children, eleven grandchildren, and five great-grandchildren, family alone had accounted for more than a few weddings in their oak-shaded backyard. The rose-scented breeze and lush emerald lawn had drawn weddings like children to candy, until the Stuart backyard wedding had become a treasured family tradition.

As Dorothy stood gazing out her second-story bedroom window, she knew that a moment's respite from the flurry of preparations was to be savored. Her family, who had gathered early in the morning to set up for the afternoon nuptials, had finally gone home to ready themselves. Her eyes scanned the yard. White wooden-slat chairs formed tidy rows, facing the latticed gazebo, with a wide path cut between for the center aisle. Ivory heather hung down in frothy sprays from huge baskets suspended from nearby branches. Her eldest daughter Nancy had outdone herself this time.

Dorothy glanced up at the gathering sooty clouds. If only the weather would hold off. Nancy, who wore optimism like a regal crown, had insisted there would be no need for a canopy and, at this point, it was too late to rent one.

Dorothy moved to her tiny vanity, plugged in her curling iron, then withdrew her hairbrush from a drawer and pulled it through her short, milky-white hair. It was black years ago and had hung in flowing curls to the small of her back. On her own wedding day she'd piled it high on her head just the way Edward had liked it. A simple wedding they'd had, just a small gathering and a forget-me-not bouquet, not at all like the full-scale productions of today, complete with videographers and all-you-can-eat buffets.

Simple and quick. A smile tugged at her lips as she remembered how her own wedding had come about. She and Edward had been dating for almost a year, but the uncertainty of war had held them back from serious commitment. *She* was serious. Oh, my, how she was serious. One evening as she finished supper, her father called her to the front parlor.

"What is it, Daddy?" The smile on her face widened as she rounded the corner and saw Edward standing by the front door. "Hi, Eddie."

"Dorie."

"Heart and Soul" played on the radio, and she thought how accurately the song described her feelings.

Her father left them alone, and she allowed her gaze to feast on Eddie. It had been too many days since she'd seen him last. Truth be told, one day was too many. But a close look at him revealed something was amiss. Unspoken pain shadowed his eyes; his countenance teemed with anxiety. Worry clawed at her insides, the terrible feeling you got when you feared the worst. "What is it?"

He motioned her to sit, and she commanded her quaking knees to lower her to the sofa. He sat beside her and took her hand. "I got my draft papers."

She sucked in her breath. The war. Her beloved was going to war. How could she bear to be apart from Eddie for God only knew how long? What if he never came home? Her stomach clenched, threatening to expel her supper. She studied his face through a veil of tears. Those sweet, caring eyes that caressed her with each look; the endearing crook in his nose; the soft, pliable lips that even now kissed the back of her hand. With gentle strokes, he brushed away the tears that fell haphazardly down her cheeks.

"When?"

Anguish spread across his face like darkness across the sky at dusk. "Next week."

Marry me before you go. The thought stuck in her throat, a jumble of words she wasn't brave enough to say. Didn't know if he'd welcome.

His gaze raked boldly over her features, then he rested his palms on her cheeks. "I know this is sudden, but…I want you to be mine before I go." His eyes flashed with intensity. "Marry me, Dorie. Make me the happiest man alive."

Shivers of joy danced along her spine as his words filled her heart. Marry him. He wanted her for his wife. She flung her arms around his broad shoulders, and he held her while she whispered her answer over and over, unwilling to relinquish this moment's joy for the fear she knew would come later. She inhaled the musky scent that was all his own. He would be hers forever.

The wedding had been rushed and simple, a union of two souls who cared little about the process but much about the purpose. They'd had only a few short days together before his bittersweet departure. While he was gone, her heart was tormented by cruel thoughts. What if she never saw him again? What if those few days together were all they would get?

Dorothy pulled the brush to a stop and stared at her own reflection as a smile tilted her lips. Oh, how the Word was right when it said, "Who of you by worrying can add a single hour to his life?" Her worry had done naught but made her miserable for the four long years of separation. Somewhere in the attic, a box of yellowed letters remembered those days.

She laid aside her hairbrush and began applying foundation to her face. The fine lines she'd fretted over in her thirties had blossomed into full-grown wrinkles until her skin more closely resembled used parchment paper than the satin of her youth. Ah, well. She would not trade it for the wisdom that came from years of living. And years of struggling.

When Eddie returned from the war, jobs were scarce in Fort Wayne, and he had spent months searching for a job. She was four months pregnant, and they were on their way home from a doctor's appointment when the accident happened.

He'd only taken his eyes off the road for a moment. "Look out!" But her warning came too late. The force of impact sent her head banging into the dashboard of their used Buick. She looked up, disoriented, watching smoke hiss from under the hood. Feeling a trickle on her forehead, she swiped it away, surprised to find blood on her hands. *Dear Lord, we've caused an accident.*

She turned to check Eddie just as he turned to her. "Dorie!" He reached up and touched the open wound above her brow. "Are you all right?" Then more frantically, "The baby!" His hand found her gently swelling stomach.

"I'm fine. We're fine," she assured, but her head ached fiercely.

"Good grief, man, why don't you look where you're going?" Outside Eddie's window stood a man with a high forehead that was made more predominant by a receding hairline.

Eddie reached for the key to shut off the engine, then drew his hand away as if just realizing that the engine was not running. He exited the car. "I'm sorry, I just looked away for a minute—"

"I'll say you looked away! Look at this." He motioned to the rear of his car, specifically to the mangled chrome bumper and cracked brake light.

"Is anyone hurt?"

"I hope you're insured, young man, I expect to be fully compensated."

Insured! They had no money for insurance. Barely had enough for the necessities, for heaven's sake.

"Name's Eddie Stuart, sir." He extended his hand.

The man recoiled at the sight of his bloody fingers, and Eddie let his hand drop.

"I hope you have a way of paying for this, sonny."

"Look, I don't have any money, but I'd be glad to work it off, mister."

The man's eyes snapped with anger. "I don't need an employee, I need my auto fixed. And if you can't oblige, I'd just as soon see you rot in jail."

"Please, mister, my wife's—"

"Excuse me." A well-dressed man had approached silently. Dorothy noticed the crinkles extending from the outer corners of his eyes. "May I be of some help?"

Eddie simply stared at the stranger, but the other man began a lengthy diatribe of accusation. Finally he finished, and Eddie met the stranger's eyes.

"No insurance?"

"'Fraid not. I haven't found a job since I returned from the war."

The stranger contemplated his words, then asked, "What kind of work you looking for?"

"Most anything. I was working in a factory before I was drafted. I have some carpentry skills and retail experience, too."

"I see."

The car owner interrupted. "This is all just swell and dandy, but how 'bout getting my automobile fixed up?"

The stranger reached inside his coat and withdrew a wad of cash, then he flipped out a few bills and handed them to the other man. "This should cover it, wouldn't you say?"

The man stared back and forth between the bills and the stranger. "Sure, sure, I'd say so." Then he walked to his auto, tossing a baffled look over his shoulder before driving away.

The stranger's name was Bronson and after he arranged to have Eddie's auto towed, he offered him a job at International Harvester, where he served as vice president.

Yes, Dorothy thought as she applied taupe shadow with a light hand, sometimes God works in strange ways. Who'd ever think that a car accident would lead to a nearly forty-year career?

Someone rapped on the door. "Come in."

"You doing okay, Mom?" It was Nancy.

"The yard looks lovely, dear."

"I'm afraid it's going to rain. Looks like I should've rented that marquee after all." She sucked in the corner of her mouth, reminding Dorothy of Eddie.

"It'll be fine."

"Want me to do your hair?"

She noted her daughter's jeans and Edy's ice cream T-shirt. "You'd best get on home and get dressed. It's nearly noon."

Nancy slipped out the door, and once again the house was silent except for the rhythmic ticking of the wall clock.

Dorothy's gaze scanned the room she'd slept in for the better part of her life. She remembered the day she and Eddie had driven down Northside Drive and had seen the For Sale sign sticking in the yard. They had saved up for three years and finally had enough for a down payment. The white two-story was perfect. With a large backyard and airy kitchen, it was everything they wanted. And it was by the Saint Joseph River. Eddie was so excited to be living near the river where he could enjoy his favorite hobby, fishing. Working and fishing were his life, it seemed. His absence weighed on her more heavily each day, especially after all the children had come and she found herself bearing the responsibilities alone from dawn 'til dark. Eventually she even began to wonder if he'd found another woman.

"Where've you been?" she demanded one night when he strolled through the door after the kids were in bed. Once again he'd missed supper, and his plate of food sat on the table in a congealed lump.

"I was fishing, Dorie, you know that."

"How do I know that?" Anger, built up through months of continual waiting, burst to the surface like a buoy. "How do I know you weren't with some woman?"

She saw the shock and hurt dull his eyes, but nothing could stop the tirade that followed. Oh, how she wished later she could take back the words. It was weeks before things returned to normal. Before Eddie took her in his arms and pledged his love in tender words. "I'll never love another, sweet Dorie. You have me, heart and soul. I'll do better, I promise." And he had.

Dorothy glanced down at her age-spotted hand to the plain gold band that adorned her ring finger. The same ring Eddie had placed on her hand so many years ago. They'd stuck together through thick and thin. Not at all like couples today. The same people who recycled plastic with firm conviction, yet threw away relationships like yesterday's meatloaf.

She brushed out a strand of hair, then slid her curling iron to the ends and rolled it in. She'd probably be better off not curling it at all, given that the rainy weather and humidity would straighten it within minutes. Ah, well.

Another knock sounded and her granddaughter Laurel entered with her toddler and her preschooler, her baby girl balanced on her hip. Dorothy stopped long enough to hug her great-grandchildren and compliment them on their appearance.

"Have you seen the yard? It looks awesome," Laurel said, scooping Steven off the cedar chest.

"Your Aunt Nancy sure has the creative touch."

Laurel shooed the toddler's hands off the armoire drawers, then turned and snatched him off the stool before he could climb up on the bed. "Stevey, stay down." She looked at Dorothy with the harried expression of a mother of three. "I declare, all this child does all day is climb, climb, climb!"

Dorothy smiled fondly. "Your father was just like that. It seemed like all I did for an entire year was follow him around getting him off things."

"Mom, can I go downstairs and play with Fluffy?" asked Taylor.

"Sure." He left, and her granddaughter bounced the baby on her hip. "Sometimes it seems like they'll never grow up. Is that awful?"

She met Laurel's gaze in the mirror. "I remember feeling that way, dear. But somehow, when you look back on it, it seems they went from diapers to diplomas in a matter of weeks."

Laurel tried to interest Steven in her beaded necklace. "When did Daddy grow out of this active stage?"

"He never did. Even after he started school, you could hardly keep him still."

Laurel pursed her lips. "Thanks for the encouragement," she said, her chuckle decidedly rueful, then grabbed the toddler's hand. "I'd better get downstairs before Taylor finds the wedding cake."

After she left, Dorothy let her mind wander to the days when her children were home. She could remember feeling overwhelmed and tired of dealing with small children all day. At the time she had thought they'd never grow up; before she knew it, they were leaving the nest.

Elise, her baby, had been the last to leave. She'd lived at home until her wedding day. It had been the traditional Stuart backyard wedding, and Dorothy had fought tears all day. Finally the last guests had left, and she traipsed wearily up the stairs and stood in the doorway of her daughter's bedroom. The closet door stood ajar, revealing a tangle of wire hangers. The twin canopy bed hugged the far wall next to the vanity, and across from it stood a solitary floor lamp like a streetlight on a lonely corner. Where were the clothes that were always scattered over the wood floor? Where were the makeup and lotions that had always cluttered the vanity? They were gone. She was gone.

Tears had coursed freely down her face as she leaned against the painted doorjamb. She could almost hear the laughter and sibling bickering that had echoed through these halls over the years. Why had she wished those years away? Now they were gone and all she felt was empty.

She didn't hear Eddie approach from behind, hadn't known he was there until his strong arms slipped around her waist. He didn't say a word; he didn't need to. He had held her as she wept for all the times she'd yelled impatiently at the kids, all the times she'd been too busy to play, all the times she'd wished them older. Then finally she had cried because it was all over. Her children were grown and didn't need her anymore.

Eddie had turned her gently around and placed her hands around his neck. She had lain her cheek against his cool shirt as he swayed back and forth and began singing "Heart and Soul" in his deep, raspy voice.

As they danced in the shadowed hall, his voice calmed her spirit and soothed her worries. She wouldn't think of this stage as an ending, but rather as a new beginning: the honeymoon they'd never had.

They'd bonded in a new way during those years, and before she knew it she was busy once again with grandchildren and church. Each new stage of life brought fresh challenges and rewards.

The eighties had ushered in more than its share of adventure and change. They'd nearly lost their home in the Fort Wayne flood of '82. Only round-the-clock effort by hundreds of residents sandbagging the banks of the Saint Joseph had prevented it. In the following year, after more than sixty years in Fort Wayne, International Harvester had closed its doors and left thousands unemployed. Eddie was among them, although at sixty-three they decided it was time for him to retire.

Dorothy misted her hair with spray and slipped on the delicate necklace her daughter Annie had loaned her. Hearing thunder rumble in the distance, she moved to the window. The clouds still threatened rain, but so far it had held off. Family and friends had begun to arrive and were now mingling in groups. Two of her granddaughters tuned up their violins by the gazebo. She'd best get her new dress on.

She pulled the ivory dress from the hanger and slipped it carefully over her head. The material fell to her knees in a swirl, and as she tied the sash at her ample waist, she wistfully remembered the days when Eddie had almost been able to span it with his hands.

She stepped in front of the cheval mirror. Her ring was old, her dress was new, her necklace borrowed....

A knock sounded at the door. She slipped on her low-heeled pumps and opened it. Howard, her only son, stood in the doorway.

He handed her a bridal bouquet of blue forget-me-nots sprinkled with roses and baby's breath. "Nancy said to give this to you."

Dorothy took the bouquet and smiled. Something blue...

He kissed her awkwardly on the cheek. "Happy sixtieth anniversary, Mom."

They walked down the stairs and through the living room to the patio doors.

"All set?"

She nodded once, her mouth too dry to speak.

They went through the doorway and across the brick patio between twin terra-cotta pots of perennials. Just then the sun poked through the clouds, and a ray of light burst through the canopy of leaves, sending clusters of light across the yard. Her granddaughters lifted their violin bows and began the wedding march. The small gathering stood as one to honor her, but they faded into the periphery when her gaze met Eddie's.

On the arm of her son she shuffled down the aisle on legs unstable with age, but with eyes that saw more clearly than ever her groom, her friend, her lover...

Her perfect gift from God.

ABOUT THE AUTHOR

Denise Hunter lives in Fort Wayne, Indiana, with her husband, Kevin, and three sons. She and Kevin were relocated to Fort Wayne twelve years ago, but agree that the city feels like home and is a great place to raise a family. Denise's other works include *Stranger's Bride* (Heartsong Presents), *Never a Bride* (Heartsong Presents), and *Truth or Dare* in Barbour Publishing's Reunions collection. They can be ordered online at www.getset.com/hsal or by calling 1-800-847-8270.

COMMUNICATION

Lori Copeland

Now folks, in this crusty ole Missourian's opinion, living in the beautiful Ozarks is a gift. Most any full-fledged, dyed-in-the-wool Missourian would agree with me. Missouri's gently rolling hills and lush green countrysides have to be a little taste of heaven. And if you love water, the Ozarks' myriad of sparkling, blue-green lakes, shady coves, and lazy-moving streams can't be beat. What could be better than drifting down a secluded cove on a blistering hot summer afternoon, trailing a fishing line over the side of an aluminum boat?

Eating wet cheese and soggy crackers (that smell like fish) and drinking Cokes out a partially melted Styrofoam cooler. Sitting on those comfy boat benches, swatting flies, and sweating. Keeping a frantic eye on a water moccasin swimming along the bow of the boat.

Boy, this is living, my husband tells me.

Snakes aside, my husband and I particularly love the water; we often spend summer weekends at a rented lakeside cabin. Hubby loves to fish, and any catch over five pounds invariably results in my being awakened from a dead sleep by a breathless, outdoor, fishy-smelling enthusiast who is beaming from ear to ear with the announcement that he's snagged The Big One.

Over the years I've grown accustomed to hearing about The Big One.

I've lived with The Big One hanging in the least obtrusive location—but still visible enough to satisfy my husband—for many, *many* long years.

Eventually (and this is only after we've communicated at our best), The Big One would be respectfully relegated to the garage or workshop to take its place beside other Big Ones, to hang in glassy-eyed, slack-jawed, lucky-lure-hanging-from-its-lip obscurity.

Like all couples, communication breaks down between hubby and me occasionally.

God instructs us to love our mates unconditionally: "Nevertheless let every one of you in particular so love his wife even as himself; and the wife see that she reverence her husband" (Ephesians 5:33, KJV). Note that there's nothing in there about fish.

There's a tale going around in Missouri about a young couple that suffered a serious lack of *communiqué*. Brand New Hubby caught The Big One and stored it in the refrigerator to be taken later to the taxidermist. Then off to work he went, blissfully unaware that Brand New Wife wanted to please. She didn't know that he had planned to have the fish mounted. But she did know that freshly caught fish was his favorite meal.

"You been keepin' out of trouble, lovely lady?" John asked with a trace of smitten newlywed in his voice when he arrived home that night.

"Don't ask."

"Bad day?"

She nodded pitifully.

"Where are the little munchkins?" He glanced around the kitchen. To supplement their income, Mary baby-sat the four-year-old twins from next door.

"Attending Missy Harrison's birthday party."

"You mean we're alone?" He grinned that all-by-ourselves-alone smile.

Dragging out a large cast-iron skillet, Mary set about cooking supper. A man liked a hot meal at the end of a long day, and she intended to be a wife John could brag about over the lunch pail.

"I hope you're hungry. We're having fish for supper." She covered the bottom of the skillet with oil and let it heat while she dipped the pieces of fish into milk, then cornmeal.

"Fish? Well, great!" He looked a little surprised by the treat. "I'm starved. I haven't had lunch. By the time I finished morning meetings I only had time to grab a candy bar from a vending machine."

Mary dropped the fish into the hot oil and stood guard over the pieces as they began to sizzle and turn a crispy brown. A hungry husband was an appreciative husband.

"Hey," John said, reaching out to take her hand. "Is something wrong? You're quiet tonight."

Their eyes met, and Mary swallowed hard. He was so attentive, so *perfect*. Her happiness knew no bounds. First the beautiful wedding, then moving into the cabin on Tablerock Lake: Life couldn't get any better than this.

"Nothing's wrong. I'm just a little tired." With a contented sigh, she turned back to the fish.

"Anything I can do to help?"

"You can sit down and eat like a horse," she said, lifting pieces of mouthwateringly delectable fish onto a platter.

"I can handle that with no problem." He reached for a piece of the golden-brown fish and sampled it, rolling his eyes in ecstasy. "Terrific, honey!"

Mary smiled to herself as she laid more fish in the skillet. Marriage wasn't so hard. What had her friends tried to warn her about?

She glanced up, smiling. "I'll bet you're a little tired yourself, aren't you?"

"A little," he admitted, savoring another bite. He winked at her. "Good stuff!"

She beamed. "Thank you. Don't spoil your supper."

"Are you kidding? It would take more than a piece of fish to spoil my appetite!" He reached for another handful, and Mary frowned. At this rate there wouldn't be any left to send in his lunch tomorrow.

"I'm sorry I missed you this morning." She motioned for him to sit down at the table. "I ran next door for a minute."

"Yeah, I know. I saw the twins playing as I left. Good grief! Potatoes, salad, corn on the cob, bread…is that *homemade* bread?" He stared wide-eyed as she sliced off thick chunks and lavishly buttered the steaming slices.

"Of course. You like homemade bread, don't you?"

"I guess. I don't remember having it very often—only on holidays."

"This *is* a holiday," she teased, tempting him with a warm, buttered slice. "We've been married one month today."

"Happy anniversary." He bent to kiss her, snatching the bread from her hand. "You're going to be a great wife, Mary."

I know, Mary thought, doing her best not to appear smug, but failing miserably…

They sat down and John ate hungrily, praising every bite, every tasty morsel. The platter emptied quickly. "This is the best fish I've eaten in my life, Mary. No kidding!" He reached for the platter a third time.

"You're going to make yourself sick." She grinned, feeling very good at the moment. Very wifely. Very *good* wifely.

"Which reminds me," he said, talking around a mouthful. "After supper, I'm going to look in the phone book for the nearest taxidermist."

"How come?"

"To mount my fish."

Mary spooned au gratin potatoes into her mouth. "Your fish?"

"I'm telling you, sweetheart, I have never enjoyed anything more in my life than the feel of that fish on my line. I worked for over twenty minutes this morning to get him in the boat. If Sam hadn't gotten the net under him when he did, I would have lost him at the last minute." Eyes bright with the remembered thrill of the catch, he reached for more fish. "No kidding, Mary, I wish you could have been there. It's the moment a man dreams of. A Rembrandt on a line!" He ceased chewing long enough to exhale a proud sigh. "I spent an hour this afternoon cleaning off the wall in my office to make a place to hang him."

Mary grinned—his excitement was contagious. He hadn't said one thing about catching a big fish! "You *caught* your trophy bass! When?" He'd talked of nothing more than catching The Big One since they met.

John stuffed another piece of fish in his mouth. "This morning. Didn't you see it?

"See it?" Mary wracked her brain. *The only fish in the refrigerator…* She froze. *Oh…* She swallowed back rising bile. "Where did you put it?"

"Where? What do you mean?" He looked up, holding a piece of corn.

"Where," she repeated, "did you put your fish?" *Please God…don't let him say the refrigerator.* "Did Sam take it home?"

John glanced at his plate, then back at her. "No…I left it here." He turned toward the refrigerator. "In there…"

"Really?" Nausea built, threatening to overcome her. "Where?"

"Well, Mary, I don't see how you could have missed it. I put it right there in the refrig—" His face suddenly turned ashen and he dropped his fork and looked down at the half-eaten piece of fish on his plate.

Panic bubbled in Mary's throat; her eyes focused on the empty fish platter.

"Mary?" His voice sounded very small. "What kind of fish are we eating?"

Mary laid her fork aside, her eyes glued to the fish platter. "I don't know," she replied timidly. "Why?"

"Where did you get it?" His hand had started to tremble now. Slowly pushing back his chair, he stood up.

She rose to her feet, edging back from the table, her legs weak.

"Mary, answer me!" he roared. "*Where* did you get this fish we just ate?"

Swallowing hard, she took a deep breath. "From the refrigerator—"

"Oh *no!*" He sank back to the chair. "*Please* tell me it wasn't the fish I put in the refrigerator before I left this morning."

Mary had an uneasy feeling. John didn't look like his normal self, not at all. His eyes were wide; his faced was flushed. Mottled, actually.

"I thought you left it in there for our supper—"

"I *told* Huntley to make sure and tell you not to touch that fish!"

Her eyes widened. "He didn't say a *thing* about a fish, John! How could you have left a message with a five-year-old about anything that important?"

"Awww…*Mary!*" John laid his head on the table, a shadow of the man who not five minutes before had been praising her cooking abilities…praising them to high heaven! Now he looked shell-shocked, and he kept repeating, "Shoot, shoot, and *shoot.*"

Two sets of eyes focused on the remainder of the beautiful trophy bass's eight pounds, twelve ounces (he would be reminding her of the precise weight for years to come), all nicely browned and greasy on his plate.

The sight made them both ill.

"Oh, John!" Her heart was nearly breaking. She'd fried his fish.

Kneeling beside his chair, she tried to console the man she'd promised to love, honor, and obey; the man whose bass she'd just cooked. Would he ever forgive her? "I'm so sorry. I never dreamt that was your trophy bass. I thought it was just a really big…fish." If possible, she felt as miserable as he looked.

He lay with his head on the table, staring blankly into space. "I ate my eight pound, twelve ounce bass. My Bigmouth."

"John, listen," she soothed. "Don't worry about that Bigmouth. I'll make arrangements for Jenny to keep the twins tomorrow and first thing in the morning you and I will go out and catch another one!" She kept the mood light and upbeat; the poor guy felt bad enough. He desperately needed optimism right now. He looked so…so…pitiful.

John turned his dull, expressionless eyes toward her. "Mary, it took me twenty years—twenty *long* years—to catch a fish that size. You think we're going to go out there in the morning and catch another one—" he snapped his thumb and forefinger together weakly—"just like that?"

Of course she didn't think that; it could take all morning—so what? "I didn't say it was going to be easy." She patted his leg consolingly, frowning when she realized he was staring at her. And not nicely.

"How?"

"How?" Was this a powwow or a rational discussion between a bride and her bridegroom?

"How could you cut up my beautiful fish into tiny pieces, dip them in cornmeal, and throw them in grease…" He shuddered, his voice trailing off to a pathetic squeak. "I think I'm going to be sick!" He stood up, his napkin fluttering unheeded to the floor. "Excuse me, Mary, I think I'm going to lie down for a while. I'm not feeling well."

"Oooh, too much fish…?"

Sympathy died in her throat when he turned to give her a black look.

Helplessly, she watched him proceed to the sofa in a bewildered stupor and lie down. As if suddenly recalling his earlier vows, he glanced up at her and murmured in a polite voice, "Thank you for dinner. It was…" He appeared to search unsuccessfully for an adequate praise, apparently finding none.

"Oh, John, I feel so awful!" She hurried over to drape a light afghan over him, though it was ninety in the midsummer heat if it was a degree. "You rest and tomorrow things won't look so bad. You'll see; we'll catch another fish. Just like—"

He stopped her with another dark look just as she was about to snap her fingers. "Mary, please, let me lie here and suffer in peace. Go to bed."

She had a sinking feeling he wouldn't be joining her later. "Are you going to sleep here tonight?"

"Right now all I want to do is crawl in a hole and scream."

"Would you feel better if I stayed out here with you?"

"No."

Well. That's the thanks a wife gets for trying to please. She drew a deep, sniffling breath. "Are you mad at me?"

"No."

"Can't I do anything to help you?"

"No." His voice was flat. The word *zombie* came to mind.

"Well," she conceded, "I guess I'll go on to bed now."

Upon reaching the doorway, she turned and glanced at his morose form. He was lying on the sofa, staring blindly up at the ceiling. "Don't worry, darling. We'll catch your Largemouth in the morning." She turned, then paused and looked back again. "Won't we?"

Well, legend says they never caught that bass, but fact says that marriage is now in it's forty-second year and going strong. Which proves either of two things: The way to man's heart is through his stomach, or marriage is more important than a fish.

I never tell this story without being reminded of one of my favorite God instructions, found in 1 Corinthians 13:4, "Love is patient and kind. Love is not jealous or boastful or proud or rude. Love does not demand its own way. Love is not irritable, and it keeps no record of when it has been wronged…"

When you love a fisherman, you have to expect a few minor snags along the way. But when you love the Lord, He gently reminds us that everyone makes mistakes: "So ought men to love their wives as their own bodies. He that loveth his wife loveth himself" (Ephesians 5:28, KJV).

Note: And folks, I believe that *does* include fishing.

ABOUT THE AUTHOR

If there's one thing you can count on with Lori Copeland's novels, it's that you'll find plenty of love and laughter in them. Lori began writing in 1982 and has authored over sixty-five romance novels. She writes in both the secular and inspirational market with over six million titles in print including thirteen foreign languages. Lori's newest releases are *Marrying Walker McKay* (Avon) and *Glory,* book four of the bestselling Brides of the West series (Tyndale House).

Lori has received numerous writing awards over the years, including Waldenbooks Best Seller, the *Romantic Times* Lifetime Career Achievement Award for Love and Laughter and Reviewers Choice Awards, and a Holt Medallion. On April 27, 2000, Lori was inducted into the Writer's Hall of Fame in Springfield, Missouri, where she took her place beside such notables as Samuel L. Clemens (Mark Twain), Laura Ingalls Wilder, and Harold Bell Wright.

Recently, Lori teamed with Angela Elwell Hunt to pen the three-book series The Island of Heavenly Daze for Word Publishing about a Maine island and its charming (and heavenly) inhabitants.

Lori and her husband, Lance, live in the Missouri Ozarks. They have three grown sons—Randy, Rick, and Russ—and four perfectly adorable grandsons.

HEART'S TREASURE

Colleen Coble

*Y*ou understand the provisions of this document, Lana? Once
you agree to give custody to the adoptive parents, your rights
will cease. First you sign custody away, and then the court
will order the adoption. This is a very serious decision."

Colin Jolsen pushed his glasses up his nose and regarded Lana
through the smudged lenses. He was nearing retirement, and his kindly
air reminded Lana of her grandfather. That had made things easier. That
and the fact that he attended New Baptist Church.

Lana tore her gaze from the antique oak bookcases lining the room.
"I understand. How much money will I have when it's over?" She just
wanted to get out of here, out of this stifling little town of Wabash,
Indiana, and its midwestern values, and get on with her life. She felt as
though the beige walls of the office were squeezing the air from her
lungs. She forced herself to sit in the chair and keep her hands still.

She just had to remember the money. The money would make it easier to forget how she'd wrecked her life. And these people would make
sure her baby had everything she could never give her daughter. Her
daughter would never feel the shame of growing up without a father as
she had.

Mr. Jolsen sighed. "You're so young, Lana. How old are you, eighteen?" At her slight nod, he steepled his fingers together and pursed his
thin lips. "You'll find that money isn't everything." He rustled through

his papers. "The family is very wealthy and will be able to give your child every advantage, that's true. But I want you to think about this carefully. Have you prayed about it?"

What business of it was his? He wasn't her father. She could almost feel herself bristle with anger. Yes, she had prayed. But God hadn't answered, at least not that she could see. Maybe He still wasn't speaking to her. She'd done enough dumb things to make Him turn His back on her completely, though she knew He would never do that. And that almost made it worse. No amount of sorry could erase what she'd done. She'd asked forgiveness and knew that He had forgiven her, but she didn't *feel* forgiven. That made it very hard to pray.

He sighed again. "Very well. The adoptive parents will pay all medical costs for you and the child as well as bestow a cash sum of twenty thousand dollars into your account upon your final signature." He gave a slight smile at Lana's gasp of surprise. "More than you expected, I assume. They will double that amount if you agree never to try to find the child."

Forty thousand dollars. The amount seemed vast to Lana. She could finish school and start over somewhere else. All she knew about the adoptive family was that they lived out east somewhere. She didn't intend to try to find the baby, anyway. It would be difficult enough to give her away. She couldn't go through that more than once.

Her heart fluttered at the thought of that much money. "Why would they pay so much? Have you met them?"

Mr. Jolsen nodded. "They seem respectable. They're in their fifties and are too old to adopt through the normal channels. They want a newborn and are wealthy enough to pay for the privilege."

Lana let out her breath. It seemed too good to be true. All she had to do was sign the paper. She picked up the pen. "Where do I sign?" Her hand shook, but she bit her lip and forced it to steady. This would be over soon.

He shook his head. "I want you to go home and pray about it first. If you're sure this is still what you want to do, come back tomorrow and we'll finish it up then."

Reprieved. The sense of relief surprised Lana. She let out the breath she'd been holding and nodded. "Okay. But I won't change my mind." She couldn't do that to Gramps and Grammy. They were too old to raise another child. Raising her alone after her mom had been struck by a train had been hard enough.

Mr. Jolsen saw her to the door. "Come back around three tomorrow afternoon. I'll be praying for you, Lana. Call me anytime if you need to talk."

She stepped out onto Canal Street, and her stomach growled. She'd been too nervous to eat any lunch, and it was nearly two o'clock now. Workers were painting one of the old buildings in a painted lady treatment, and Lana skirted the scaffolding as she started toward the crosswalk. She heard someone shout her name and gazed across the street. Her best friend Marcie waved, then disappeared into the All About You shop.

Tears stung Lana's eyes. She wished she could go and try on a prom dress as Marcie was doing. No one would ask her to the prom when she looked like a ready-to-pop Pillsbury doughboy. Since dumping her, Rob had already given another girl his ring and claimed no responsibility for the baby.

After crossing the street against the light, she hurried up Wabash Street. Before anyone else saw her, she ducked into Metro Espresso for a decaf iced mocha. Sitting at the little card table, she knew she couldn't hole up here forever, much as she wanted to just breathe in the heady aroma of the dark, rich coffee and forget her worries. There were decisions to be made.

She finally got up, took her cup, and waved good-bye to Michael, the owner. He shouted something after her, but she didn't stop. She was in no mood to talk. Rolling the rich mocha around on her tongue, she turned the corner onto Market Street and wandered down the sidewalk. This aimless wandering would only succeed in delaying the inevitable. She could peruse the entire three-block-long area of Victorian shops that made up the downtown proper and be done in half an hour. That wasn't nearly enough time to make a decision…

But it was already made, wasn't it?

She wished her baby could be raised here instead of in some fast-paced city out east. This town, where people still left their doors unlocked and greeted strangers on the sidewalk, had been a good place to grow up. She used to think she'd never leave the warmth and safety of this small town, but her pregnancy had made that choice impossible. She couldn't stay here and see the stares and smiles from her classmates.

Passing J & K Pet Store, she made a split decision to go inside. She'd never been allowed to have a pet. The responsibility of another mouth to feed was simply more than her grandparents could handle. She wandered down the aisle, staring at the fish and birds, then turned into the next aisle to look at the furry pets.

A young couple knelt beside the puppy pen. The roly-poly collie inside the pen licked their fingers and whined, pleading to be picked up. The woman was lovely, with hair nearly as red as Lana's and pale, translucent skin. Her dark-haired husband hovered over her protectively.

"Let's take him home, Tate," the woman said. Her tear-stained face gazed up into her husband's with an overwhelming sadness.

He put his hand on her shoulder. "Don't, Abby. I know we're both hurting over what the doctor said, but a puppy isn't the same thing as a baby."

Abby began to sob and leaned against her husband's shoulder. Feeling like an eavesdropper but unable to move away, Lana stepped behind a display of dog food. Had the woman just miscarried?

"I know," Abby sniffed. "But we'll never have a baby, so we might as well have a puppy we can love."

"God can work even in this, Abbs." Her husband buried his face in her hair. Sobs shook his own shoulders, but he made an obvious attempt to hold them back. "Maybe we could adopt a baby."

Lana thought about Rob, about his disgust when he had learned she was pregnant. He'd even accused her of getting pregnant on purpose, as though none of it was *his* fault. Gazing at this man who so obviously cherished his wife, Lana felt a twinge of pain she didn't want to face. Sometimes life was so unfair.

Abby gave a frantic shake of her head. "Where would we get that kind of money, Tate? All our savings went for the down payment on our house. It will be years before we could save that much. By then we'll be too old." Fresh sobs wracked her body. "I trust God, but I don't understand why He would do this to us. We've served Him faithfully, joyfully. Why would He punish us this way?"

Give them the baby.

Lana's eyes widened at the inner urging. Where had that come from? She shook her head. This couple had just said they couldn't afford to adopt.

Give them the baby.

She needed the money. The college she intended to attend was expensive. Before this had happened, her best shot at college was to attend the Indiana University/Purdue University branch in Fort Wayne. She had never dreamed she could go to Stanford. Though the costs of the baby's birth could be covered by insurance, her promised spot at Stanford would evaporate without that adoption money.

Give them the baby.

The compulsion to do just that was almost overwhelming. Her throat constricted, and she fought the desire to step out and speak to them. She heard their voices fade as they left the store. Lana gasped in relief and stepped into the aisle. She was glad she didn't know their names. It was out of her hands now. Her head down, she raced toward the front door.

"Miss!" The young female clerk hurried after her. "You dropped your purse."

Lana paused long enough to grab the purse; then she hurried outside. She ran down the sidewalk as if a swarm of bees were chasing her. She crossed at the light and ran past the old Eagles Theater and up Miami Street. Home was only two blocks away. If she could reach the sanctuary of her room, she could forget she had ever seen those people.

Her grandparents had lived in the Victorian house on Hill Street since they were married fifty-two years ago. The brick home in all its fading glory loomed at the foot of one of the hills that surrounded the downtown. Lana threw open the door, dropped her purse onto the table in the entry, and raced up the two floors to her room in the attic.

Her grandparents had given her the entire attic as her own suite when she turned thirteen, and she loved it. Nearly thirty feet square, books, her stuffed bear collection, and other remains of her childhood decorated every nook and cranny. Papered in a soft rose floral and furnished with white wicker furniture, it was home to Lana.

She sat at her desk under the eaves and buried her face in her hands. The brochure for Stanford University lay there, and she pulled it forward and stared at its glossy pictures. In three months she would be in sunny California. All she had to do was sign the papers tomorrow. The minutes stretched to hours, and the battle still waged in her heart. She heard the grandfather clock in the hall chime five times.

"Lana, supper!" Her grandmother's voice echoed up the stairs.

"Coming," she called. She pushed the brochure away and went down the steps.

The aroma of roast beef and potatoes made her stomach rumble hungrily, and she remembered again that she'd had no lunch. Gramps, his denim overalls covering his protruding middle, was already seated at the table. Grammy, short and nearly as round as she was tall, carried in the plate of roast and potatoes. The corn, coleslaw, and bread were already spread out on the table.

She slid into her seat, bent her head while her grandfather said grace, and then began to fill her plate. She sensed her grandparents' eyes on her but kept her head down.

Her grandfather cleared his throat. "Did you sign the papers?"

"Um, he wanted me to think about it one more day first." She finally looked up and forced herself to smile. "If I sign a paper saying I'll never try to look for the baby, they'll give me a total of forty thousand dollars."

Her grandmother's hand flew to her mouth, and her eyes filled with tears. "Oh, Lana. What kind of people would pay for something like that?"

"This is my chance to start a new life, Grammy. Don't look so horrified."

"Bu–but it's like selling your baby, Lana, can't you see that?" Two tears spilled from her green eyes and followed a soft wrinkle down her cheek.

Lana flushed. Her grandmother had placed her finger on the very thing that had been bothering her. "At least she'll have everything a family like that can give her," she began.

Her grandfather cleared his throat. "And just what is that, Lana? Money? Is that what you think is important in life? I had hoped we'd taught you better than that. Have you missed out on so much, girlie? We've always gotten by."

She swallowed hard at the disappointment in his voice. "I—"

He cut her off. "Did you even ask what faith they held? Will they raise her in a Christian home so we have some hope of seeing her in heaven? The Bible says, 'Where your treasure is, there will your heart be also.' You need to evaluate where your treasure is, Lana. All the money in the world won't matter when you stand before God."

Tears sprang to her eyes. "You don't understand!" she cried. She pushed her plate away. "I made a mistake, a bad mistake, but no one sees how sorry I am. I've been labeled loose and easy, and that's all I'll ever be in Wabash. Here I'll see reminders of my mistake all my life. I'll see Rob, too, and I can't take that."

"You're better off without him," her grandmother said adamantly. She began to cut her meat fiercely, as though she might cut the plate itself in two.

"You can't run from your problems, girlie." Gramps sighed and folded his big hands in front of him. They were hands that Lana had always loved: rough and callused, but tender and loving, too. "I'm not saying to keep the baby. Your grandma and me, we're too old to help you much. You've made a responsible decision, a loving one. Your baby deserves a momma *and* a daddy, and I know it cost you plenty to give up what you wanted to do so you could do what's best for the baby. But take a long, hard look at what's important in life, Lana. God will show you if you ask Him."

They ate the rest of their meal in silence. Lana didn't know what to say or do. The food was tasteless, but she choked it down. Finally her grandfather rose from the table heavily and plodded to the living room.

Lana jumped to her feet and began to clear the dishes away, fighting tears. Giving this baby away was the hardest thing she would ever do. Was it wrong to fulfill another dream as a tiny compensation for the pain? The plates clattered in her numb fingers.

"I'll do that, sweetheart," her grandmother pushed her toward the door. "Go spend a little time in prayer."

Prayer. What good would that do? God never answered back. Lana started toward her room and stopped at a sudden thought: Was that inner compulsion she'd felt in the pet store from God? Was it possible He really cared about her situation? Thoughtfully, she walked through the library and into the entryway. She stopped to get her purse on the table. The only thing on the table was a navy leather purse. Grandma must have bought a new purse.

"Grammy, have you seen my purse?" she called.

Her grandmother's voice floated through the hall. "It's there on the table, darling. I like your new one. Very pretty."

Lana stared at the purse. It wasn't hers. She picked it up and opened it. Rummaging through the contents, she pulled out the wallet and flipped it open to the driver's license. That woman in the pet shop, Abby, stared back from her photo. Her heart thudded in her chest, and Lana dropped the wallet numbly. She took the purse with her and mounted the stairs to her room.

Curling up on her bed, she took out the wallet again. This couldn't be a coincidence, could it? What *did* God want? She'd failed Him enough; she didn't want to do it again. Leaning back against her pillow, she closed her eyes. "I'm listening, Lord. What do You want me to do?" The minutes ticked by, and she began to feel silly. "Lord, are You there?" she whispered.

Sighing, she took the Bible and began to flip through the pages. Was she wrong to take money for her baby? It's not like it was hurting anyone. The bulletin from last Sunday was stuck in 1 Timothy 6. She smoothed the pages and began to read.

For we brought nothing into the world, and we can take nothing out of it. But if we have food and clothing, we will be content with that. People who want to get rich fall into temptation and a trap and into many foolish and harmful desires that plunge men into ruin and destruction. For the love of money is a root of all kinds of evil. Some people, eager for money, have wandered from the faith and pierced themselves with many griefs. (1 Timothy 6:7–10)

Had she fallen into a snare? The snare of thinking money would solve all her problems instead of leaning on the Lord every day in faith? Lana's heart sank when she realized what had happened to her. She had nearly given in to the temptation. Picking up the phone book, she found a listing for Tate Mitchell and wrote down the address. She would go right now before she lost her courage.

She glanced around her room. This was home. Grandpa was right—she couldn't run away from her past. She would stay and face the future. The talk would die down sooner or later.

Placing a hand on her belly, she whispered to her baby, "let's go meet your mommy and daddy."

ABOUT THE AUTHOR

Author of seven novels and five novellas, Colleen Coble's newest release is a novella in the anthology Heirloom Brides from Barbour. Colleen and her husband, Dave, reside in Wabash, Indiana, where they are restoring a Victorian home. They have two grown children, David and Kara. While they have no grandchildren yet, they do have a grandpup and two grandcats.

FENCES

Neta Jackson

Chicago, 1980s

I don't like the looks of that dog."

I dropped the box marked Gwen and Ray's Bedroom onto the back porch of the cozy brick bungalow we'd just bought on Chicago's north side and followed my husband's gaze into the next yard. The large black German shepherd had been barking nonstop since we'd started unloading the truck from the alley. Now it was momentarily silent, sitting on its haunches and panting hugely.

"Aw, we're just strangers. See? She's getting used to us already." I couldn't understand Ray's reaction. He was a dyed-in-the-wool dog lover from childhood. In our old neighborhood, every dog within whistling distance went nuts when Ray came in sight, knowing it would get an enthusiastic rump scratching.

"Yeah, but they don't take care of her right. Take another look, Gwen. See that short chain? That's no way to treat a dog. Water bowl's tipped over. And the yard's not totally fenced, either." A chain link fence ran the length of the yard between our two houses, but stood alone, not connected to either house. It wasn't even clear whose fence it was.

I saw Ray's eyes search out the swing set where our three-year-old Erika was happily draped over the U-shaped rubber seat like a limp noodle, dragging her feet in the patch of dirt beneath. Okay, so he was feeling protective. "But honey, we chose this neighborhood for its diversity. We can't let a dog keep us from getting to know our neighbors. Maybe we can invite them to church."

The north side of Chicago along Lake Michigan was known for being a melting pot of races and cultures and ethnic groups. Corner grocery stores run by Pakistanis and Koreans were mixed with two- and three-story flats, big old frame houses, and family bungalows. Ray and I found it exciting, a chance to raise our children in a more colorful world than the monochromatic suburbs we'd both been raised in. When we looked at the attractive brick bungalow on Kelsey Avenue, with its front porch big enough to harbor a porch swing, and discovered that our neighbor on one side was a retired Polish cop and our neighbor on the other was an African-American grandmother with a large family, that was icing on the cake.

Or so we thought.

"Yeah—" Ray's tone was decidedly glum—"but one of the first things I'm going to do is fence in our yard."

Which was a good thing, because it turned out I was wrong. The dog didn't get used to us. Sheba, they called her. Well, *called* was relative. "Sheba! Shut up!" the grandmother would yell from the back door, then turn around and disappear inside. Sheba, of course, ignored the periodic yappings of her people and continued to leap against her chain and bark furiously whenever we went near the useless fence.

But the house was full of friendly children who hung over the wire fence and ventured into our yard from time to time to ask if they could play on Erika's swing set. I wanted to say yes, but it never turned out to be that simple. One or two children coming over to play with Erika was one thing. But if I said yes to the constant requests, it usually meant seven or eight children of all sizes suddenly swarming all over the yard. No way could I work inside, not even with an occasional maternal glance out the back window to make sure two toddlers were not eating the sand in the sandbox. No, it meant full-scale supervision.

So I usually made up some lame excuse, wondering, *Who are these kids' parents?* I saw a menagerie of men and women flow in and out of the house, but had no idea who actually lived in the big, three-story frame house.

Except for the grandmother, the matriarch. "Mrs. T," the neighbors called her—T for Thomas. But she rarely ventured outside, appearing at the back door only to yell at the dog or the kids or one of the lanky men tinkering with one of the cars in the back alley. On the few occasions I saw her walking through the backyard to the garage, moving heavily as though her back and knees hurt, I called cheerfully, "Hello, Mrs. T!" But she was either hard of hearing or ignoring me. She never said hello back. How could I be a good neighbor if she wouldn't even say hello to me?

Joe, the retired Polish cop on our other side, approved of our plan to build a fence. "Good fences make good neighbors." He jutted his chin slightly in the direction of Sheba, who was doing her chain dance. A row of scraggly bushes from the alley to the front sidewalk divided his property from ours. "These old bushes wore out a long time ago!" He laughed. "Go ahead. Pull 'em all out!"

Joe had an invalid wife and seemed hungry for conversation. He "supervised" construction of the fence and was generous with both his post-hole digger and his advice. "They don't mix much with the rest of the neighbors," he informed us one day as Ray plunged the post-hole digger into the knotty ground at eight-foot intervals. Joe always referred to the big family on the other side of us as *they*.

"This neighborhood used to be all Polish in the old days, but the old ones died off and the young ones moved away. I'm glad to see young families like yours moving in. Keeps the neighborhood alive." Another jerk of the head in Sheba's direction. "They're the only ones on the block—you know, black. But they keep to themselves and we all get along." He gave a knowing nod. "Just be careful. Keep your car locked. If something wanders away…"

I caught Ray's eye. Did Joe know something we didn't know? Or was he just a gossip…or a bigot? But we said nothing. We were new here. We didn't want to have to choose sides.

The sturdy cedar fence went up, right along the old chain-link, until it enclosed our backyard. We chose a style called the "good neighbor" fence. It was tall enough to give a sense of privacy, but the top of the fence was scalloped to allow for friendly calls between yards. Surely Joe was right: Good fences would make good neighbors.

With his daughter safe from Sheba's potential jailbreak from the short chain, Ray occasionally wandered behind our garage to talk to the guys tinkering on cars in the alley. Ray could talk cars. Soon he was referring to the guys as Mort and Kenny and Rod, all sons of Mrs. T. They were friendly in a weather-and-cars-and-baseball-scores kind of way, and even returned my greetings when I came into the alley to take out the garbage.

But I still hadn't figured a way to actually speak to Mrs. T or to any of the other female members of the household. (Wives? Sisters? Mothers of the kids?) Everybody in this neighborhood used his back door to go in and out because we all had garages standing back by the alley. But I certainly wasn't going to venture into their backyard and knock on the back door, not with Sheba ready to leap in mad frustration on the end of her chain, announcing me like the barbarians attacking Rome.

Once I went over and rang the front doorbell, trying the old trick of borrowing a cup of sugar, but one of the kids answered the door and simply yelled my request inside. "Gram! The lady next door wants sugar!" Then the boy shrugged. "She ain't got no sugar."

I went home feeling foolish. "Melting pot" was certainly a misnomer on this block. More like stew vegetables thrown into a pot—but somebody had forgotten to add water and seasoning.

As the summer months brought more people out of their houses and onto their porches and sidewalks, we started getting to know a few more of the neighbors along the block and even behind us on the other side of the alley. Parents of preschoolers can sniff out other families with preschoolers like the giant at the top of Jack's beanstalk: "I smell the blood of a possible playmate!"

We'd found several PP's in the neighborhood and, to Erika's delight, located some "play exchanges"—the popular term for "I'll take care of your kid for two hours today if you'll take care of mine Thursday." We snapped them up like premium lottery tickets.

Daylight was fading fast one evening in late August when I headed down the alley to pick up Erika at a new playmate's house. It had been a muggy summer day, but the breezes off the lake were rustling the leaves of the big old elm trees that arched over the alley, giving the impression of cooling off. I picked up Erika and we walked back down the alley, pointing out the old garages that had been horse stables in the "old days," as Joe often told us.

In the twilight I didn't see the shadow that moved out between Mrs. T's garage and our own until it stood in my path.

Sheba.

I swung Erika high up on my hip and froze. But Sheba must have smelled my fear because the shadow moved quickly, and then I felt sharp teeth sinking into my thigh.

Erika's blood-curdling screams must have startled the dog because the shadow backed away. I seized the chance and, with Erika screaming on my hip, made a break for the back gate in our fence. Fumbling with the latch that seemed reluctant to open, I felt curses rise in my throat. The fence that was supposed to keep the dog out was keeping us out as well!

Where was Sheba? Was she going to attack again? I began to panic. Finally the gate fell open, and I banged it shut behind me. As I ran down the walk to the house, I saw Ray bolt out the back door toward us. "The dog bit Mama! The dog bit Mama!" screamed Erika. I wanted to fall into Ray's arms—but all he said was a terse "Get inside" as he passed us and headed for the back gate. Didn't he want to see if I was okay? What was he going to do?

"Honey, honey, we're safe now," I soothed Erika, grabbing a cookie from the Mickey Mouse cookie jar and practically shoving it into her mouth. Delighted with a cookie before dinner, she wandered off. Trembling, I locked myself in the bathroom and peeled off my jeans. Angry red welts circled an area the size of my hand on my right thigh. I examined the area closely. No broken skin! My jeans had saved the day.

Now that I knew I was all right, I started shaking like a leaf. That dog! Even our fence had been no protection. Maybe Ray was right. Maybe buying this house had been a big mistake.

Suddenly I was aware of Ray yelling in the yard next door, "Keep that dog inside or I'm going to call the police! She bit my wife!"

Other voices rose and fell in the yard next door. And then Ray's angry voice again, "Just do something about that dog, or *I'm* going to do something about it!"

I cringed. What if our friends at church heard him making threats like that? But I jerked my jeans back up, wincing in self-righteous anger. Any self-respecting husband would react the same way if his wife got bit by a huge dog.

Later, after Erika was in bed, we sat together on the porch swing, listening to the cicadas in the elm trees practically drowning out the evening traffic on our one-way residential street. I felt comforted by Ray's arm around my shoulders, even though my leg was throbbing. But he was strangely silent.

"Whatcha thinking?"

He shook his head. "Oh, I dunno. Just feeling kinda bad about how angry I got. It's taken me months to make friends with those guys next door. Now what? They're our neighbors, after all."

I pulled out of his arm. "Hey, wait a minute. It's not my fault Sheba bit me. You're the one who wanted to build a fence between us and that dog."

Ray reached out and snuggled me back under his arm. "I know, honey. It's just that…. What does 'love thy neighbor' *mean?* We have to live next door to them for…years!"

Guess I should have been glad when I saw Ray talking to the guys under their car hoods the next evening, but my pride was wounded. Did my husband regret rising to my defense? But he came in the back door looking relieved. "I apologized for getting so angry last night. Mort said he was real sorry about Sheba biting you. Those guys are really all right, Gwen. I'm sure they feel bad about it. But I told 'em I was serious that they need to do something about that dog."

By the time the bruise on my leg had faded, things seemed pretty much like they'd been before. The guys next door had accepted Ray's apology, said they understood and that they'd have done the same thing, and bantered with him as they puttered with the cars back by the alley. We never heard boo from Mrs. T, but like I said, things were pretty much the same.

Except one day we realized we hadn't seen Sheba in the backyard for a couple weeks. When Ray asked about it, Mort just shrugged and said his mother "got rid of the dog."

I felt kind of bad in spite of myself. Maybe Mrs. T was upset about having to get rid of her dog. I couldn't say I was sorry the dog was gone, except that now there was nothing standing in the way of me going to her back door and getting acquainted. So what was stopping me?

Then my opportunity to mend fences landed in our mailbox. I unfolded the garish pink flyer announcing a Neighborhood Block Party the last Saturday of September. The city would block off the street, the kids could skateboard or ride their bikes and trikes, everybody was supposed to bring something for the grill and a "side dish to pass."

I showed it to Ray and grinned. What a great way to meet and get to know our neighbors better!

On the day of the Block Party I brought out my three-bean salad and set it on the makeshift plywood table. Ray helped Joe drag out his big charcoal grill and ended up flipping the steady supply of burgers and hot dogs donated by various neighbors. Keeping one anxious eye on Erika, who was riding her tricycle in the middle of the street amid flying two-wheelers, I wondered if our neighbors from next door were going to show up. Mrs. T didn't come out; neither did Mort, Kenny, or Rod.

But the kids showed up. No meat for the grill, no side dishes, no paper plates or liters of pop. Just big appetites. They cleaned out my bowl of three-bean salad.

Well, I was going to make the best of it. At the Block Party I could be friendly to the kids without all of them ending up in my backyard. With my soggy paper plate in my lap, I sat down on the curb beside the kids from next door and tried to memorize the names they generously offered up: Kendra and Kevin and Mikey and D'Angelo and Damen and…well, it was a good start.

"So. Are you all brothers and sisters?"

Giggles. "Well, Mikey and D'Angelo are my brothers," said Kendra, "but Damen and Kevin are my cousins…well, actually, Kevin's mama is my big sister, so I'm actually his aunt…"

We resumed the sorting process after the watermelon had been cut. Erika sat in Kendra's lap and happily consumed slice after slice that the other kids shared with her as I tried to sort out the mamas and papas. Mort was Damen's daddy, but Uncle Kenny and Uncle Rod were single. Kendra's mama was Mrs. T's daughter, but she was at work all day, so Mrs. T seemed to be raising most of the kids.

"Those kids are cute," I told Ray later that evening, after all the grills, plywood tables, wooden saw horses, and lingering neighbors had disappeared off the street. "Polite, too. I think I've got the family pretty well sorted out."

My smugness was reinforced the next day. As we came home from church, I saw Mrs. T hanging some dishtowels out on a line in her backyard. I called out cheerfully, "Good morning, Mrs. T!" The heavyset black woman actually looked up and started to come my way. My grin widened. This was great! We were actually going to speak over the fence. What a great testimony this would make at church! Better still, maybe I could invite her and the kids and—

"Why are you asking all my kids so many questions, huh?"

Mrs. T's tone felt like a slap. My grin slid off my face.

"Wha…uh, I was just…just trying to get acquainted with them." My words felt like they were tripping all over my tongue.

"You got questions? You ask me. Don't you go using little kids to be pryin' and pokin' into our business, you hear me now?"

Almost before I knew what was happening, she had turned her back and was stalking back to her laundry basket, muttering under her breath.

I fled into the house. Ray was somewhere helping Erika get off her Sunday dress and into play clothes. Escaping down into the basement playroom, I threw myself on the old couch and burst into tears.

"That old witch!" I raged. "What did I ever do to her? All I've ever done is say hi and try to be friendly." My shoulders shook. I felt humiliated. Rejected. Persecuted. "After all, I'm the one who got bit by her stupid old dog," I yelled into the empty air. "She's angry at me? I'm the one who has a right to be angry!"

Fresh sobs rose from my gut, and I threw a pillow across the room.

"Honey?" It was Ray's voice calling down from the top of the basement stairs. I didn't answer. But in a few moments I felt his comforting presence on the couch beside me. "What happened, honey?"

I poured out what Mrs. T had said to me, the injustice of it all. "We'll never be good neighbors. She's just a sour old woman who doesn't like anybody."

Ray held me until I quieted down in his arms. Then he said, "I don't know if this makes any difference at all, but Mort told me something the other day that maybe we should think about."

I pulled back and looked at him. I knew my eyes were red and my nose was runny. "What?" I sniffed.

"Mort told me that when his mother was a just a girl of fifteen, she saw her older brother lynched by the Klan down in Georgia, back in 1930, I think."

I just looked at him.

Upstairs we could hear Erika calling, "Mommy? Daddy?" Ray kissed me on the forehead and went back up the basement steps.

I don't know how long I sat down in the basement. For the longest time I couldn't think. I just wanted to be angry. But slowly the face of a terrified young girl, watching a mob of white-hooded terrorists—white people—put a rope around her own brother's neck and strangle him over the limb of a tree for who knows what reason, replaced the bitter image of Mrs. T's face yelling at me over the fence.

The tears started again. Helpless tears, because the fence between Mrs. T and me had been building for generations—a fence of fear and prejudice and injustice and suspicion and distance. A fence of history stood between us, just like the sturdy cedar fence we had built between her life and ours.

What made me think I could cross over that fence in just a week, a month, or a year?

The calendar said November, and the leaves from the big elms were all on the ground before I worked up my courage to face Mrs. T again. But the day before Thanksgiving I stood on the back steps of the house next door and rang the doorbell. For a long time I thought no one was coming, but then the door opened a few inches and Mrs. T peeked out.

I thrust out the apple pie I had made. "Happy Thanksgiving, Mrs. T," I croaked. "I hope you like it. Ray says I make pretty good pie."

The door opened wider. Mrs. T took the pie. I thought I saw just the hint of a smile on the wrinkled old face.

"Thank you," she said. "Happy Thanksgiving to you, too." And then the door closed.

But as far as I was concerned, that day the fences started coming down.

ABOUT THE AUTHOR

Neta Jackson would like to thank her many sisters and brothers in Christ, both black and white, who have taught her the importance of building bridges instead of fences.

Neta and her husband, Dave, are a husband/wife writing team, the authors of the award-winning Trailblazer Books of historical fiction, introducing young people to great heroes and heroines of the faith. Transplants from the West Coast, the Jacksons have lived in the Chicago area for most of their married life, which is going on thirty-five years.

PRAIRIE LESSONS

Deborah Raney

I shooed the dogs away and carried my breakfast out to the back
deck. It was a tradition Grant and I had shared for most of our
married life, and I had just recently been able to enjoy the deck
again without it bringing back too many difficult memories.

I set my whole wheat bagel and steaming, oversized coffee mug
down on the wobbly table and stepped to the rail to appraise the day.
The air was April-cool, but the bright sun climbing over the hedgerow at
the edge of the farm promised to warm things up in a hurry. The sapphire skies of that Kansas morning and the greening wheat fields that
rolled across the prairie should have filled me with hope. But hope had
become a rare commodity.

While Buster and Lad trotted off to the barn, King, our old mostly-
collie, came to the rail beside me, cocking her head, watching to see if I
would allow her to stay. She must have been close to a hundred in dog
years and she walked with an arthritic limp. Like half a dozen other
lucky dogs over the years, she'd been dumped off in our yard when the
boys were small. They had named her before we discovered she was a
she. No amount of cajoling could convince them to call her Queenie, so
she'd spent the past fourteen years happily answering to King, while
Grant and I'd had to explain to every casual visitor to the farm our reason for calling our obviously female collie "King".

As though she knew I was thinking about her, King pressed her wet nose into the palm of my hand and whimpered. I knew exactly how she felt. We'd both been abandoned, first by three boys off to college in quick succession, and then by Grant. As far as King was concerned, Grant had been just another overgrown boy. King was the one who'd discovered Grant in the barn that awful morning. I wondered if dogs remembered the way people did. For her sake, I hoped not. The vision of my husband's crumpled form at the foot of the hayloft ladder still haunted me.

After the funeral Eric had offered to quit his job, and Jon and Mitch had both offered to quit school and come home to keep the farm running. But I couldn't ask them to do that. It wasn't like the farm was our entire livelihood. The economy had long ago dictated that Grant take a full-time job in town. His hours at the lumberyard had paid the bills and in truth had allowed us to stay on the farm. His life insurance had left me in decent shape financially.

Eric was on his own, and Jon would be soon. Mitch, our youngest, still had two years of college, but between his savings and a couple of scholarships he'd be okay. It was the farm that needed supporting. Like an indigent relative, Grant's home place couldn't take care of itself. The smart thing would be to sell it, but when I thought about telling the boys, I knew that would never fly. They loved this place. It was the only home they'd ever known, the only thing they had left of Grant. I loved it, too, for that matter. I couldn't imagine ever leaving, but neither did I see how I could possibly keep the place up by myself. The boys did what they could when they were home, but three or four weekends a year—even times three sons—just wasn't cutting it.

I pulled out a chair and started to sit down, but King's ears stood on end and she barked at a small cloud of dust rising half a mile or so up the dirt road to the west. It was too small to be a car, and as the dust rolled closer I realized what—or rather *who*—it was. I grumbled viciously under my breath and seriously considered whisking my breakfast inside and pretending not to be home. When you live ten miles from the nearest city limit, you aren't supposed to be a prisoner in your own home.

I ripped off a bite of my now soggy bagel and chewed furiously. My stomach had turned sour by the time I heard the annoyingly familiar sound of the rusty old bicycle chain clanging against its even rustier frame. King limped off the porch and greeted Robert J. Simmons with a wagging tail and a friendly bark. *Traitor,* I thought, glaring at King. But for Mitch's sake—and for Grant's—I forced myself to be civil. "Good morning, Robert J."

"Mornin' Mizz Keene," he muttered, gazing lazily at the sky. "Nice day, huh?"

Well, it was, I thought, draining my coffee mug. *Before you ruined it.*

"Mitch was just home last weekend, Robert J. He probably won't be back till school's out now."

"Yeah, he told me that." Robert J. stood at the bottom of the deck steps, unconsciously rubbing King's head with one hand, holding his kickstandless bicycle up with the other. His jeans were what the boys would have called flood pants, the hems ending just above the tops of his striped athletic socks. The lenses of his eyeglasses were smudged with I-didn't-want-to-know-what, and the earpiece on one side had been mended with black electrical tape. Dark, greasy hair sprouted every which way from his head and curled, unfashionably long, over his ears.

Mitch had befriended Robert J. when they were in junior high. Robert J. wasn't exactly retarded, but he wasn't the brightest bulb in the marquee either. Socially retarded was probably more accurate. Grant and I had been so proud of the way our youngest son had stood up for this social misfit against the other kids' cruelty. Of course Mitch had had to endure Robert J.'s undying loyalty ever since. After Mitch went off to college, Grant had taken Robert J. under his wing, letting him tag along while he did farm chores and sometimes letting him work on the old Chevy truck that was Grant's pride and joy.

"The kid's not as dumb as you'd think, Annie," Grant had told me more than once. "He's got a good mechanical mind. Shame he doesn't have much chance to put it to use." I'd tolerated Grant's little charity project but had drawn the line when he tried to get Robert J. involved on a repair job inside the house.

I hadn't counted on Robert J.'s loyalty transferring to me once Grant was gone and Mitch had headed back to college. It was not an inheritance I relished.

Now Robert J. stood, head down, still patting King, still holding up his bike. After three interminable minutes I picked up my breakfast dishes, hoping he'd take the hint. He didn't. Finally I said, "Well, thanks for stopping by. I'll tell Mitch you were here."

Robert J. nodded—and stood in his tracks.

I harrumphed louder than I intended and went into the kitchen and put my dishes to soak. When I came back out Robert J. hadn't budged. I couldn't bring myself to kick him off the farm, but I was determined not to let him ruin my day either. I had several projects lined up and he wasn't going to stop me.

I started toward the barn where I was planning to put together a plant stand to hold my flowers out on the deck. Grant had ordered the kit from a mail-order catalog, apparently a surprise for my birthday. UPS had delivered the box two weeks after Grant died. I was not handy with a tool kit, but I was determined that I was going to put this thing together if it killed me. And it just might. Though the blurb in the catalog promised "easy assembly," I'd been shocked to open the box and find no less than ten different wood pieces, assorted screws and bolts, and a list of instructions that might as well have been in Swahili. It had taken weeks to psych myself up for the task, but I'd awakened this morning feeling up to the challenge and had actually been looking forward to it. That is, until Robert J. had shown up.

I walked past him without speaking, but my jaw tightened as I heard him lean his bike against the deck and come after me. King trotted after both of us, panting happily. I looked over my shoulder and saw that she was smiling in the peculiar way of collies.

I opened the big sliding door at the end of the barn and wrestled an oversized slab of plywood onto two sawhorses to form a work surface. Robert J. stood and watched while I took the premeasured boards out of the packing box and smoothed out the instructions on my makeshift table. After I had stared vacantly at them for several minutes, the illustrations started to come into focus—like one of those computer-generated 'magic' pictures—and I began to see how these ten boards could, given time, become the attractive display piece pictured in the catalog.

Following the instructions, I anchored the bottom slat between the two boards that would form the sides of the shelves. I found the Phillips head screwdriver in Grant's toolbox, selected the screw pictured in the directions, and set to work.

Robert J. sniffed loudly and wiped his nose on the back of his hand. "Uh…you want some help?"

"No thanks, Robert J."

"I could hold the boards for you."

"No thanks," I repeated firmly. "I'm kind of looking forward to doing this on my own. It was a gift from Grant—for my birthday." At the words, I teared up unexpectedly and wondered why I felt I owed this intruder an explanation.

"Oh," Robert J. grunted.

After five minutes of blister-raising effort, I was still turning the first screw and it still protruded from the wood a good inch and a half. *If that idiot weren't standing there watching every move I make I probably wouldn't be having so much trouble.*

I kept turning the screwdriver, the resistance growing stronger with every twist of my wrist. "Surprised it ain't countersunk," Robert J. mumbled.

"Huh?"

"Surprised it ain't countersunk," he repeated in the same monotone.

"I don't even know what that means, Robert J.," I said politely through clenched teeth.

He picked up a small plastic packet of wood plugs from the pile of screws I'd lined up on the worktable and proceeded to explain. "Usually if they give you these plugs, the screws is countersunk."

That told me exactly nothing. I laid down the screwdriver and wiped the sweat off my forehead with the tail of my T-shirt.

Robert J. took a hesitant step forward. "I could turn it for a while. I'm pretty strong."

I was seething now and angrier yet that my conscience had begun to prick painfully. *Why should I feel guilty? Is it a crime to want a little peace and solitude on my own farm?*

"Do you want me to turn it for a while?"

"No, Robert J., I don't." I felt bad for the way that came out, especially when I saw him slink back a few steps.

I continued putting in screws, turning them until I couldn't turn any more, bad-mouthing under my breath the imbecile who'd packed screws in this kit that were half an inch too long.

Every so often I'd look over at Robert J. He watched me in silence, but I could tell by the way his hands twitched nervously that he was dying to get hold of my screwdriver.

I was being selfish; I knew that. I felt sorry for the kid, I truly did. The oldest of six children of an alcoholic father and a worn-down mother, Robert J. had had a rough life, no doubt about it. *But Lord*, I prayed, knowing suddenly where I needed to take my anger, *he's not my problem. And in case You hadn't noticed, I've had it a little rough lately myself.*

I pretended to pore over the instructions, but in truth I was praying—and confessing. *I was wrong, Lord. Forgive me.* And I thought I heard the Lord's voice in reply:

Robert J. needs to help you, Annie.

Okay, okay…I got it, loud and clear. I had a lot to be thankful for. This kid needed to be needed. Surely that was the least I could do for him.

"You thirsty, Robert J.?"

He nodded.

I held out the screwdriver. "Tell you what: You work with these screws for a minute, and I'll go make us some lemonade." I could always undo the damage later.

When I returned to the barn bearing two icy glasses of lemonade and a much-improved attitude, Robert J. was beaming. "Turns out they *was* countersunk, Mizz Keene," he crowed. "You had both them boards on there backwards! See? But don't worry. I fixed it."

I examined the beginnings of my plant stand and saw that each screw was now sunken neatly into a hole drilled just for that purpose, leaving an indention that would be nicely covered by the wood plugs provided in the plastic packet. *So much for idiots and imbeciles.*

That's when it hit me like a cyclone. I'd heard the Lord's voice all wrong. He hadn't said *Robert J. needs to help you.*

What He'd said was, *You need Robert J.'s help.*

My throat filled and I wanted to fall to my knees in humility—or on my face in humiliation. *I'm so sorry, Lord.*

But for Robert J.'s sake I simply said, "Well, I'll be, Robert J.! You're right. I should have let you have a go at it a long time ago."

His ear-to-ear grin was all the forgiveness I needed.

While I sipped lemonade in the shade, Robert J. built me the sturdiest plant stand I've ever owned. It sits out on the back deck to this day, and sometimes—when he's not too busy with the farm chores—Robert J. even helps me water the colorful geraniums and begonias that spill over the edges of its shelves.

The old adage may be true most of the time, but I have a sneaking suspicion that Grant is smiling to know that his last gift taught me that once in a while it is more blessed to receive than to give.

ABOUT THE AUTHOR

Deborah Raney's latest novel is *Beneath a Southern Sky* (WaterBrook Press). Her award-winning first novel, *A Vow to Cherish,* was the inspiration for World Wide Pictures' highly acclaimed film of the same title. Although "Prairie Lessons" is fiction, the story is based on a humbling lesson the Lord taught the author.

The oldest of five siblings, Deborah had a fairy-tale childhood growing up on a farm in Rice County, Kansas. The rural setting of this story is especially poignant for Deborah since her parents sold the family farm this year in order to move closer to their children. Deb and her husband, Ken, an illustrator and author, have four children and continue to make their home in the Sunflower State. Visit Deb's web site at www.deborahraney.com.

LONELY CHRISTMAS
IN CHICAGO

Lyn Cote

The Christmas morning sunshine glowed rosy through Jenna's closed eyelids. Its cheeriness made her want to pull the covers over her head and bawl.

Opening one eye, she read the bedside clock: 6:37 A.M. She groaned. "I've prayed and prayed I wouldn't have to spend Christmas alone," she said aloud to her empty flat. She waited, wishing some voice would reply.

When none did—of course—she gave herself a stern lecture. "I'm the one who decided to take a new job far from home only four weeks before Christmas. I knew I'd only get Christmas day off, so no crying now."

She gazed out her front window at the deserted city street below, so different from western Iowa. She stiffened her will against the images of home, the fields of dried, broken corn stalks, the wide front porch of the white farmhouse her grandfather and his brothers had built, and the open sky over the harvested prairie. She pictured her family rising soon and dressing for her home church's annual Christmas morning service. Last night over the phone, she'd wished everyone Merry Christmas and asked her mother not to call until the day after Christmas, already dreading the lonely holiday. She didn't think she could bear talking to family, hearing all their voices and the family holiday sounds in the background when she was so far away. She didn't want to spend Christ's birthday weeping in self-pity.

She rose and stepped close to the large window, the focal point of her second-story apartment. Across the street stood the old stone church, regal but a bit grimy—like a grand lady who'd aged and couldn't keep up the high standards of her youth. The city church was the complete opposite of the small, white prairie chapel she'd attended all her life.

"I should have started attending church by now," she scolded herself. But somehow going to a strange church during the holiday festivities had filled her with dread. She had felt too homesick to prompt bittersweet memories of Christmases past—a blond child trembling while lighting a purple advent candle, hot cocoa in the church basement after the caroling party, the children's nativity play. She'd missed everything— the sound of "Silent Night" being sung by their tiny choir, the scent of cinnamon candles, the red-cheeked faces.

She wrenched herself from her memories. "Six months from now I'll be settled in a new church family. I'll visit a church next Sunday." The digital clock unsympathetically registered 6:38 A.M.

She looked out the window. "Lord, thank You for Your wonderful birth. Though I'm alone today, let me somehow be a blessing to someone." Her daily prayer had been learned from a sampler her grandmother had cross-stitched in vivid gold and royal blue, "Make me a blessing to someone today." The prayer lifted her spirits enough to get her moving.

Taking a deep breath, she literally shook off the blues. She pulled on the loose-layered navy and white outfit she power-walked in each morning and let herself out quietly, not wishing to disturb the landlady and her husband downstairs. Outside in the chilling crystal air she started through the nearby park.

She'd fallen in love with this park at first sight, with its silent fountain and mature trees. The park beside the church was the old neighborhood's pride. The neighbors didn't wait for the Chicago Park District to keep it clean. They picked up the litter and called the police to rout any unsavory element that tried to gain a toehold. Jenna's landlady, who spoke with a strong Slavic accent, had told her, "You be safe in our park. Don't worry. Anybody gives you trouble, you run right to the grocery. Tell Martin, he'll call police."

Jenna smiled at the memory as she ran on the path between towering evergreens and old spreading oaks, which still clung to their dried brown leaves. A trace of snow lined the path. For days everyone had bemoaned the meager snow. Would Chicago have to endure a Christmas without a fresh frosting of snow on the rooftops?

An hour later she approached the church. Its recorded bells chimed eight times. In the holiday silence, an unexpected whimper stopped her.

She listened. The whimpering came again. She skirted some evergreens to the church steps. There against the bright red double doors sat a baby carrier, its high handle draped with a pink blanket. As if in a dream, Jenna lifted the blanket and peeked inside. A tiny, round, rosy face grinned up at her. Shocked, Jenna sat down on the top stone step, letting out an "Oof!"

The baby smiled, then flapped its mittened hands. Jenna tried to think. The infant appeared about a month old, spotless and healthy. Jenna felt around the baby for a note, but found only a disposable diaper and a small commercial bottle of formula. Her mind tried to make sense of this, but in vain. When she felt the below-freezing temperature nipping her cheeks and nose, she said, "I'd better get you in out of the cold."

Jenna lifted the baby carrier and conveyed it across the still barren street. Would anyone glance down from a flat above the old stores? Inside her warm apartment, she stripped off her jacket, unzipped the infant from her snowsuit, and pondered the situation. "A baby left at the church steps on Christmas morning. That only happens in movies," she whispered, still amazed. "I should call the police." But she made no move to pick up the phone by her bed. *What should I do, Lord? Why was this baby abandoned at the church?*

Jenna recalled a long-ago high school friend who had panicked when she thought she was pregnant. She'd come to Jenna's house weeping. Fortunately, Jenna's mom had heard the girl and had come in. Her mom's words and support had helped the friend tell her parents. A delighted, childless couple in the next town had adopted the baby.

Jenna traced the baby's round cheek. "Your mother has taken good care of you, little one."

Then Jenna remembered her older married sister slamming hysterically into their home after having her first baby. Jenna had been shocked and worried. Her sister had been ready to leave her husband, something Jenna hadn't been able to believe. But their mom had soothed her sister and then called the doctor. Mom and Jenna had visited Sis daily until she had begun acting like herself again. Mom had later explained post-partum blues to Jenna.

"Your poor mama," Jenna murmured. Obviously, some woman—probably young and unmarried—had panicked and deserted this sweet baby in a weak moment.

Jenna finally forced herself to the phone to dial the police. But she still couldn't make herself pick up the receiver. Instead she turned, looking back at the church. She picked up the soft baby. The scent of fresh baby powder filled her nose. "It won't hurt to wait an hour or so. If I call the police now and your mother comes right back for you, she'll be in worse trouble than she already is. She's probably already regretting what she's done." Peace and a kind of possessiveness settled over Jenna.

There was plenty of time to call the police. It wasn't as if she'd seen the mother and could give them a description. All they could do was call the Department of Family Services to take the child. The social workers could come a few hours later. How much better if the young woman sought help with the child, instead of facing charges or—having to live with guilt and regret. Maybe God was using Jenna to bless this poor mom with a second chance.

Patting the baby and humming "What Child Is This?" Jenna made herself a cup of tea, watching people arrive for services and then later leave. A firm, intuitive conviction grew within her: She should wait. Then a plan occurred to her.

Feeling as though God had whispered it to her, she smiled at the baby. "Everything's going to be all right. Your mom will be back soon. But if I got this wrong, I'll call the police then."

Before long, the baby, which Jenna had nicknamed Noelle, and she were fast friends. Keeping one eye on the church front, Jenna watched an old movie on TV, *Christmas in Connecticut*, with Barbara Stanwyck, one of her favorites. But soon the one diaper and small bottle were used up. Even though it was Christmas, she knew of a couple of neighborhood stores that would be open for a few hours.

Jenna bundled the baby up and hurried down the steps and outside. The street where she lived was where the neighborhood did its shopping and socializing. The quaint old storefronts included a laundry/dry cleaner, a watch repair and gift shop, a tavern, a corner grocer, a cafe, and a Slavonic Hall. Jenna had immediately felt a homey atmosphere in this corner of the large metropolis, the "city of big shoulders," that Sandburg had written about. And even though it wasn't a trendy address, after only a week she'd known that she'd made the right decision in moving above the watch repair shop. This area was like a cozy little town inside the big city.

With the baby carrier over one arm, she hurried into the corner grocery and selected formula and diapers. Turning quickly, she ran into another customer and dropped the diapers.

He stooped, picked up the soft diaper package and handed it to her. "Jenna?"

"Jack! Didn't you go to visit family?" It had never occurred to Jenna that she might meet someone from work while taking care of Noelle. On her very first day at the bank, where they both held officer positions, she'd noticed Jack Worth. He'd been the one who'd told her about the flat. Jack's handsome face had caught her eye, but his spontaneous smile had kept her shy interest.

"Where did this little one come from?" He tickled Noelle's chin.

Good question! "I'm just taking care of her for a neighbor for an hour or so." Though technically true, she felt a little guilty. If her hope didn't pan out, she would have to call the police soon. Nervously she glanced out the front window, keeping watch on the church steps.

Wishing Jack a Merry Christmas, she paid for the items and stepped outside. On the chill breeze, the scent of cinnamon rolls and coffee snared her. The café next door was open for breakfast for another hour, and she suddenly felt ravenous. Inside she took a booth, which gave her an unobstructed view of the church.

Jack appeared beside her. "Mind if I join you? It seems silly to sit in separate booths on Christmas morning."

Not really wanting his company with the baby on her mind, Jenna nodded anyway. He was right. She smiled at him. "I take it you don't have family nearby or vacation saved either?"

"Something like that." His face crinkled into a wry smile.

The cook's plump wife bustled over to take their orders. Along with a cinnamon roll and coffee, Jenna ordered scrambled eggs and bacon.

"Ditto." His eyes beamed at her. "I didn't know we had so much in common. How old is…?"

"Noelle. About a month."

"She looks a lot like you."

Jenna grinned. "We're just good friends." She changed the topic. "Where is your family?"

"Nebraska. This is my third move since college…"

Over breakfast, they chatted about work and Christmases past. Jenna bit into her roll. Melted butter ran down her chin. Reaching over, Jack caught it with his finger. Jenna held her breath. When he drew his hand away, he unexpectedly brushed the underside of her chin, making her blush.

Don't be silly. He's just a coworker.

But eating breakfast with Jack made the morning feel just a bit festive, and Jenna found herself smiling at him. Though her eyes kept straying to the church, she took her time eating. Jack seemed to be in no hurry either. He told her about his college years and how he'd chosen this ethnic neighborhood over an apartment downtown. A warm glow chased away her concern over Noelle.

Finally their last cup of coffee had been drained. The cook and his wife were shutting down. Jack stood. "I have to get going."

"Where?"

"I'm helping serve Christmas dinner at the Salvation Army nearby. If you didn't have to take care of the baby, I'd ask you to go with me."

"If I didn't have Noelle, I'd accept." She toyed with telling him the truth about Noelle, but instead tucked away the knowledge of his unexpected volunteer service, which spoke of compassion.

To Jack and Jenna's parting "Merry Christmas!" the cook and his wife wished them the same in Slovenian: *"Wiesela Boschna Prasnika!"* Jenna and Jack parted outside with smiles and friendly waves.

As she mounted her steps, she murmured, "I'm getting worried, Noelle. I'd hoped your mom would return by now."

Back in her apartment, Jenna went to the window, once again keeping vigil. She put on a CD, settling back to listen to the majestic strains of Handel's *Messiah*. Then she watched the 1936 version of *A Christmas Carol* with Leo G. Carroll as Marley's ghost. During all that time, no one approached the old church. The long shadows of the short winter afternoon lengthened. Feathery snowflakes floated down on the deserted street. Jenna's confidence waned.

I must have gotten things wrong. I'll have to call the police soon.

But she still couldn't pick up the receiver. She found herself doing something of a dance as she paced the apartment and occasionally approached the phone only to turn away from it.

At early winter twilight, a knock came. Jenna started up from her window seat. "Who is it?"

"Jack."

She opened the door and looked up at him.

"I decided to come...." He glanced at Noelle. "You still have the baby!"

"I found her this morning on the church steps," Jenna confessed miserably.

"What?"

"I'm just about to call the police."

"Why haven't you done that already?"

His words stung her conscience. "I hoped her mother would come back."

"But—"

"Wait! Is that someone in the shadows?" Jenna rushed to the window. "Someone's there!" Within seconds, she had her coat on and Noelle in her arms. Jack ran after her, asking questions with every footstep. Ignoring him, Jenna scurried across the silent street. For the first time that day, Noelle cried out.

"My baby!" The girl who'd been feverishly searching underneath the tall evergreens around the church snatched the baby from Jenna. Frantic words poured from her. "I kept listening to the radio, waiting to hear that someone had found her, that she was safe! But they never said anything! I've been so afraid some awful person snatched her before the church opened." Sobbing, she railed at Jenna, "Why didn't you call the police?"

Jack put his arm protectively around Jenna's shoulder.

Smiling, Jenna sagged against him with relief. She'd gotten it right after all. "I almost called them right away, but then I got a feeling I should wait and give you a chance to come back for her. Then I realized that if you loved her...." Jenna cleared her throat. "You'd have to come back if you thought she hadn't been found by the authorities. A good mother would return—if she thought her baby wasn't safe. I thought you'd be waiting to hear on the TV or radio." Jenna swallowed with difficulty. "I mean, a baby found on church steps on Christmas morning would be all over—"

The young woman exclaimed, "I couldn't make myself turn on the radio until afternoon. I was sure it would be on WBBM, the news station. I waited…and waited.…" The young woman broke off, sobbing.

"It sounds to me like the plan worked." Jack's arm tightened around Jenna.

The young woman, dressed in ragged jeans and a torn jacket, still gasped for breath between sobs. "I've just been so worried, frantic.…"

Jenna stepped close and put an arm around the girl. "You're fooling yourself if you think you wouldn't have been worried if the police had taken her to child welfare. You would have worried about her for the rest of your life."

"Jenna's right." Jack's voice softened. "Come with us."

"Where?" The young woman buried her tear-stained face in her baby's neck.

"To the Salvation Army," Jack replied in a kind voice. "We'll take you to the chaplain. Whatever your problem, he'll know what to do. If you still want to give up your baby, he'll help you. Then you'll know everything's been done right and you can be at peace about it."

"Please come with us." Jenna smoothed back the girl's tousled hair. "Noelle is too special to give up like this."

"Noelle?"

Jenna smiled. "That's what I've been calling her. Please, you panicked. That's all. You just needed time to change your mind."

Tears still streaming, the young woman nodded.

After taking the young mother and her baby to the chaplain and eating supper at the Salvation Army with her, Jack walked Jenna home through the silent streets. A lazy snow floated down around them. He walked with his arm around her and she didn't demur. His touch comforted her after the long, wearying day.

In front of the watch repair shop, he faced her, resting his hands on her shoulders. "I've got a secret to tell you."

"What?"

"I could have taken a few days and flown home, but I stayed around…because I knew you would be alone today."

"But you never said anything!"

"You never seem to notice me much at work—"

"You never seem to notice me!" Jenna couldn't help herself. She gave him a brilliant smile.

They stood staring at each other. The sound of "Silver Bells" played in a nearby apartment, and snowflakes collected in Jack's eyebrows. Jenna brushed them off gently.

"That girl and her baby will be all right now thanks to you."

Jenna shook her head. She put her faith into words, "God gave me a plan."

"He gave me something, too. Someone special to spend Christmas with."

Remembering her own prayers, Jenna drew in a sharp breath. *Thanks, Lord!* "Me, too."

"Do you ever play make-believe?" Jack asked impishly, leaning toward her.

Jenna's breath caught in her throat. She could only nod.

Jack held his hand over her head. "Make believe there's mistletoe." Closing his eyes, he bent and pressed his warm lips to hers.

Jenna closed her eyes, too. *Oh, Lord, when You answer a prayer, You don't kid around!*

ABOUT THE AUTHOR

Though Lyn Cote and her husband raised their son and daughter in Iowa, they themselves both grew up in Waukegan, Illinois, a suburb of Chicago. While Chicago overshadows its suburbs, the Big City itself possesses ethnic-rich neighborhoods, little towns within the metropolis— which Jenna discovers in "Lonely Christmas in Chicago." In true Chicago style, Cote wishes her readers *"Wiesela Boschna Prasnika!"* And with a nod to the late Harry Cary, Chicago's favorite baseball announcer, she adds, "Holy Cow!"

THE COWARD

Athol Dickson

Perfect love drives out fear.
1 JOHN 4:18

The boy stood on the catwalk of the water tower high above the Grand River valley and wished that he was dead. The silver cylinder at his back straddled Garrison Hill on four spidery legs like a spacecraft poised for takeoff. The moon was bright. He could clearly see the roof of his grandparents' imposing three-story home below, just a few hundred feet to the right. Their house had turned a century old that summer, the summer the boy turned thirteen.

In the days when Oklahoma was an Indian Territory their house had been the officer's quarters of old Fort Gibson, a famous jumping-off point to the American West. Washington Irving had camped within shouting distance before departing civilization with a Frenchman in the 1820's, knowing the land toward California was alive with Comanche but going anyway, living life. Sam Houston also lived at Fort Gibson once upon a time. Disenchanted with Eastern society and a shrewish blue-blooded bride, he took to drink and a common law marriage with a Cherokee woman. They called him Big Drunk, but Sam Houston went down from Fort Gibson a few years later and took Texas from Santa Ana.

The boy knew these things because, like his grandfather, he was a student of history. He thought about Washington Irving and Sam Houston often. He wondered if people would remember his own act of bravery someday. Maybe they would say, *That boy climbed the water tower. Only thirteen, and he climbed it all alone.*

From up on the catwalk he looked further away, down toward the river where the Works Progress Administration had erected a replica of the first fort. It was the stockade of his schoolboy dreams: a four-square log structure standing where the original fort had been, with blockhouses on two corners, firing slots for rifles, wide wooden gates, and a parade ground on the interior containing a covered water well and a pair of stocks for the punishment of thieves and laggards…

And cowards.

If folks knew the truth, they would say, *That boy? Ain't he the one climbed the water tower and got too scared to climb back down? Stood up there all night long.*

History kept the boy from thinking about what he was.

Down on the Grand River, the moon's reflection rippled near the old fort site. The boy thought about malaria forcing the soldiers up the hill, where they built a different kind of fort. By then the Indian troubles were almost over. The five Civilized Tribes had adjusted to this green country at the end of their Trail of Tears, farming it, raising cattle on it, building homes of wood upon it with columned front porches and wide friezes in the Greek revival style. They had even elected their chiefs with blind ballots—the white man's way—and sent them off to lobby Congress.

Military duty at Fort Gibson became more a matter of politics than defense, so the second fort was built with comfort in mind. On the hill above the river's buzzing cloud of mosquitoes, the officer's quarters were erected, with limestone walls a foot and a half thick, imposing walnut staircases, a ballroom, four chimneys, twelve fireplaces, and a widow's walk high up on the ridge of the roof. From up there they said you could see row after row of long, blue hills rolling toward the Ozarks like frozen tidal waves. But the boy had to rely on other people's descriptions of the glorious view, because of his disgrace.

It had happened just that morning. A shaft of light boring down through the open hatch had pinned him starkly in place upon the ladder as darkness whispered accusations from unseen corners of the attic with breath that reeked of dust and very old things. His grandfather stood above him on the widow's walk, smiling down, his face framed by the deep blue sky and racing clouds, his wide polka-dotted tie fluttering in the breeze.

His grandfather's world was mythical in proportion. The old man told stories of ancient Indian burial grounds in the grove by the fence along the pasture. He took the boy fishing on Corral Branch, that magical stream where clear water gently rippled over a flat rock bed, wide and staggered down slab on slab, like giant stair steps. In his grandfather's world, each underwater crack in the stone became a hiding place for arrowheads, each hole in the bluffs above them a lost gold mine.

The boy loved the way his grandfather whispered to the fish, inviting them to bite. He loved the way his grandfather laughed—a gravelly sound that rumbled around in his big belly and erupted contagiously into the Oklahoma air.

His grandfather had flown in machines of wood and cloth during the First World War. He had once landed on Wrigley Field in Chicago in a stunt designed to get young men to enlist and fight the Kaiser—a very dangerous thing to do, brimming with bravado. Standing astride a widow's walk fifty feet above the ground was nothing for such a man. He had found his place in history long ago.

"Come on, son. Just a few more steps."

"I can't."

"Don't be afraid. There's a good solid railing up here."

"I can't."

The boy remembered gripping the stringers of the ladder like his fingers were forged of steel. Although he badly wanted to move, he had been stuck ten feet above the attic floor, five feet below the hatch to the widow's walk. When he looked up again, a crow had flown across the patch of sky just above his grandfather's head, and the boy had known that only birds belonged in such high places…birds, and brave men like his grandfather.

"All right," said the old man. "Go on back down."

Again, he had willed his hands to move. They would not.

"Go ahead, son," said his grandfather.

"I can't."

"You'll be fine. Just do it one step at a time and don't look down."

As much as the boy loved his grandfather, he had not trusted the old man enough. In the end, his grandfather had called to the family gathered at the annual reunion on the fieldstone patio far below, and the boy's father had come up to help. He too had been a soldier, a sergeant in the infantry at Omaha Beach. He wore lace-up boots and a flat-top haircut, and he preached every Sunday at the Baptist church in the small Texas town where they lived and he broke horses during the week for money.

His father climbed the ladder until he stood just below the boy, ready to catch him if he fell.

"All right," he said. "I've got you now."

The rest of the day had been a humiliating progression of aunts and female cousins clicking their tongues and petting him as if he were a soft little animal, assuring him that *they* would never go up on the widow's walk. The male cousins had flung barbed remarks whenever the grown-ups weren't listening. *Sissy. Scaredy-cat. Girl.*

Now, up on the water tower in the middle of the night, the catwalk railing shivered in the boy's hands. He heard a low flutter, the sound of his shirttail luffing like a sail in the stiff breeze. He told himself it was the wind that brought these tears to his eyes. He wondered what would happen next. The boy could think of only two possibilities. He could stay there until the sun came up, then call for help, allowing everyone to know he had done it again.

Or he could simply jump and get it over with.

The boy longed to join the ranks of Washington Irving and Sam Houston and his grandfather and father. After the widow's walk disgrace, he had known his only means of redemption lay in doing something brave. He had come to this decision while lying in his bed, tucked beneath the third-floor eave of his grandfather's house, just a few feet away from the attic steps. There had been some consideration of climbing up to the widow's walk, but his parents were sleeping nearby and would surely hear him in the attic. The boy did not want to make them angry. On the other hand, he needed everyone to know what he had done; otherwise, what was the point? And whatever he did, it must involve something tall, something like the widow's walk.

That was when he had thought of the bad word on the water tower.

The boy had dressed in the dark and slipped down the stairs, careful to step close to the wall so the treads and risers would not squeak. Outside he had run barefoot across the grass to the old summerhouse. A minute later he had emerged from that building with a bucket of white paint and a brush, then slipped back across the yard to the water tower.

It had loomed over him, pale in the moon's reflected light. Away up on its side, someone had painted the bad word in tall black letters. The boy remembered the grownups talking about it. The word had made his grandfather angry every time he looked up in the air. The boy remembered his grandfather standing in his front yard, shouting up at the bad word and shaking his fist, as if the water tower could hear him. Nobody else paid any attention. His grandfather often did strange things like that. "Get down off of there!" he shouted.

The old man did not want his family to see such words.

Remembering that, the boy had climbed the chain link fence around the water tower's base. It had been frightening and hard to do while holding the bucket, and the wire had hurt his naked toes. On the other side he had run to the closest leg of the tower, which was built of steel bars welded together in a crisscross pattern. A ladder had been fastened to the water tower leg. It would be like climbing through the attic to the widow's walk, except twenty times taller. The boy had slipped his foot onto the lowest bar. The steel had been warm to the touch, having soaked up heat throughout the August day. Grabbing another bar higher up with his free hand, he had lifted himself onto the leg of the water tower. He remembered what his grandfather had told him on the widow's walk ladder; he did not look down.

Halfway up, when the boy felt fear beginning to take control, he had become a soldier in Coronado's exploration party, scaling a tall pine to get the lay of the land. A little further and he had been a Cherokee brave, climbing a sheer rock face to watch for invading horse soldiers. Near the top, one hundred feet in the air, he had been his grandfather, soaring in a biplane high above the French trenches. And when he had reached the top, the boy was certain he had climbed into his own place in history at last.

It had taken longer than he expected to paint over the bad word. From the ground, the letters had not looked so large. When he was done the paint was almost all used up, so he threw the empty bucket over the side.

That had been his only mistake.

A sudden gust of wind had caught the bucket on the way down, carrying it several yards out away from the tower base. It seemed to hang in midair for a moment. The boy held his breath and watched as the wind actually lifted the bucket upward a foot or two. Then, suddenly, the air itself seemed to change, becoming a malevolent thing, bent upon destruction. The boy felt a chill as the bucket plummeted to the earth, hitting bottom with a loud bang.

He had stared down in shock. The bucket had been utterly flattened by the impact. A small trickle of white paint flowed from its horribly mangled mouth.

Since that moment, the boy had known he could not climb down.

Even when the wind carried clouds across the stars and moon, even when it began to rain in the slow, steady, straight-down way it rained in Oklahoma in the summertime, the boy remained at the catwalk railing, high above the valley, waiting. Slowly, the eastern horizon had begun to dimly glow. Soon now, the sun would rise beyond the clouds…and he would still be up on the water tower, unable to release the railing, even to wipe the rainwater from his eyes.

The gentle downpour became a drizzle and then stopped altogether. Almost immediately, as if he had been waiting for a dry opportunity, the boy's grandfather appeared down below in housecoat and slippers. *Don't look up,* thought the boy. The old man crossed the yard and knelt to pick up his morning newspaper beside the road. *Don't look up.* His grandfather seemed to hesitate, still kneeling. *Oh, please, don't look up!*

Then his grandfather did a strange thing. Slowly, in little jerky motions, he dropped to the wet ground, face up, with his feet together toward the water tower and his head toward the rising sun. It was impossible to tell for sure from so far up, but the boy thought the old man's eyes were closed. He could see his grandfather's hands clasped together over his chest. Was he clutching at his heart? The boy could not be sure.

What if it was a heart attack? What if he was dying?

The boy filled his lungs to call down, but at the last instant he stopped. *If I call, everyone will know…* He let a few more seconds pass by, watching the old man on the ground. His grandfather did not move. *I can't just stand here.* And so he screamed, loud and long, but the old man did not move, and no one came outside the house. The boy screamed again, with no response. He thought about the wind lifting the bucket a foot or two. Maybe it was lifting his voice like that, carrying it away from the ground, while down below his grandfather's hands were still laced together over his heart.

The boy looked toward the water tower ladder. He looked back toward his grandfather. He looked back at the ladder. Slowly he moved his right hand to the side, slipping it along, fingers still encircling the rail. Then he moved his right foot, sliding the bare sole across the wet metal catwalk until he stood with legs spread wide apart. Next he moved his left hand along the railing, not letting go, but getting it close to his right. Finally he slid his other foot across the catwalk, and now he stood two feet closer to the water tower ladder. Moving his right hand again, he began to the repeat the process, and in this way he inched along the catwalk without releasing the railing until he reached the place just above the ladder. There he froze again.

Down below, his grandfather had not moved at all.

"Oh, God, please help me," whispered the boy, and ever so slowly he began to bend his knees. Both hands remained firmly wrapped around the railing as he sank beside it on the catwalk, until he was squatting there, head below his upraised hands, peering beneath the railing.

Still his grandfather had not moved.

He inched his right foot forward, slipped it out along the metal deck until his toes hung over the edge. Without warning and against his will, he sobbed aloud. But he pushed his foot out further. Now his leg was straight, with his foot and lower calf out in midair. Shifting his weight, he did the same thing with his other leg until he sat upon the deck with both legs straight in front, hanging over the edge, and both hands still gripping the railing up above his head. "God," he whispered. "Please."

Shaking from the fear of it, the boy released the rail and slid out off the catwalk.

Ten minutes later, standing on the ground, the boy looked back along the water tower leg, shooting straight up toward the dawn, tapering as it went until the sides of it came together in perspective, far away. Forgetting his grandfather just for a moment, the boy laughed out loud, even though the rain had washed the paint off of the bad word, and with it, all proof of what he had done.

Then, remembering, he ran to the fence and climbed it and leapt to the ground from the very top, unafraid for himself. He dashed across the road to kneel at his unmoving grandfather's side.

"Grandfather! Are you all right?"

"I am now," said the old man, rising easily.

And without another glance at the water tower, the two of them walked toward the house that had once been part of old Fort Gibson, a famous jumping-off place for historic deeds, brimming with bravado.

ABOUT THE AUTHOR

Athol Dickson is the author of two published novels, *Whom Shall I Fear?* and *Every Hidden Thing*. A third novel, tentatively entitled *They Shall See God*, will be released soon. The *New York Times* Sunday magazine wrote the following about *Whom Shall I Fear:* "Readers get moonshine, a crooked sheriff, and a redneck crucifixion scene that would put Flannery O'Connor to shame." *Library Journal* wrote: "Novels such as this are willing to explore realistic issues while also offering readers a sense of hope…"

AUNT PERT'S FOLLY

Lois Richer

Annie Pert took one look at the Victorian monstrosity some distant relative had named Pert's Folly and prayed as she never had before.

Oh, dear Father, I've lost my mind. Moving to Hasten, North Dakota, was clearly the decision of a crackpot. Sure, she was a woman of the new millennium and all that, but buying this dump suddenly seemed all the proof anyone could possibly need to call the whitecoats. *Please, God, let this be just a bad dream.*

"Uh, 'scuse me. You okay?"

Annie whirled around. Unfortunately, her ankle-length skirt didn't follow. It snagged on what had once been a white picket fence and resolutely refused to move. Annie grabbed a handful of the offending material and tried to free herself without tearing the blue-sprigged cotton.

"More like a nightmare, Lord," she muttered, her fingers working against the death grip of a rusty nail. "You could wake me up anytime now, preferably *before* the shock treatments."

"You'll wreck it pulling like that." A big brown paw closed over hers and squeezed, halting the frustrated activity of her useless fingers. "What's your hurry, anyway? You see a fire somewhere? Slow down, take your time."

Annie peered up into the soft brown eyes of what first appeared to be a bear. His face was barely visible beneath a thatch of bristly brown hair. Not a bear—Grizzly Adams, she corrected herself.

"I'm Deken Jones. Just stand still and we'll have this fixed in a jiffy."
His friendly grin parted the overgrown mustache from the brown bush
of scraggly beard covering the bottom half of his face.

Annie gulped. With a smile like that, Deken Jones would make more
in Hollywood than on the back forty.

"There we go. Good as new." He let her skirt go. Annie figured his
burly frame stood at well over six feet. He frowned down at her.
"Something wrong?"

"Uh, no. Not at all." She gulped again. Now he would think she was
nuts! "I'm Annie Pert. I just bought that—that thing." She jerked a
thumb over her shoulder toward the tumbledown Victorian house.

Jones frowned. He turned, gave the structure a once-over, shook his
head, then switched his gaze back to her. "Just one question: why?"

Annie bristled. "To live in, of course. To run my business from. Why
else?"

He held up both hands as if to stem her tirade. "Fine by me."

Annie was getting tired of this. Clearly the man had something to
say. Why didn't he just come out with it? "Is there a problem?" She
glared at him.

"Is there *a* problem? As in just one?" He burst out laughing—a laugh
that crumpled up what she could see of his face and sent his shoulders
shaking. "Yeah, just a tiny one or two—*thousand,* that is." He broke out
in delighted glee again.

How dare he? She wasn't going to stand there and be laughed at by
some—some gorilla! She already knew she'd messed up buying the
place sight unseen. Trusting the realtor to tell the truth had been a mistake. All right. Annie got that. But she didn't need some Neanderthal he-
man from Sticksville rubbing salt in her wounds.

"Good-bye, Mr. Jones." Annie swept her eyes over his burly body
once, raised an eyebrow at the tattered coveralls he wore, and gave him
her deep-freeze look.

The laughter stopped. "Hey, I'm sorry, okay. I shouldn't have
laughed." One hand found a strategic place on her forearm and
squeezed, halting her departure.

Annie glanced at the hand and tilted one perfectly arched eyebrow
until it dropped away. The she turned her back on him. Except she
couldn't leave. Her foot was stuck. *Nightmare* wasn't the word for this day.

"Can we start again? I promise I'm not the jerk you probably think I am. Actually, I'm a carpenter."

Understanding dawned. Annie's eyes narrowed.

"Softening me up for a nice high bid, no doubt." She wiggled her heel to free it from the crack in the sidewalk. "Trying to make me believe I need a total revamp, which would line your pockets for the next few years, maybe?"

The light drained out of his eyes, his hands tightened by his side, and his whole body seemed to go still. "Where are you from, Miss Annie Pert?"

"My last residence was Chicago, but I was actually born in this house," she informed him, nose in the air. "Why?"

"Well, in Shee-Caw-Go maybe everyone is out to get you. That is not the case here."

His exaggerated drawling of the city's name was her first clue that Deken Jones no longer found her amusing. He glanced down at her wiggling foot, then returned his piercing gaze to her face. Annie shifted uncomfortably.

"Homer and Pete at the hardware store told me you were moving in today. They asked if I'd make sure the place was safe first. They're the boys who sold the place." He frowned as she shifted once more. "You're going to break that shoe." He tugged a hammer out of his back pocket, hunkered down and rapped firmly against the back of her heel.

One second Annie was imprisoned, the next moment her foot slipped free of its hold and would have sent her toppling into a patch of prickly sow thistle if he hadn't grabbed her.

"Th-thank you," Annie managed, easing herself away. Her nose twitched. Cedar? She loved cedar. "And I'm sorry." Her cheeks burned. "I had no right to say those things to you. No right at all. I'm afraid I'm a little, er, surprised by the condition of the place."

He nodded, good humor restored in his friendly smile. "I'll bet the agent sent you pictures of this house. Ronald Brown is like that, not always truthful. He's from the city."

From the city. Apparently, that one description said it all in Deken Jones' mind.

"Don't matter if it's 2001 or 1901, folks in Hasten don't try to trick anyone. There's not much point. Everybody knows everybody else, and the guy you mess with today is the guy you need to help you tomorrow.

It's better to treat people like you want to be treated."

Annie blushed and looked away. Talk about making a first impression!

"So, Miss Pert, do you want me to go in and take a look, or would you rather handle that yourself?"

He was giving her a second chance.

"I'd like it very much if you would inspect the house and give me a list of what needs doing," she told him quietly. "I don't know whether or not I can afford it all, but at least I should be aware of the priorities." She dug a notepad and a pen from her bag. "I'm ready."

Deken nodded. He shoved open the gate and blinked when it fell to the ground. His eyes met hers. "Item one, Miss Pert. Fix gate."

Annie couldn't help it; she burst out laughing. And she kept laughing as he led her through the house room by room. It was either laugh or bawl her eyes out.

"There doesn't seem to be a single room that doesn't require extensive work." She glared at the faded plaster, wobbly woodwork, and dangerously dangling chandeliers. "I don't know where to start!"

"Well, you mentioned your business. Why don't you start there?" He thrust his hands in his pockets, leaned back against the only piece of oak paneling that didn't need repair, and waited.

"I'm an artist. I illustrate children's books. Perhaps you've heard of them—the Mrs. Biddle books?" He shook his head; obviously, he wasn't familiar with children's literature. "Never mind."

Annie took another look around and wished she hadn't. How could she possibly live in this place and meet her deadline for next month? The plumbing dated from the dark ages!

"Drawing probably means you want lots of light and space to lay out your drawing equipment. Best place for that'll be the top floor. It's got a great view of the park and the river and lots of windows. Also needs the least amount of work once the roof is fixed."

Was it really so easy to retile turrets and towers and replace gingerbread trim with bites out of it?

"H-how much is that going to cost?" Annie held her breath, watching his face as he mentally conducted whatever mathematical manipulations were needed. The figure, when he said it, sounded very reasonable to her. "Okay. I can do that." She let out her breath. "What next?"

"Kitchen. If you intend to live here—?" He waited until she nodded.

"Okay, then, you need to get it working. It'll be expensive. The cabinets are oak and will just take time to scrape and refinish, but the floor's rotten." He went on describing the room's all-too-numerous problems.

Annie stood there listening, marveling at the depth of Deken's knowledge about Victorian-style buildings. "Are you some kind of a restoration expert?"

He shrugged. "I worked on a lot of older homes when I apprenticed in San Francisco. Comes in handy sometimes."

"Why would you move from San Francisco to Hasten?"

"My dad was sick; he needed help. After he died, I'd become part of the place. The people are great, there's steady work, and I like knowing I won't get mugged if I take a walk at night. Besides…" He glanced at her sideways, hesitating.

"Besides what? Did something else make up your mind?"

Deken nodded. "Yeah. I guess you could say I stayed mostly because of the church." He grinned at her curious look around the neighborhood. "No, not the building. It's more the people who inhabit the church. They made me really dig to know what I believe, to understand what Christ was about."

Annie wanted to ask more, but the words stilled on her lips as the tired front door creaked open and three elderly ladies peered inside.

"Helloooooooo!" Their voices echoed around the circular staircase to the floors above. "Anyone home?" They stepped inside and smiled at Annie. "Oh, there you are. How nice to meet you, dear. Howard said you'd be arriving today."

They tumbled into the house like eager children. Each lady carried an object wrapped in a white tea towel. Annie's stomach rumbled at the delicious odors that wafted to her as they set their gifts down on a dilapidated old table. She could only blink in shock when they enveloped her in three lilac-scented hugs.

"I'm Esther, this is Nona, and this is Tiny. We live across the street, dear." The speaker had pure white hair, dancing blue eyes, and a smile that warmed Annie to the soles of her feet. "It's almost lunchtime and I know you must be hungry. Young people always are."

Young? Twenty-seven was young?

"We're so glad you're here." The woman called Nona stepped forward and pointed to the dishes. "We've brought roast chicken, a salad, fresh bread, and boiled carrots."

"I brought some blueberry pie." Tiny giggled as she waddled forward and stood on her tiptoes to pull Deken's ear. "This boy just loves my blueberry pie."

Annie stifled her laughter with difficulty. Deken's face was a mixture of comic dismay and little-boy innocence. She wanted to paint him for the book—Harvey Hedgehog with all those bristles.

"This is so kind of you." Annie tore her gaze from Deken and smiled at the old girls. It had been so long since someone had cooked for her— and way too long between hugs. *Thank you* hardly seemed enough. "You went to so much trouble. I don't know how I'll ever repay you."

"Nonsense! We'll find a way. Just you wait." Esther winked, her chipmunk cheeks grinning.

"They will, too," Deken whispered loudly, his voice brimming with laughter. "These three ladies can charm the socks off of just about anyone with their cooking."

"Hush up, boy. Don't you be telling tales out of school." Tiny took one look at the mess, made a face, then marched up to stand directly in front of him. She wagged one finger over his nose, which was just about as far as she could reach.

"You've hardly gotten anything done, Deken. The place is a mess. Don't tell me those boys sold the place in this condition?" She clucked in irritation. "Old coots should have married years ago. Good thing they're at that home where a woman can keep 'em in line." She turned to her two friends. "Come on, girls. Housecleaning party."

They nodded, then turned and raced one another to the door.

"Oh, please, you don't have to do that." Annie worried about the determination she saw in Nona's eyes. "Really, it's too much. I don't expect you to—"

"I thought she was a painter or something. Aren't artists supposed to be the quiet type?" Esther glanced at Deken for confirmation. Then she abandoned her post as leader and walked back to pat Annie's arm. "Honey, you've got a big job ahead of you and not a lick is gonna get done until this place is cleaned up. We've waited a long time to see this old girl shine again and we'd like to have just a little part in making that happen."

"But…you'll wear yourselves out!" It was the nicest way Annie could think to tell them that they were too old to be shoveling the debris she'd just purchased.

"Of course we won't. We'll supervise." Nona pulled a cell phone out of her pocket and waved it. "I can speed dial a dump truck in a jiffy, if we need it." She pointed toward the food. "You two get your lunches eaten. By one o'clock we'll have a team firmly in place."

And having issued her edict, she hurried the others out the door and down the stairs.

"Don't worry. They're only trying to help. They'll do anything for a party." Deken lifted the covers on the dishes, sniffed, and grinned. "I'm pretty hungry. How about you?"

Annie was starved. They carried everything out to the back patio and placed it on a tarp Deken had spread out over the stones.

"I hope spring comes soon," Annie muttered, leaning back with her coffee, replete from the delicious food. "The air feels warm but it doesn't look like spring."

"Don't fuss. It's on its way. Just looks a little bleak until the leaves start. You want any more pie?"

Annie shook her head, but couldn't help staring as he served himself the last of the scrumptious dessert. It was his fourth piece. He caught her looking and laughed.

"Hey, there's a lot of me to feed. Besides, I don't get pie like this every day."

She realized that she knew nothing about him. "Doesn't your wife bake?" It was an obvious ploy, but how else did one go about finding out personal details?

"My wife?" Deken shrugged. "I don't know."

"You don't know?" Annie stared. "What do you mean you don't know? How can you not know if your own wife bakes?" There were some odd characters in this town, no doubt about it. Even odder marriages, from the sounds of it. And some people thought Chicago had problems!

"I don't know if she bakes or not. I haven't found her yet." Deken continued eating as if that problem didn't particularly bother him one way or the other.

Haven't found—? Annie rolled her eyes as his meaning suddenly became clear. "I see. Do you have other family around here?"

Deken licked the purple juice from his lips with a delighted smack that needed no explanation. His fork shrieked across the plate, hunting down the last delectable morsel. When his eyes finally met hers, a strange glimmer glowed in their chocolate depths.

"My sister moved away after high school. She lives in Minneapolis with her husband and kids. My brother is a foreman on the oil rigs in Texas. I'm twenty-nine, six foot three, two hundred and forty-five pounds. I run my own carpentry business, pay off my loans on time, and live in a little house on the other side of town. Oh, and I drive a red half-ton that's ten years old." He put his plate in a bag with the other dirty dishes, then straightened to his full height. "Anything else?"

Annie bristled. "I wasn't prying."

"Sure you were." He grinned. "Everybody in this town pries. You get used to it after a while. Thing is, you could have just waited. Your neighbors would have filled you in about me—and everybody else—before the day was out."

At least he didn't sound offended. Annie swallowed the last of her coffee and handed over the cup. "I suppose now you think I should reciprocate," she muttered as she got to her feet.

"If you want."

"I don't." No way was she discussing her desire for a family.

"Fine." He seemed more interested in the sagging back porch than any answer she might have. Annie felt a twinge of hurt that he wasn't curious about her and then lectured herself for being silly.

"Annie Marie Pert. You were born here when your mother came to visit her mother around twenty-seven years ago. They quarreled; your mother left and never returned. Your grandmother sold the house to 'the boys' and moved into a nursing home in Grand Forks." Deken folded the tarp methodically as he spoke. "You attended school in Detroit, L.A., Miami, and a couple of other places. College was at some fancy place. Your mother died five years ago. You never knew your father. You just signed some big deal with the Tabor company and your fiancé took off with another woman. Did I miss anything?"

He stared down at her from his superior height and waited.

"Yes! I wear a size eight shoe and pick my teeth with straw from a corn broom, if anyone's taking notes," Annie sputtered indignantly.

"Uh-huh." He picked up the empty dishes, the tarp, and the thermos that held the coffee and loped toward the house. "Want to get back to work now?"

"Ooh!" There was nothing to do but follow his broad back. But as she did, Annie decided that Hasten, North Dakota, was in for a change.

What right did the people in this town have to pick and probe through her life as if it were some kind of specimen? What right did they have to know all these personal details, information she might have wished to keep confidential? Nobody was going to snoop into her life, speculate on her lack of relatives, or anything else. She was a private person, and she simply would not tolerate snooping from the locals.

That thought was thrust out of her brain at the sight of the chattering crowd that now filled her living room. Men and women stood holding mops, pails, paper towels, rags of all descriptions, and a vast array of cleaning products, waiting for directions.

"What is the entire town doing in my house?" she whispered from behind Deken's back. He simply stepped aside.

"Thought we'd lend a hand getting your place shipshape." Tiny bustled forward and began ordering the dispersal of the troops, dishing out the appropriate equipment as she spoke.

Annie watched, her mouth hanging open, as the hum of helpers filled the old house. She grabbed Deken's arm. "I can't afford to pay all these people," she hissed, beseeching him with her eyes. "It'll break me. How do I get them to go?"

"I s'pose you could just ask them, but that'd kind of defeat the purpose." He took pity on her confusion. One finger brushed a cobweb from her cheek. "They don't want to be paid, Annie. Think of it as a housewarming. They're glad you're here and this is how they say welcome. It's a gift; all you have to do is accept it."

"Deken, you get yourself out on that roof! Carter Prescott insists on doing some repairs and he won't wait." Nona turned to Annie and winked. "Problem is, there'll be more to repair when Carter's done. Hammering just isn't his forte." She bustled out to the kitchen, mumbling all the while.

"Mercy! Child, you can't wear that to houseclean! Let's pop over to Maynelle's and see if she's got something she can lend you." Tiny took possession of Annie's arm and tugged.

Now they were picking apart her clothes? Annie stopped their forward motion by digging her heels into the only bit of carpet that still retained any nap.

"Actually, I have work clothes in my car, Mrs.—er, Tiny. But I'm not really comfortable with this—this invasion. It just doesn't seem right to take these people away from their own work." Godly tact was a lot more difficult than she'd thought.

Tiny frowned. "Doesn't seem right?" A hint of dismay washed over her face. "Of *course* it's right. The good Lord said a body should love her neighbor just like herself and folks in these parts try to obey God." She studied Annie for a moment, then let her hand drop away from the arm she still clung to.

"Of course, if you don't want us here, we certainly wouldn't want to *invade* your private life. We respect privacy, same as folks in your big cities do." Her fingers knotted together. "I'm very sorry we intruded."

Annie watched Tiny's thin shoulders slump, her plump cheeks lose their color, and her eyes dull as the animation drained away.

"I'll get everyone out of your way right now," she offered quietly. "I'm really very sorry I butted in. I should have asked first."

Feeling like a miserable party pooper, but knowing she had to set the parameters for future visits, Annie followed the old lady out into the foyer. Her eyes widened when Tiny's wrinkled mouth emitted a piercing whistle. Suddenly the laughter from upstairs stopped, and the chatter of young mothers comparing notes faltered to a halt. Even the men on the roof stopped their pounding.

"Folks, I'm afraid there's been a mistake." Tiny's voice wobbled to a stop, her eyes meeting Annie's once more. The hurt and the rebuff were as plain as the sadness that covered her tired face. Her joy had been stolen.

"What's the matter, Tiny? You forget to put the coffee on?" Laughter bubbled down the stairs, percolating through the cheerful grins and sparkling eyes of Annie's new neighbors.

Except for Deken. He stood at the top of the stairs and peered directly into Annie's eyes, asking a question: *Why did you come here?*

Suddenly, like a gull swooping down to grab a fish, Annie understood. These people could become the family she sought. There were no strings; they weren't busybodies looking for a thrill. They wanted to be friends. They wanted to include her in their circle, to let her know that they were there for her, even down to the dirty job of cleaning this house.

They asked nothing in return, only that she accept their friendship. How could she refuse such a gift?

"Well, out with it, Tiny. We haven't got all day to be lollygagging around." Nervous laughter spilled out as the silence stretched ominously through the rooms.

"You see, the thing is, I made a mistake." Tiny's double chin quivered as she spoke.

"You?" "Don't believe it for a minute!" "Never happen."

"But I did, Horace. And it was a bad one. I hope none of you will hold it against me." Her voice whispered to a halt. She gulped.

Love one another. How many times had Annie printed those words while brainstorming illustration ideas for *Mrs. Biddle's Birthday Blast*? And now, as she looked around, she saw exactly how the sketches should be.

Buying Pert's Folly a mistake? Not hardly. This was a God thing.

Annie took a deep breath, stepped forward, and grinned at the group.

"Actually, Tiny made two mistakes. The first was sending over those three extra pieces of pie and not warning me first. Deken ate them all." Laughter and good-natured teasing followed. Annie waited until most of it had died away; then she took a deep breath, her gaze moving from Tiny's tear-filled eyes to Deken's approving ones.

"Tiny's second mistake was not letting me tell you how very much I appreciate your kindness. I've never lived in a small town, never known neighbors like you. I'll probably make a lot of mistakes while getting to know you. I hope that doesn't ruin the friendship I'd like to have with each one of you."

They called out their denials in firm, assured voices. Annie felt a blanket of peace settle over her heart. Pert's Folly was a blessing, not a curse. It was God's way of teaching her how to put His words into deeds. She was finally home.

"By the way," she called, grinning for all she was worth, "my name is Annie Pert and you're all welcome to visit me any time you want. I think it's high time this house got a life!"

Annie moved toward Tiny, her heart bursting with love for the sweet woman. But instead of a hug, her head connected with a brass fixture and the hundreds of dangling crystals that were part of the elaborate chandelier. The entire group tried to smother their giggles. Annie didn't mind.

"One little thing I forgot to mention," she told them, rubbing her bruised temple with one hand. She grinned at Deken's shaking head. "I'm a klutz. Will that make a difference?"

"Not a bit, honey. Not one single bit." And dear sweet Tiny wrapped her in the kind of hug Annie had longed for for years.

ABOUT THE AUTHOR

The local butcher shoveling their sidewalk, tea parties with a teacher who loved kids, all the peas she could pick when there was no garden at home…those are just a few of Lois Richer's small-town memories. Neighbors are necessities on the prairie. Blizzards, forest fires, floods—battling such things takes a community. Neighborhoods change, but neighboring never does. Says Richer, "So many hearts long for someone to listen, to share, to love. So who is my neighbor? Come on over for coffee. Blueberry pie's gone, but I promise we'll talk."

Richer's nine novels include *Stained with Love* and *Blessed Baby* (Love Inspired).

THE SMELL OF
GREEN APPLES

Nancy Moser

*Let us hold unswervingly to the hope we profess, for he who
promised is faithful.*
HEBREWS 10:23

I have good reason to laugh as I sit in the garden with day lilies nodding at my left and nasturtiums teasing my right. I'm dying.

If only my daughter would stop eyeing me through the kitchen window, her hand to her mouth and her husband close as a shadow. Getting blubbery over nothing, they are. Well, dying ain't nothing, but it ain't worth having a hissy-fit about neither.

There she goes, blinking the porch light at me again. She doesn't think it's proper, me being out here by myself after giving them the news. I'm supposed to be inside, slumped over the kitchen table with a cup of tea steaming my glasses as it soothes me in my time of sorrow. They feel a need to hover close, pushing pain on my shoulders till all of us end up crying.

I'd rather laugh.

I admit this laughing business doesn't make much sense. I certainly didn't know I'd be one of the odd ones who found a giggle in death. But how was I to know? Folks don't spend time figuring such things. Dying ain't a proper subject to bring up at dinner over mashed potatoes and creamed corn.

Doc Martin didn't appreciate when I laughed at him this afternoon, but I wasn't laughing at what he said so much as the way his cheeks hung limp when he told me I was dying. Looked like a hound dog ready to howl at a rabbit in the bushes. Then he said, shaking his head real slow, "There's nothing we can do, Matty."

That's when I cackled—really cackled. Fiddle-dee, don't he know there's always something to do? God's let me live through five wars, the Great Depression—and a few other piddly ones—a fire in the kitchen, the death of a babe, and a whole mess of too hots, too colds, too drys and too wets. There's always something to do.

Like now, sitting in my garden. There are weeds to dig and lilies to divide. Good idea. It's still plenty light.

I grab my gloves and a bucket and sit down by the daisies. Ornery things have a habit of growing like weeds themselves. The stones on the path are cold and hard—not one bit comfortable. But I don't mind. They're real. They're here and now. The future will be set soon enough. At least I know where I'm going to forever and eternity…

The truth is—though only my roses know it—there's another reason I feel like laughing. It's because I'm old and I'm finally having to own up to it. That's a tack of a lot harder to do than accept the fact I'm going to die. Almighty thunder, I've known that fact of life since my feet dangled from a chair. But the fact I'm old—now that's a different ponder. Who thought I'd be wearing pull-on pants and ugly shoes of my own free will? Somehow my mind stopped aging me at fifty. Yup, that's where I've been sitting, mental-wise, for the last thirty years. Too bad my body couldn't sit there a spell longer.

Whatever. Digging in the garden always makes me feel better. Getting my hands wrist-deep in dirt makes me think deep thoughts.

Thoughts of my husband. Thoughts of Edgar.

The big question that pushes itself front and center is this one: Will Edgar be up in heaven waiting for me?

I never was certain whether that old kumquat came to know Jesus before he died. And it wasn't for me not asking. The bottom line was Edgar was too stubborn to let me know anything I really yearned to know. He was a teaser who spent a lifetime pulling my leg—I wouldn't be surprised to find one was longer than the other. Edgar wasn't one to talk serious. Ever. Whenever I had a weighty subject needed tending to, he'd make a Red Skelton face or tell a joke about a rabbi, a priest, and a Baptist minister that would make me roll my eyes and either forget what I wanted to talk with him about or handle it myself. He pushed the limits of my love a good bit of the time, but I suppose I did the same to him.

Sometimes I figure God put the two of us together to provide the heavens with a little entertainment. Never a dull moment with Edgar and me. Not a one. Tomato, to-mah-toe; potato, po-tah-toe—that was us. If I was sitting at one of life's red lights, Edgar was racing through a green, and never mind being careful to watch any caution light. Edgar believed in one speed: full-out fast—until this tendency led him through a red light and into the side of a semi. I shoulda known he'd go out dramatic.

Me? It appears I'm going quietly, though not without giving death a bit of a scuffle. I have my moments too, you know.

Golly, I miss Edgar…the old coot. Which leads me back to my question: Will he be meeting me at the pearly gates? Waving me in? With all those preachers up there, I bet he's got himself a passel of new jokes. I suppose there are worse ways to spend eternity. Actually, I bet God will be glad to see me so I can take Edgar off His hands for a while, keep him occupied so the Almighty can get some work done. I *know* how distracting Edgar can be when there's work to be done.

Except for this garden. It was the one place Edgar and me jibed—as long as he kept his attentions on the fruits and vegetables and left me the flowers. That's why I like working here even now. The memories of our life are my friends; annoying sometimes, but steady and comforting too. And here in the garden I know how to turn them on quick as a whisper. The feel of fresh dirt and the smell of green apples are my strongest trigger. Maybe that's why I have the best garden in Minden—the only one with an apple tree smack dab in the midst of it. It only takes one dig in the dirt or bite of an apple and I can see Edgar with dirt all over his boots. He's crunching on a green apple as he looks at the sunset, at that time and place where dreams and reality run together. And I'm standing beside him, sharing the apple as well as the dream. Then he turns to me and—

"Matty?"

I hold my breath. *It's Edgar's voice!* Lord have mercy, have I gone and died right here with a bunch of weeds in my hand? Am I in heaven with Edgar coming to meet me?

His voice sounds from the left behind the zinnias. The blue glow of dusk makes his shape soft and hazy.

"Fiddle-dee, Edgar. What are you doing here?" I squint to get him clear. It doesn't help much, but I see enough. He moves onto the path. He's wearing those awful navy pants with the saggy backside. And a green—

"Isn't that the green flannel shirt I gave you for Christmas back in '72? I thought I gave that thing away."

"It was always my favorite, Matty."

"Fiddle-dee. You wore that thing till the elbows were bare and the dye looked like lettuce gone bad." I take a hard look at him. "I put that thing in the ragbag. I know I did."

"They got me a new one."

Then it hits me. "Am I dead?"

"Soon, Matty, soon." He stuffs his hands in his pockets. "I came when I heard. I've been waiting for you the longest time."

"You don't look too good, Edgar. Kinda ashy. You eating right up there?"

"They make a cherry cobbler better 'n—"

"Better 'n me?" My voice rises and I feel stupid being insulted by a…a…what is he anyway?

Edgar takes a step closer. "Matty, I—"

I put up a hand. Talking to him is one thing, but I don't want him touching me. "Now you go on, Edgar. I ain't ready to die yet and I don't want you making me go sooner than I needs. I'll be coming time enough."

I hear the scuff of his toe against the path. "I miss you, Matty."

I'm afraid if I say I miss him too I'll be whipped away before my proper time. "I'm busy, Edgar. I gots stuff to—"

He turns to the left, toward the place where the tomato plants used to grow. "Too busy to set in tomatoes?"

I catch a whiff of garden dirt and let its spice push back the regrets. "That was your job." The blue light has faded to black, making him harder to see. A blessing. "I guess I need you and—"

"You miss me."

The cicadas start a verse. A porch door slams. I open my eyes and find my cheek nestled against the path, my garden gloves its pillow. *Have I been dreaming?*

Of course I have! Dead people don't show up to talk to the living easy as a pesky neighbor at supper time.

"Mom?" It's my daughter calling from the back door. "You coming in, Mom? It's dark."

I stand up too fast and feel a stitch in my side. I walk toward the house, eager to be inside, choosing to have a live daughter hover over me rather than have a dead husband hurry me along.

My time has come. Sooner than even Doc Martin expected. Although Edgar stayed out of my dreams after our meeting in the garden, I suspect he had something to do with me getting an earlier dying date. An impatient man he was. So thanks to Edgar, I'm in the hospital ahead of schedule with tubes gurgling, machines beeping, and a bedpan guarding my bed. My daughter and her shadow stand beside me. See if her hand isn't by her mouth again. Probably best, covering up that sickly Cabernet Crimson lipstick she's always wearing. I've told her that color makes her look like a fast woman, out to leave her mark. Don't she know she's pretty enough without it?

She tells me she loves me. Fiddle-dee, I don't need her to say it. I know. I want to tell her so but—

I clutch at my middle. Not because of pain but because…because there isn't any pain. Lord Almighty, praise Jesus! The pain's gone! Quick as a word, like the flip of a switch. I take a breath, testing it out. I feel good. Real good. I have a mind to sit up and tell the nurse to turn off that blasted elevator music in the hall and bring me a man-sized wedge of cheesecake with cherries on top. I have a mind to do it…but my body won't answer. Almighty thunder with lightning on the side! Feeling feisty with no place to go!

My daughter and her husband jerk their heads toward the monitors. Then back at me. She sucks in a breath and digs her face into his shoulder.

"Matty?"

A man's voice. The room fades…

Oh. So that's it. I'm not better. I'm past being better.

Well, fiddle-dee. Now's as good a time as any. God's been very patient with me.

I sense someone nearby. "Edgar? Is that you? Don't you go tapping your foot and pointing at your watch, mister. I won't take your chiding for being late. If I had my choice, I wouldn't—"

What's that smell? Biting and sharp. My eyes are open but things are hazy, like a mist covers the edges. A breeze whispers through branches nearby. The sun—the Light—is warm and inviting.

Splotches of color peek through the mist at me, tempting me to come closer. I move away from my daughter, following the path.

There's a bench up ahead. Someone's there. Waiting.

I walk faster. My body is young again, agile, eager. The mist pulls away from the path. Day lilies nod to my left and nasturtiums tease my right.

I hear a noise. A crunch. The smell grows stronger, inviting cozy thoughts.

"Hey, Matty. I've been saving you a place." Edgar holds out an apple and smiles.

"You're here." I smile at him.

"You expected otherwise?"

I punch his arm in the way I'd done a thousand times. "You never would tell me whether you believed or not. I asked plenty. I begged you to tell me."

Edgar scuffs his toe and shrugs. "I shoulda told you, Matty. It was wrong of me to keep you guessing. We coulda shared a lot of stuff—"

"You bet it was wrong. You can be so exasperating sometimes, Edgar, that I don't know what I'm going to do with—"

Edgar puts a finger to my lips, stopping my tirade. I quiet myself, embarrassed. Sniping at my husband is not a good way to start eternity. "So, now what?"

Edgar grins and I brace myself for his latest joke. But then he gives me his arm, just like a gentleman. I take it.

"Where we going?"

"I've got Someone for you to meet, Matty."

I follow the direction of his gaze and see where the path is leading. *Ah, so that's it…*

I have good reason to laugh as my Edgar and I sit in the garden, for now our two has finally become one as together we walk toward the Master.

Better late than never…

ABOUT THE AUTHOR

Nancy Moser is the author of *The Invitation, The Quest,* and *The Temptation,* the first three books in The Mustard Seed series of contemporary fiction (Multnomah). She has been married twenty-four years—to the same man. She and Mark have three children. She kills all her houseplants, can wire an electrical fixture without getting shocked, and loves antiques—humans like Matty and Edgar included.

The South

THE BLUE CONVERTIBLE

Terri Blackstock

he prisoner looking through the bars was right good-looking, even with dark, stringy hair that hadn't been washed since he'd lost his skirmish with the law. The stubble on his jaw was a couple days thick, giving him the look of one of the regulars that woke up on the sidewalk in front of Jared Sellers' bar. From his basement cell, the young man peered up through the bars of his window, toward Winona Barlow's pink beauty shop across the street, as if one of the patrons would get the idea to bail him out and prance right over with her hand in her pocketbook.

But Laura Ruth had seen the car the man drove—a powder-blue '67 convertible that was now parked out in front of City Hall. She could see it from her grandma's beauty shop window, and all the ladies who had come in had taken a peek out and wondered what would bring a man like that to the Picayune jail.

Laura Ruth climbed higher into the oak beside the beauty shop, trying not to be seen, and wondered if the prisoner's mama knew where he was. It happened sometimes. Boys just barely eighteen, or even younger, speeding down Mississippi highways on their way to New Orleans…or worse, on their way back after a party that left them with circles under their eyes and a green cast to their skin. They'd come off the interstate to find a bathroom, and the next thing you knew one of the rookies would be hauling them in for driving too fast. Then they'd smart off to him, and he'd get mad, and find reason to search their car. Almost every time a marijuana cigarette would turn up, and their fate was sealed—at least for the next few days until somebody bailed them out.

"Hey, kid. Come here a minute."

The voice startled Laura Ruth, and she realized he had seen her. She pulled her feet up to the limb and tried to look smaller, as if it would render her invisible. She peered through the leaves to the small window just above the lawn at City Hall. He must be hot down in that basement. The August heat gave no relief. It just hung there like an invisible fog that made your skin sticky and your clothes wet and your hair dirty.

She didn't want him to see her with dirty hair.

"You ain't foolin' nobody," he said. "I can see you clear as day."

She knew her cheeks had that blotchy pink look she got when she was embarrassed, but she hoped he would think it was just the heat. Slowly she climbed down to one of the lower limbs. "What do you want?" she asked, like he'd interrupted her from important business.

"Come here, and I'll tell you."

She dropped to the dirt, her bare feet sending up a little black cloud. She stood there looking straight across at him, not more than fifty feet away. She knew he must be standing on the bench in his cell or else he'd pushed his cot up to the window. She'd been down there and had a look before, when her cousin worked for the city. The barred windows were about seven feet up. The thought of him balancing on some perch like that made him seem less threatening to her.

"I don't talk to prisoners," she said, knowing that the minute she crossed that street one of the ladies from the beauty shop would scream like she'd been bit by a wasp, and her grandma would shoot out and snatch her back. "How do I know you ain't an ax murderer?"

He laughed then, and she had to admit he sounded more like a next-door neighbor. "An ax murderer? How old are you?"

"Almost thirteen," she said, stretching to her full height. She set her hands on her scrawny hips and tried to look tough. "Not that it's any of your business."

"When people stare at me it's my business, and I been watchin' you stare at me for hours."

Now she was insulted. "I *ain't* been starin' at you. We got prisoners there all the time. Just last week we had Junior Harkins in there for killin' his next door neighbor's dog. Said he barked too loud, so he up and killed him. He was right there, in that same cell, so what do I need to stare at you for?"

"I don't care if you stare at me," he said. "When I get out, maybe I'll march over there and give you a real good look, head to toe. Let you take a picture of me."

She knew that should scare her, but instead she was amused. "You come over here and you might wind up at the funeral home. My grandma don't take chances, with all the criminals comin' and goin'."

"So she's a gun-totin' glamour guru?"

Again, she couldn't help grinning. "I'm just sayin', I wouldn't be too bold about comin' to pose for no pictures. Not unless you got a taste for formaldehyde."

He gripped the bars and leaned his forehead on them like a child peering through a banister. "What did they do with my car, anyway? They out joyridin' in it or somethin'?"

She looked over at that blue convertible, sitting in its place as shiny as you please, like some movie star had just put the top up and popped in to see the mayor. "It's in the parking lot."

"How do you know which car is mine?"

She shrugged. "Heard talk."

He strained to see off to the side...the wrong side.

"Not over there," she said. "You're lookin' toward the church. Parkin' lot's on that side."

He strained in the direction she pointed, but gave up, then peered back toward the church. "Perfect little town. Everything you need right in one place. City Hall, police station, jail, all packed into one, sittin' in a little triangle with the beauty shop and the church."

"You got somethin' against church?"

"No, I got somethin' against beauty shops."

She smiled again, but turned away to hide it. She broke a stick off of a limb and tapped at the dirt. "You spent more time in church, maybe you'd spend less time in jail."

"Hey, it's my first time," he said. "Last time, too, you can bet on that."

"Yeah, that's what they all think. Ax murderers and all."

"How many ax murderers you met?"

She used the stick to swat at some Spanish moss hanging from the tree. "All I want to meet, if you have to know."

He laughed then, and she thought it had a nice sound. Kind of like her daddy's laugh when he got going. She thought about what day it was and how many months it had been since the funeral. Her mama still lay in the back room of her grandma's house, staring at the dark walls. Laura Ruth knew things would never go back to normal.

"Come on over here," the prisoner said again. "I'm tired of having to yell across at you. We can talk in regular voices."

"I ain't got nothing to say," she said. "Besides, I'm not allowed. My grandma—"

"The Colt-packin' cosmetologist."

She grinned again. "You don't want to mess with her."

He draped his wrists over the hot cement at the bottom of his window, and she could see that he was losing his zest. "All right then, but would you just do me a favor?"

She dropped the stick and dusted off her hands. "What favor?"

"Go get me the preacher."

She looked over at him, trying to see if he was joking again. "What preacher?"

"The preacher who runs that church. You said there was a church over there, didn't you?"

"Brother Baxter don't bail folks out of jail, so you're wastin' your time."

"I can't be bailed out, anyway. The judge didn't set it. I'm just waitin' here 'til they transport me to Parchman."

"Parchman?" The word came out as a whisper, and she took a slow step to the edge of the street, getting closer. She had never spoken to a prisoner bound for the state penitentiary. She wondered if the ladies in the shop knew it yet.

"Don't look so shocked," he said in a quieter voice. "I ain't some thug. All's I did was get in with the wrong crowd down in New Orleans."

"You don't go to Parchman for runnin' with the wrong crowd."

"No, but you can if you buy up a mess of dope from 'em and try to take it back home to sell. Don't never get messed up with drugs, kid. Take it from me."

She just stared at him now, no longer amused.

"I need a preacher, kid. Would you go ask him to come?"

She looked back at the door to the beauty shop and wondered what her grandma would do if she poked her head in and told her she was going to get the preacher for the prisoner who drove the convertible. The roof would blow off with her grandma's shrieks, and then the whole building would tip off its blocks when the ladies getting their hair done ran to see out the window.

She had strict orders against crossing the street to talk to the men in jail but nothing about walking over to the church to see the pastor. Not that she'd ever wanted to before.

It would make an interesting story, she thought. She could prance back into the beauty shop afterward and announce to the ladies that the convertible-driving convict had asked for a preacher before they transported him to Parchman. She made up her mind right then: It was worth any trouble it might cause her. "All right," she said. "I'll go tell him. But I don't know for sure he'll come."

"Ain't he a decent guy?"

She looked toward the church, running the question through her mind. "I don't know nothing bad about him."

"Well, that's good, at least." He leaned his forehead on the bars. "We had a preacher back home who sat up with my mama 'til morning, the night my daddy died."

The words stopped her. She could tell by his low voice that the death had torn him up. She knew that feeling of losing somebody when it wasn't even your fault.

"I'd call that preacher, if I was home," he said. "But this one'll probably do. Go tell him."

The jail was catty-corner to the church; she started silently across the street. She found the heavy door near the offices and pulled it open. A fan-blown breeze lifted her hair as she stepped barefoot into the hallway. She scanned the office doors, and then made her way to the one with a sign that read Brother Baxter. Nervously she reached for the knob.

"You're Winona Barlow's grandbaby, aren't you?"

Laura Ruth swung around like she'd been caught sneaking and saw the preacher standing in the hall. "Yes, sir."

"To what do I owe this pleasure, young lady?"

She felt real important bringing this message. "The boy with the convertible who's in jail?" It came out as a question.

"Uh-huh." He leaned down, looking almost as interested as the ladies in the beauty shop.

"He sent me to get you. Don't tell my grandma."

His forehead wrinkled. "He wants me?"

"Yes, sir. They're takin' him to Parchman. I don't know when."

"I'd better hurry then, huh?" He didn't even bother to go into his office, just headed for the door.

Laura Ruth hurried behind him. He opened the door and waited for her to go through. "After you, young lady."

She marched through and led him back across the street to the door of City Hall; then she crossed again to the beauty shop. She looked down at the basement window. The prisoner wasn't looking out anymore. "Hey you!"

He came back to the bars. "Yeah?"

"He's comin' down. He'll be there in a minute."

"Thanks, kid."

He disappeared again, and she stood staring at the window, wondering if Brother Baxter had made it down yet, what the man would say to him, why he wanted him to come. She glanced back at the front door of the beauty shop and didn't see anybody looking out the window. Slowly she crossed the street and stooped closer to the bars so she could hear what was going on inside.

The preacher was there, and she could hear the convertible driver talking like he had saved up the words his whole life and had just a few minutes to spill them all out. She heard the prisoner telling of drinking and taking drugs, of wild parties and fast driving, of girls he'd known and wrongs he'd done.

Then she heard him tell about his daddy's accident, the night in the hospital, and how mad he'd been at God for taking him away.

She lowered to the ground and sat down, head to her knees. She didn't want to cry, not here, right out in the open, where the next lady out of the shop would see her for sure and run back in shrieking for her grandma. But she couldn't seem to move. She wondered what the preacher would say about being mad at God, about blaming things on Him, about missing daddies…

A van passed, and she looked up and saw the gray bus with bars on the windows, the one that came to get the prisoners moving up to the state prison. She had seen it many times before and watched as they paraded the inmates out in their orange jumpsuits with hands cuffed behind them. Always before she had sat on her grandma's front steps feeling all superior, thinking they must be low-down good-for-nothings if they were being sent to Parchman. But she'd never known what car they drove, and she hadn't talked to them through the bars, and she hadn't run to get the preacher for them.

She wondered…were there other prisoners who drove convertibles and missed their daddies and were sorry for what they'd done?

The bus pulled into the parking lot on the other side of the building, and she got to her feet. She thought about running over and telling them he wasn't ready yet, that they had to wait 'til he'd finished talking to the preacher, that what he was telling him was real important.

But she didn't have the nerve. She just stood there as the two guards got out and went inside.

In a few minutes, she heard the bars of his cell opening, and she knew the talking was over. She got closer to the bars and tried to see inside, but the sunlight made the darkness seem too deep. She swiped at her eyes and tried to stop her bottom lip from quivering. What would the ladies think when she went back inside? *You been cryin', Laura Ruth? You ain't been botherin' your mama again, have you, girl?*

She waited a small eternity, sweat dripping through her bangs and into her eyes, until they came out with him. She saw the preacher trailing behind. The prisoner didn't look like anybody who'd driven a blue convertible. He looked lonesome and scared, the same way she looked when she caught herself in the mirror.

Without thinking, she crossed the hot street toward the parking lot and came up beside the preacher. She stood next to him as they led the prisoner onto the bus.

"I almost told 'em," she said under her breath. "I almost told 'em you weren't through. They coulda waited."

He patted her shoulder. "I think I said my piece. They don't wait, anyhow."

She swallowed and looked up at him, fighting the tears in her eyes. "But he's sorry."

"Sorry goes a long way with God."

"But…they're taking him off…" She wanted to tell him that she knew how he felt about his daddy, that sometimes she couldn't sleep at night for laying there with her stomach aching and her head remembering. "Can't you do somethin'?"

"It's in God's hands, but He won't forsake him. You can count on that."

The bus started up and began to move. Laura Ruth met the convertible-driver's eyes as he passed. She hoped the sun didn't catch the wet on her face.

He lifted his fist to the window…and gave her a thumbs-up.

The bus pulled away, and she watched it until it was out of sight. When it had turned the corner, her gaze drifted back to the convertible, parked—so shiny and important— in the parking lot where it had been left.

"What'll they do with the car?" she asked the preacher.

"His mama will prob'ly come get it," the preacher said. "It'll prob'ly be waitin' for him when he gets out."

She stared at it for a moment, trying to picture him going home when his time was up, getting behind that wheel and cranking it up just to hear it run.

"Laura Ruuuuuth!"

She turned and saw her grandma standing at the door to the beauty shop and she wiped her face real fast. "Thanks for comin'," she said to the preacher and launched off across the street.

"Where have you been?" her grandma asked, craning her neck to see who she'd been talking to. "You know better than to cross over there. I've told you 'til I'm blue in the face—"

She thought of telling her about the man who drove the blue convertible. Her grandma would get over the anger of her going that close to the jail, because she would be so interested in why he was headed to Parchman. The ladies under the dryers would forget their perms, trying to get the story.

But she didn't want to tell it anymore.

"I was just talkin' to the preacher. I figured it was okay to cross, since it was him and all."

"Well, you just stay put from now on, you hear? I don't want you strayin' off like that, even if it is to see the preacher. Why'd you want to see him, anyway?"

Laura Ruth stepped inside the door of the beauty shop, and breathed in the scent of fingernail polish, peroxide, and hair spray. The Formica was cool on the soles of her feet. "I just like him."

She held the door open, but her grandma didn't come. "Brother Baxter? You've never listened to a word that man's ever said."

"Well, I will from now on."

But her grandma's attention had strayed, back to the parking lot at

City Hall. "That car's still there. I'da thought they'd let him go by now."

Laura Ruth just looked back at it. She hoped when his mama came for it that nobody would be there to stare and point, to talk about how it was a downright shame. She hoped his mama would come when it was late night and all the ladies were on the phone talking about some new scandal.

She hoped they would miss the whole thing.

"I think Miss Sadie's just about dry," she told her grandma. "Don't you think?"

Her grandma's attention shifted, and she darted back in.

Laura Ruth just left it at that.

ABOUT THE AUTHOR

Award-winning author Terri Blackstock has published eleven Christian novels since leaving the secular market, where she had 3.5 million books in print under two pseudonyms. Her bestselling projects include the Sun Coast Chronicles series, the Newpointe 911 series, and *Seasons Under Heaven,* a novel cowritten with Beverly LaHaye. Terri has appeared on national television programs such as *The 700 Club* and *Home Life,* and has been a guest on numerous radio programs across the country. Though "The Convertible Driver" is fictitious, the setting is real. Blackstock spent many childhood summers in Picayune, Mississippi, at her grandmother's beauty shop, directly across from City Hall with its basement jail and catty-corner to the First Baptist Church.

The State of Incorporation

Angela Elwell Hunt

In her twelfth-floor office overlooking gorgeous Tampa Bay, Victoria McMillan brushed a smattering of orange cracker crumbs from her polished desktop, pulled a palm-sized mirror from her purse, and checked her smile. She couldn't let her one o'clock know that lunch had been a package of peanut-butter crackers—not in a firm where corporate lawyers regularly conducted million-dollar deals over power lunches that stretched for two hours. Bad enough that her secretary had even scheduled a one o'clock appointment—lawyers shouldn't begin working again until at least two-thirty. Clients were supposed to realize just how valuable those highly billed hours were.

Satisfied that her appearance wouldn't frighten her new client away, she stood, brushed her skirt lest any tell-tale crumbs remained on the soft navy fabric, and then settled back in the black leather chair. Sighing, she looked at the folders on her desk. She ought to open a file and start reading, but as soon as she did the phone would chirp with news that her new client had arrived.

Frowning, she glanced at her calendar, freshly printed just that morning. The one o'clock slot had been reserved for Bob Hopkins, who wanted to discuss incorporation.

Good. She pulled out an application and a copy of the fee schedule, then centered them on her desk. *Look at me now, Mom and Dad—just one week on the payroll of Loundon, Stock, and Whitlow, and I'm looking like a regular lawyer.*

She felt the corner of her mouth rise in a wry smile. In a few weeks she'd probably look as bored as the other members of this firm, but everything still felt new to her. During all those months of law school, all that time as a paralegal before she passed the bar, she'd dreamed of the day she'd sit behind a desk and entertain anxious clients who paid for the pearls of wisdom that fell from her lips.

The phone chirped.

One of those anxious clients had just arrived.

She pulled one of the case files she'd inherited onto her lap, opened it, and picked up the phone. "Yes?" she asked, trying to sound distracted.

"Mr. Hopkins has arrived."

Victoria released an audible sigh. "Send him in, please."

Bob Hopkins seemed to be an amiable sort of man—he came straight toward her desk, with none of that awkward hesitation other clients seemed to adopt when in the presence of legal experts. His hand was over the desk before Victoria had a chance to put away the file she was pretending to peruse.

"Bob Hopkins. Nice to meet you," he said, a sheaf of sandy hair falling into his eyes.

Victoria stood, struggling to hold onto the heavy file with one hand as she met his handshake with the other. "Victoria McMillan. A pleasure to meet you, Mr. Hopkins."

"Call me Bob. If we're going to be working together, I figure we ought to be on a first name basis."

"All right...Bob." *Please, don't call me Victoria.*

"Well now." Glancing behind him, Bob spotted the guest chair and lowered himself into it, then reached out and smoothed his khakis with both hands. "I'm really glad you could fit me in. I hear this firm's the best, and I had to get the best lawyer I could for this incorporation deal."

"Well—" Victoria felt her cheeks burn beneath the praise, not one iota of which she had earned—"this firm does have a fine reputation, but incorporation isn't really complicated. It all depends upon what you have in mind, of course, but these things are fairly routine."

Bob Hopkins exhaled loudly, a relieved smile spreading over his face. "That's *such* good news. My wife thought I was crazy, but I always listen to my pastor. If he's behind something, so am I. I mean, he's got the ear of God, right? So if he says *jump*, I say, *over what?*"

Victoria forced a smile. If that was a joke, she'd definitely heard better. "So…your pastor recommended that you incorporate? How interesting. I don't know many ministers who are savvy businessmen."

Hopkins made a face. "Well, I don't know if Pastor Charlie is a businessman, but he prays a lot, and I trust him. So when he started talking about incorporation last Sunday, I decided to find the best corporate lawyer I could. So—here I am!"

"Indeed you are." Victoria folded her hands and tried to maintain a properly serene expression. Why had this rube come to *her* office?

"Well, Mr. Hopkins," she began, "perhaps we should talk about why you want to incorporate. Other than the fact that your pastor recommended it, of course."

Hopkins' grin widened. "Well, I hear that incorporation gives protection, right? I mean, if I incorporate, I'm protecting myself—"

"Against lawsuits, to a point, certainly. And incorporation usually results in protective tax benefits as well. You can also set up a medical plan for your family and a retirement plan for yourself and your employees."

"Oh," Bob said, "my boss has already arranged for an unbeatable retirement plan. And I'm not here to speak for any other employees. Just me."

Victoria frowned. "So…you're thinking about a single-proprietor corporation? You plan to own 100 percent of the stock?"

"Shucks." A blush blossomed from beneath Bob's knitted shirt collar. "I'm not going to own anything. I'll do the footwork, but my boss will own everything."

Victoria drew a deep breath and tried not to lose her temper. She really ought to be speaking to the corporation's owner, but she might as well start somewhere…

She pulled her legal pad closer and picked up a pencil. "So you'll be the employee of the corporation. That's fine. Is this boss of yours a family member?"

Bob grinned. "I guess you could say he's my father."

"You guess? You're not sure?"

"I was adopted into the family."

Victoria nodded carefully. This man was a little slow on the uptake, but work was work, and she needed to put in some billable hours this week…

"That's fine, Mr. Hopkins," she said, making notes. "Before you begin, either you or your father will want to transfer some assets into the corporation." She forced a laugh. "You can't even buy stationery without some seed money."

"Oh, I'm prepared to fork over a chunk of change. And stationery would be nice. Right across the top it could say, *Bob Hopkins, Faith Investor.*" He leaned forward and gave her a conspiratorial smile. "Kinda has a ring to it, doesn't it?"

Victoria's hand stopped moving across the paper. Was this some sort of joke? A welcome-to-the-firm prank from her coworkers?

Better to be sure before calling their bluff. Some clients were more than a little eccentric.

"Faith investor?" She permitted herself a frown. "Is this an investment venture you want to incorporate?"

Bob thumped the arm of the chair. "You bet. My church is starting a new building program, and everyone wants to invest in it. I've been encouraging all my friends to become involved. My father protested that he was too old, but I told him you can never be too old for incorporation!"

A shadow darkened his eyes when Victoria didn't reply. "I was right, wasn't I?" he asked. "Age has nothing to do with it, right?"

"Right." Victoria inclined her head. "As long as you have business to do, you can incorporate at any age."

"I thought so." Again he thumped the chair. "My son—he's eighteen—thought he was too young to incorporate, but I told him, nooooooo. My sister-in-law and her husband thought they were too poor, but I told them, hey—everything you own is God's anyway, so what's the big deal? Incorporate, and place it all back in His hands!"

Victoria closed her eyes. "Your entire family wants to incorporate?"

Bob was shrugging when she forced her eyes open. "I hope so, but I can't speak for them. All I know is that I'm dead serious about doing this thing by the book and for the record. So I'll sign whatever forms you give me, and I'll pay whatever fees are appropriate. I want the world to know I'm serious about this thing."

Victoria had brightened at the words *fees* and *forms,* but Bob's last comment thrust her back into darkness. Well, when it doubt, fill it out. Things always looked clearer in legalese.

"All right then—" she pulled out the State of Florida incorporation application—"I'm going to help you do several things. First we'll draw up a business plan that outlines exactly how you plan to run your corporation, who your official representative will be, and where your place of business will be located. Second, we'll file for a certificate of incorporation from Tallahassee. Third, we'll choose a fiscal year that will give you the maximum tax-deferral advantage." Looking across the desk, she gave her client her brightest smile. "Let's get started, shall we? Exactly what sort of business are you in, Bob?"

Hopkins crossed his legs at the ankles. "I'm an elementary schoolteacher," he announced, his voice as confident as a man with the winning answer on "Who Wants to Be a Millionaire?"

Victoria dropped her pen. "Um, most schoolteachers don't incorporate. They are employees of the school. So you must be interested in incorporating a side business."

Hopkins' face clouded in confusion. "Seems to me that would defeat the point. Pastor Charlie seemed to imply that my incorporation would be a full-time occupation. You know—a twenty-four/seven situation." He grinned. "That means twenty-four hours a day, seven days a week."

"I know what it means." Victoria sighed. "Suppose we begin at the beginning. Exactly what is it you wish to incorporate?"

Lifting his chin, Bob met her gaze straight on. "My faith. Pastor Charlie said we should incorporate faith into every aspect of our daily lives."

Beneath the desk, Victoria clenched her fist, resisting the urge to reach out and slap sense into the man. "I'm sorry, Bob," she said, smiling, "but you can't incorporate something like faith. It's intangible. Incorporation is for companies that produce services or goods. If you were producing a product—faithmobiles or something—okay, but you can't incorporate a feeling—"

"Faith is not a feeling," Bob interrupted. "It's a solid thing. It's a...a noun."

"It's an intangible attitude. You can't see it."

"I beg to differ with you, ma'am, but yes, I can. My church is standing because of faith, and my country exists because of my forefathers' faith. I visit older folks in a nursing home every Thursday morning, and I can see faith shining in their eyes—"

"Mr. Hopkins—" Victoria pushed the legal pad away—"I don't think the state of Florida would recognize a corporation based on faith. I wouldn't know where to begin the application process. Who would own the corporation?"

"God."

"But who would be the official representative if the state wanted to call? The commissioner of corporations can't knock on heaven's door!"

Bob straightened in his chair. "They can knock on mine. I'd be happy to tell them anything about God they want to know."

Thick silence settled over the office for a long moment, and then Victoria glanced at her paperwork again. If this was a joke, it was a good one. And if it wasn't…well, one didn't trifle with God.

"What's the purpose of this corporation?" she asked, looking at the application. "What goods or services will you produce?"

Bob leaned forward in his chair, his eyes alight. "Whatever the boss wants me to. Who am I to argue with God?"

Victoria lifted a brow. "Good point." She felt her mouth tip in a small smile. Her mother had been a flaming Christian, and if she were here, she'd be in Bob's corner, urging him on.

"Well—" Victoria pulled the application closer—"we can always file the paperwork and see if it flies. But I'll bet the folks in Tallahassee have never received anything like it."

Bob settled back in his chair. "It just makes sense to me. If you're going to incorporate anything, you should do it right." He grinned at her, then suddenly leaned forward and lifted his hand. "Before we get into the details, I wonder if you could tell me the name of a good doctor in this area?"

Victoria felt a jolt of alarm. "Why? Are you ill?"

"No, I'm fine." Bob grinned as if to prove his words. "But Pastor Charlie said we should follow our incorporation of faith with an injection of joy, and I'm ready to roll up my sleeve!"

ABOUT THE AUTHOR

Angela Elwell Hunt began her writing career in 1983. After five years of honing her craft working for magazines, she published her first book in 1989. Since then, she has authored over eighty books in fiction and non-fiction, for children and adults. Among her picture books is the award-winning *The Tale of Three Trees*, with more than one million copies in print in sixteen languages.

She and her husband, Gary, make their home in Florida with their two teenagers, three dogs, two cats, and a rabbit.

This short story was originally conceived as a skit for her Florida church…pastored by the real Pastor Charlie.

DIARY OF A FARMER'S WIFE

Patricia Hickman

Diary Entry One

Love has always eluded me. Just as my mother named me after a flower that always eluded her efforts to make it bloom, love packs up its bags and walks away from me. I always hated the name Violet anyway. Marry my first name, Violet, to my surname, Little, and what you get is a fistfight every day after school. I always lost.

Violet has never fit me. I always imagined the name typified some demure, auburn-locked beauty queen from Atlanta.

We Littles lived on the fringe of city life, but never fully tasted its fermented elixir. I remember in sugar-fine detail the day I announced I would leave behind our town of Oblivion, North Carolina, and end my stint as an invisible participant in its nothingness. Two plump bags full of my tattered life sat sentry against my bedroom door. While I rested my head upon my pillow, my thoughts so enrapt with my trip ahead, I was blinded to the long journey I was about to make. Blindness is my cold companion.

My eyes closed and I felt the same uncomfortable restlessness I sometimes felt when, as a young girl, I boarded a bus to my Aunt Sophie's. But the lull of drowsiness finally paced my thoughts enough to walk me out onto the sands of my dream state. It was then I heard a rattling sound so distant I struggled to catalog it, believing the sound to be the creaking of an old ship against an ocean wave. Perhaps I had pressed too many thoughts of travel and escape into my subconscious and somehow forced my dreams to place me on a ship. But a long, thin sliver of light seeped from the direction of the sound, penetrating either a fold or maybe just creating a sort of tear in the fabric of this other world so that I could see beyond myself and glimpse inside. Not many mortals lay claim to such things, but even us Littles have our secret hope of touching something grand.

I kept my eyes on the filament of light, holding on to it with nothing but the sound of my own breathing. At once the light broke into a thousand pieces and converted to sunlight glinting off the rain on tree leaves. The rattling was nothing more than a farmer's tractor.

"Why, it's nothing more than mere life," I said. "But why am I here? And what has happened to Oblivion?"

Diary Entry Two: Date Unknown

The remains of the long thread of light now stretched in front of me, a pathway that had seen some use. Beside it, on either side, tall rows of white and golden wheat stood swaying in the midst of a dance between the morning sun and a pleasant breeze that carried a faint hint of perennials on her skirts. The heat left me feeling parched. But all at once the wind picked up and I could see a storm building just beyond the northern horizon. The storm rose as a great stack of indigo clouds, situating itself in such a way that I knew to try and escape its swelling train would be futile. The threat of this squall sent me skittering down the narrow path, past a mailbox full of letters.

An old well, perhaps dug before modern irrigation stretched its legs across primitive farming operations, stood imbedded in flat terrain between the two fields. I might have run past the well in search of shelter, but the idea came to me first to banish my thirst and then to find refuge. The well, a circle of stone and mortar encrusted with crisp algae, was fashioned with its own small covering, a simple roof. A tin ladle hung from a nail and, helpless against the wind, banged against the joist. I was no stranger to well water. The rope that attached the pail easily descended, and I soon had my water in tow. I sipped from the ladle.

The wheat tops bent against the wind, but I found it a gratifying sight, as though a song were being whispered—but one I did not know how to sing. If the sea of wheat had been all that I had confronted on that day, I might still be journeying outside the bounds of those fertile hills, a lost tourist. But my gaze followed the path into a clearing.

That is when I first saw the farmer.

Attired in worn overalls, he stood with sleeves rolled to the elbows—a sign of his continual toil. I could not muster a single word and now wonder if he must have found me rude. But he met me with such purpose, as though he had been waiting for me. Girls like me are always caught off guard by purpose. I found the farmer more comely than any man I had yet encountered—and believe me when I say I've encountered my share—but it was what was hidden from me that intrigued me. If ever I encounter a person of supreme importance who shrouds himself with lowliness, I'll admit only then it is more common than I realized to find such an anomaly. He stood upon the fertile loam and owned it. And everywhere his eye fell, he owned that too.

I have known men who have never found their kingdoms, who instead wander the roadways emasculated, their souls half eaten away. Believe me when I say that he was made of something much larger than a human soul, but had made himself small enough for a woman of bad reputation to see.

"My name is Violet," I said.

"Follow me," he answered.

My feet lifted, and I hurried to keep up with this farmer, wondering why it felt so natural to chase after a stranger who had not even bothered to tell me his name.

Diary Entry Three: Time Has Disappeared

The farmer spoke little, but when he did break the reverie of silence, his words had the same effect as a large, ancient church bell tolling to break the languor of a sleeping village. Behind him an old home beckoned visitors with its rocking chairs and quaint stone foundation.

"You travel alone, Violet. I'll bet it gives you a lot of time to think."

"I'm no great thinker. Who would want to listen to me?"

"I'm listening."

"I'm no good with words."

"I write my words down," he said.

"In a book?"

"In a book. On a heart."

"Is that your house?" I asked. "It's a nice house."

"Come see."

Before I could utter "I don't want to impose," the farmer led me up steps graced on either side by winding roses. "Is your wife about?"

"Come inside. I'll show you around."

My heart nearly stopped. His eyes locked on mine, and I could see my past as easily as a child can dip a soiled finger into a dark pool. I wanted to live inside that gaze of his, inside those eyes that could see me without shouting out my dark past to the world. He did not look like a man who harbored dark secrets himself, yet he kept all of mine without pointing a finger my way.

We walked past many rooms until he guided me into one with an open door. As I surveyed the room, I felt as though I had been standing in that very place at one time.

"Something has happened in here," I said. Strewn across the floor were objects of beauty that had fallen into ruin, beautiful statues, and pieces of art crumbled and scattered to the floor. Marble sculptures, once priceless pieces, were becoming one with the dust.

"This room belongs to my wife," he said.

"If this were my room, I'd not allow such a thing to happen." I felt angry with the woman. The farmer had given her priceless treasures, yet none of them had been given the care they needed. I saw nothing of the woman and yet sensed her all around me.

He invited me to roam freely about the home, but nothing drew me like the room of broken treasures. I stumbled over every piece to find the next broken vessel or statue. The damage was beyond hope of repair. It was then that I found a gravestone lying face down amid the ruins.

The farmer found me crying, slumped against the doorpost to this room.

"Have I troubled you?" he asked.

"I've sought someone like you my whole life," I said. "You're caring and gentle, and you find good inside of me where everyone else sees nothing but empty vanity. But in this room I find the remnants of a woman who lived her life so selfishly as to throw away the most priceless treasure of all. She has forsaken the very one who wooed her, called her his own, and sacrificed so that she could taste of life's finest treasures. Now amid her own ruin lies her gravestone, awaiting her final breath."

"You mourn her death?"

"No. I'm selfish like that."

"If not her death, then whose?"

"I mourn my own. If I cannot leave behind my own life of ruin and remain solely yours, I am dead."

"You wish to be my wife?"

"I do."

"Turn over that gravestone and read her name, Violet."

The stone, however small, was weighty and rough to touch. When I lifted the marker, it left me breathless. I felt small. Deep in the stone were etched the two homely words I had hated my whole life: Violet Little.

"The inscription, it's my own name." I turned and saw the eyes that had once more read my life. I felt so foolish. On the pathway he had known me. Beside the well, gazing from the blowing wheat field, or standing between the thorny rose—I should have known His name. "It's You," I said. Blindness fled my side.

"You are My bride, once dead, now alive in Me," said my Lord.

"Is that my life amid the rubble?"

"It is."

"I don't deserve You."

"I'll never leave you."

"Somehow I know it's true."

"Thirsty?"

"Strangely, no."

"I knew that, Violet."

I know some may think these words to be the remnants of dreams, but if they are the foolish whimsy of a girl of bad reputation, know this to be true: I will never return to Oblivion. But I will invite all who live there to come and visit the rooms of my Lord and see if they find their life an open grave as I did.

He will take you from the stench of your mistakes and give you new things to wear and a new place to call home. And you will never have to visit nothingness again.

I'll stake my life on it.

Come see.

ABOUT THE AUTHOR

Patricia Hickman, an award-winning novelist, speaker, mother of three, and pastor's wife, began her published career after being mentored by bestselling novelist Dr. Gilbert Morris. Patricia has written ten novels, all of which have earned critical acclaim from both the Christian and secular world, including *Affair de Coeur* magazine, *Romantic Times* (Top Pick Gold Medal Rating), *Moody* magazine, *Shine* women's magazine and the West Coast Review of Books. Her most critically acclaimed work, *Katrina's Wings*, has captured enthusiastic praise from such popular and bestselling authors as Francine Rivers, Terri Blackstock, T. Davis Bunn, and Patsy Clairmont. She is one of four authors selected to pioneer a line of high-quality women's fiction for the nationally popular Women of Faith conferences presented to packed out stadiums across the country.

Hickman has won two Silver Angel Awards for Excellence in Media, has been a guest on numerous radio programs across the country, and speaks on topics from women's issues to the craft of writing fiction.

BROTHERS

Randy Alcorn

The gray sky pressed down on two men, huddled close in the faint twilight.

Stoop-shouldered and leaning forward, Obadiah Abernathy stared off into empty space. He was ninety-two, the son of a sharecropper, the grandson of a Mississippi slave. His son Clarence, a 260-pound former college lineman, leaned over and looked into his father's eyes. They were moist and deep-welled—eyes that had seen more than any man should have to.

Obadiah shuffled toward the front porch, Clarence holding his hand. It still felt callused and leathery from picking cotton, milling grain, shoeing horses, and scrubbing floors. But now it was feather-light, a ghost of the hand that used to whip a baseball to first, grip a chopping maul for hours on end, and overpower young Clarence in arm wrestling.

"How you feelin', Daddy?" Clarence asked as they gingerly ascended the stairs to his brother Harley's front door.

"'Bout a half bubble off level. When you gets to be my age, if you wakes up in the mornin' and nothin' hurts, it's a sure sign you're dead." He laughed with a delightful hiss that sounded like air escaping a balloon. "Been hard since Dani's passin'. Man shouldn't have to see his baby girl die. Lijah tell me that when he lost Bobby. Couldn't have made it without my sweet Jesus. No suh."

Two weeks after his sister's funeral Clarence could still hear the wail-

298

ing. Nobody wept like black folk. They'd had centuries of practice.

A sports columnist for the *Trib*, Clarence had knocked on many doors. But the door in front of him now was the hardest. He let his wife Geneva do the knocking.

"Here they are, *black* by popular demand!" Malcolm X-style glasses framed Harley's face. A professor at Portland State, he often wore his suit and Black Muslim bow tie, but tonight had on a striking brown and yellow kente cloth.

While Harley hugged his daddy, Clarence brushed past him to his sister Marny's embrace. Clarence followed her into the kitchen, lured by the smell of ham hocks. Geneva stepped into the kitchen, put down her sack, and poured in bacon grease. She'd threatened to stop this, to keep the men from dying of heart attacks, but they'd said if she did, she might as well kill them outright.

Aunt Ida added greens to the ham hocks. Obadiah poked his head in beside Clarence, eyes closed, nostrils flaring, breathing in the aroma with conspicuous delight. Harley stood behind both of them, trying to lean in too.

The women turned and shot mocking looks, like queens to court jesters.

"You manfolks jus' get away, you hear me now?" Aunt Ida shooed them off as though they were stray cats. "Go discuss yo' politics and solve the world's problems so we can do what's important—fix dinner!"

After forty minutes of small talk at twenty decibels louder than any white family gathering, they sat down for the meal. Mama's dressing, loaded with onions and peppers and celery, sat at the table's center. Huge plates surrounded it—collard greens, mustard greens, and turnip greens. Big bowls of macaroni and cheese, candied yams, butter beans, and crowder peas sat alongside ham hocks and turkey, the full bird. A heaping plate of Mississippi catfish raised Clarence's eyebrows, as did a bowl of succotash and a mess of cornbread and black-eyed peas.

There was fried chicken, fried okra, fried potatoes, deep-fried pork chops, and fried green tomatoes. After Daddy said the blessing, Clarence took one slick, rubbery chitlin for nostalgia's sake. Chitlins objected to being eaten, but some eye-watering Cajun pepper helped him get it down.

Nothing could bring Mama back for an evening like the smells and tastes on this table. And now they were reminders of Dani, too. His precious little sister, taken so suddenly, so violently. His neck bowed low under the weight of his thoughts.

Clarence dug into the comforting fried channel catfish and Biloxi shrimp. It was enough to get the Mudcat goin', to dredge up the deepest memories, sweet and sour, of Yazoo Basin, Black Prairie, the Bluff Hills, and the Flatwoods.

Mississippi. Dusty towns with overdressed old men sitting on porches, plucking their suspenders and pronouncing judgment on all that didn't suit them. Corn whiskey stills. Backwater towns where the women spent their school years looking for a man to marry and then spent the rest of their lives wondering why they'd married such a fool. Clarence envisioned the magnificent antebellum mansions about which whites were so proud and blacks so angry. He lived in Oregon now, but Mississippi was his home. Yet it never had been home and never could be.

Clarence picked up cornbread and mixed it into the collard greens with his fingers. The salty, grease-soaked greens attracted stray crumbs. He licked his lips.

"This is livin', that's sure," Obadiah said.

"These are serious vittles, ladies," Clarence added.

"Just keep that pig meat on the other end of the table," Harley said. The air filled with a sudden but familiar tension.

"You always have to get that in somewhere, don't you, brother?" Clarence ignored Geneva's pleading eyes. "This family isn't Muslim, and *pig meat* is as black as coal at midnight. So if you have all that black pride, just join in or be quiet. You know that deep-fried dish there you been eatin' from? Bet you thought it was chicken, didn't you? Truth is we bought it just for you at Bits o' Pig!"

"Just keep it goin', *brother.*" Harley said the last word as if any black man off the street were more a brother to him than Clarence.

Harley's voice sounded to Clarence like an out-of-tune guitar. It didn't help that he was brilliant, one of the few people who could keep up with Clarence in an argument. The dinner continued in hushed tones before cautiously regaining its carefree mood.

"Let's go to the family room," Marny said. "Time for the menfolk to work off their dinner tellin' stories."

"Powerful good dinner, ladies, powerful good," Obadiah said. "Menfolk gotsta come up with some pretty big whoppers to match this!"

Soon the stories flowed like melting butter on steaming okra.

Obadiah, sitting in a rocking chair, was in the thick of them, his stories a string of pearls without the string.

"You remember ol' Reverend Charo? Dat man had more points than a thornbush. Used to say from da pulpit in this big voice, 'Ain't no disgrace to be colored.' Then he'd pause and lean forward and wink at us and whisper, 'It's just awfully inconvenient.'" Obadiah laughed until his eyes watered. "Sundays, now they was sumpin'. Mama, she'd put wheat starch in my collar to glue down the threads. We'd walk four miles to Sunday school, rain or shine. And did we have fun? Ol' Lijah and me, we was always cookin' up mischief. Mama'd say, 'Don't let them boys tease your sisters at church.' Like askin' a couple o' rottweilers to guard the barbecue!"

Clarence was warmed and stung by his father's love for his brother Elijah. Obadiah always wanted Harley and Clarence to be that close, but they couldn't be in a room for an hour without tearing each other apart.

"Reverend Charo say, 'Remember yo' mama? How she used to hug you and tuck you in? But she gone now. Can't tuck you in no more.' He'd carry on till we was all snifflin' and sobbin'. He'd keep remindin' us of our grandmammies and all our kin that died till we was in a frenzy. Then he'd shout, 'But someday you goin' to see yo' mama again. Someday you goin' to heaven, if you loves Jesus. There she be—arms awide open, waitin' fo' you. How many o' you can't wait for that day?'"

Obadiah's hand shot up. "People, they be shoutin' and clappin', twitchin' and tremblin'. Now, chu'ches today, they don't preach 'bout heaven no mo'. Maybe nowadays we thinks this world's our home. Maybe that's whys we's in so much trouble."

Obadiah's eyes clouded. Was he thinking about Mama? Dani? Old times with Uncle Lijah? Low and quiet, he started singing, voice wobbly.

"'I don't understand my struggles now, why I suffer and feel so bad. But one day, someday, He'll make it plain. Someday when I His face shall see, someday from tears I shall be free, yes, someday I'll understand.'"

It was awkward. Nobody knew quite what to do when Grandpa edged off into his other world.

"Tell us a story, Grampy," Keisha said. "Tell us about playin' in the Negro Leagues." Her sweet voice reeled in her great-grandpappy.

Obadiah smiled. "Shadow ball, folks called it." He laughed like a little boy, and the children laughed with him. "We was barnstormers. Played three games a day, travelin' by bus. Couldn't stay in most hotels. Wrong color. But lotsa folks come to see us. They cheered us and wrote us up. Played every city. They'd hitch up the team to come see us. If they didn't have a buggy, they'd ride two to a mule. If they couldn't find a mule, they'd ride an armadilla."

Obadiah's eyes sparkled. "One year I'd be with the Kansas City Monarchs or the Indianapolis Clowns, next year the Birmingham Black Barons."

"Tell us about Cool Papa Bell, Grampy."

"You want fast? Only man who could hit himself with his own line drive. I watched Papa Bell run from first to third on a bunt. I saw him hit three inside-the-park homers in the same game. His roommate swore Cool Papa Bell could flip off the light switch and be in bed before the room got dark."

Everybody laughed, revving up Obadiah's engines.

"Tell them about Ty Cobb," Harley said.

"Played against him in exhibition games. Cobb was an ol' sourpuss. You could put his face on a buffalo nickel and nobody'd notice the difference."

"What about Josh Gibson?" Ty asked.

"You want a slugger? Josh hit more five-hundred-foot home runs than Ruth. Only man to hit a ball clean out of Yankee Stadium. One season Josh hit seventy-five home runs."

"If Gibson was playin' in the majors today," Harley said, "what do you think he'd hit?"

"Oh—" Obadiah paused, pondering—"maybe .280, with thirty home runs."

"That all?"

"Well, you has to understand…he'd be eighty-five years old!"

When the laughter stopped, Ty asked, "Was Josh Gibson the best?"

"No. No. *Satchel*. Satchel Paige." He nodded vigorously. "I's not just black as coal, chillens, I's *old* as coal! Played with Satch on two teams, and played against him more than I cares to remember. No man never pitched like Satchel. He'd go into a game sayin' he'd strike out the first nine men. Usually he did. First baseman didn't touch the ball for three innings. Once we put a batboy out on first 'cause we knew he'd never have to do anything. Another time all us infielders sat down around second base and played poker till somebody finally got wood on the ball. It was the fourth inning. When I was with the Clowns, the catcher would sit in a rockin' chair. Ol' Satchel, he could pitch a greasy pork chop past a hungry coyote!"

Geneva passed out the sweet potato pie. Obadiah smiled broadly. He held it up under his nose. "Um, um, um." He placed it on his lap so his hands were free to talk.

"My son, the sportswriter," he looked at Clarence, "always told me he'd take me and his brother to Cooperstown one day, and we'd look at those pictures, and I'd show 'em Satch and Josh and Cool Papa. Even find ol' Obadiah Abernathy in some of them Shadow Ball pictures, I reckon."

Clarence squirmed. He'd promised his daddy they'd go to the Baseball Hall of Fame. He'd thought about it every year. But Cooperstown, New York, was on the other side of the country. There were always reasons not to go. And Harley was the biggest.

"We was sharecroppers in a bitty Mississippi town," Obadiah said, "so far down they had to pump in the sunshine. Lived in an ol' shotgun house. We chillens slept with each other, cuddlin' to stay warm."

"Yuck," Jonah said.

"No yuck about it, boy. Sometimes my nose so frozen, don't know what I'd done if brother Elijah hadn't been there to snuggle. They was hard days, but good ones." His eyes watered again. He looked up at the ceiling as if trying to peer beyond it. "I miss eatin' sowbelly and corn pone and slicin' up the catfish fresh out o' the river and sittin' on the porch those warm nights—Lijah and me and Daddy and Mama and the rest. We'd jus' watch the lightnin' bugs, lookin' magical, like somebody sprinkled livin' pixie dust in that ol' creek. We'd listen to those hound dogs bark and look up at those stars and see the face of God. True brothers, me and Elijah. Went through that Depression together. Couldn't find no work in Mississippi, so we rode the rails. We'd get off town to town, search for work all day. Most nights we was outside or on the rails. We'd find newspaper, lay it over us, curl up and put our arms around each other jus' to keep from freezin'—grabbin' on to life, like when we was little. We'd pray, quote the Good Book, talk and laugh the night away, just Jesus and me and Lijah, brothers through and through."

"I wish Uncle Elijah could come for Christmas," Clarence said.

"You and me both," Obadiah said. "Miss Lijah, surely I does."

"Where we meeting for Kwanzaa?" Harley asked.

"Don't know about Kwanzaa," Clarence said, "but *Christmas* is at our place, right Geneva?"

Harley shook his head. "You celebrate an independence day that didn't consider blacks worthy of independence. You celebrate a Thanksgiving of hoodlums who stole America from its natives. And you celebrate a Christmas about a white man's religion that oppressed your ancestors."

Clarence's eyes burned, but he held his tongue.

"I'm an African. That's why I celebrate Kwanzaa, not Christmas."

"Well, I got news for you," Clarence said. "Kwanzaa isn't from Africa. It was invented in Los Angeles, by Americans!"

"It was invented to commemorate what Africa is about. Which you've obviously forgotten."

"Our ancestors came from Africa. But we're Americans. If our kids are going to make it here, we've got to quit telling them they don't belong."

Harley put his hands up. "Now that the wood's all split, the water's drawn, the cotton's picked, and the rails reach coast to coast, now that the ditches are dug and there's just shoes left to be shined, *now* they tell us they'll give us a chance. Well, they've been liars all along and they're still lyin'! So excuse me if I don't join you in shufflin' for 'em, Tom!"

Clarence stood, shoulders tense, well aware that his two hundred and sixty pounds cast a formidable shadow. "To you, anyone who makes a living outside of a government agency or a black studies department is an Uncle Tom." He ducked into the kitchen and slammed his fist on the counter. Right about now, he knew, Dani would have come in, cooled him down, reminded him he and Harley were brothers.

Clarence breathed deeply and returned to the family room as his father said to Harley, "Nossah, son, that's poppycock, pure and simple. Not all white people's like that. Yeah, there's racists—white *and* black. You raised in the garbage, you can't help but stink. Some gots it so bad they'll never change, and you just got to let 'em go. Like Pappy said, 'Don't never try to teach a pig to sing.'"

"What?" Geneva asked, laughing.

"It wastes your time, and it annoys the pig."

"Daddy, I wish you'd come to the true faith of the black man," Harley said.

Obadiah sucked in air and sat up straight. Every back in the room tensed. "Hear me, son, and hear me good." The voice was clear and firm. "I *knows* the true faith of the black man, the brown man, the red man, the yellow man, the white man. *Every* man. It's a faith in Jesus. He say, 'I am the way, the truth and the life; no man comes to the Father but by me.' The only train that's goin' to take you to the Promised Land is the glory train, and Jesus is the conductor. When he hears *that* whistle, ol' Obadiah Abernathy's gettin' on board. I'm gonna make it to that Promised Land." His thin voice started singing, "'Git on board, little children, git on board. De gospel train's a-comin', git on board.'"

Clarence looked down uneasily, but suddenly Daddy's eyes cleared and he pressed his hands on the arms of the rocking chair, gazing at Harley.

"I won't let you attack the faith that's been the foundation for this family, for your mama and my mama and daddy, and their mamas and daddies before them. You hear your papa talkin', Harley?"

"My name's Ishmael Salid."

"Don't tell *me* what yo' name is, boy!" Obadiah stood up with startling force, shaking his finger. Daddy looked like he was about to bring out a hickory switch, and Clarence relished it. "I'm the one that *gave* you yo' name. Me and yo' sweet mama. I love you, son, but you'll always be Harley Abernathy. Somebody else can call you Elijah Mohammed or Kareem Abdul Jabbar or Sister Souljah, but *I* gave you yo' name and I's gonna call you *Harley* till the day I die and then some. Nuttin' you say's gonna change that. You hear me, boy?"

"Yes, Daddy," Harley said. "But when you've been emasculated by white Christians for four hundred years, you want to do something that affirms your *black* manhood. Islam is Afrocentric; Christianity is Eurocentric."

"Baloney," Clarence said. "Both of them started in the Middle East, and there were black Christians in Africa six centuries before Muhammad."

Harley ignored Clarence. "Let me ask you one thing, Daddy. Those Mississippi cops nearly beat you to death for bein' black, didn't they? And that place was full to the brim with Bible-believin' church people, wasn't it? Does that tell you something? One of those crackers was a deacon in the Baptist church, remember? Now I want you to tell us all, Daddy, did you ever hear any white Christian church leader stand up and say to the community, to the black churches, to the newspaper, to anyone, 'This is wrong. We're sorry. We will no longer tolerate the lynchings, the beatings, the humiliation, the cruelty! We'll kick the Klansmen out of our churches and help the oppressed and stand up for justice'? Did you *ever* hear that from a white church leader? I want the whole family to hear your answer."

Seventeen family members sat in breathless silence in the crowded living room, all of them looking at Obadiah. He sat silently for a long time, eyes down. Tears fell into his lap. Finally he looked up.

"No. I never did hear that. I wish to Jesus I would have." He fought to gain control of his voice. "But that's not God's fault, son. And my faith's in God, not men. Not white men, not black men. My faith's in a God who ain't black or white, but who made both and died for both."

Obadiah looked at Harley, then Clarence. "It grieves this ol' man to see my sons fight. I don't want my Ruby or my Dani lookin' down here and havin' to see it neither. You're brothers—don't that mean nothin' to you? I'm old as dirt, but I ain't mulch on the flowers yet. I gots me a third-grade education, but I seem to know some things you college graduates don't. I's still your daddy. Now I gots a few things to say, so shut up yo' mouths and listen, both of you."

Everyone sat wide-eyed and attentive. "Clarence, you should show more respect for your brother. Yeah, I disagrees with him too, but sarcasm and venom ain't the way to convince him. I wish I heard more love in your voice, more kindness to your brother. Yo' mama would want that. You knows the words of the gospel, boy. But I's sorry to say, you's missin' the music."

Clarence looked at the floor.

"Bein' angry 'n bitter won't bring your sister back neither. Truth be told, she wouldn't *want* to come back. Now you, Harley," Obadiah said. "You read Revelation, last three chaptas. Almighty ain't gonna adjust His plans to fit your beliefs or Minister Farrakhan's or nobody else's. You better start changin' your beliefs, 'cause the Almighty ain't gonna change His."

Little Keisha stared up at her great-grandfather. Catching her eye, his voice became gentler. "Now, the rest of you, hear this old man and hear me good. Not all my dogs is barkin' anymore, but I can tell you what I knows, and I knows this—there's bad Christians and there's good Christians; there's phony Christians and there's real Christians. The devil can go to church once a week. Nothin' to it. It's livin' it that counts, and the people that live it, those are the real Christians. The way I reads my Bible, anybody who hates a man for the color God made him isn't filled with God, he's filled with the devil. There's real money and there's counterfeit—don't let the counterfeit stop you from believin' there's the real thing. People's always gonna let you down."

He'd been talking fast, but now his speech slowed to a crawl. "But my Jesus, He won't never lets you down. *Never*. Yessir, my Lord tooks my daddy and mama, my Ruby and nephew Bobby and now my Dani, He tooks them all away from me, and Moses and all my brothers and sisters 'cept ol' Lijah, but He never *once* tooks away Himself from Obadiah Abernathy, and that's the gospel truth."

A hush permeated the living room. Clarence and Harley, both ill at ease with the tears flowing down their father's cheeks, lowered their heads.

Geneva got up and collected dessert plates. The other women followed.

"Close to God, my Ruby was," Obadiah said to no one in particular. "And now she's in His backyard. When the chillens in bed, we sat on our porch countin' cricket chirps and watchin' stars. Used to ring that ol' porch bell, Ruby did. Meant it was suppertime, time to come home. Sometimes this ol' boy hears that bell a ringin'. Time to come home."

Obadiah tilted his head, then hummed. While Clarence and Harley squirmed, Daddy listened to the music no one else could hear. Obadiah looked boyish, as if running unrestrained through the meadows of childhood. Was he remembering childhood, Clarence wondered, or anticipating it?

"'Oh Freedom, Oh Freedom, Oh Freedom over me,'" Obadiah suddenly sang. "'And before I'll be a slave I'll be buried in my grave, and go home to my Lord and be free. Git on board, little chillen', git on board. De gospel train, she's comin', git on board.'" His voice changed. "'Amazin' grace, how sweet the sound that saved a wretch like me; I once was lost, but now am found, was blind, but now I see.'"

Most of the family sang along. Harley picked up a newspaper from the coffee table and buried his nose in it.

"'When we been dere ten thousand years, bright shinin' as da sun, we've no less days to sing God's praise, dan when we first begun.'" The tears poured down the old man's cheeks as he stared out the window.

Clarence followed his daddy's gaze.

He couldn't see anything outside but darkness.

Clarence rushed into the hospital room. His father looked so small lying on that bed, tethered to an oxygen tube.

"How are you, Daddy?"

"If I was a hoss, they'da shot me already." Obadiah chuckled feebly. "But I's still a man."

"You're the *best* man I've ever known."

"You should get around mo', son. Meet mo' people."

"I mean it, Daddy. You were always a hard one to disobey, but you've been everything I could ask for in a father. If I could be to my children and grandchildren what you've been to me…"

"Give 'em yo' *time*, son. No substitute for yo' time. Learn those young-guns God's ways. Teach 'em who they is—*chilluns* of the King. Some man treats 'em like a dog, he gonna have to face their Daddy, the King. Chilluns grows up real quick, and grandbabies too. Don't miss the chances you got now. Won't get 'em again, boy. Won't get 'em again."

"I called Uncle Elijah this morning. Wanted me to tell you he's prayin' for you."

"Best brother a man could have, Lijah. Kept each other warm those cold nights. Had us some fine times, we did. Wish I could be home with 'im. Miss 'im terrible. A true brother. Wish you and Harley could…"

"I know." Clarence choked. "I'm sorry we never got to Cooperstown."

"It ain't too late."

Clarence looked at him, not sure what to say.

"I wants you to take Harley. You can do it. They gots ol' pictures. Look for me. Twenty-two years in Shadow Ball. Your ol' daddy's gots to be in some of them pictures!"

"But it's you I wanted to go with, Daddy."

"Don't worry none about me, son. I's goin' to the *real* Hall o' Fame." He laughed and looked at Clarence with soulful eyes, the light inside flickering in eternity's winds.

Harley walked in the door. He stood on the opposite side of his father's bed.

"My boys." Obadiah smiled. "Brothers," he whispered. He lay still, closing his eyes. The brothers stood there, not looking at each other, both wondering if those eyes would open again. Three minutes later, they did.

"I hears that whistle blowin'," Obadiah said. "Train's a-comin'. Folks a-gatherin'." Eyes closed, he said, "Who's dat walkin' beside me now? Tall as an oak. Where'd ya come from, big fella? These ol' legs don't feel so sore. Now who's dat up ahead? Whose face I see? O, my sweet Jesus. It's You. It's You!"

Obadiah grew quiet. Clarence checked his pulse. Suddenly Daddy's eyes popped open, not blinking, but watering up, focused on something beyond the room.

"Who dat, now? Daddy? O *Daddy,* what you told me was true. And…Mama? Yes, me too, Mama. Me too. Terrible much." Silence again. "Moses! How are you, brother? How long's it been? But where's my Dani? There she is! O Dani, I hasn't stopped cryin' for you, little girl. And who's this one? Bobby, that you? Leukemia's gone now, ain't it? O sweet Jesus, sweet Jesus. I never knowed such joy. Thank You, my sweet Jesus."

Clarence and Harley stared, wide-eyed, as the tears streamed down their father's face. "He's hallucinating," Harley whispered. Clarence nodded, then moved over to Harley's side because his father's head was turned that way. The brothers stood shoulder to shoulder, leaning over their father, wanting to hear the fading voice.

"My oh my, can't believe my eyes. Who's dat woman? Uncommon pretty, she is. Missed you terrible, Ruby. Gets lonely jus' me and the fire-flies, countin' cricket chirps and watchin' the stars all by ourselves."

Clarence looked at Harley. Was it possible…?

"Wait a minute, there." Obadiah said, "Who dat behind you? *Lijah?* That you, brother?"

As Daddy went on, Clarence and Harley let out their breaths at the same moment. The old man's body jolted.

"You all come out to get me, didn't you? I hears that ol' porch bell a ringin'. Time to come inside, ain't it? Gospel train's a comin'. Obadiah Abernathy's on board. Time to cross dat ol' Jordan. Time to…"

Obadiah's eyes grew big, but his pupils contracted as if seeing a bright light. Then his eyelids fell over them, like blinds suddenly tugged shut. He gasped air like it was his last breath.

Or his first.

Clarence and Harley looked at each other in disbelief. Only an instant before, the empty shell in front of them had still contained a man.

"Oh…Daddy," Harley sobbed, taking off his glasses.

Clarence fell to his knees, laying his head on the bedspread. "We gonna miss you, old man…" He choked out the words. "We gonna miss you terrible."

After ten minutes, Harley and Clarence helped each other out into the hall.

"Antsy?" Harley said. Clarence hadn't heard his brother call him that for twenty years. "Must have been the painkiller or something. But for just a moment, I thought maybe Daddy was really…I don't know. Did you…?"

"Yeah, I did. Up until he thought he saw Uncle Elijah. But I just talked to him a few hours ago. Lijah's still in Mississippi."

"One thing's for sure," Harley said, "Mississippi and heaven aren't the same place."

Clarence nodded and cleared his throat. "Harley?"

"Yeah?"

"Would you mind comin' to my house for a bit? I'd like to talk…if that's okay with you."

"Well, I got papers to grade and I need to tell my family about Daddy. But…yeah, I guess I could come by. Let me call home first."

When they got to Clarence's they sat in the living room, eight feet apart. Geneva brought coffee to Clarence and tea to Harley. The phone rang. Geneva answered. Both men listened.

Geneva put down the phone, face pale. "It was your cousin Jabo in Jackson. I left him the message about Daddy half an hour ago. He called about Uncle Elijah."

"I'm sure Lijah's taking it hard," Clarence said. "They were so close." Harley nodded.

"It's not that," Geneva said.

"What?" Harley asked.

"Uncle Elijah passed away."

The two brothers stared at each other across the room.

"When?" Clarence's voice was hoarse.

"Four o'clock this afternoon, Mississippi time."

"That means he died…" Clarence stopped.

"An hour before Daddy." Harley put his hands on his face. Clarence did the same.

Clarence made the long walk across the living room and knelt next to his brother. He put his arms around him. They embraced for the first time in twenty years, the first time since Mama died. They hugged each other like two freezing men in a railroad car, hanging on to life.

Clarence could only think about going two places. One, to where his daddy and mama and Dani and Uncle Lijah were.

The other, to Cooperstown's Hall of Fame.

ABOUT THE AUTHOR

Randy Alcorn is the director of Eternal Perspective Ministries (EPM). A pastor for fourteen years before founding EPM, Randy is a popular teacher and conference speaker. He's spoken in many countries and has been interviewed on over three hundred radio and television programs. He's the author of fourteen books, including the bestselling novels *Deadline, Dominion, Edge of Eternity,* and *Lord Foulgrin's Letters.* His most recent novels are *The Ishbane Conspiracy* and *Safely Home.* Randy lives in Gresham, Oregon, with his wife, Nanci. They have two grown daughters, Karina and Angela.

The Northeast

A SEED FOR TOMORROW

Doris Elaine Fell

ew York City. Fifth Avenue and Times Square. The Empire State Building and the Statue of Liberty. Glamour and glitter and the mayhem of crowded streets and subways and the marvelous complex people. New York, New York. I loved it. I hated it.

What had happened to my first thrill of living here? Four years and as many winter snowstorms had dimmed my love of the theater and the excitement of life in the city that never slept. A city on the move. A city where I could dine out night after night and never repeat a menu. Pushing through the door to Babies Hospital in Manhattan, I determined to be out of here, to be back home on the farm in sunny California before winter really set in again. Except for my job as a pediatric nurse—except for the children—I would have been out of here long ago.

One could almost taste the threat of winter around the corner and feel its icy fangs reaching out. The bite of autumn stung my cheeks as I hurried down the corridor to the nurses' station. I flung my fur-lined car coat and scarf over an empty chair.

"Sorry, Alice, the subway trains were running late." A likely excuse, but the night nurse didn't seem to hear me.

"Jeromy is back," she announced huskily as she began her report at the nurses' station. I shot a glance at her as she flipped the cardex and nodded toward the private room across from the station. An isolation rack stood ominously outside the closed door. Alice's mouth twisted in an effort to smile. "Jan, I think it's his last trip in."

"Not Jeromy." Not this on top of the threat of a bitter winter. Not this to swallow when I was already homesick. My plans to go home shattered. Jeromy needed me.

"I'm sorry, Jan," Alice said. "But you knew it was coming."

Jeromy had come to us a year before, walking in, solemnly clutching his mother's hand. A handsome five-year-old with a Yankees baseball cap tilted rakishly over his dark locks. His sturdy legs were dimpled at the knees, and the toes of his sneakers were scuffed from play.

"This is Jeromy Evans," the Pink Lady had said as she handed me the papers from the admitting office.

"Hi, Jeromy," I greeted him as I scanned the admission sheet for his diagnosis. His cheeks were drained of color and I remember thinking, *Oh, no, not another leukemic.*

"His older sister had leukemia," Mrs. Evans was saying.

Her distraught expression seemed to shout: *His sister died from leukemia.*

Jeromy's eyes, dark and beautiful and watchful, moved from the Pink Lady to me and then to his mother.

"It's all right, darling," Mrs. Evans said as she knelt beside him. She was petite, too thin to be pretty, too anxious to hide her fears. She pointed to me. "This is the nurse who is going to take care of you, Jeromy."

But not the nurse who took care of his sister. That was before my time. Two years before I reached New York City. I knelt beside him. "We've been expecting you, Jeromy."

Tears welled in his eyes. He seemed to be drowning in them. I didn't try to rush him or touch him. My smile grew bigger with his hesitancy. "I'm Miss Cullen."

"Hello, nurth," he lisped.

Afraid to entrust Jeromy's fears with someone else on my staff, I left the desk to usher him and his mother to the ward. We stopped by the bed, folded back fresh and clean for its new patient. "This is your bed, Jeromy," I told him.

He edged closer to his mother. "No, Mommy. No."

Several patients in the children's ward took stock of the new arrival.

316   The Storytellers' Collection

Zach stuck out his tongue. Tammy, our battered child, pressed her face against the bars of a neighboring crib, and Ramon limped over to check Jeromy out. The others were too small or too busy—or too sick—to care that another small boy had arrived.

"Mommy, I want to go home," Jeromy whimpered. "I want to go home for Christmas."

It was obvious that his frightened whimper expressed the cry of her own heart. "As soon as you're well, darling."

"Mommy, I'm not sick."

She hugged him gently before lifting him onto the bed.

"Mrs. Evans, the doctor scheduled a bone marrow test for tomorrow," I told her as she removed his cap and began to unlace his sneakers. "And some more blood tests."

She nodded, refusing to look at me as she folded her son's clothing. I watched her polished fingernails gently press out the wrinkles. "Yes, I know." It was barely a whisper.

I glanced again at the admission sheet and recognized the name Evans at last. Jeromy's father was a photographer, well known in our city. His sensitive pictures of children around the world graced the walls of more than one gallery. Aware suddenly of my own surprise and silence, I asked, "Is Mr. Evans coming?"

"He's away on one of his photo shoots. I've tried to contact him to let him know that…Jeromy is sick."

"I'm not sick," Jeromy protested as he grabbed one shoe and tried to shove his foot back in. "Daddy will be mad if you leave me here."

That had been almost a year ago—in December, with Christmas only days away. And now Christmas was coming again in a few weeks, and Jeromy was back in the hospital on his fifth admission. When the night nurse finished her report, I moved toward the isolation stand at Jeromy's door, gowned, and went quietly to his bedside.

He slept fitfully, his respirations shallow. Hemorrhagic bruises marked his wasted body. His right arm lay limp over the distended abdomen; the left one was restrained as the platelets dripped into the microdrip chamber. His Pooh Bear lay on the sheet beside him. I fondled the bear in my gloved hands and read the smudged tag around Pooh's neck: "To Jeromy, with love."

Mr. Evans had given Pooh to Jeromy on the day the bone marrow report came back. "Not Jeromy, too," he had said as he pounded his fist on the nurses' desk in unrestrained fury. "Wasn't the loss of our daughter enough?"

Back at my desk, I felt someone touch my sleeve. "Miss Cullen, the reverend is coming," my LVN warned in a loud whisper.

I groaned. "Not first thing in the morning?"

I looked up in time to see the chaplain, a retired minister, push through the swinging doors at the end of the hall and bounce toward us. He caught up to the first boy in the corridor and told him, "Story time right after breakfast."

The boy swung his lollipop in the air; it stuck to the reverend's gray hair. He separated child and candy with a shake of his head, eyeing the offender with merriment, and hurried on toward Jeromy's room.

"Lollipops before breakfast," he scolded. "Miss Cullen, Miss Cullen, you're spoiling the children."

"And now you are here to help me, Reverend," I responded, picking up on our endless verbal battle. "But I believe you handed out those lollipops yesterday."

His brow wrinkled. "So I did. So I did."

He looked pleased as he shoved his glasses in place and rubbed the bald spot on the top of his head. He allowed his gaze to sweep past me to Jeromy. "Let me know when he wakes up."

And with that he turned like a pied piper toward the playroom, the ambulatory children scurrying behind him. It was like Sunday school every day when the reverend was around.

My LVN shook her head. "What that preacher does to the walls of Jericho and to Joseph's brothers tearing up that coat of many colors glues them kids to their seats like it was Star Wars."

"Well, Sherri, he's got them sold on Jonah, too, and that one about the fiery furnace." I stomped toward the babies' ward. "And if we don't watch out, we'll all be believing what he says."

Sherri shrugged her shoulders. "Well, the kids sure do."

"Yes," I snapped, my stomach knotting. *If he'd just keep story time for kids only. Little folk like Jeromy.*

But Jeromy was too bruised to cuddle long on the reverend's lap, too weak to hold the Bible storybook. Yet day after day the minister sat with the child while his mother went home to rest—or down to the chapel to pray. He was with Jeromy on Friday when I led the lab technician into the room to take another blood sample.

Jeromy screamed when he saw the technician. "No!"

The reverend peeked over the top of his mask and reached out to steady the frightened child. "Must the technician jab him again?"

"Doctor's orders," I reminded him.

He pressed his cheek lightly against Jeromy's. "Jeromy, my boy, you heard Nurse Cullen. Try to be brave like Daniel in the lion's den."

The woebegone eyes widened. The sobs subsided.

"And now let's get on with Daniel," the reverend said, smoothing out the bandage on Jeromy's finger. As we turned to leave, the reverend picked up the threads of the story as though there had never been a break.

Without realizing it, I had canceled my plans to go home before winter. Canceled them indefinitely. I had to stay on for Jeromy even if another snowstorm hit us. On the first of December Jeromy had been back in the hospital two weeks when a new batch of student nurses, stiff and starched in their new uniforms, rotated to our floor. After their first morning with the children, I gave the students my worn-out lecture, adding at the end, "We have a number of very sick children on this floor. Some are dying. You'll tend to get too involved. Try not to; but remember the dying child is still living. We will treat him that way on Babies Five. We will help him to live his last days and hours to the fullest as much as his illness will permit."

I especially wanted this for Jeromy.

The reverend acted as though Jeromy would live forever. His hands were full as he hurried toward Jeromy's room. "It's planting time, Miss Cullen," he greeted as he disappeared into the room. It was actually rest period. He reappeared moments later, apologetically reaching for the isolation mask and gown that I held out to him. "Such a barrier to children," he blurted out. "I can never remember to wear them." His eyes twinkled above the mask. "Jeromy and I have to get a garden planted before Mr. Evans arrives with the camera."

I glanced out the window at the dismal gray outside. A garden in New York City? With the housing complexes crowded together and space for planting gardens all but gone? "It's not the season for planting, Reverend."

He nodded toward the boy. "In God's plan of things, it's always the right season, nurse. Come and help us, Miss Cullen. Surely you can spare a few minutes for that."

Come and hear another nugget sermon. I started to protest, but Jeromy turned that thin frail body toward me, his dark eyes like saucers in his pallid face. "Hi, Nurse. Mommy's here."

I smiled as I joined them, swallowing the lump in my throat and holding up a new IV bag as my excuse for being there. I winked at Mrs. Evans. She knew I should be tossing the preacher out of the room and throwing the sandbox out behind him. I bit my tongue, hating the rules of isolation, knowing that the chaplain needed to be with Jeromy and his mother. Knowing that Jeromy needed them both.

It was easy to love this boy. The chaplain had propped him up, but his body lay limp against the pillows. A planting box rested on Jeromy's tray. The sunken eyes followed as the reverend furrowed the ground with his forefinger. Then Jeromy reached out with his free hand and dropped the seeds into the freshly dug soil. I kept thinking, *Jeromy, you'll never live long enough to see them grow. You'll be gone before Christmas…gone before your birthday.*

As the reverend patted the soil around the seeds, he talked. He spoke of God, of seeds dying—"and sprouting to life!" His voice overflowed with assurance. He talked of Jesus loving little children—"especially you, Jeromy, my lad." Then the old chaplain straightened his back and surveyed the garden. "Jeromy, those seeds are going to grow right where we planted them."

He brushed his hands clean. "I think we're ready for the camera now. Where's that daddy of yours?"

Jeromy glanced toward the door of his room, framed with strands of Christmas tinsel. His dark eyes, lined with deep circles, were open, expectant. His cracked lips cut short the smile. The reverend's big hand rested on the boy's forehead, then brushed through the sparse, thinning hair. "There's new life in your garden, Jeromy. It's going to bud and grow."

"In time for Christmas?" Mrs. Evans asked.

The reverend nodded. "We'll ask God about that."

He cocked his head thoughtfully at Jeromy. "May I be in the picture with you and your garden?"

Jeromy pursed his dry lips. "No," he lisped, "I want to take the picture." It was more than he had been able to say for a long time.

Mrs. Evans still sat curled in the armchair, her fingertips touching her son's arm. The reverend put a firm hand on her shoulder. "God wants you to bloom where you're planted, my dear." His voice was soft, filled with compassion.

The tensed crinkles at her temples eased. Tears glistened. In her silence she was agreeing with him, thanking him for the hope that he had given.

Reverend, this is too much! I scooped up the empty IV bag. *Her child is dying, and you're telling her to have hope.*

But I had to admit that he was getting under my skin too. He was making promises to Jeromy about new life. And the reverend always kept his promises. I looked down at Jeromy's garden, unable to speak.

We watched it together after that, Jeromy and I, waiting for the bud. It just had to sprout while he was still alert enough to see it. It had to sprout before Christmas.

When I pushed through the swinging doors to Babies Five after my long weekend off, "Silent Night, Holy Night" played softly in the corridor. But the notes turned sour when I saw the suitcase outside Jeromy's room, his unwrapped Christmas presents lying beside it. Pooh Bear lay crumpled on top. Jeromy's room was very still. His IV pole was pushed back in the corner, the unit shut off. The isolation equipment had been removed. Jeromy lay motionless on his back; his mother wept beside him as she brushed his still brow.

The night nurse met me in the hall. "Cullen, the chaplain is on his way." She smothered her feelings with a sigh, her gaze avoiding mine.

"When?" I managed.

"An hour ago."

"You should have called me—"

"There wasn't time. He started to hemorrhage. And he was gone just like that."

"Alone? I wanted to be here with him."

"His parents were with him."

Tears stung the back of my eyes. I brushed them away. *Don't get involved with your patients,* I had told the student nurses.

"Look, Cullen," the night nurse said. "Why don't I stay on for a few minutes? I'll cover for you. Give you a chance to—"

"To get hold of myself? I'm all right."

She nodded and, with a final glance toward Jeromy's room, left me. I straightened my shoulders and stepped calmly through the door and crossed the room to Mrs. Evans. I slipped my arm around her and squeezed her shoulders, my eyes on Jeromy. His lifeless hand was cupped in her own, his chalky face still and peaceful. I wanted to touch him, to kiss him good-bye, to brush those sparse strands of dark hair in place. Instead I looked down at his grieving mother.

She glanced up and met my gaze. The darkness under her eyes had spread across her cheeks. Her voice sounded hollow as she said, "Bob went to get the car, but…Miss Cullen, before he comes back, would you take Pooh Bear and give him to one of the children? To Tammy, maybe."

"Surely you'd want to keep—"

"To bury with my son? No." She shook with the inevitable, then caught her breath and rushed on. "It would be easier on Bob if you took Pooh away."

"Of course…. Could I get you something? Coffee? Tea?" Even with words, it was impossible to break the stillness.

She didn't respond. Instead she reached over and touched Jeromy's garden. "Did you notice this, Miss Cullen? The tiniest bud has broken through. The chaplain must see it."

We heard his footsteps in the hall before we saw him, heard him breathless from running as he reached the room. He barreled in. Jeromy's mother stood, took a step toward him on her trembling legs and collapsed into his arms. "My dear, my dear," he said. "I thought we had a little longer."

Her sobs were smothered as he held her against him. "He was a good boy, Mrs. Evans. He's safe now, my dear, in the arms of Jesus. No more pain."

I left them, picking up Pooh Bear at the door.

In the children's ward, the little battered girl who had been with us for so long pushed her nose through the bars of the crib. "Mornin', Tammy," I said.

She was instant smiles, her fattened cheeks bulging. I lowered the rail and scooped her up, soggy britches and all. The scrubbing of Pooh would have to wait. "Tammy's Pooh Bear," I said, pressing Pooh into her hands.

I carried her to the window and stood there holding her as the moments ticked away. Outside, yesterday's snowfall still painted the city in a downy white. On the street far below, Bob Evans opened the car door for his wife.

"A remarkable woman, that Mrs. Evans," the reverend said, slipping up beside me. We watched as the car pulled away from the curb, the tires making slushy tracks down the empty street.

The winter air was crisp and clear. Pastel ribbons from the morning sun glinted off the Hudson River and highlighted the skyline of Manhattan. Patches of blue crowded in between the old hospital buildings and the cancer research complex next door.

But hope was there.

The reverend saw it all in its creative beauty. He pointed to the clear blue sky and the white fluffy cloud that floated there, a different shape to everyone who saw it. Behind it, other clouds spread like waves at the ocean shore. "Ah, Miss Cullen, it's as though all of heaven's gates have opened to welcome Jeromy home." He cocked his head and beamed at me. "I'm sure the angels are singing the way they did on that first Christmas morn."

I could barely nod. The card from Pooh Bear was still in my hand. I crushed it against Tammy's leg, struggling for words. And then over the lump in my throat I mumbled, "God must be saying, 'To Jeromy, with love.'"

The chaplain patted my arm. "And maybe to Miss Cullen with love." He chuckled low and distinctly. "Yes, it's all for the asking. And do you know, Miss Cullen," he said as I started for the station to answer the phone, "Jeromy is already blooming where he is planted."

ABOUT THE AUTHOR

Doris Elaine Fell's travels and interests are as diversified as her careers in nursing, writing, and as a missionary teacher in a bamboo schoolhouse. A Christy Award finalist for *Blue Mist on the Danube,* she brings humor, the spirit of adventure, and exotic settings to her writing. She is a teddy-bear collector, not to mention an avid fan of the Tour de France. She and a traveling companion once became ensnared in a cycling race in France when the *gendarme* drew back the barricade and waved them into the race. With jeering crowds on either side, they dashed for an escape.

Fell chose New York City, the city where she took her nurse's training, as the hometown for her story of a homesick nurse, a story as current today as when it first appeared in *Home Life,* a Southern Baptist Convention publication. Her love for the Lord weaves a scarlet thread of forgiveness through all her novels. Doris is currently under contract for her seventeenth book, a novel for Fleming Revell. She makes her home in southern California.

IN THE MATTER OF GRACE

Judith McCoy-Miller

Groveton, Pennsylvania, 1944

Grace stared down at the dark pinstriped suit. Bob's knotted navy tie lay in a straight line, hiding the row of buttons down the front of his crisp white shirt.

I should have chosen sky blue, Grace absently concluded as she stared at the ivory satin lining surrounding Bob's body. The quilted pearl-white fabric cast a gray hue on his already discolored complexion. Reaching into the casket, she carefully moved her husband's wire-rimmed glasses into a more familiar position along the bridge of his nose.

"He looks real good," Aunt Zanie said as she approached Grace and peered into the rectangular box. "And that's a real purty suit he's wearin' too. But don't you think you shoulda saved your money instead of spending it on a suit that's just goin' six foot under? Ain't as though you can afford to be wasteful."

The words startled Grace. How could Zanie be so callous and judgmental? It had taken four years of scrimping and saving to lay up enough money for Bob's new suit. And now, only five days since they had gone shopping in Pittsburgh, she was burying him in the long-awaited garment. Except for the fact that the pants needed to be shortened, the suit was a perfect fit. Not that it mattered now. The ivory satin would keep her secret hidden from the gaping eyes that viewed her husband's remains. She pulled an embroidered handkerchief from the pocket of her dress and wiped away a tear that threatened to spill over and run down her cheek.

"Shoot, Grace, I didn't mean to make you cry. Bob looks real nice." Zanie sighed as she shook her head back and forth. "You shouldn't let them bury him with his glasses on."

"Why?" Grace asked, her gaze never leaving Bob's face.

"He didn't sleep in his glasses, did he? It's uncomfortable having glasses on when you're asleep. Crimps your nose." Zanie pinched at the bridge of her nose.

Grace's head slowly turned, and she looked at Bob's Aunt Zanie, one of several relatives who had driven from West Virginia to attend the funeral. "He's not asleep, Zanie—he's dead!"

"I know that, but still…" Her voice trailed off momentarily and then, with renewed interest, the older woman changed the subject. "Earl said he never heard of anybody dying because of troubles with their spine. But I told him you should know, cause you surely woulda talked to the doctor. Ain't that right?"

"Spinal meningitis, Zanie. He died of spinal meningitis," Grace patiently murmured, her attention already returning to her dead husband's face.

A baby cried somewhere in the distance, and Grace felt the milk begin to let down in her swelled breasts. Dampness seeped through her gray and black print dress as the sounds of the crying infant grew more demanding.

"Grace, come away from the casket. Come feed the baby; she's hungry," her sister-in-law urged.

"I can't nurse the baby. I have to stay with Bob. Do you like his suit, Patty? We bought it on Saturday; it's only three days old. A perfect fit— that's what the salesman said. It is, too, except the pants need to be hemmed. Look…" She began to pull back the satin cover that lay across her husband's legs.

"No, Grace! Don't do that. Come over here and nurse the baby." Patty pulled on Grace's arm, forcing her away from the casket. "There's a room back here where you can sit with the baby."

Grace allowed herself to be pulled along to a small sitting room and obediently sat in the overstuffed chair that Patty pointed toward. "I was going to keep it a secret," Grace said as she unbuttoned the front of her dress and put the baby to her breast.

"Keep what a secret?" Patty asked.

"Bob's pants needing to be hemmed. You won't tell anyone, will you?"

"No, Grace, I won't tell," Patty promised. "But you need to pull yourself together. You've got these three kids to take care of and you've been talking like a crazy woman ever since Bob died. It's time you straightened up!"

"Straightened up? Pulled myself together? Of course; what's wrong with me? I need to get my emotions under control." Grace's voice sounded shrill to her own ears. She finished nursing the baby and rose from the chair. "It's almost time for the service to begin," she stated in a measured voice. Determinedly she strode out of the room and beckoned toward her seven-year-old son. "Come sit with me, Tommy," she instructed, taking her son's hand and moving toward the front of the funeral home chapel. Passing by the wooden folding chair where Zanie sat holding her other child, Grace nudged the older woman. "Zanie, bring Mary Kay up front with us."

The preacher's words faded in and out; Grace couldn't keep her mind from wandering back to three years ago when they had made their decision to leave West Virginia. Would Bob still be alive if they hadn't moved to Pennsylvania? But Bob had said they needed money, and the move had provided him with a good opportunity—a job at Neville Island helping construct Navy ships for the war that continued to rage overseas. There had been no jobs in Fairview, she reasoned.

But there was no spinal meningitis in Fairview, either.

"I know Grace takes comfort in the fact that Bob accepted Christ as his Savior only a few short weeks ago," the minister said, his words pulling Grace back to the present.

The remark echoed in her mind. The preacher's statement was true. She was genuinely happy that Bob had been saved, but was this his reward? Being snatched away from his wife and three children? And what of her? Was this her reward for becoming a Christian and spending countless hours praying for her husband's salvation? So much for a loving God.

Her gaze strayed to the preacher. What would the man think if he knew what she was thinking? Worse yet, what would God think? Well, she didn't care what God thought. It was obvious to her that He wasn't worrying about the burdens she was facing.

Grace ignored the sharp knocks that were breaking the early afternoon silence of the red brick tenement apartment. Mary Kay and baby Judy were finally napping, and Tommy was busy playing with his erector set. But the beckoning sound of company sent the boy scrambling toward the door before she could manage to hold him back. Without thought to her appearance, she trudged toward the kitchen where Tommy stood holding open the front door and permitting Birdie McGeary, the nursery worker from church, entrance into their living room.

Grace leaned out and grabbed the storm door that refused to close, evidence of a missing spring that Bob should have replaced months ago. "You can go back inside, Mrs. Maskie," Grace called to the next-door neighbor who had come outside to investigate. "There's nothing to see, and I sure wouldn't want you to catch pneumonia on my account."

"These are nice apartments. I've never been to the Projects before—always wondered what it was like," Mrs. McGeary said, ignoring Grace's stinging remark to the neighbor.

"Now you know." Grace raised her arm in a sweeping gesture. "Acres of brick walls dotted with windows. They're all alike, except for the one-stories at the end of each row. Those are for couples only, no upstairs and only one bedroom. The two-stories have three bedrooms and a bath upstairs, living room, kitchen, and utility room downstairs. Different linoleum in each row of apartments—that's our claim to individuality," Grace replied in a flat voice.

Birdie remained in the kitchen clutching a large cardboard box while her purse dangled from one arm. "May I set this on the kitchen table?" she asked, nodding toward the burden in her arms.

Grace sighed as she slumped into one of the padded metal chairs surrounding the table. "That's fine."

"I've missed you and the children at church on Sundays, so I thought I'd drop by and see if there was anything I could do to help. Our Sunday school class sent the box of food, and this is from the church." Birdie pulled a long white envelope from her handbag. "I assure you that the church members want to do everything we can to help you and the children. And it looks as though what you need the most is someone to keep an eye on these youngsters while you go and take yourself a nice hot bath and get freshened up." So saying, she peeled off her gloves and removed her red wool coat.

The comment caused Grace to run slender fingers through her mass of unkempt dark brown hair. "I can take care of the children. You don't need to stay," she argued as Birdie began picking up the toy-strewn living room.

"I won't take no for an answer, Grace. Go take a bath, go shopping, or do whatever you'd like. I'm going to stay and watch the children. I'm even going to fix supper for all of us."

"You can't do that! Go home to your husband," Grace commanded.

"He works the three to eleven shift, so I'm afraid you're stuck with me. I have the car if you need to go to the grocery store or run some errands," Birdie offered in a gentle voice. "The preacher mentioned that you had to sell your car. Okay if I put these things in the refrigerator?" she asked, having already unloaded the remainder of the groceries onto the shelves that lined the utility room wall.

Grace nodded and stood mute as Birdie placed butter, cheese, assorted produce, and several packages of meat wrapped in white butcher paper into the small refrigerator.

"Go on," Birdie urged, waving her arm and shooing Grace toward the steps. "Go take a bath. Tommy and I are going to make something special with his erector set." Tommy smiled at the remark, beaming his approval when Birdie pointed her index finger toward the picture of a crane on the printed instruction sheet. "Of course, we may need a little help from Mr. McGeary if I can't figure out how to make the motor work," she added with a laugh.

Grace said nothing, but she did as she was told. It was obvious that Birdie was staying. Besides, not worrying about the children while she bathed and washed her hair would be a luxury, and the baby didn't need to be nursed for at least two hours.

When she emerged an hour later in a fresh housedress, her damp hair combed into soft waves and a tint of color on her lips, she looked and felt like a different woman. The aroma of a savory stew wafted up the stairwell into the hall. It smelled wonderful…

How long had it been since she'd actually cooked a meal? Oh, she had thrown things together for Tommy and given Mary Kay finger foods, but she hadn't really prepared a decent meal since the day she had taken Bob to the hospital.

"It smells good down here," Grace said as she walked down the steps. Birdie was holding Mary Kay on her lap and was using her left hand to hold a piece of the metal erector set in place while Tommy diligently tightened a small bolt. Judy, up from her nap, was lying on the couch waving her hand back and forth in the air, her baby eyes attempting to maintain visual contact with the mysterious moving object.

"I hope you and the children like stew. I had some leftover roast beef and gravy at home, so I brought it along. I thought I'd stay and join you for dinner if that's all right." Birdie smiled.

It was more of a statement than a question, and Grace knew she had no choice. Tommy was already nodding his head in wholehearted agreement—he wanted to finish building the crane and sensed that Birdie was the only one who was going to help him accomplish this feat.

And so it went. The days moved by, melting into each other, dissolving into some unknown void, just as the mounds of snow had melted and given way to spring and then the heat and humidity of what promised to be a scorching summer.

"So how are you really doing?" Birdie asked one evening after the children were tucked into bed.

"Not so good." Grace surprised herself with her honesty. "It's hard. After the funeral, everybody went home and returned to their normal lives. But my life isn't normal anymore. I resent being left like this—it's not fair."

Birdie nodded. "Lots of things in life aren't fair, Grace. We don't know why situations occur the way they do, but I can tell you that growing bitter and wallowing in self-pity doesn't help."

"That's easy enough for you to say. You've got a husband, a nice home in Coraopolis, a car to take you where you want to go, and money to buy groceries and pay your bills. It's easy to have a good attitude when things are going your way."

"That's true enough. I do have all those things you've mentioned. God has been good to Ted and me. But you have something I don't have, Grace. Something I very much want, something I earnestly pray for."

"What could I possibly have that you want?" Grace asked, her question leaving a note of bitterness hanging in the air.

"Children. You have three beautiful children." Birdie surveyed the room, her gaze resting upon the worn maple high chair.

A momentary pang of shame shot though Grace but dissolved almost as quickly as it had arrived. "Yes, I have children. But I also have the responsibility of raising them without the benefit of a husband. And they have the disadvantage of growing up without a father."

"True enough." A warm smile turned up the corners of Birdie's mouth. "Grace, I'm not going to get preachy, but you may need to read-just your thinking just a bit. If not for you, then for the children. It's that old principle of whether a cup is half full or half empty—a matter of atti-tude."

"Attitude? Well, right now my attitude is that my cup is completely empty, so I don't need to spend much time thinking about half any-thing."

"You're wrong, Grace. Your cup is full to overflowing. Don't you see that you've filled it with anger and bitterness? I'm afraid that grief and resentment are going to bubble up and spill over to your children. As unfortunate as your situation may be, you're the only one who has the ability to change your attitude. With God's help, I know you're going to succeed in doing that. I can feel it—in here—" Birdie pointed toward her heart—"because I've watched you with your children. I know you love them enough to sacrifice your own self-pity and get on with your life. And I'm going to help you whether you want my help or not," Birdie added in a voice filled with determination.

Grace didn't answer. She didn't know what to say, and besides, she didn't have the stamina to argue. Birdie took Grace's hands in her own and began to pray—a soft, pleading prayer. Grace bowed her head, intending to listen and then add her own petition to Birdie's prayer. Instead her thoughts wandered back to the days when she was a carefree young girl playing on the wooden sidewalks in front of their home in West Virginia. Back to the days when she had no worries, no concerns; back to the days when she had been totally dependent upon her mother and father to meet her needs. She had never given a second thought to her needs back then, never questioned where her next meal would come from, where she would live, or if she would have a new dress for the first day of school. Those were the things that her parents automatically took care of just because they loved her. She had always trusted them to provide—and they had always done so. It had been a trust built on her childlike faith.

Like raindrops filtering through leafy branches on a warm summer's afternoon, Birdie's words of supplication trickled in and out of Grace's consciousness as she asked God to be caretaker, companion, manager, father, provider.

Grace flopped onto her left side and tucked the cotton sheet under her chin. Sleep wouldn't come, no matter how she positioned her weary body on the lumpy mattress. Birdie's prayer continued to echo in her mind. Could God really be her companion, a father to her children, a provider for all of them? Was that the truth she had been unwilling to believe all these months? It was an incredibly simple idea. Yet wasn't that the way of God?

Early the next afternoon the sound of a car door slamming sent Grace rushing to the kitchen. She was holding the front door open before Birdie had stepped out of the car. "I thought you'd never get here." She grasped Birdie's hand and pulled her toward the kitchen table. "Sit down."

Grace patted the back of a chair and quickly positioned herself across the table. She rested her arms on the table, palms flat and outstretched toward her friend. "I think I understand now!"

Birdie's face was etched with confusion, but she nodded affirmatively. Grace took that as her cue to continue and leaned across the table, her eyes flickering with a newfound excitement. "I couldn't go to sleep last night. I kept thinking about your prayer. The words kept tumbling around in my head, until I finally realized what you've been trying to show me all these months. What I need to do is trust God to care for me just like I trusted my parents to provide my needs when I was growing up. That's it, isn't it?"

Birdie nodded and smiled. "That's it."

"And all this time since Bob's death, God has been providing. Through each of you at the church giving me food, and rides to church, and babysitting. Why, I'd even venture a guess it was the church that paid my rent last month, wasn't it? How could I have been so dense?" Grace asked, a tear rolling down her cheek.

Birdie took hold of Grace's hands. "It's certainly true that you had an unwilling spirit, but you're not dense, Grace. I learned a long time ago that God is perseverant when it comes to His children. He faithfully woos us back to the fold, no matter what the cost. It is His greatest pleasure to welcome us back, no matter where we may stray."

"I guess I took the long way around, but at least I've finally found my way. Now I've got to remember that this is where I belong and not go wandering off again. I have a feeling I may need some help, so I hope you plan to stick around," Grace said. "I don't know how I'll ever be able to repay you for all you've done."

"Oh, Grace, the pleasure has been mine. The joy of being around your children is all the payment I'll ever need. Amazing how God found a way to provide just the right thing for both of us at the same time. But that's just like God, isn't it?" Birdie whispered as she pulled her friend into a warm embrace.

ABOUT THE AUTHOR

Judith McCoy-Miller is an award-winning author of inspirational romance fiction and also writes children's inspirational fiction. Although Judy, her family, and their ancient dachshund now live in Topeka, Kansas, she grew up in Groveton and Coraopolis, Pennsylvania, thankful for a widowed mother who knew the Lord and a church family that practiced benevolence. In addition to her writing, Judy works full time for the legal division of the Kansas Insurance Department.

JUST FOURTEEN DAYS

Gayle Roper

*Y*ou can do it, Hal. You can, I told myself as I tucked my beach chair under my arm. *Today is Saturday. We go home two weeks from today. Just fourteen days. That's not long. Nothing bad can happen in fourteen days.*

I wasn't certain I believed myself, so I quoted Patti's favorite verse, what she called the theme verse for parents of teenagers: "So don't worry about tomorrow, for tomorrow will bring its own worries. Today's trouble is enough for today."

Don't think twenty-four/seven. Take it one day at a time. My self-directed pep talk made me feel like I was the only attendee at one of those double-letter meetings: *Hi, my name is Hal, and I'm a worrier.*

I looked at my much-loved family as we gathered on the porch of our four-bedroom, second-floor beachfront rental on Central in the Thirty-eighth Street block in Ocean City, New Jersey. We'd come to Ocean City for vacation every year for as long as I could remember and beyond. Originally a Methodist camp meeting, it was still a dry town on a barrier island below Atlantic City. We all loved the place with its white sand beaches and crisp sea, and I only had to survive for fourteen days.

If it were just two generations, Lord... Even though I'm not the best people person, I can do two generations. It's trying to balance three that gives me heartburn. Help!

"Your mother and I loved the shore," my father said suddenly in my ear.

I jumped. The man persisted in sneaking up on me and dropping one of his "your mother and I" statements. He'd been doing it ever since Mom died fifteen months ago. Then his eyes would fill with tears, he'd look at me with a sad, hound-dog expression, and he'd sniff. The picture of pathetic.

When Mom had first died and he'd started this routine, my heart had broken for him every time. After all, I missed her dreadfully too. I'd start sniffing with him in sympathy pain, sort of like I'd groaned with Patti when the girls were born. But his act had gotten old after several months, and my well of sympathy/empathy had long since run dry.

Dad looked out over the beach to the sea with his patented hound-dog look. "We met here in Ocean City, you know." As if he hadn't told me a million times, about half of those times on the two-hour drive to the shore today. He turned his tear-filled eyes to me and sniffed.

I bit back a very uncharitable retort and asked as mildly as I could, "Do you have your beach tag, Dad?"

"Beach tag?" The tears disappeared, his shoulders straightened, and a militant light gleamed where seconds ago the tears had glistened. "I don't believe in beach tags. The beaches should be free to all!"

"Unfortunately the town fathers don't agree. You have to pay your money and wear your tag."

"Your mother and I never wore tags." With that, he stalked downstairs. Sighing, I slid his beach tag—which actually came free with the rental—into the little pocket on my swim trunks. If the poor kid unfortunate enough to be the tag checker happened by, I'd whip Dad's tag out and save us an embarrassing confrontation. After all, it was just some kid trying to earn college money, not an issue over which to take an unflinching stand for liberty.

"I've got my tag," announced my nineteen-year-old daughter Cass as she pinned it to her modest blue suit just above a bosom that threatened to overflow its moorings. Every time I looked at her in a swimsuit, my blood pressure went sky high. Not that she flaunted herself; she did not. Truth be told, she was very self-conscious. I just remembered what it was like to be a boy her age, hormones raging, imagination firing on all pistons, and my parental imagination went berserk.

"But you're not allowed to lock your daughters away until they're fifty," Patti had told me when I first suggested the idea a few years ago. "I think it's against the law."

"Law, schmaw," I told her. "A father has certain duties and responsibilities."

"And I've got my tag," eighteen-year-old Zusi announced. Zusi was wearing a few scraps of material that she called a bathing suit, the designer called a summer fantasy, and I called an expensive rip-off. How could so little material cost so much money? Thankfully, Zusi wasn't built like Cass.

"She's going to give me a heart attack, but at least it won't be over her figure," I told Patti when I first saw the suit.

"A lot you know," my wife answered unsympathetically. "Slim is in. Besides, her legs are incredible."

And I'd been so happy in denial.

Zusi's real name was Suzi, but when she was thirteen, she decided it was too common. "My name is now spelled Z-u-s-i," she announced one evening at dinner.

"Zoo-see?" I asked incredulously. "You think that's better than Suzi?"

"Oh, you still say it the same way," she said in casual disregard to all the rules of pronunciation. "It's just spelled different."

"That's crazy, Suzi," I said with my usual tact and understanding of the teenage feminine mind.

"But it's only crazy, dear." Patti patted my arm. "Save your spleen for something that actually matters."

So I saved my spleen, whatever that is, and tried with limited success to determine what those things were that actually mattered.

As I started down the stairs with my beach chair and Dad's beach tag, Zusi squealed, "Look, Cass! Boys!"

"Where?" Cass sounded contained, controlled as always, but I knew she was salivating almost as much as Zusi. They tore down the stairs and across the dunes, then sauntered oh-so-casually toward a blanket and the three muscle-bound apes lying on it.

"Patti," I said, trying not to whimper.

"Two weeks," she said, patting my arm. "Only fourteen days, Hal. You can make it: 'Don't worry about tomorrow, for tomorrow will bring its own worries. Today's trouble is enough for today.'"

"I'm biblical," I said. "It is today's trouble I'm worrying about."

We located Dad near the water's edge and settled beside him. When I opened my chair, I put my back to the girls so I wouldn't have to watch the apes drool over them.

"Come on, Hal." Dad climbed to his feet. "Let's go into the water."

"But I just sat," I said. "I have a new book to read. Besides, it looks cold."

"It always looks cold," he answered, staring at me until I twitched.

I sighed, clambered to my feet, and followed him to the water's edge. We began to wade in. It was cold.

"Your mother used to love the ocean." Dad gazed at the horizon, tears forming in his eyes. "We'd hold hands and walk in together. She'd always gasp when the first wave hit her tummy." He turned to me, as hound-dog as they come. He sniffed.

I rolled my eyes, at least metaphorically. "Dad, I seem to remember Mom standing in the shallows while you raced past her, swatting her on the rump and yelling, *Chicken!* Then you'd head for the deep water, where you'd float and play until either you were a prune or the lifeguards whistled you in for going out too far, whichever came first."

Dad looked at me with concern. "For a relatively young man, you have a very faulty memory. Watch for premature dementia."

I left him to become a teary-eyed prune all on his own.

"Daddy?"

I looked up from my book on full alert. It was the *daddy* that did it. Cass and Zusi stood there with the three apes drooling behind them.

"The guys are going to take us to the boardwalk tonight." Zusi was grinning from ear to ear.

"How nice," Patti said, smiling like she actually meant it.

"The boardwalk on Saturday night?" I stared, aghast. "You want to fight the congestion, the crowds? I wouldn't go near the boardwalk on Saturday night."

Everyone was polite enough to refrain from reminding me that I hadn't been invited.

The phone rang at eleven P.M., minutes after I had discovered several new gray hairs when I looked in the bathroom mirror. I don't think it was just my sun-reddened nose making those I already had more obvious. They were honest-to-goodness new ones brought on by the drooling apes.

I managed to beat Patti to the phone, thanks to the hip I threw at her as I sped past. "What's wrong?" I yelled into the receiver.

"Dad!" Cass's voice was nearly drowned out by the noises around her. Superman wasn't the only one who missed the old-fashioned phone booths where you could actually shut out the noise as well as change an outfit. "Can you come pick us up?"

"Where are you?" My heart thrummed as I waited for the answer. I just hoped I could find the deserted road where the apes had taken them and molested them. I hoped they weren't scarred for life. I hoped the police didn't badger them. I hoped I could be calm and supportive.

"At Tenth and the boardwalk. We'll walk out to Wesley and wait on the steps of the Baptist church."

"Where are the apes—the guys?"

"They wanted to go to Somer's Point to go drinking. We didn't."

This time I was the one with tears in my eyes, tears of pride.

We all went to the Baptist church service the next morning. As we walked up the front steps, Dad said, "Your mother and I used to come here all the time." Tears filled his eyes. He gave a lusty sigh, and his hound-dog face brought a look of concern to the usher who handed us our bulletins.

We four took our seats while Dad fished in his pocket for his hankie. He blew his nose with panache and great volume, then took his seat—where he slumped, woebegone. He didn't move the whole hour, not even when we stood to sing.

Patti patted me on the arm when the service ended. "Don't let him bother you." She smiled.

"Have I told you recently that I love you?" I thanked the Lord for one sane member of this family. And she was cute, too. Cuddly. And all mine.

"Warren Lipton!" a chirpy voice called. "That is you, isn't it, Warren?"

Dad shot out of his seat, his face alight with wonder. "Betty Ann Mercer!"

Dad and Betty Ann met in the aisle and embraced enthusiastically. Then he gave her a great noisy kiss on the lips. The hound dog and the sniffles were nowhere in evidence.

"Betty Ann and I used to date," Dad told us as he introduced his friend. "That was before she married old Whatshisname."

Betty Ann punched him playfully in the arm. "Tommy Williams, as if you didn't know."

"So where is old Tommy?" Dad asked, looking around.

Betty Ann suddenly looked teary-eyed. Dad nodded in understanding. "Alice too." He sniffled.

Then they looked at each other, and the electricity could have lit the boardwalk.

"It's not right," I told Patti as we walked down the church steps. "He's still crying over Mom."

"It's wonderful," Patti said. "And it's about time. I hope he asks her out."

I was still reeling at this remark from my traitorous wife when the girls came tripping up.

"Guess what?" Zusi asked, her moussed hair standing up in little spikes.

"We met the neatest guys!" Cass's eyes shone as she tugged on her long braid. "They're coming to the beach this afternoon and bringing some friends!"

Only thirteen days. Only thirteen more days.

We all came back to town that evening, rosy and glowing from the sun. Dad was also glowing over his coming dinner date with Betty Ann.

"We're going to Mack and Manco Pizza for dinner," he said.

"I know you haven't dated for a long time, Dad," Patti said, "but isn't that a bit déclassé for a first date after all these years?"

"Memories," was all he said. It was the smile with which he said it that worried me.

The girls glowed because the guys were meeting them for a walk "from one end of the boardwalk to the other."

"Aren't they the cutest?" gushed Zusi.

They hadn't spit into the sand or scratched impolitely during their visit with us that afternoon. Good signs, I guessed.

"And they don't drink," Cass said.

Wonderful lads, all.

As soon as we parked, the girls were off. "The guys will bring us home, Dad," Zusi called back over her shoulder. "Don't wait up."

Patti patted my arm. "So don't worry about tomorrow, for tomorrow will bring its own worries. Today's trouble is enough for today."

"Have you ever thought of getting another verse?" I asked. "Maybe 'Trust in the Lord with all your heart' or something?"

There followed a long discussion with Dad about the use of the car. It had seemed such a good idea when we'd all driven down the shore in our van. Who could have imagined Dad would need wheels for a date?

"Do you have to drive her home?" I asked.

"Of course I have to drive her home. A gentleman always takes a lady home."

"That's sweet," Patti said, patting me again. I was beginning to feel like her pet dog.

"I meant, can't we all drive her home?"

"I do not want my children along when I say good night to Betty Ann. Whatever would she think of me? That I need chaperones?"

I didn't let myself touch that one. "But you're only taking her for pizza!"

They both stared at me like I lacked understanding, and truthfully I was beginning to wonder how I'd ever managed to marry Patti, let alone help raise the girls, given my obvious level of interpersonal ineptitude.

"Okay," I said grumpily. "Meet us here at ten. You can take us home, then take Betty Ann. Where's she staying?"

"At the Port-O-Call."

"But that's right on the boardwalk. You can *walk* her home!"

"See you at ten," he said as he walked toward the Port-O-Call to get Betty Ann.

I saw Patti's hand move and prepared for another patting session. Instead she rubbed soothing circles around my back.

"Come on," she said softly. "Let's go get a tub of Johnson's caramel popcorn. That'll cure what ails you."

I leaned over and kissed her temple. "I love you," I whispered.

"I know," she whispered back. "You love us all."

We were halfway through the tub of popcorn when we walked past Mack and Manco's. I almost choked on a particularly tasty kernel when I looked in the window and saw Dad and Betty Ann sitting in a booth.

"They're sitting on the same side," I said as people parted around us like a river around a rock in its way. "Who sits on the same side?"

"We used to," Patti said, leaning close.

"Did we stare at each other like that?"

I could hear the laughter in her voice. "Probably."

Then she gulped—just as I did—when Dad leaned over and kissed Betty Ann. In Mack and Manco's. In a booth. In public. Then Betty Ann fed him a bite of pizza.

"I can't stand it!" I walked on, oblivious to the swirling crowds.

"It's better than tears and sniffles," Patti said, taking my hand.

"I don't know. He scares me even more than the girls do."

We met Dad and Betty Ann at the car at ten. They came sauntering up holding hands and giggling. It's hard hearing your father giggle. They dropped us off and went back to where we had just come from.

"Let's read in bed," Patti suggested. "All that sun and sea air has made me tired."

"I'm not going to bed until everyone's home."

"You can still read in bed. Just don't go to sleep."

Foolishly I agreed. The phone by the bed woke me at 12:30 A.M.

"The girls!" I gulped and grabbed for the receiver. "What's wrong?"

"Hal." It was Dad, wide awake and brimming with energy. "I locked myself out of the van."

I blinked, trying to get my mind around this unexpected scenario. "What?"

"I'm at Betty Ann's and I locked myself out of the van."

"So what am I supposed to do?"

"Bring me another set of keys." Betty Ann laughed in the background.

"But you've got the car."

"So get a cab. I can't stay here all night. Betty Ann's grandchildren are here. *I* know nothing wrong would happen, and *you* know nothing wrong would happen, but what would *they* think if they found me here in the morning? Kids don't need any excuses these days."

Tell me something I didn't know.

I climbed out of bed and lurched across the hall to the bathroom. When I emerged, I noticed the low murmur of voices from the big porch overlooking the beach. I grabbed a pair of shorts and went to investigate.

Cass, Zusi, and five guys sat on the recliners and chairs. Soda cans, chip bags, a pizza box, and my Johnson's popcorn tub—now empty—littered the floor.

"Hey, Dad," said Cass, smiling her sweet smile. "Hope we didn't wake you."

"Hey, Dad," Zusi said. "You remember the guys."

I nodded vaguely as they sketched little waves in my direction. "I've got to call a cab."

Cass followed me into the kitchen where I rummaged for a phone book. A tall, skinny guy with a formidable beak of a nose followed her in and came to rest very close to her. Very, very close.

"But he worries me," the guy said to Cass. "He's too sensitive to be Arminian in his theology. He'll spend his whole life in fear over losing his salvation."

"So you want him to be a Calvinist and spend his whole life worrying over those who aren't elect?"

"At least he'll know his own place in the scheme of things."

I stared at Cass and the young man. Arminian? Calvinist? "Who's too sensitive?"

"Pete," they answered together, pointing to the porch. "He's having trouble with predestination and election," Cass clarified.

Zusi walked in. "I told him he doesn't have to decide right this very minute," she said, pointing to the refugee from the World Wrestling Federation who trailed her in. Pete, I assumed, the sensitive one. She turned to him. "I mean, if great men of God like Calvin and Wesley didn't agree, what makes you think you'll come up with all the answers?"

"Well," Pete said defensively, "I like order."

"Too bad," Zusi said. "No one else has reconciled 'Jacob have I loved, Esau have I hated' with 'whosoever will may come.' I don't think you'll be the first."

Pete looked downcast until Zusi laid a hand on his arm and began patting—just like her mother. The boy brightened immediately.

"Just trust the Lord, Pete." Zusi smiled. "He loves you whether you have all the answers or not."

I looked at my daughters, totally confounded. When had they begun discussing theology with their dates? How had I missed their maturing, their depth?

"Why are you calling a cab at this hour?" Cass asked as I thumbed through the yellow pages.

"Granddad has locked himself out of the van. I need to call a cab to take me and Mom's car keys to the Port-O-Call."

"Hey," Pete said. "I've got to leave. I have to be at work at 5:30 this morning. I need at least a couple of hour's sleep or I'll burn everyone's eggs and pancakes. I'll drive you in."

I smiled at Pete, sensitive man that he was, and didn't even mind when he asked Zusi if she'd be free tomorrow night.

That's how I came to be riding on a motor scooter that sounded like a giant mosquito, clinging to the waist of a Goliath with a sensitive spirit, waiting for someone to reach out with a humongous flyswatter and squish us.

When I finally climbed back in bed with the sleeping Patti, Dad safely rescued, I leaned over and kissed her sloppily on both eyes. I figured that if I had to be awake, so did she. Fair is fair, even if he was only her father-in-law.

"Interesting day," she muttered after she punched me in the gut and dried her eyes.

"Understatement," I said as I slid down onto my pillow. "My whole perception of everyone but you has changed."

"Huh?" She blinked sleepily, trying to focus on what I was saying. Wonderful woman.

"The girls are arguing theology, and Dad is dating." I shook my head. "Life just doesn't get any stranger."

"Trust in the Lord with all your heart," Patti muttered.

"Yeah," I agreed. "Only twelve more days. How very sad."

ABOUT THE AUTHOR

While Gayle Roper didn't grow up in Ocean City, she is a New Jersey girl, raised in Audubon just across the Delaware River from Philadelphia. She did, however, spend many a summer "down the shore," first as a child at her grandparents' boarding house on Park Place, then as a college student waitressing for the summer at the now-demolished Raleigh Hotel at Tenth and Wesley, catty-corner to the Baptist church.

In fact, Gayle met her husband, Chuck, at that Baptist church. A generation prior, her mother met her father in Ocean City when he played his trumpet in a band at a restaurant on the boardwalk. As Gayle's mother tells it, every night the trumpeter would play a song just for her, looking soulfully at her the whole time. She fell hard and never recovered. (Says Gayle, "Thank goodness.")

Such civilities as live music during dinner have disappeared in today's casual vacation setting, as have the dresses and gloves, suits and ties everyone once wore at the shore. Gayle admits she prefers comfort to class. But the sand and sea and sun, God's contributions to the shore, haven't changed. It's almost like He says, "Everybody, come on down!"

THE CRAB GARDEN

Lisa E. Samson

Not many out-of-towners have ever heard the term *crab garden*. The very phrase sprouts pictures in their minds of some animated root crop, crabs growing under the ground only to claw their way through the soil to the humid air of summer and a Maryland sky bluer than a museum quality. We don't live our lives beneath high, wide skies here in the snug confines of the Chesapeake watershed. More approachable than a Western sky, our heavens rarely shake the soul. But during the balloon races around the Preakness they're a friendly backdrop, bowing in homage to the floating carnival of silk enchantment that hovers above the tidy cornfields and white-fenced horse farms.

We Marylanders know a crab garden serves up its own brand of enchantment. Summer has officially arrived when the crab gardens begin to open in June, and we take comfort that there's a place where life slows down, where folks that haven't met before become neighbors for a time. Its picnic tabletops piled with back issues of the *Sunpaper* or heavy, brown, woody-smelling butcher paper, its mallets lined up in neat rows, its pitchers collared with the foaming beverage of one's choice, the crab garden welcomes anyone daring enough to crack a hot steamed crustacean.

Unfortunately, crabs are about as adventurous as I get. As the younger daughter of Joe Fitsch, second-generation owner of Fitsch's

Seafood in the Highlandtown neighborhood of Baltimore City, I grew up with heavy canvas gloves on my hands, the rough fabric ending halfway up my skinny arms. Mom died when I was three, so I quietly accompanied my father through life. I'd cruise through classes only to chuck my bookbag beneath the counter and wind down the day with a sharp knife clutched between my stubby fingers while the transistor radio by the mallet bucket crackled out whatever sport happened to be in season. Joe Fitsch and I never met a sport we didn't like. Pop taught me to sever the nerve of a dozen live crabs in less than minute. "No one shucks oysters faster than you, Brenda Louise Fitsch," he assured me on many a sweaty afternoon before he finally air-conditioned the shop.

Pop taught me pretty much everything I know. And when that terrible Linda Lipinski told me I was flat-faced and got all the girls in the class to laugh at me, Pop just said, "Let's face it, Bren; it's always been us anyway. Right? Who needs those girls?" Then we walked down to Baskin-Robbins and he ordered two triple-dip Jamocha Almond Fudge ice-cream cones. We'd talk about ratcheting Fitsch Seafood a little, making it better. We'd talk about opening a crab garden: how many tables? What color should the awning be? Concrete, decking, or indoor/outdoor carpet? Picnic tables or tables and chairs? Newspaper or butcher paper?

"Maybe someday, Bren," he'd say with a wink as we walked home, looking at the movie posters by The Grand and then crossing the street to chat with the boys at the fire station. "Maybe when you're older."

I talked about how great it would be. A bigger business. More money. Maybe even getting to move out to the country.

Joe Fitsch smiled a lot at that and said, "Never forget your customers, Bren. Don't ever look at them as dollar signs."

I never needed anybody but Joe Fitsch. And when he died ten years ago, the worst day of my life since the Colts were kidnapped by that scoundrel Bob Irsay and taken to Indianapolis, I wanted to follow him to heaven. Then one day, while I cried on the front stoop and sipped a cherry Slurpee, I realized that I wanted to keep on going and that God wanted me to do that too. The kids down the street were hopping like crickets in the water of the fire hydrant.

I'd like to open that crab garden here on Eastern Avenue. But hand-cuffing myself to Maryland National Bank just to tear down the property next door doesn't seem to make much sense, really. I don't know. Pop and I never did decide on a blue awning or a green awning, anyway.

Don't get me totally wrong, though. Life's not all that bad.

I'm up six days a week at 4 A.M. for a trip down to the boats and the distributors. I live to argue with those snooty foreign chefs over that particularly impressive bushel of clams. And sucking down real Cokes with oysters really gets me ready for a day with my regular gaggle of customers. I've been doing this full time since I graduated from high school over eighteen years ago, the day after I torched the ugliest school uniform known to all-female Catholic education. I stayed on with Joe Fitsch, our ears glued to WBAL during the day when a game was on, our eyes stuck to Home Team Sports at night as we sat and ate our supper together off of our TV trays.

Every day it's the same, you know.

But a dream gathers inside me, a crazy kind of dream: skippering the wheel of my own little boat. I yearn to fly above the fishy smell, ride the crests of the Chesapeake Bay, and head right out to sea away from this dying neighborhood…to putter past the estuaries and the lonely, white vacation homes skirted by large screen porches that stare out over the gray waters with dark, multifaceted eyes. Just go on, Brenda, go without any plan other than saying good-bye. And maybe not even that.

Who would really miss me?

My family? Nope. Don't have any.

My customers? Well, I do a nice little business, but food is food. And I have a sneaking suspicion I rely on them a lot more than they rely on me.

Georgie Farone, a serious Catholic, tiny, energetic, and one generation away from the old country, skitters in on freshly laundered Keds every Friday for codfish cakes. She complains about her heart problems—five medications, hon, seventy-some percent blockage, and let me fill you in on the *real* scoop about balloon catheterizations!

Boyd Horn's visit ends my week, usually. Saturdays at 5:55 he huffs out an order for two crab cakes ready for frying and a pint of coleslaw. He asks about my old cat Stinky Girl, glotches in his smoker's voice about how the Orioles are faring this year, about his bum shoulder, and about the jokers and losers down on Baltimore Street where he bounces at one of the girlie clubs.

Boyd is nice, but maybe one day I'll meet a man like Joe Fitsch, and he'd better watch out!

My favorite customer, though, is Solomon Schwartz. He shuffles in

sideways through the door at Friday noontime for the bag of claws I collect for him all the day before, the ones that fall off in the steamer. He
says the guilt about eating shellfish urges him to temple every Sabbath.
Without it, he'd never go. That's what *he* says, not me. I don't know
much about the Jewish religion. I just make sure I'm at Moravia Road
Community Church every time the doors open because, well, I hear so
many curse words and various combos thereof down at the docks and
all every day, it's nice to go to a place where I can hear God speaking. So
far He hasn't said anything pro or con about the crab garden. Or my trip
out to sea for that matter.

So Sol brightens my day in his moth-eaten black suits. He hangs his
battered cane on the lobster tank and tells me about his grandchildren
who all live far away as he pulls out the latest snapshot creased into the
shape of a tricornered shallow bowl. It's hard to hold them flat when
you're shaking and your hands are bent into thick jointed claws by
arthritis, I guess. He slumps like a musty, wrinkled Victorian doll in the
faded old director's chair near the cash register while I make up crab
cakes, padded oysters, cocktail sauce, and my own special blend of
seafood seasoning for the brave souls who steam their own crabs, not to
mention shrimp, coleslaw, and macaroni salad. When I'm finished con-
cocting the salads, we sip Cokes together and complain about everything
from the crowds at Harbor Place to Haussner's Restaurant closing down
and for cryin' out loud, Eastern Avenue will never be the same again,
will it? That new Walgreen's might be snazzy, but it won't be enough to
save the neighborhood, that's for sure!

Sol knows it's time to go when my only employee arrives. I hired Bea
Armistead for Friday afternoons because she's so mean. Herds the customers in and out in record time like some sheepdog in a competition.
Dad dubbed Friday afternoons the Catholic Rush Hour years ago. God
bless every single one of them!

Bea straps on her apron, samples a spoonful of each salad, and either
proclaims "Tastes pretty good today, hon" or "Horrible, Brenda, you're
actually going to sell this garbage?" and then she bends herself in half,
making sure the double-knots in her shoelaces will stand the test of
time.

I don't say a word. I just fill the orders while she attacks the cash register for the next five hours. We don't flip the sign over until eight on
Fridays. But when the last surface is hosed down, the final switchplate is

swiped, and the door is locked, Bea and I allow ourselves sideways grins as we stroll up the avenue to the Eastern House Restaurant and order a nine o'clock steak.

Bea likes to talk about the neighborhood and I just let her go on. Sacred Heart's Church, which she faithfully attends every morning at eight o'clock for mass, is dying of old age. So after we've taken the last bite of steak, chewed, swallowed, and paid the bill, we go our separate ways. I guess I'm most lonely when I walk through the front door of my narrow row house on Friday nights.

Life is way too quiet here on Conkling Street now. I want that crab garden more than ever these days. People coming and going in happy spurts, pounding their mallets and talking about their lives. And it would be something I did all by myself. I'd sure make Joe Fitsch proud with that one. I'd sure be able to look myself in the mirror at night and say, "Brenda, you done good."

Monday morning there stands good old Georgie Farone as I unlock the door. She comes in a lot during the summer. Fitsch's Seafood first and then on to the Value Food because they have a blood-pressure machine back near the rest room. When her doctor finally decides to Roto-rooter those blocked arteries, I don't know who will sit in the waiting room. Me, probably. And Sol. He won't mind having something to do.

"Hiya, Georgie. What's new?" I say, wondering what the response is going to be because Georgie goes on a lot of bus trips so she's always got something new to say. Georgie knows everything, you see.

"Hiya, Bren. Guess where I went this weekend?"

"You really want me to guess?"

"No. Knowing you, hon, that'll take too long. Just a figure of speech. I went lighthouse hunting."

I start spooning out the quarter-pound of potato salad she always orders. "I'm making shrimp salad today. All I've got to do is add the mayonnaise. Nice big shrimp. How 'bout it?"

"Okay. I'll take half a pound. Anyway—" she peels off the clear plastic hair bonnet with white trim she always wears on cloudy days and plops down in the director's chair—"we took a boat outta Havre de Grace, right near the lighthouse. I suppose you know that's right where the Susquehanna River meets the Chesapeake Bay."

I do know that, but don't have the heart to tell her.

"We took the clipper ship out," she continues, her voice fading inside my head.

Clipper ships out of Havre de Grace? Do they ever go out into the ocean?

Georgie blathers on about screwpile lighthouses as I mine the bottom of the plastic mayo jar. "How much did it cost to go on the boat, Georgie?" A little trip out onto the Bay couldn't hurt, right?

"Twelve dollars plus tax. They sail every evening. And a couple of times a day on Saturday and Sunday. As long as the weather's fit."

Georgie is a walking brochure for the state of Maryland. Sometimes know-it-alls come in handy. Georgie went to school with Joe Fitsch and I have a sneaking suspicion she liked him for years. I sometimes think most of my customers come in and chat because they loved Pop so much they can't bear to let him go. If I'm the next best thing, well, I feel a little sorry for them. It must be like having your mouth set for filet mignon and finding out the only available choice is olive loaf on Wonder Bread.

After Georgie scurries away, a few more regulars slide breathlessly into the cool of the store. They complain about the heat. They complain about the humidity. They complain about their health, their wealth, their kith, their kin. And I just go right along, hopping aboard my own skiff of disgruntledness and sailing along with them. Poor old Billy Hipschman burps and belches and talks about Prevacid, and Big Francie McHenry slams in before lunch with a copy of her new will. "I've cut every last ingrate out! If they can't give me their presence, I can't give them no money when I go. And that's the truth."

The next Sunday I rent a motorboat after church and putter about the Magothy River. Just practicing for that big trip out into the ocean. The dream has become more real these days. I'm reaching middle age with no one to show for it. No husband. No kids. No best friend. Not even a crab garden. With the money I've saved, maybe I can buy a little outboard motorboat and buzz down to the Outer Banks in North Carolina or something.

That could work. I could just plaster a sign on Fitsch's front window that says Closed Indefinitely, collect my savings, buy that boat, and use the rest to live on until I find work. I just hope it's something other than being an attendant at a miniature golf joint. I've never been all that fond of miniature golf, even though some people swear it's a real sport.

I bought that boat at the beginning of July. Couldn't believe it myself. So now, step one is out of the way, even if it is a used boat that smells like my shop. And blast, if I didn't go and blurt the news about the purchase to Bea who tells everybody she can.

"Brenda bought a boat! Now why in the world does a young, single woman…?"

That gossip!

Every one of the last four Sundays, a different customer has chopped through the bay with me. How am I ever supposed to get away now?

Sol loves it, though. He sits in his suit in the heat, hands folded in bony lumps on top of his cane, and just pushes his barky old skin full into the wind like an old hound out for a joyride not caring that the car isn't at all respectable. We quietly sing old Irving Berlin tunes and nibble away at the turkey and cheese sandwiches I packed. And when I drop him off in front of his house around eight o'clock, he invites me inside for coffee.

"Are you sure that's no trouble, Sol?" Nobody's ever invited me in for coffee before.

"You've done so much for me all these years, Brenda, the least I can do is fix you a cuppa coffee."

Is he serious? What have I ever really done for Sol?

It's August the twenty-sixth, and I am setting out. Behind me in the boat sit two duffel bags, a cooler, and a strongbox stuffed with all my legal papers. I'm going to arrange for the business to be sold after I get settled in North Carolina. But for now, subterfuge is necessary. If old Sol—or even Bea—found out, well, I just wouldn't know what to say.

Glad I kept my big mouth shut this time.

It feels strange, the water getting wider and wider as I putter on. Stinky Girl suns herself on the seat near the back. Not a care in the world. I'm scared, to be honest. Pop would have never done this, but I know I'll never have that crab garden. I never will.

God is still silent about everything, so I figure how can asking for some kind of sign hurt? So I ask Him. "Is this right or what, God?" And I say, "If You don't want me to do this, give me a sign." I figure it's best to leave lots of room for interpretation.

Nothing happens. What a shame that I can escape so easily; how many days will it be before someone reads the detailed note taped inside my screen door?

"Gone for goodness knows now long," it starts out.

And then I hear a voice.

"Brenda!"

A still, small voice.

"Brenda! Brenda!"

I turn off the motor and fall to my knees, remembering the story of Samuel. "Speak, Lord, for thy servant heareth," I say, as though God needs a hearing aid.

"Brenda!" The voice is louder now. "Is that you out there?"

Is it me out here? Would God need to ask?

"Oh, for pity's sake," I mumble, scrabbling back to my feet.

And twenty yards away a boat much like my own weaves toward me. Bea at the helm looks madder than a hornet. Boyd the bouncer argues with Georgie the know-it-all about something or other. And Sol gestures toward me, his ancient eyes so round they would swallow up his reading glasses if he had them on.

Talk about a sign from God. Definitely one of His more unusual ones!

"What in the world do you think you're doing?" Bea shouts. "The least you could've done is told me I was out of a job!"

"And what about my crab cakes?" Boyd hollers.

"What about them?" I yell.

"I'm going to need them even more now that I've taken a new job," he says.

"Oh, yeah?"

"Yeah! Down at Bethlehem Steel in Sparrows Point."

Sol yells, "A much more respectable job, isn't it, Brenda?"

And Boyd nods furiously.

Georgie hollers, "Do you know for sure if that motor is in good enough shape to take you all the way down to goodness-knows-where? That kind isn't well-rated in *Consumer Reports*!"

"You never answered my question!" Bea accuses.

"I can't remember what it was!"

"What do you think you're doing?"

"I'm leaving."

"Why?" Sol asks as their boat inches up alongside mine. Boyd hops aboard and begins tying them together.

"I don't even have the courage to start my own crab garden."

There, I said it.

Sol looks at Bea, and they burst into scruffy laughter.

Boyd shakes his head with a chuckle, looks me square in the eye, and says, "You're crazy, Bren, you know that?"

"Well, why not?" I snap. "Having no one but you gripers to hang around all these years."

"You go right along, Brenda," Sol reminds me, his blue eyes catching the sun. "You crab right along with us."

"I know. I can't help myself."

Bea crosses her arms. "So now, what was it about a crab garden? Would that mean I'd have to work more than one day a week?"

"Most new business ventures fail in the first six months," George prophesies.

Boyd sits down at the driver's seat of my boat and thumbs at the crew in the other boat. "Seems to me you've already got a crab garden, Bren."

Sol says, "Come home, Brenda. We need you."

"No, you don't. You really don't."

But he reaches out his gnarled old hand and wiggles his knotty fingers. I place my hand inside and, with a wince, he squeezes as much as he can, which isn't much.

But it's enough.

Boyd jerks his head toward the other boat. "Climb on in there, Brenda. Stinky Girl and I will follow behind you guys."

And so I do. Bea smacks me on the behind and says, "Silly girl," as Sol hugs me tightly.

Georgie blinks at me (ooh, I like that!). "You sure had me scared, hon. What would Joe Fitsch have said if we had let you go?"

"Joe's dead, Georgie!" Bea says.

Sol lets me go with a pat on my shoulder.

"Let's go home, then, you crazy bunch!" I shake my head.

"But I'm still driving," Bea barks, snapping us all to attention.

"Do you know how many gallons of water are in the Chesapeake Bay?" Georgie asks.

Sol rolls his eyes. "No, but I'm sure you're going to tell us."

"I didn't think you'd know."

"Oh, for cryin' out loud, Georgie, be quiet!" Bea nips.

I decide right then I'm not going to sell my boat. I'll just have a good time with my friends, and we'll cruise the waters together, complain together, and spend the rest of our lives together in a garden we've been growing for years. Its crop may not look or sound beautiful to the rest of the world, but it's all we've got, and really, that's just...well, just fine. Right, Joe Fitsch?

I'm guessing the answer to that question is yes.

I'm guessing Joe Fitsch learned the answer to that question years and years ago.

ABOUT THE AUTHOR

Lisa E. Samson grew up in the Baltimore area. Highlandtown, the city neighborhood she describes in "The Crab Garden," is where her father, Dr. William Ebauer, grew up with his older siblings, Dr. Lawrence Ebauer and Loretta "Sis" Ebauer. Lisa and her family spent many happy holidays in the company of her grandparents, Dr. John T. and Elizabeth Ebauer. Aunt Sis still lives across the street from Sacred Heart's Church, and they attend the Sour Beef and Dumpling supper together every November. Row houses line each street, their white stone steps parking their square footprint on the cement sidewalk. And if you go there at Christmastime, you'll catch whimsical scenes in the basement windows. Lisa still lives in the Baltimore metropolitan area with her husband, Will, and their three children, Tyler, Jake, and Gwynneth. Lisa would eat steamed crabs once a week, if she could afford it!

Multnomah Publishers®

The publisher and author would love to hear your comments about this book. *Please contact us at:*
www.multnomah.net/storytellers